Praise for Amanda Boyden's **BABYLON ROLLING**

"*Babylon Rolling* is many books in one—a brilliant, nuanced portrait of pre-Katrina New Orleans; a passionate defense of the city; a clear-eyed critique of the problems that remain. . . . Boyden shoots right to the heart of a fabulous, flawed city."　　　　—*The Times-Picayune*

"[*Pretty Little Dirty*] hinted at the author's literary promise. With *Babylon Rolling*, that promise is fulfilled."　　—*St. Louis Post-Dispatch*

"Complex and compelling. . . . Boyden has so fully and generously imagined Orchid Street and its inhabitants. Her writing acknowledges the depth of race and class divisions . . . but she's also aware of the ways people break out of their assigned roles."

—*San Francisco Chronicle*

"Few contemporary novels are, at their root, as compelling about the relationship between a city and the people who live there. Boyden's *Babylon Rolling* is a love letter, sometimes sad, sometimes angry, sometimes beautiful, between New Orleans and five people who live on one of its streets."　　　　—*The Globe and Mail*

"Big and rich. . . . One of those books you want to share."

—*The Palm Beach Post*

"It is possible that New Orleans is the perfect setting for the post–9/11 American novel. . . . Like the characters in the gorgeous and tactile *Babylon Rolling*, our survival hinges on our ability to cope with the lack of a universal culture and common body politic, the truth that natural disasters and random violence are a fact of life."

—*Mother Jones*

Amanda Boyden

BABYLON ROLLING

Amanda Boyden was born in Minnesota and raised in Chicago
and St. Louis. Formerly a circus trapeze artist and contor-
tionist, she earned her MFA from the University of New
Orleans, where she now teaches writing. Her first novel, *Pretty
Little Dirty*, was published in 2006.

Also by Amanda Boyden

Pretty Little Dirty

Amanda Boyden

BABYLON ROLLING

VINTAGE CANADA

VINTAGE CANADA EDITION, 2009

Copyright © 2008 Amanda Boyden

Published in Canada by Vintage Canada, a division of Random House of Canada Limited, Toronto, in 2009, and simultaneously in the United States by Vintage Books, a division of Random House Inc., New York. Originally published in hardcover in Canada by Alfred A. Knopf Canada, a division of Random House of Canada Limited, Toronto, in 2008. Distributed by Random House of Canada Limited, Toronto.

Vintage Canada and colophon are registered trademarks of Random House of Canada Limited.

www.randomhouse.ca

This is a work of fiction. Names, characters, places, and incidents either are the product of the author's imagination or are used fictitiously. Any resemblance to actual persons, living or dead, events, or locales is entirely coincidental.

A portion of the definition of fatal familial insomnia on pages 278–79 is taken from Wikipedia, http://en.wikipedia.org/wiki/Fatal_familial_insomnia.

Library and Archives Canada Cataloguing in Publication

Boyden, Amanda
Babylon rolling / Amanda Boyden.

ISBN 978-0-307-39682-2

I. Title.
PS3602.O934B32 2009   813'.6   C2008-905503-9

Book design by Wesley Gott

Printed in the United States of America

2 4 6 8 9 7 5 3 1

For Joseph and our city

But the people cannot have wells, and so they take rain-water. Neither can they conveniently have cellars, or graves, the town being built upon "made" ground; so they do without both, and few of the living complain, and none of the others.

—Mark Twain, *Life on the Mississippi*

BABYLON ROLLING

PROLOGUE

We choose New Orleans.

We choose to live Uptown on Orchid Street inside the big lasso of river, though we rarely look at it, churning brown, wide. Giant catfish with eyes the size of salad plates cuddle down in its soft mud. They eat bicycle inner tubes, sometimes tin cans, like goats. Divers who work in the river with headlamps and wet suits say a catfish will suck your arm in and gum it up to the elbow.

We shoulder the rummy, pissy weeks before Lent when our city goes into heat. Squawking for titties, wearing cameras, the magpies come in throngs, overload branches, mate and shit, everyone swooping at glittering strings of nothing worth fighting for. After Ash Wednesday a chain of doughnut shops accepts grocery bags of beads, and we trade in sacks of greasy sins for a dozen glazed each. Sprinkles, mixed. So many mistakes get repackaged for the next year.

We acknowledge that spores of racism and mold grow here, recede, disappear to hide behind wallpaper. We keep track. Do nothing. We are good at watching: On a dank summer night, a pack of feral dogs shreds a girl's pet bunny in her backyard. At the start of his second grade, a poor boy kicks a pigeon that cannot fly, spits at it, and kicks again. New Year's Eve, a rotted balcony buckles and spills drunk tourists onto pavement splatted with sticky blots of their own daquiris.

But, oh, the comeliness. We have fallen for snowy egrets and high ceilings as naturally as we would our own mothers on the days of our births. Weak-kneed, we lunge for oysters and musty authors and mean-tongued rappers with gold and diamond teeth worth more than our homes. We swoon for the glassy surface of our shallow lake, the one that appears in photos taken from the moon; traipse, loopy, behind brass bands on the street; slurp on crawfish heads for their yellow fat, our favorite. It is the more than enough of, the flooding of, everything that we must have, even though not all of us know this. Our want wears out our sleeves.

If we decide to, we can tell you who New Orleans is. New Orleans is the old man who cannot read. Still, he buys the paper every day. He touches the faces of murderers and commits them to memory. And New Orleans is the slack-jawed woman, too full of Sunday dinner to move from the table, staring at her haystacked pile of turkey neck bones. And New Orleans is also, always, the terrible child, our *enfant terrible,* the one who never makes it home on time, the one whose parents never care why. Four-letter lyrics, a cornerstore scuffle. Music and violence. The kid craves both.

We love a place that cannot be saved by levees. We are brilliant losers. But, of course, those of us living Uptown on Orchid Street do not know this yet. Katrina is a year away.

1

Fearius stare from the car at Stumps Grocery and Liquor. Painted on the siding: Package meat Fried rice Cold drinks. He might could drink a strawberry cold drink. Orange. Fearius like cold drinks better than malt liquor when they smokin the hydroponic, but Alphonse be inside Stumps for Colt 40s, and Fearius, his bankroll thin as a spliff now. Thin as quarters and a dime thin. Juvey dont pay, dont he know.

But Fearius, he be patient. He learnt it. He waited to make fifteen full years of age inside juvey, waited four months sitting in there. Finally turned legal for driving on a learner permit when he caged up in Baby Angola with no wheels nowhere. Now he borrowing a license till he take the test. Why he hafta take a test to drive when he been driving since he made twelve, Fearius dont know. Maybe he just go buy a license. He be working soon, back tight with everybody, two weeks, three, fatten up the bitch bankroll.

Fearius flick the cardboard tree smell like piña colada on the rearview, rag the sweat off his shaved head. He open the glovebox and touch Alphonses Glock. Pretty thing, hot as they get. Stinkin like firecrackers.

Alphonse walk out Stumps and pass Fearius a 40 in brown paper, wet on the bottom, sweatin. Everything sweatin. Fearius dick sweatin in his drawers.

"You want it?" Alphonse ask about the gun. Or maybe the beer.

"I earn it," Fearius say about the Glock and the 40 both.

Alphonse nod, get in, take the Glock and shove it in his pants.

Two hours still before Shandra off work. Shandra gots a friend, she say. Fearius need, need, *need* a friend. He just gone take a friend soon, he toll Alphonse. Alphonse said, "Be patient." Fearius remember he know patient. And Alphonse gots the Glock. Patient be way easier with a gun.

Autumn is running around in a circle at the end of its tether, Ariel May decides, as far away as it can get from the stake of New Orleans. She misses fall with a pang, squints against the thick afternoon sun, licks salty sweat from her upper lip. The streetcar stinks of too many bodies and is full of noise, and the junior high school kids in their uniforms and blue braids and attitudes with music leaking out of the little speakers crammed into their ears irritate Ariel enough so that she uncrosses her legs and takes up more room on the wooden seat, presses her hot thigh beneath her wrinkled linen skirt against the loud girl next to her. The girl can't be more than twelve, Ariel surmises, but she has C-cup tits at least, maybe Ds. How does a body so young grow those things? Maybe the girl is older. Maybe she's dumb and has failed a couple of grades.

The girl doesn't notice Ariel's leg at all though. Instead, she busily rubs some kind of pale salve the consistency of mucus onto the propped-up elbows of the girl squatting on the seat in front of her and blathers on about what another girl did. She'll bust her fuckin skinny-ass face if she thinks about fuckin doin it again. A cursive tattoo shows on the second girl's upper arm through the short sleeve of her thin white uniform shirt. Ariel wants to swat the tub of goo out the open window. She's tired. Hot, hot. Here, inside this streetcar, perpetual summer drapes itself around Ariel's neck like a stole. Like a giant piece of raw bacon stole.

The streetcar squeals to another stop. Two waiters in their black and whites squeeze on. The junior high kids jammed up front fan their noses and talk about the waiters' pizza funk and pepperoni faces. When the streetcar takes off again, the little breeze that snakes its way past the salving girls is a drooly lick. A breeze almost worse than none. Ariel sighs and remembers woodsmoke, brown leaves dancing across a sidewalk. The people who have lived here their entire lives can't have any idea what they're missing.

She wonders what Ed will make for dinner. She wonders about her commitment to public transportation in a city like this.

Ed hollers hello from the kitchen. Miles and Ella bicker above the somber narration of Animal Planet surgery: "Lucky's femur is broken in five places." Ariel saves her breath. The instant she'd confront Ed about their children watching surgical gore is the instant he'd take the remote, change the channel, and say, "What gore? There. Look. PBS." And smile. She's given up on training him to greet her at the door with a martini.

"Changing!" Ariel yells, ascending the stairs. The house groans out its age with each footfall.

In September, cold water only runs cool. Ariel drops her head in the shower. She waits, knows that the water temperature won't change, feels nostalgic, considers where, exactly, the best place is to apply a cold pack to drop body temperature. Wrist. Throat. Sliceable places. Once, in Jamaica, a man put shell-shaped ice chips in her vagina in some form of misdirected foreplay. The ice melted. Even then, young as she was, the island and the guy alike felt fake to her. Practiced. She tries to remember the guy's name, knows she can't, not even to save her life.

The soap rests in a soupy muck in the holder. Ish. If Ed is going to tend house, then that's what he should do, but he just doesn't see things. Giant snot soap. How do you miss it?

She should be fair. Ed cooks. Ed listens to NPR.

What's His Name, the ice chip man, had a washboard stomach. Ariel didn't come. She knew she wouldn't the instant he stood at the end of the bed and caressed his own waxed chest in some staged, amorous gesture. She has no recollection of whether his was a name that suited him or not.

Names hold too much power, she thinks, or none at all. Everyone should have a chance to name themselves. Just today "Miss Sugar

Enspice" checked into the hotel. Ariel recognized the woman with crispy yellow extensions from her music video, the one where her plump ass cheeks hang out the bottom of a pair of kiwi-colored shorts.

Jesus, some of the pseudonyms that the celebrity guests use. Axel Savage. Rod Doe. Ha! Everybody behind the front desk busted guts. Rod Doe. Nameless Cock. The pubescent musician had no clue, it seemed, as he gave her, the general manager, very specific instructions on who could and who could not know his room number, what calls could be put through. He took off his dark sunglasses, stared directly into Ariel's eyes the way some men's magazine must have told him to do, and said *she* could use his room number. She felt at once mildly flattered and sick to her stomach. His dyed black hair stood in carefully spaced spikes all over his puny head. Ariel nodded politely. She bet he had acne on his back.

The idiotic name of the hotel itself can't be beat: La Belle Nouvelle, a Barcelona-modern hotel through and through smushed into the French Quarter at the edge of the Central Business District. They don't even have enough curb footage on the street to get zoned for valet parking. The bulk of the property rises orange and lime green, a contemporary cyst, in the center of the block between a department store and three empty buildings being forever renovated, the continual drilling and pneumatic hammering deafening to everyone but touring bands and the feckless groupies for whom the hotel has become a favorite. Ooh, and she can't forget the proms. Or the frat and sorority formals. Somehow, Ariel is supposed to change the clientele. A year ago April, when the new owners called Minneapolis and made the offer she couldn't refuse, she thought the name La Belle Nouvelle was likely reflective of some sort of New Orleans charm she hadn't yet experienced. Ah. Well.

Their own family's names always hover, too. Fruit fly names that won't leave. Ariel kept her surname when they married, and they gave it to their kids. Ed, fortunately, has always believed the decision to be best. But then Edgar Allan Flank is a toughie of a moniker. Ariel and Ed couldn't break completely from family tradition though. They chose two classics for their children: Miles Davis May and Ella Fitzgerald

May. Ella will answer to the nickname Fitzy when she has no choice. Drying off, walking naked into their warm bedroom, Ariel again hopes they haven't burdened their children with expectations of greatness.

Fearius sit, full-up tired of patient. His ass sore, done molded to the car seat by now. Shandra and Alphonse fighting and fighting on her stoop. "I say I finish for *seven*!" she scream at him.

Alphonse dont care, mixed everything up. Now Fearius not gettin no Shandra friends pussy.

Alphonse got the Glock in his pants still, in there for hours. Fearius feel like his dick a gun, feel like shooting big old lumpy Shandra with her witchy claws that cost more than Dom Pérignon. Except Alphonse got the Glock, so Fearius not getting no fat Shandra neither.

Fearius decide to quit Alphonses company till tomorrow. Tonight Fearius gone make a girlfriend, no matter what, make sure no Glocks nearby.

It a hot night, time he make hisself a girlfriend in the Channel by Annunciation. Lots of them over there when it hot, clucking, all together on corners like hens. Bunch a chicken heads.

Kissin between houses can turn into a lay down in no time.

"The goopas are purple," Ella says, kicking the table leg. Ariel's daughter peels cheese from the top of her lasagna with her fingers. Her chipped nail polish has disappeared.

"Guptas," Miles enunciates.

"What?" Ariel understands her kids less each day. She knows she should be frightened by this fact. "What are guptas?"

Miles, Ella, and Ed giggle. "Who," Ed says. "They're a *who*."

"What?"

"Mah-um!"

"Ed?"

"We say 'people of color,' " Ed instructs Ella, and Miles rolls his eyes. So does Ariel.

"Ed?"

"Uh huh." Ella nods. "Dark dark purple."

"Nah *ah.*"

The junior high people of color on the streetcar today gyrated in the aisle. Ariel tries to remember dancing at twelve. A table for twelve. A party of twelve. Here in this city she's learned everybody says, about a time, I'll be there for twelve. I have to be there for six. We need a reservation for nine for seven. In such instances, Ariel has yet to figure out which way they want the reservation. A bellhop told her it comes from the French, which automatically means it doesn't make any sense to Ariel. Sadly, no matter what Ariel tries, La Belle Nouvelle's high-end dinner-bar retains a reputation for serving underage drinkers.

The dancing kids filled the aisle. They seemed to want to rile people of non-color on the streetcar. Why did she have to be a non-color? She has color. "Ed?"

"Our new neighbors," he answers.

"They're Indian," Miles says knowingly.

Ed lays his hand on the table in front of Miles' plate. "We say *East* Indian," Ed corrects. This from the man who didn't notice his daughter chewing on the end of the grape magic marker till the ink had covered her entire front in a purple indelible apron. Now Ella's favorite color seems to be a shade of Gupta.

"Where?" Ariel asks, meaning which house. Two houses on their street have sold recently, the big one immediately to their right and a little one across the street next to the ratty community garden.

"Next door!" Miles yells.

"Next door!" Ella echoes and kicks the table leg again. "Next door!"

Ariel looks to Ed to see what he thinks. "Real new neighbors, then," she says. Ed, the local stay-at-home dad, keeps a close watch on the neighborhood. He recognizes everybody. He knows the names of the teenagers who live on the block. He waves hello to some of the afternoon regulars who frequent the neighborhood bar, Tokyo Rose. Sitting diagonally across the street from their house, the little ugly thing looks like a residential shack decked out in Christmas decorations year-round. She could kill the realtor for not pointing it out to her as an up-and-running bar when she flew down to check out properties, but then again, kudos to Numbnuts for fooling her. She didn't think to ask about it, and he didn't offer. Kudos to New Orleans too for burying its bars so well that outsiders don't even recognize them sitting square in the middle of a neighborhood block.

"They seem like real neighbors," Ed says. He nods but doesn't smile. He's always preaching diversity.

"Reserving judgment?"

"India is . . . ," Miles says and grins, *"the largest worry of global over-population."*

"You're quoting?" Ariel asks.

"It's true. We learned it."

Well, the May-Flank union isn't in danger of sending global population over the precipice. It's been a hard year and three months.

Ever since school started up again, Ed observes, the kids have been praying for the beasties to come while they sleep. Lately Miles calls on Yahweh. Ella begs Buddha. At bedtime, Ed requires only that they acknowledge a higher power, and they're currently running with the classics.

Miles, firstborn, prayed to the Jolly Green Giant in August. Ed had already nixed all superheroes, but he didn't think to include fictional grocery characters. His son's running list of deities strikes Ed as both laudable and absurd: hockey great Wayne Gretzky; pirate Johnny Depp in long earrings and scarves; Santa Claus; Miles' kindergarten teacher from two years ago, Mr. Zabalbeascoa (it took Ed three months to say it right); buffoon Jim Carrey; SpongeBob SquarePants; soccer magician David Beckham; and not a single woman at all, which bothers Ed somewhat.

Ed reminds himself to initiate a discussion with Miles about his gender issues, then questions yet again if Miles really has any. Miles loves his sister, after all. And Ariel, of course. It's just the age, maybe. Miles is only seven. Or maybe his boys' club list comes from the Catholic school they had very little choice about when they moved here. Ed's found out that the school has assigned God a gender—although fortunately they don't seem to be shoving religion down the kids' throats.

No matter how Ed tries, though (Ariel, too, when she has the time), the kids won't warm up to New Orleans. Ella and Miles hate the Southern city, nearly all of the school and neighborhood kids, their backyard full of biting red ants. Ants that attack. Roaches that fly. Somehow it's harder here to respect all the earth's creatures. Without question. Ed watches rats run across the power lines at night when he sits on the front porch with his single Scotch after the kids have gone to bed. He feels for them, his good, sad kids, and sips at his Scotch.

The cafeteria women at Miles' school pick on their Yankee kid for not recognizing the food names, or even the food itself. Jambalaya is not goulash, of course, but he seems to have trouble differentiating. Miles claims mean hairnetted women call him a Yankee and laugh. To Ed, it sounds much more like a word his teacher would employ.

Miles and Ella say New Orleans is sticky, and Ed agrees. Tonight, like every night, he listens to them pray.

Ella implores God for a hurricane to give them a day or two away from it all. She says, "Dear Bood-ah. Please send a beastie so there's not going to be any school yesterday and tomorrow and the next day and the next and the next." She itches at the back of her head resting on her purple beaded princess pillow.

"Is that it?"

Ella nods.

"Nothing else? No thank-yous?" They're supposed to give thanks too. And acknowledge sorrow.

Ed himself continues to pray for the survivors of the Beslan school. He can't rid his brain of the Chechen terrorist attack on the Russian grade school children. Ella and Miles are too young to be told about it, but it thumps at his chest like a knocker. The thought of those people, the terrorists, repulses him. Little children sweating to death in their underwear only to be shot and exploded and burned. It unhinges him.

His daughter shakes her head no, and Ed wonders how it is he got here, to fatherhood and New Orleans. To having children who summon a tooth-fairy Buddha: bring me something.

Ella's imitating Miles, of course. Ed really wishes their son would dig in his heels. Step up to the plate, all that. He's a brave kid at home, funny, fun. He used to be the most popular kid in kindergarten in Minneapolis. What a difference a place makes. "I'm off to your brother's room then," Ed says. " 'Night, Fitzy." He leans over and kisses Ella, her hair already tangled in the beads of her princess pillow. She knows better than to sleep on it, so he won't tell her again.

"Goo'night, Daddy."

Same as always, Ed's heart melts. Something about a daughter, they say, softens a man forever. Ed's softened enough, he supposes, but he'd love another daughter. Or son. Ariel won't think of it, though. "Don't let the bedbugs bite," he says.

"The purple ones can, right?"

Since she learned her colors, Ella has thought everything purple to be good. Purple bedbugs are allowed to bite; they only nibble and don't have teeth. "Right. I love you, Ella."

"I love you."

In Miles' room, Ariel wraps up a book about a boy who accidentally gets onto a subway car in Manhattan without his mother. It's a happy ending, but Miles likes the adventurous middle part best.

"The End," Ariel says.

"I wish *I* could ride on a subway," Miles says.

"There are subways all over the world, you know," Ed tries.

"Not in New Orleans," Miles counters.

"We have streetcars here," Ariel says. Ed can hear the faux optimism in her voice. He can't fault her. At least to himself, he can admit to having trouble with the brightly dressed tourists that often ride the streetcar through their Riverbend area. He can find little genuine about them. Many wear Mardi Gras beads no matter what the season. Some don kinked smokestack hats in purple and acid yellow velvet. They sweat alcohol. Their faces shine red. Pink Vs of needless sunburn point down from their throats. As hard as he tries, Ed cannot find a way to see the tourists sympathetically. Not even his usual tactic of looking to the youngest, the most innocent of a species helps in this instance. He used to find warthogs reprehensible creatures till he saw a documentary on them that concentrated on a single family on a reserve in South Africa. The youngsters trotted everywhere—never walked—tufts of head fur catching the breeze. He feels a mild affection for them now. But the tourists: the youngsters are loud, whiny, rude, often fat. Ed needs to work on his acceptance of overweight humans. All at once he feels compressed by his personal weaknesses. He has so much work to do yet to become good, to become a better man.

"You choose," Ed tells his son. "Where's the first city you want to ride a subway?"

"What are my choices?" Miles asks.

Ed glimpses the teenager to come. Ed will need to be a very good man by then, he knows, to deal with this child. "Let's see," he says, thinking fast. "There's London. They call it 'the tube.' Paris has their metro. And Chicago has the El. It's short for 'elevated.' "

"Aw, come on," Ariel says. "Besides those, Miles, you have choices all over the rest of the world."

Ed hates it when she does that. Undermines him. He breathes in slowly, breathes out. His mindfulness, the result of meditation, helps him recover. He chooses to give his nightly thanks right then. He's glad he has a penis. He's glad he has stomach muscles that show when he flexes them. He's glad he can run a mile in under ten minutes. He's glad he could cook his way out of a shipwreck. Ed tells Miles, "Actually, many cities and often whole countries don't have the ability to construct subways due to the water—"

"Do dead people float out of the ground here?" Miles has jerked away from subways, but Ed follows his son's train of thought. Miles is thinking about digging underground.

"Who told you that?" Ed asks.

"Nobody." Miles fiddles with some sort of latch on one of his converter plane-robot toys he's chosen to take to bed. "They were teaching us about Louisiana."

Ed glances at Ariel. She seems not to be listening. "What about Louisiana?" Ed tries.

Miles shrugs. "Do they float?"

"Did you learn about water tables today?" Ed asks and watches Ariel yawn.

"That's dumb, Dad. There's no such thing as a table made with water!"

Ed wants his Scotch badly. He has little idea how to make this place more appealing for Ella and Miles, and right now his failure is exhausting him. "Why are you asking about corpses?"

"Does it happen to dogs that people bury in the backyard?"

Bingo. That's where it's coming from. Ed questioned whether or not he should let them watch the Animal Planet program, but he decided that they were ready for some reality. Another mistake to chalk up. What could he have been thinking? Especially Ella. But she seemed just fine a minute ago. "No, Miles," he says. Ariel lies down next to Miles and closes her eyes. "Neither animal nor human corpses come out of the ground," Ed says, "here or anywhere else."

"Tameera Michaels says they do. She says her uncle floated out of the ground."

"I don't think that Tameera is telling the truth."

"Yah huh. After it rained for forty days and forty nights. She said so."

"I think Tameera is getting her stories mixed up."

"The uncle was covered in goo like a monster. And his pet dog that was in the, in the—what are they called?"

"Crypts," Ariel mumbles, her eyes closed.

"And his dog in the crip was all, all hanging hair in strings and with sores all over his body and a eyeball hanging out."

Ed can see Ariel quiver with silent laughter. "Ariel."

"What?" She opens just one eye.

"Ariel," Ed says again.

"He's just having fun," his wife answers. "There aren't any subways for him to ride here, *Dad*."

"Well, I'm sure if the water table weren't so close, New Orleans would have a wonderful subway."

Ariel elbows Miles conspiratorially, and they both laugh out loud. Why does Ed even try?

Miles, with his mother's permission now, runs with it. "The uncle had a axe in his stomach, like, like halfway out."

Ariel laughs harder.

"Good night, you two. Don't forget prayers, okay?"

They don't answer as Ed flops his hand good bye. He leaves as Miles presses on, "And two swords. In both his legs."

It's how he feels, Ed thinks. Two swords in both his legs.

Time for Scotch.

Fearius be knowin the chicken heads from the streetcar back when he still in school. They right where he know they gone be with their thick thighs and big backsides. It alright. Give Fearius more to push up on, ya heard. He know they all visit the Planned Parenthood over by Magazine. They all baby makers with protection, perfect for Fearius. They be sharing him, climbing all over him with they tongues, turn it into a juicy sandwich. A arm and leg and ass and pussy sandwich. They gone fight over Fearius he been away so long. And if they dont fight, they still know they cant say no, not when the peoples on his list include Alphonse, right at the top.

Fearius walk up, casual like.

"Wooooo, lookit here." It hafta be that dark bitch Kenyata talk first. "Little Danny *get out*!"

Why she say that? "It Fearius, bitch."

Every chicken head laugh. Cackle like they old and dried up.

"How you get that name, Little Danny? You grow big inside juvey? You grow *fearius*?" Kenyata ugly. Ugly mouth. Ugly words. Fearius decide to look straight through her like Kenyata a window. Aint nothing there.

"Hi, Danny," Teesha say, but she say it nicer. Teesha have a floppy bottom lip and yellow tiger eyes. Teesha gone do just fine tonight.

"Call me right, Teesha," he say, serious.

Teesha smile, and the others make noise. Fuck if they dont make Fearius hate they own all the easy free pussy he know about. "Alright, Fearius. Why not you tell us how you be Fearius now."

So it gone be Teesha. He gone talk the talk and she gone take him somewhere. Best be soon.

Kenyata say, "You tell us, *Fearius*." Kenyatas brother dead two years now. A dead brother earn rights or else Fearius smack her. Her brother just be dead one day in bed. A vein pop in his brain or some such.

Fearius touching Teeshas shiny belt.

"Ooooooh," the hens say.

It just gotta be easier than this, Fearius think.

"I'm thinking of driving to work," Ariel says from bed.

Ed pulls off his dirty T shirt. Ariel checks him out with a measure of objectivity. He's getting hairier, she concludes. Most men do. Her dad did. The two-night fling with her high school sweetheart revealed the same thing. She and Ed were only engaged at the time; still, she feels a tug of guilt at the memory. Ed never even suspected. Jesus, Charlie could kiss.

"Hey, I thought we agreed, A," Ed says, stepping out of his pants. Ariel can't remember a time when she's seen him step out of his underwear too before getting into bed. If and when the rare occasion arises for him to do away with his boxers, he snakes out of them under the covers.

She'd like to see him standing in the light of the bedside lamp with a raging hard-on for her. See proof of his desire for her after all the years. "Yeah, I know. We agreed that we would be 'environmentally responsible citizens,' " she says, "but I'm gonna kill somebody on the streetcar soon. Shit, Ed, these kids are awful."

"It's cultural," he says. "You know that."

"So? It's a fucking ridiculous culture. The boys take off their belts and pull their uniform pants down past their asses. Their entire asses, I'm not kidding. I mean, I'm staring at full-blown asses in their fucking underwear. Inches from my face. I got bumped in the head by a fucking ass yesterday." It's a lie, but it could have happened.

"You sound like a sailor, Wifey."

There's the word. When he wants to irritate her under the guise of being sweet, he pulls out 'Wifey.' "We have two perfectly good cars that sit in the driveway all day," Ariel counters. "You sure as shit don't go anywhere. Hubby."

Ed crawls into bed, a look of mild amusement on his face. "Don't be a racist, Ariel. Try imagining being one of those kids. Try to understand why they do what they do. Practice tolerance." He leans over and kisses her cheek.

"Your breath reeks." She hates the smell of Scotch on Ed, though it doesn't bother her on others, which says something, she supposes. Shit, he knows she's no racist. She dated plenty of Ed's *people of color* before they married. "Racial issues and cultural issues can be completely separate, and you know that. And you know full well what I'm bitching about is the cultural."

"Let's make love. In the morning you'll feel like helping the environment again."

"You're going to fuck me into riding the streetcar?" Now she's actually pissed. He doesn't even mean it. They haven't had sex in a month.

"Where's all this anger coming from?" Ed props himself up on his elbows.

"Never mind." Ariel rolls away to the edge of her side of the bed and turns out the light. Where is all her anger coming from? The streetcar, maybe. This slippery straw of a city they've drawn.

Two minutes later she says into the dark, "I'm sorry."

Ed doesn't answer.

They kissin and Teesha making moaning noises, leaning against her real baby crib, against the rails. She *so* not be no virgin, not no how. But her tiger eyes way pretty. Fearius press up on her face, but he dont wanna turn her around. He dont wanna bend her over, look over her shoulder at her baby, her baby daddy proof, sleeping right there. Lookin at the future. Looking at a mess.

She be wet, Teesha. His fingers say so. "Come on," Fearius tell her.

"Come on what," Teesha say, not much asking in her voice.

"Come on," Fearius say and push her down on the ratty carpet smell like macaroni and cheese.

"Danny, no," she say, but it too late. It gone be too late now.

She try bein a boxer, try to say she already drunk.

He cant care now. Fearius take what he want.

2

Cerise Brown drinks her caramel latte nutritional shake on her porch and watches. She's a watcher. Always been one, but now she can do it from her own property rather than from behind that tired register. She's discovered she's invisible to people who don't know to look for her, sitting still. Like a bird, or a bug. Or a woman old as cane dirt. This morning she sits in her canvas director's chair and watches the new neighbors. They're darker than Cerise, but they got noses shaped like white people's noses, and the mother wears a dot on her forehead and a sari the color of a cucumber's insides, shiny in the morning sun. The new neighbor lady makes Cerise think of dew.

Why people would come all the way from another country to New Orleans is beyond her. Crime and air-conditioning bills for newcomers, mostly. But it is her place. Move away from your people and you have exactly not much at all. You need family and friends around you. Circled. Like wagons, Cerise thinks and smiles.

Orchid Street holds her wagons, although not so many anymore. She and Roy have lived here almost since they moved up from swamp country, moved up in money too. When they bought their first car, they went back to Bayou Blue once every month for lunch with her mother. Always the same duck gumbo, greens, sweet tea. The place still fitted like home, then, but by the time the sun melted towards the trees, Cerise missed the freedom of New Orleans. Missed walking most anywhere she wanted.

As a girl, she never imagined being able to live on a street with whites, never imagined that they could all be mixed up on the same block. But that's what New Orleans gave her and Roy. Freedom. Freedom to just be human beings. Sure, their house was one of the smaller ones, and the big houses across the street all held white families, and if you looked at it a certain way it might seem that they worked for the white families, that they were their gardeners or help—like when Lenore Watts worked cleaning and leaving dinner in the oven for that bachelor Mr. Parker—but still, it amazed Cerise back then that nobody in the city looked at her as though she'd done something wrong just by being born in her skin. Now, of course, some of the houses on Orchid that need the most tending belong to white folks, renters, and some of the biggest, like the one the new family is moving into, they belong to dark people.

Cerise has watched the city change. Some days she worries for it. Not enough money to go round, and the children boss the parents. The young people come up troubled, like the Harris kids next door. That gaggle of Nate and Sharon's is all troubled, Klameisha and Debutanté with their own babies already, Angelique hanging out of boys' cars night and day. But it's the sons, Michael and Daniel, what with their ridiculous street names, Muzzle and Fearius, who are the hornet's nest of pain for their parents. Those boys are part of nothing good. Guns, Cerise knows. Worse. Both in juvenile half the time running on three years now. Cerise has not one idea how to change young men but to send them to war. Too bad no draft can save Nate and Sharon from their own boys.

Last month, Michael cracked his sister loud and clear then said she shouldn't backtalk. Imagine. Hitting your own sister. Cerise heard him plain as day from her porch through the Harrises' thin tarpaper wall. For two years since the water damage, Nate says he's replacing the siding, but even when they had siding, Cerise could hear all of them fight. She's happy her oleander bush hides the gap between their houses from the street. It hides the ugliness you can see, if not the kind you hear.

Roy steps out onto the porch and lets the screen door slap, same as always. It's his rebellion, Cerise thinks, what he does to get back at her for coming on fifty years of her complaining about him doing exactly that. That's the way it goes. It makes her smile inside her head, though no way she could let him know she's onto him.

"Cherry Baby. Marie on the phone, says she needs to get Lil Thomas to the pediatrician tomorrow. Not eating."

Cerise shakes her head. Their only child, Marie, is a panicky new mother. Came to it too late. She spent too much time educating herself and then being finicky about finding a husband, needed him to be smart *and* handsome. Always sounded like a dangerous combination to Cerise. Since having their son, Thomas, in February, Marie can't stop taking the boy to the doctor. Cerise tells Marie that the boy just needs to get hungrier and he'll take her nipple just fine. The child's developed a taste for the bottle. Marie puts a noisy pump to her swollen breasts while Cerise watches the plastic container fill with bluey milk. Immunities, Marie says.

"That boy's fat," Cerise says to Roy. "She needs to stop worryin' and let him be." Cerise sips on her nutritional shake.

Roy shakes his head. He nearly toppled over when he found out their forty-two-year-old daughter had got pregnant. No small miracle that Cerise herself had become pregnant with Marie at thirty-four. Cerise knows he believed that their daughter's wedding was the last big ticket they'd ever have to pay out, but now, with Marie and her husband, Big Thomas, both taking turns staying at home with Lil Thomas, they hint at wanting money help, and Roy and Cerise just give it. Not like they need much of their retirement, though they'd always had hopes of a camp or a time-share down in Grand Isle, maybe, or a regular vacation someplace. The big Key or Clearwater, maybe.

"Talk her down, Cherry. You know otherwise they'll be asking for donations again." Roy looks at Cerise. His same old warm eyes. Who'd have thought you could love somebody's eyes your whole life?

Cerise rises from her director's chair. She's happy the skinny legs she's got still work well enough. Not as much to look at now, but they're sturdy. In the kitchen, she picks up the phone from the counter. "Marie, now, when's the last time Lil Thomas *didn't* eat? You've got to calm down about that boy or you're going to kill him with worry."

"Mom, I don't have the energy for one of your extended metaphors. He hasn't eaten, well, almost anything, for over six hours."

The girl is going to kill the poor boy. Choke him with her worry. Drown him with her worry. "And how many hours you've got till his appointment tomorrow?" Cerise asks.

There's a pause. "Twenty-three," Marie says.

"Tell me he has a fever."

"Do you think if Thomas had a fever I'd even be at home? Mom?" Marie has that special tone of indignation in her voice, the one reserved just for Cerise.

"Don't be burdening that doctor, Marie. She won't like Lil Thomas and not even know why. Just from seeing him too much, she won't like your boy. You don't want a doctor ignoring your child." It's worth a try, anyway.

"Why must you always exaggerate, Mother? You take things ten degrees past where they make any sense and I—"

"What'd you call me for, Marie?"

Another pause. "Why won't he eat, Mom?"

Cerise sighs.

Philomenia Beauregard de Bruges resquares the proper stacks of towels in the linen closet. She walks down the stairs to her husband Joe's room. She looks inside. He lies there. She can smell it growing in him. It smells like mold. She will bleach the room when it is over. She will return the room to the parlor it is supposed to be. She walks to the kitchen.

Philomenia has told the new neighbors that her name is Prancie. She thinks it sounds like ponies. A name light and dancy. A name to cover her fifty-seven years like a long silk scarf. Prancie sounds like there is wind around.

She should have had a nickname coming up. All caring parents should give children nicknames. She tsks.

The new neighbors burn incense. The smoke travels down the narrow and through her kitchen window in the evenings when she lets the air in. The smell taints the taste of dinner. This bothers Philomenia. The incense and the neighbors' appearance both bother her. But they took her praline cheesecake with many thank-yous. She had difficulty not staring at the woman's third eye.

Philomenia will start a journal for them.

Joe calls out from his room. "Philomenia," he croaks.

Philomenia turns on the faucet. The rice needs rinsing and picking. Prancie cannot tolerate pebbles, Philomenia thinks and smiles. Oh no, Prancie cannot stand pebbles.

Cerise watches surfboarders on cable TV. She's amazed most when they finish, how they dive into the curling waves and give themselves up to that power. There's skill there.

She's seen two dark-skinned boy surfers so far. And one dark-skinned girl looks strong enough to lift a car off a grandmother's back. Makes Cerise chuckle. But the rest of them are white. Maybe the native Hawaiians have puffed up too big these days and don't surf but for fun. On another show she saw how they eat too much and are all getting fat. Spam and gravy and piles of food for very little money. Mountains of noodles and fried fish and pork chops. Sandwiches the size of your backside. No wonder why they don't win surf awards anymore.

Marie's on her way over with the boy any minute. Cerise would like to keep watching the surfers instead of comforting her daughter, work in her sudoku puzzle book, take a walk around the block. She's too old to have to look after Marie. Lil Thomas is one thing, but Marie won't leave him alone with Cerise, not for more than five minutes. Cerise swears that boy'll get smothered.

A knock sounds.

"Since when do you latch the screen door?" Marie asks when Cerise answers.

"You think it would prevent anything but a cat from getting in?" Cerise asks her daughter. Cerise glances at Lil Thomas. He's wide awake, his brown curls pretty and tight. He could be a little girl for how long his eyelashes are.

"Well, *I* couldn't get in," Marie says, already with The Tone, and here Cerise hasn't said a thing to her bad, anything that should warrant it.

They stand on the porch, and Cerise diverts out of instinct, "Lil Thomas looks fine."

"This neighborhood isn't getting any better, Mother. You really shouldn't leave your door open."

Hadn't Marie just complained she couldn't get in? "Well, hello there, Lil Thomas," Cerise says to her grandson.

The boy chortles, and Cerise's belly warms all the way through. She could jog around the block the way the boy makes her feel. Maybe she'll get one of those speed buggies she sees, the ones that look like off-roading bicycles with nubby tires, the buggies that could do cross-country tours. Cerise could take Lil Thomas through the Smokies, through the Grand Canyon! Up and down the Hawaiian mountains when the surfers aren't in contests.

"Hello to you, too," Marie says. She swings Lil Thomas in his car seat and looks around at the neighborhood.

Cerise smiles at the thought of jogging Lil Thomas through Audubon Park in an off-roader. She'd take it on the grass, under the live oaks older than anything she knows. She'd run over the edges of picnic blankets and dawdle by the youngsters smoking their weed in the gazebo, playing bad guitar. "Why, hello, Marie," Cerise tells her daughter and leans to kiss her cheeks times two.

"People don't do that outside of Europe, Mother."

Marie used to love their French greetings. God knows why the woman got pregnant. She's old-dog cranky, ready to snap at a petting hand. "Come on in out of the heat then," Cerise tells Marie.

They sit at the kitchen table, Lil Thomas in his car seat on a chair. Cerise needs to bring up the childcare article she read in one of her women's magazines this month about the shape of babies' heads. Their heads can get flat on the back, sometimes even sort of square-shaped when they're left in the same position, in the same carrier. Cerise doesn't want any grandson of hers to be a squarehead, but she'll have to find a way to get at the subject later, after Marie settles some.

Marie stands and opens cupboards in that reflexive way she has, looking for food. Cerise smiles at her daughter's old habit. "Rice pudding left over in the fridge," Cerise tells her. Of course Marie already knows there won't be junk, but she can find real cooked food any day of the week in Cerise's kitchen.

"I want salt," Marie says. "I can't get enough salt these days. Is that normal?"

"It's normal if it's what you want. Listen to your body. It'll talk—" Cerise stops herself. Her advice isn't working well just now.

"My body says 'I'm a cow,'" Marie says. "'Milk me, feed me, milk me.'"

At least Marie still has some sense of humor, which makes Cerise happy. "Salt holds water," she tells her. "You need water to nurse."

Marie opens the cupboard with spices, dried peppers, sugar. "I feel laden, Mom. I'm a donkey with saddlebags."

"It'll pass. Eat what you want." Cerise watches her daughter pick up the little sacks of bulk spices tied with their handwritten twisty ties from the health store up the way. Marie presses her nose into the plastic flower blossom that tops one of the bags. "Mmm. Curry powder."

She's still Marie. "Mmm is right," Cerise says back. "Nice with goat, or so they say." Cerise's never made a thing with goat in her whole seventy-plus years.

"You'd never!" And then Cerise gets her daughter's smile. Good as gold, Marie's is.

Cerise glances to Lil Thomas and sees him stick something into his mouth the color of a purple crayon, shaped like an eraser. "Get that out," she tells him, grabbing. It's a tear-away ticket from somewhere. Cerise holds it up to Marie. "What's this from?"

"What?"

"Lil Thomas."

"Oh, damn it." Marie walks over and takes the gooey ticket. "There's a raffle. For a house out in Metairie."

Cerise has listened to Marie talk about wanting to move to the suburbs ever since she was a girl, always wanting to live like somebody in another place. But Metairie is the suburb of Anywhere, America, one of hundreds of identical suburbs across the country. Suburbs from sit-coms. Metairie reminds Cerise of one big shopping mall. It's at least as ugly. "How much one of them cost?"

Marie wipes the ticket on her pinstriped skirt and turns away. "He can put a raffle ticket in his mouth but damn if he nurses," she says into the cupboard.

"Those raffles for houses cost money," Cerise says.

"A hundred dollars, Mom. The raffle ticket cost a hundred dollars." Marie goes back to the refrigerator. Lil Thomas begins to fuss.

Cerise bites her tongue. It took her more than a long shift behind the register to make that kind of money. And a hundred dollars is the clean sum, a lot of times in multiples, that they always give to Marie and Thomas. "I see that playing poker is popular these days."

"Can you just stop it? Please?"

"Is the raffle house nice?"

Marie removes a jar of pickled okra from the fridge door. Lil Thomas squawks, working up to a cry. Cerise's daughter puts the jar down on the table and cups her breasts. "He makes me leak," she says.

"That happens," Cerise says. "It's natural." What are the odds of winning one of those raffle houses?

Marie picks up Lil Thomas and bounces him, makes shushing sounds. He works himself up into a full baby wail.

Marie huffs and plunks her donkey self into a chair. She starts unbuttoning her blouse.

"Sometimes, Marie," Cerise says, "you have to put up with crying."

Marie rolls her eyes, actually scoffs. "Mother, that's inane. Yes, I know I have to put up with crying." She jostles Lil Thomas, trying to undo her fancy-label top. Lil Thomas' head wobbles.

Cerise wipes at crumbs that don't exist on the table. "Some women back at the store lost their whole paychecks to the casinos in a single night. Mississippi might could be a bad place."

"Might could," Marie says to Lil Thomas, trying to stuff her nipple into his mouth. He twists his head back and forth. Marie's breasts look about to burst, and suddenly Cerise wants to cry too. Poor boy. Poor mother. " 'Might could' is a colloquialism, Lil Thomas," Marie says.

" 'Might could' *might could* ruin your chances of a scholarship when you grow up."

Lil Thomas shoves Marie's nipple out of his mouth with his tiny tongue. Who wouldn't? How did Cerise ever raise such an awful daughter? Cerise yearns for an afternoon with surfers on ESPN2. The zebras and antelopes on the Animal Planet channel would do just fine too. They make babies that trot religiously behind their parents. And then they finally leave. They don't borrow money. They don't make fun of their parents.

Cerise looks up from her hand circling on the kitchen table to see tears running down Marie's cheeks. Lil Thomas wails and wails, a high-pitched bleat punctuated with chokes, hitches. The padding of his car seat is a stylish leopard print. Cerise knows that she is wrong. She is seventy-six years old. Enough. She can help her daughter somehow.

"The house isn't even built yet," Marie says. "The raffle house." She stares at screaming Lil Thomas as if he's an asteroid, a thing flung out of the sky. "But the drawings of it are beautiful."

The Hollywood people play poker so well because they're actors, Cerise thinks. Sometimes they make more money in a hand than Cerise ever made in a year. She can act, for sure, same as all married women, but she's not sure she can hide everything from a daughter. It's hard to hide all that you need to.

Prancie, as Philomenia has decided to sign at the bottom of her journal entries, resquares the stacks of towels in the linen closet again. The toad has not left his bed since his last treatment. Their insurance is standard, but it is not perfect. Gaps will exist in their coverage in six months. Joe has five months, then, to die.

Prancie decides that she will make another cake for the neighbors. She will make a cake that allows her into their house. Likely they have done terrible things to the traditional interior. Poke-holes and whatnot. Terrible things. Who has a last name that sounds like fish in an aquarium? Gupta. It is simply not right. Prancie is appalled at the smells that waft from their kitchen. Still, they take her cakes, and she is certain that the coconut cream will warrant an invitation inside. Damage is damage, though. Wrongs already done. Wallpaper smells like its inhabitants for years.

The neighborhood has taken one turn after the next. Prancie thought that the block was again making strides when the Minnesota family moved in, but, alas, the father has turned out to be a drunkard. Prancie has seen the man—Ed—drinking at night on his porch. Imagine. With children inside the home. She has made certain to note his appearances in her journals. He is already cross-referenced. What else does a person drink so slowly, with ice in a tumbler? It took Prancie only two nights of observation to decide she had concluded correctly.

Joe must be checked, she reminds herself. The air in the house will be better without Joe in it. She removes the bag of finely shredded coconut from the pantry.

No money paid out to Marie, Thomas, and Lil Thomas equals a celebration. Marie's finally left with Lil Thomas and a promise to call later. Cerise tends to side dishes in the kitchen while Roy does his thing outside, having wheeled out the grill in honor of the evening. His ribs don't zing like they used to, but his chicken has gotten better. He's got a batch of thighs on for tonight. Roy's scare with his heart makes Cerise even happier to have nights like this, the sun clinging low and muggy to the skyline, the quiet whoosh of Carrollton traffic up the way. She has it in her to ask Nate and Sharon, the whole Harris family over, even those troubled boys if they're around, for dinner. The drive to the Winn-Dixie isn't terrible. They have double coupons on beef all month.

She walks to the porch where she can see Roy standing at his big oil drum grill at the curb. They always feed anybody comes around, same as usual, but they don't usually manage the proper invites. The older two of the little Harris grandchildren will be by regardless, and one or two hungries from Tokyo Rose. "Roy," Cerise calls out, screen door in hand, "we need more meat? Invite some people?"

"Cherry, we not feeding no army." He smiles. Cerise can see the dark place where the molar used to be. They're only missing four teeth between them, not too bad. She never did order herself the bridge, though. For just one missing tooth, way in the back, it wasn't worth it. Roy, his bridge fits fine, he says. Maybe or maybe not they'll get a new one for this last-gone tooth of his. A seventy-eight-year-old with most of the teeth in his mouth is finer than fine for Cerise. Never, really, did she think she'd love a man so much. All those fights, the times with others messing in their marriage. But now Cerise lays her body down again after her bathroom trip in the mornings, watches Roy breathe, and thinks herself the luckiest woman around. Most of his front teeth are still pearly white, too. Lucky, lucky.

Roy's smile fades at the same time they both hear it, one of those miniature motorcycles. They look like they're made for dwarves in the circus, those things. The Harris children have friends who bring them round, and then they all whiz up the one-ways the wrong direction. Their heads barely poke up over the hoods of cars on those little machines. Cerise fights her clucking. She watches Roy cross his arms, his usual response. They try not to let what they can't control get them down. It's a good life philosophy, she thinks.

Cerise steps to the curb next to Roy. The miniature motorcycle sounds like a weed whacker on crack. Their neighborhood, a maze of one-ways, is usually safe enough, but you never know. The machine carrying a young man more than twice its size zooms around the corner from Poire Street and up the wrong way of Orchid. Cerise and Roy watch it wobble over the permanently grooved pavement. It's Michael Harris, Cerise can tell. She recognizes his particular slouch.

"Boy's going to kill himself," Roy says, hefting the lid of the grill.

"Should we feed him before he does?" Cerise asks.

"Winn-Dixie?"

"No harm in food for the neighborhood." Cerise waves at Michael Harris as he caroms past, nearly bouncing from one parked car to the next. The boy'll take his head off with a rearview. The tires of the tiny motorcycle are nearly round and flat black, no tread in sight. "Maybe we can get the new neighbors outside."

"Doubt it," Roy says. "But we can be neighborly."

"Yes, we can."

Cerise walks back to the porch. "Dogs? More chicken?"

"Dogs, Cherry. No sense wasting."

It's true kids like hot dogs best, but more and more Cerise hates feeding anybody junk. And she bets the new neighbors don't eat them, although she might be wrong. She'll pick up more chicken too. She thinks Indians eat chicken. And probably chicken dogs. She could split the difference.

Cerise goes inside and checks on her mustard greens, her black-eyes. Almost done. Her cholesterol's dropped since she quit with the pork. That and taking her Lipitor. She cheats both dishes using turkey bacon now. Nobody, Marie and Roy included, seems to notice, so Cerise keeps with her new recipes and stays quiet.

She pulls her handbag from the hall chifforobe and the keys from their bowl, and as she checks her hair in the mirror, Cerise can hear the whining motorbike again, the streetcar ringing its bell down on Carrollton, a Harris grandkid crying next door, a dog barking, the refrigerator kicking in, the rhythmic ticking of the overhead fan, and she understands, she understands it all, the way it's supposed to be.

Outside on her steps, Cerise sees Michael Harris up the block, hunkered over the mini motorcycle, winding it out at full speed. If the boy had a wig on, it'd fly off. He reminds her of a buzzing bee coming down the road, a big brown bee in a white T shirt. Cerise laughs at the thought when the boy starts to bobble over the grooves in the pavement again. He doesn't let up, though, just keeps on speeding, only this time she can see he's losing control. He's getting closer and weaving wider and wider like a water hose left on, snaking back and forth. Roy lowers the grill lid. The boy sits up tall in his seat, and Cerise can actually see his fingers squeeze the brake lever before he plants a foot on the asphalt. It happens so fast, and it takes an hour. It takes a lifetime.

The sitting up and the braking and his foot do something to Michael Harris' course. His movements make him fly. Michael Harris and the motorbike somersault in the air, the boy hanging on to the bike as if the thing will save him, as if it's a parachute.

Cerise backs up her steps despite herself. Her body has the sense before her brain how to react, what's about to happen.

Michael Harris flies straight at Roy.

A thud, a terrible noise. Barbeque sauce strings out into an arc in the air.

Roy and Michael Harris land on their little patch of lawn near the curb. The boy crawls onto his knees, long shorts down around his thighs, his drawers showing. The miniature bike is gone. But the oil drum grill is there. There, there, there. The grill is on top of Roy.

Cerise rushes down the stairs and goes to lift the grill. Her body and her brain both have nothing to do with it. She lays her hands on.

3

Ed rushes from the dishwasher to the front window.

"What the hell was that?" Ariel calls down the stairs.

"I don't know." He opens the front door.

"What was that noise?" Miles asks, magically at Ed's side.

"What was that noise?" Ella echoes, chewing on fruit leather, fingering Ed's pant leg.

"I don't know. Stay here." The kids bunch up next to Ed anyway as he steps down to the sidewalk. He can't quite see over the cars lining the street, but there's a white tennis shoe in the gutter, and then Cerise Brown begins screaming. Ed's scalp tingles. He clutches the kids, shoves them together. "Stay *here*. I mean it." He races across the street to where old Roy Brown lies. His big barrel grill pins him to the ground.

"Get it *off*! Get it *off*!" The old woman holds her hands in the air. Something is wrong with her palms. One of the Harris boys sits on the grass a few yards away with his long shorts leg pulled up, staring at his socked foot. It flops loosely to the side. A pink bone pokes through the boy's dark shin. In a sick second Ed realizes that the flesh on Cerise Brown's palms is charred, one of them white and grotesquely red where pieces of it have been pulled away. Something very wrong has happened. Roy moans.

Ed bends to lift the grill, stops.

"Get it *off*! Oh, my Roy!"

Ed sees that the grill rests with the lid's handle on Roy's waist, both his arms trapped beneath. The lid is still closed, the charcoal evidently contained within. Ed risks it spilling all over the old man, though, if he does not do this right. Roy wears cotton workmen's pants, a T shirt. Surely they have not saved Roy's skin beneath them. Ed has seconds. Roy has seconds. Ed needs to help, but he can think of no easy way to free Roy without risking the lid opening. Ed looks down, tries to open his mind, sees his rubber-soled sandals strapped on his feet.

"Roy," Ed says firmly, crouching, unstrapping.

"Help!" the woman wails.

"Roy," Ed says again. "Roy Brown. Can you hear me?"

The old man nods, surely in shock, but his unblinking eyes hold Ed's gaze.

"Roy, if you can help me," Ed says as he scrambles to put his sandals on his hands, "I want you to try to scoot backwards exactly when I say. Do you understand?" Ed is vaguely aware of other neighbors coming their way.

"Dad?" Miles asks, his little feet appearing inside Ed's small circle of vision there on the grass.

Roy's eyes move from Ed's in the direction of Miles. "Back, boy," the old man actually says, and suddenly Ella is there next to her brother.

"Daddy?"

"Get back!" the old man roars, and the kids turn and run, and Ed puts one sandaled hand on the lid near Roy's torso and the other opposite, on the bottom, and begins to tip the grill back up towards its wheeled legs. His arms shake with the weight, the pressure of trying to keep the lid from opening. The grill's wheels pivot and slip. Ed feels something knot in his back.

"*Now*," Ed tells Roy. "Scoot. *Move now.*" Ed won't be able to hold it long.

Arms freed, the old man drags himself backwards and out from under the grill. Ed drops the heavy barrel. Gray and orange-hot charcoal spills out the opened mouth. Some kind of meat sizzles in the pile.

Ed stands and looks around. Other neighbors jog up now, the bartender from Tokyo Rose, the Tulane students from three doors down. "Call 911," Ed tells them.

"I'm pre-med," the bartender says and bends down to Roy. One of the Tulane students takes out her cell phone.

Ariel runs from across the street, her hair wet, a look of panic smeared across her face. She stops at the kids, grabs them, runs her hands over them, makes them turn around.

"Oh, my," Cerise Brown says. Her palms are something from a horror movie. Ed immediately knows that he will be a better vegetarian for a long time to come.

"Ed?" Ariel asks.

Ed lunges at his family with his flippered paws, hugs them, and then sees him, sees the neighbor kid. Michael Harris still stares at his foot the way he might at an algebra equation that makes no sense whatsoever.

Prancie steps carefully across the street in her mules. She holds her coconut cream cake aloft. She has waited patiently. Finally the second ambulance left containing that terrible older Harris boy, Michael. Prancie has noticed that the Harrises have not allowed him in their home for the last two weeks and four days exactly. He comes round, however, most days. Too little too late, she thinks. But the parents' decision does show a surprising bit of gumption.

So many folks dapple the Browns' lawn that it feels almost festive. A wonderful mood, really. Prancie looks for the Guptas. She saw through her ginger leaves that they arrived on the scene shortly after the drunk had removed the grill from Mr. Brown. Now the entire street's worth of neighbors mills about. Children intermingle. Adults converse.

Where is that Mrs. Gupta? Certainly Prancie's ruse will work. What could the woman do but ask Prancie into her home? No one would dare hold a coconut cream in the street for long.

"How kind of you," Mrs. Gupta says in her thick accent, appearing in a flash out of the neighborhood tableau. "Now that the emergency has abated, a cake is exactly what this situation calls for." The woman takes the cake from Prancie and gives it directly to Sharon Harris. "Let me get plates and forks," she tells Sharon and then bustles across the street in her abominable orange sari.

Prancie stands with her mouth agape. She had not expected such a possibility. *Catching flies, Philomenia?*

Sharon Harris nods, acknowledging Prancie's presence. "Philomenia," Sharon says.

There is no use in allowing Sharon the new nickname, Prancie thinks. The mother has daughters whose names resemble venereal diseases. Sharon would not understand. "Sharon," Prancie provides back, staring at her own cake, enrobed in its perfect angora blanket of coconut. It does not play well against the background of Sharon's overly snug T shirt advertising the photograph of a passed-away Harris relative. Behind Prancie's cake, the dates of the boy's short life stretch across Sharon's drooping bosom.

Watching through the ginger leaves, Prancie was not surprised to see that Sharon Harris did not climb into the ambulance as well. Indeed, Prancie admits a fluttering of admiration for Sharon mustering such reserve. Perhaps the two of them are a small bit alike. Addressing what they must.

Prancie turns at the sound of the drunk's voice. He retells his tale. The man is a farce. A charlatan. But who on the block would know this besides Prancie?

"I did the only thing I could think of," Ed Flank says. Prancie clenches her teeth at the man's boasting. He is circled by neighbors and fellow drunks from the block's barnacle, Tokyo Rose. "What else could I do?"

"Dude," one of the Tokyo Rose parasites says, "you're a frickin' hero." The young man sways and holds a bottle of beer aloft to Ed Flank.

Prancie considers returning home to her phone to report open glass containers on the street. Only cans and plastic are allowed, despite what the containers might hold, much to Prancie's consternation. That Mardi Gras continues to rob the state of millions of dollars' worth of interstate highway repair because the city chooses to ignore drinking outside of preordained establishments vexes Prancie daily. But she will not make that phone call just yet.

"It red or white inside?" Sharon Harris asks.

"Pardon?"

"The cake."

Clearly Prancie has made a coconut cream, not a red velvet. "How are your grandchildren?" Prancie asks. She would very much like to have lost count of the number of illegitimate children across the street. Regrettably, she has had no such luck.

"Growing faster than you can feed 'em. Klameisha's boy, aw. Apple of my eye." Sharon looks around at the Browns' lawn. "Terrible, just terrible."

Prancie wonders if the woman feels even one tablespoon of guilt for the fact that her son caused the tragedy. "It is," Prancie says. "Will you be going to Charity Hospital?" All New Orleanians know that Charity is the sole place for true emergencies.

"Michael ridin' to Touro," Sharon offers cursorily. "Just broke his leg. He act like a man, he can be a man."

Sharon works at Touro hospital in some capacity or other that requires her to wear those ill-fitting purple and patterned hospital workers' garments. She must still carry insurance on her Michael, being that he is not yet eighteen. Prancie considers, for a short moment, how hard it must be for Sharon to practice her version of tough love. Mothers always love their first boys best. "I suppose he will need a—"

"How Joe treatments going?" Sharon asks about Prancie's husband.

Where is that Mrs. Gupta? The woman and her husband scurried with impressive speed across the street for the Brown emergency. "He says hello to everyone," Prancie says. "Joe says hello."

"So he doin' alright?"

"Yes."

Tectonic plates have shifted inside Ariel's skull. If Ed is not always the passive man she has painted him to be, then he has to be somebody different. She watches Miles run around happily with the other kids on the block for the first time since they have moved here. The boys and girls both stop and heft random objects, a tiny potted azalea losing its leaves, a baby's car seat. They growl and pretend the things weigh hundreds of pounds. Superheroes in hand-me-downs. A little girl, no older than two, squats in her loaded diapers and yanks a dead banana frond from a tree in the Harrises' yard, holds it over her head, and shows her new teeth, looking for others to see.

Ella clings to her father, and Ariel knows their daughter won't leave his side now for days. Word is that Ed may well have saved old Roy Brown's life. Ariel still can't believe what her husband managed.

Ed displays his sandals, soles up. On one of them, a melted groove marks the dirty surface. "I can't imagine what Cerise must have felt," Ed says to the group of neighbors and barflies.

Ariel can't either. To lose the use of your hands . . . Would Ariel try to do the same for Ed? She could lift a tractor trailer off Miles and Ella, but she has to wonder what she would do for the man she married. Ariel feels shame creep up her neck. "Amazing," Ariel says.

"Palm skin is way different than skin on the rest of your body," a customer from Tokyo Rose offers.

Ed nods.

"Her lines will change," Ganesh Gupta says.

"Sorry?" Ariel asks.

The man displays his own pink palms. "Her life line. Head and heart lines. I would like to see what the grafting process does. She will be a child. Her hands will say that she is a girl again."

Such a strange and terrible welcoming party for the Guptas, Ariel thinks. Indira and Ganesh Gupta seem extraordinarily intelligent. She's happy to have them on the block. Their children, Elizabeth and William, are nearly the same age as Ella and Miles, in reverse gender order. Ariel's already seen Miles purposely including Elizabeth in their play. A good son. Her good son.

"Come," Indira says, returning to the group, her arms full. "There is cake." Ariel has learned Indira is a new women's studies professor at Loyola University. Ganesh works as an environmental researcher, specializing in reptiles. He has a temporary position with the Audubon Zoo.

They all bump and jumble over to Sharon Harris, who holds a coconut-covered cake. "What a beautiful cake," Ariel says. It looks like something from the cover of a magazine. "You could bake those for our restaurant."

Sharon grins. "Miss Ariel," she says in greeting.

"Hi, Sharon."

Philomenia stands awkwardly next to Sharon. She offers a half-smile. Ariel doesn't understand the woman at all. She feels like a puzzle piece from a different box. "Hi," Ariel says to her.

"A lovely sweet," Indira says. "Thank you." She carries a large knife and plastic forks and plates. "Where shall we cut it?"

The kids, smelling sugar on the air, appear fast as sharks to blood.

Sharon parades the cake to the Browns' tidy porch. "Little pieces," she says. "A lot to go around."

Ariel rubs Ed's back through his shirt. "Did you lock up their house?"

"Not yet." Cerise Brown entrusted her house to Ed with so much sense and calm Ariel could hardly believe it. The thin, proud old lady gestured with her elbow at her dropped bag and key ring on their front walk, her raised hands such a mess Ariel winced. All of it, such a crazy, horrible mess of an accident. The Harris kid's little motorcycle was still running, lying on its side in between the banana trees, before somebody killed it.

A grungy man with a blond beard, a guy Ariel recognizes from Tokyo Rose, says, "We need to bring flowers."

Indira cuts into the furry icing. People agree with the bearded man.

"We should lock their door," Ariel says, holding out her hand to Ed. He gives her the keys.

"Balloons always make me smile," Sharon says.

Ariel looks at the woman's T shirt. She wonders what the relationship of the boy on it was to Sharon. Ariel cannot imagine. Truly. "Balloon bouquets," Ariel says blankly. Her head feels screwed on wrong. She sips at her free bottle of beer from the bar. She should lock the

Browns' door now, but she checks herself, thinks that locking it in front of all the friendly people, the caring people who rushed to the old couple's aid, would give the wrong message.

She looks down. Cerise Brown's key chain contains only three keys. How simple life must be with three keys. Between the hotel, home, and cars, Ariel herself is the begrudging bearer of dozens.

Indira and Sharon feed the littlest ones first. Philomenia stands slightly apart from the rest. "Prancie," Indira says, "come, please, have some of your cake."

What? What is Indira calling Philomenia? The strange neighbor's face colors. She takes a tentative step towards the vying children. Philomenia made the cake? "It's your pretty cake?" Ariel asks.

"My childhood nickname," Philomenia says. The woman's posture astounds Ariel. Straight as a ballerina.

"Wow," Ariel says. "I mean, the cake's really pretty."

"Thank you." Philomenia takes a sliver on a plastic plate and stares at it.

"How old is Roy?" somebody asks.

"He's gotta be in his seventies," the bearded man says, bellying up for his piece, Heineken in hand.

"Good thing Pedro's pre-med," somebody else says.

"Pedro's his bartending name. He's really Thurston."

"What?" Ariel doesn't follow.

"Thurman, not Thurston. Some kind of family name."

"He knew what to do."

"Yeah," one of the lingering Tulane students says, "but not like how—like what *you* did." Ariel watches the girl nudge Ed with her silky young shoulder. Is she flirting? Is Ed good-looking to college students?

"Well, you were pretty quick on the draw," Ed says back. He whips out an imaginary cell phone and holds it to his ear. "911."

Ariel's not sure she wants any cake. What was she thinking? Same old Ed.

Only he's not.

"Bigger," a kid says.

"Eat that first," Sharon tells the boy. "Git."

Ariel admires Sharon's chutzpah, helping to pass out cake after her son's caused a terrible accident. Ella stays glued to Ed's leg. "You want cake, Fitzy?" Ariel asks.

Ella glowers at Ariel. Ariel's used the wrong name in public. Ella purses her lips, barely says, "Yes." It really is a pretty cake. It reminds Ariel of something from a fairy tale. A Cinderella cake. It must be four layers tall.

"More," another kid says.

Dark grows in from around the edges, from under the raised houses, drips in from the leafy canopy of live oaks. In the distance, the streetcar screeches around its turn from St. Charles to Carrollton, and Ariel knows in a strange instant, surrounded by hot bodies once again, that she has lost her tether. Something more than Michael Harris on his mini motorcycle has run amok.

"I'm going to lock their door," Ariel announces, deciding that all the Good Samaritans should hear her. "But, hey, if anybody talks to them before we do, and they need anything, Ed's around with the keys, okay?"

A couple people clap Ed on the back again, for the fiftieth time. Ariel locks the Browns' door. She wonders if she should check the house later when everyone has gone home. Water any plants or do dishes.

"The ambulance people seemed to know what they were doing, at least."

"Paramedics."

"Yeah. They were good. That woman paramedic was way real good."

"We should pray tonight."

"An' order flowers. Yo, Charity let in flowers, right?"

"Somebody needs to be in charge of flowers."

Ariel stands on the Browns' porch and takes in the view. Cerise Brown was always out on this porch, with a wave to Ariel, by the time she left for work in the morning.

The view is better from this side of the block.

Ed needs to mow their lawn.

Ed feels something other than peace and understanding flowing through his veins, and he worries about it. He's nearly clogged with mixed emotions, and he considers going to Tokyo Rose for a Scotch. The beer he tries not to gulp isn't even registering. He knows it has to be adrenaline, of course, but more than that, he's concerned that he's proud. He can't help himself for talking about what he managed to do with Roy Brown, and he sees that Miles is proud as well, which only perpetuates the issue.

Ella has glommed on, too. How frightening for her to see the Browns burned and in pain. Ed can't go into the bar, of course, but he also can't stop running the looped tape of the rescue, over and over. Something seems injured in his back, but damn if he can feel it at the moment.

Considering his sandals, Ed thinks that Roy Brown might actually end up being alright. Well, that he might make it with injuries not much worse than his wife's. Ed's thought it through: if the charcoal sat for however long on the bottom of the oil barrel while Roy grilled food, the bottom was going to be much hotter than the lid. And it was actually the side of the barrel that had rested on Roy, not the bottom. The charcoal shifted, obviously, but the barrel itself buffered the heat for a while. Roy might be okay.

"Daddy, I don't want it," Ella says, holding her plate of cake up to Ed's chest. The old man could have sustained significant injuries from the collision, however.

"Okay, sweetie. You don't have to eat it."

How tenuous life is. Ed recognizes the toddler wandering around, dragging the dead banana leaf. She's Debutanté's little girl, Arlet. The girl's maybe two, the mother no older than seventeen. Ed thinks about getting new palm lines, how he could change his future with new creases in his hands. Be a different person.

But he's already a different person. He's a man who has rescued another.

"Daddy." Ella tips her plastic plate towards his shirt.

Ariel stomps down the stairs. "Give me that," she says to Ella. "Wasting when others want more isn't right. Here, Sharon." Ariel gives Ella's plate back to Sharon. "She didn't touch it."

Ed can't figure out Ariel's short temper the last number of months. He should let her brusqueness go without comment. "Moo-*deee*," he says for some reason instead.

Ariel smirks. "Were you going to simply let her smash it on your stomach?" She does the cocky head thing she's learned since moving here. "All zoned out from being a hero?"

He wishes she would be kinder to him, especially in front of others. He hasn't done anything wrong. On the contrary.

"We should have dinner before dessert anyway," Ariel says to Indira and Sharon.

"I don't even try stopping 'em from getting into the sugar," Sharon says. "Can't stop 'em so I join 'em." She laughs.

Indira chuckles too. "Children have a much higher tolerance for sugar than adults."

"Fruit works, sometimes," Ed offers.

"The last number of days," Indira says, "my children have been eating far too many of Prancie's treats."

Ed wonders when Philomenia changed her name. Likely she's trying to get herself invited over for dinner at the Guptas' house. She did the same to them when they first arrived.

"Moving can be such a trying experience," Philomenia says. "I thought it might be nice to have something you need not bake yourself."

The Tokyo Rose customers dribble back into the bar, and with them goes Ed's buoyancy. He would like to go home. "Time for dinner, then?" he asks Ella.

His daughter nods and raises her arms to be picked up.

"Ella, that's enough," Ariel says. "You can walk."

Ed stoops to lift Ella and winces. "Daddy's back is sore," Ariel says. "You walk, young lady."

"Sorry," he says to Ella.

Ed, Ganesh, and Indira agree to go to the hospital after her morning classes. Ariel has to work, of course. Sharon Harris busies herself with a grandson, wiping his face. Philomenia nibbles at her sliver of cake. Neither says a word.

After typing in Ed and his family's home phone number and Ariel's cell into his own, Ganesh agrees to collect donations for flowers at the bar. Miles trots over, and Ed brings his family back across the street.

The new night sighs. Glossy leaves rustle. Ed takes the stairs to their porch in his bare feet and notices how warm the bricks still are. He hopes Ariel will give him a back massage later, that the kids will go to sleep easily, that Cerise and Roy Brown will be alright.

And then Ed thinks of the Harris boy again. He never cried out in pain. Ed will make sure the kids pray for Michael Harris tonight too.

Ariel finds Ed on the porch. She sits next to him, leans over and takes a goodwill-gesture sip of his Scotch, then realizes he's been crying. "What is it?"

"That kid. Michael Harris." Ed turns his face away from Ariel and sniffs.

"He's a shit," she says. And he is. Ariel has seen him be downright cruel to his younger brother, the one who looks so much like Michael that you need to see them together to realize which is which. Michael is taller, but they both wear their drug-selling uniforms, white Ts, droopy blue jeans, white-white running shoes. Both have the same shaved heads and attitudes. Ariel considers her husband, considers this Rescue Ed. "Please tell me you're not feeling bad for him."

Ed turns to gaze at Ariel. "Why shouldn't I? Why don't you? Who knows how long before he walks right again, if he even will."

"He nearly killed two people—two *old* people—being an idiot."

"You never had any fun as a kid?" Ed asks, and suddenly Ariel doesn't like his tone, doesn't like the condescension in his voice. Rescue Ed. She has to work tomorrow.

It's all she can manage: "I'm glad you were able to help today. I need to get some sleep."

Ariel has no idea what time Ed opens the bedroom door, but the sharp crack of hallway light jolts her awake. Ed reaches back around the doorjamb and flicks the light off. Their room fills again with a browny-black.

Fumbling, Ed sheds his clothes and crawls noisily between the sheets. He doesn't seem able to lie still, wriggles and twists, trying to unobtrusively force the tucked-in cover out from the foot of the bed.

"Ed. *Please.* I have to work in the morning."

"Can we make another baby?"

Ariel is so tired she can hardly think. Environmentalist Ed. Rescue Ed. They don't jibe exactly. Do firefighters recycle? Does Superman take the streetcar to the grocery store? "Babies drain the environment," she says, too wiped out to care if she makes sense.

"That's true." Ed seems to consider. "But can we practice?"

"Ed," she says. It's all she needs to.

4

In the morning, Alphonse break the news. He give Fearius good work, tell Fearius he gone sell Avon again. Not no lookout, not no runner. Fearius be taking over his bros blocks in Pigeontown, deep the other side of Carrollton, while his bro lay up over by Touro in a cast and those ropes and what. His bro text messaged Alphonse late, toll him to tell Fearius about his leg. Alphonse say they drive over by the hospital when it get dark.

After they grown and out from under the thumbs of Moms and Pops, Fearius bro Michael go by Muzzle, a name like what a fighter pit got to wear before he get into the ring. Like there no taming him. Or Muzzle like on a gun. Fearius think it a good name. It done took Fearius a long time come up with his own, have to be like his bros but different.

This morning Fearius find out he have to give Muzzle thirty percent his take each day. Alphonse get fitty, less than normal but lots after Muzzles share. It leave Fearius twenty percent. It how it is when a nigga comes out juvey. But it change soon enough if Fearius play the game good, careful. Fearius spose he should be happy the runners and look-outs be paid outta Alphonse pocket, not his own.

Now Fearius hoof it back and forth between the dead house stoop to the cars rollin slow down the street. Nobody in the house for over six months. Muzzle done tore down the For Rent sign a long time ago after he heard the owners live by Florida, dont even check it. The dead house be painted pink and peeling brown, and it make little kids want to eat the curls like they chocolate. Fearius stopped two kids already, toll them eating paint make them stupid. Toll them not to come around no more, that it his house now. One the boys dripped snot out his nose and asked where Muzzle be. Fearius raised his hand like he ready to smack him and they both ran round the corner, made Fearius smile.

Now he hoof it, sellin his Avon, two for ten on the white, three for ten on the lime green. He look enough like Muzzle most customers dont notice or care, just pass him money in a handshake, a palm slide like they friends sayin hello.

Muzzle done got his blocks the easy way or the hard way, depend how you look on it. It Alphonses hood. Mostly only Alphonse flesh and blood work Pigeontown. Muzzle worked years to earn Alphonse protection, only now there aint no getting away from it. Muzzle stuck with Alphonse. Fearius now too. It be part of the code. Fearius belong to Alphonse, best never cross him, never cheat him. The Glock aint all the power Alphonse carrying. Fearius understand lucky too, ya heard.

Fearius sit on the dead house stoop and wait, watchin the street, watchin for Alphonse. Fearius figure Alphonse be checkin on him at least a couple times his first day, come pick up the cash money, maybe give him a pager if he see Fearius a good worker. But it a matter of trust, so it hard to say.

The back door of the dead house kicked in. Floor covered in all kinds of things, aint nobody ever cleaned out what be left from before. Piles of clothes, brown water in the toilet, place smells like cat piss and rotten Popeyes maggot wings. Junkie needles. Fearius try not to look at the garbage inside, the tags all over the walls, big spray paint dicks and ghetto work like what they say come from Los Angeles. Fearius try to breathe out long and slow when he go to his supplies in the hole over the door, not have to take the place into his lungs. Out in the sun with a rag on his head be way better than inside. Plus it be a rule. They got to see him, know he there. See his clean kicks, his clean clothes. Trust. Trust the Alphonse supply clean. Worth it to come back again a second time in one day, some of them three times, a couple even more.

Alphonse make Fearius hoof it longer than Muzzle, give Fearius a double shift his first day makin sure Fearius prove hisself a good solja. Fearius know patient, know hard work. He work school hours and then some, past dinner. When it get dark later, Alphonse real blood bros be taking over nearby. Customers know they suppose to skip over three blocks where the streetlight busted out.

Not everybody be so lucky to sell Avon for Alphonse. And not every-body have the sense Fearius do, even if it be a rule. Dont touch the shit. Dont be stupid on the product. Never mess with the supplies, Muzzle toll Fearius. Fearius only smoke when Alphonse offer up some his own, and then only the lime green. Fearius never look at a gift horse. And Alphonse, he never smoke less he got a lieutenant watching. Alphonse be high yesterday, wont be no more for the rest the month.

It a little quiet over this way, Fearius think. Not bad quiet for busi-ness but quiet like he dont know nobody yet. Some peoples hang back when they see he not Muzzle, stroll away, stroll back a half hour later, look all casual, stroll away again.

Fearius here with no defense, but he aint scared. He gone prove to Alphonse he grown big as Muzzle, big enough. Hang with Alphonse, get protected by Alphonse. Everybody know it in Pigeontown. Anybody fuck with Fearius, they fuck with Alphonse.

But it like what they say? Fearius stare down at the stoop and spit. A rock and a hard place. It good and not good. Best he live rich or die try-ing. What else he gone do, shove fries out a window, be poor all the days he get? Fearius gots plans. He gots big plans. He dream of spinnin rims, paying somebody else to detail his ride. Baby blue glitter paint, but tasteful. Speakers under the seats they so many, so loud. Nobody gone miss Fearius coming or going. Not Moms or Pops neither. He be show-ing them why school aint gone happen and why he right. Fearius gone buy Moms some sparkling Christmas presents, yo.

Fearius nod at himself, nod at his *vision,* when a skinny white bitch roll up in a yellow truck covered in brown like a banana gone soft. Rust enough to make him sneeze. Fearius stroll up slow after he check the street. Whitey got a sweaty twenty she pull out her brassiere. The look fo sho in her darty eyes. She want five for twenty. She say, "Muzzle.

Muzzle knows me. He lets me. Five for twenty. Where's Muzzle?" She be jonesing bad.

Fearius think on if he should make his mark now, early, make Alphonse happy or mad. If she gone take four for twenty, Fearius make Alphonse more money, even if Alphonse give a okay to Muzzle to deal the bitch. Her hair look like a ol stuff animal drooping over her red eyes. Like tangly fur. Fearius make hisself stop looking at her hair and say, "I ain't Muzzle. No deals." He tip his head like the cornerstore Chinese motherfucker did when Fearius done be little and dint have enough money for candy. Fearius practice that look. He remember it, done made it his. Like he the man. And now he be the man. "Maybe next week I make a deal," Fearius say all warm and fake, like on purpose fake, like she best know it fake. "Four for twenty," he tell her. Fearius put his hand on her banana truck roof, casual, but he feel the rust. Rust be worse than dirt. He take his hand off the roof and shrug, start backing off.

"Bullshit!" the bitch say, but Fearius know he got her. They aint no heart in her, her eyes ziggin and zaggin, her jaw going. She be chewing on her own tongue. "Where's Muzzle? That's fucked up."

Fearius shrug again and back away more, rub his hand on the leg his pants, casual, get her rust off him. He actually turn and then she call at him, "Gimme four."

Bitch must not know where else they selling safe or she already trust Muzzle, trust Alphonses product. Fearius give her four, pocket the twenty, keep rubbing his hand on his pants. She drive away too fast. She gone kill a kid speeding on her way to go smoke up.

Fearius draw a lil line in the air. Muzzle taught him it be keeping count, it be like saying 'I remember.' Fearius feel good to do it. He remember the banana truck. He done got one customer good already, make the bitch come back faster.

But now Fearius need a hose for his dirty hand. Alphonse forgot to tell Fearius where he might could wash up. Fearius have pride. Clean be important. He be representing Alphonse. And Fearius, it his first day back at work.

"Mom?" Marie asks.

Cerise opens her eyes to her flesh and blood.

"Mom, look what people brought you."

Cerise tries to focus on the enormous bouquet. She glances at the IV needle taped to her arm, at her hands wrapped in so much gauze they look like mittens. The burn people explained to her last night about the procedures to come, how the skin can't heal even close to right without scrubbing it away over and over again. They call it debridement. Every two to three days. Cerise shivers.

"Are you cold?"

Cerise shakes her head. The pain medication's making her feel sleepy and dumb, but the flowers are dreamy, like that painter's garden, a mass of summer blooms in all the colors of the rainbow. They had to have cost a fortune, Cerise thinks, more than her normal measure, more than she made in a day standing behind the cash register. "Who?" she asks Marie.

"Your neighbors. Three of them came to visit. You were sleeping." Marie gives Cerise a look only a mother could, and Cerise worries she will cry yet again. That Marie would look at her own mother like her child now is too much. Cerise couldn't stop crying last night when Marie told her Roy's burns weren't as bad as Cerise's. Second degree only. Pure tears of joy. Roy'll be home nursing his fractured ribs without Cerise within the week. She can see him trying to change his own bandages, patting cream on his burns. The crying starts again, dribbles out of Cerise's eyes.

"Don't cry," Marie says and frowns. She plucks a tissue from the box on the bedside table and pats Cerise's cheeks. It is a gesture that makes Cerise cringe. She realized last night that she will be at the mercy of the nurses for a long time to come, will be humiliated, bathed and wiped after the toilet, fed and have her teeth brushed by strangers. Roy has never had to clean her bottom, and Cerise is determined to never have him do such a thing all the rest of his days.

"Which neighbors?" Cerise asks, worried that Marie might soon have to hold a tissue to Cerise's nose and tell her to blow if she can't stop blubbering.

"The father of that nice family across the street. And a couple I didn't recognize. They said they just moved onto Orchid. Next to the nice family. They were very nice, too. And before I forget—"

"Ed. He's the one who saved your father." Ed is the one who saved everything. Cerise loves the man. Forever.

"*That* guy?" Marie asks.

What does she mean? "Ed, the man from directly across the street," Cerise tries.

"With two kids. They came from Wyoming or Wisconsin or some-place."

"That's Ed," Cerise says.

"*That* man?"

Would Marie just stop? "What are you after, girl?" Cerise asks, irritated.

"I'm sorry you're in so much pain," Marie says. She squinches up her brow. She'll be getting herself ugly forehead wrinkles if she's not careful. "He's quite thin is all. Sort of. For some reason I expected a bigger man."

"Lil Thomas eating?"

Marie looks a touch guilty at the question, Cerise thinks. "Not enough," Marie says. "Certainly not enough, but yes—before I forget, Mother, you and Daddy are getting moved into a room together tomor-row. They found one for you to be together in."

"You think they might could—you think they might move us tonight?" Cerise saw Roy for only a short time last night, and her heart aches for him bad as her left hand, a constant throb. It took the second-degree burns. It can still feel. Most of her right, though, is just plain numb. They told her she killed the nerves. They told her she could end up with a claw if the tendons don't recover properly. It's what normally happens.

"I doubt tonight," Marie tells Cerise. Marie's breasts look like balloons.

"Are you wearing a nursing bra?"

Marie looks down at her chest. "Victoria's Secret. They had a sale." Marie smiles at her balloons, lifts her head to Cerise. The smile droops away. "Mom, I'm so sorry. I'm just so sorry. I don't know what else to say." She sits in the chair pulled up to the side of the bed, rubs her hands together, looks at Cerise, stops.

"I'm happy to hear Lil Thomas is eating," Cerise offers. She tries at a smile. "I wish I'd been awake for Ed's visit." She stares at her gauze mittens. "I don't know the new people's names."

"Ganesh," Marie offers. "And get this: Indira. Ganesh and Indira Gupta."

"It's pretty. Indira."

"Some big footprints," Marie says.

"What?" Cerise asks. The hospital food is terrible. When will she ever be able to cook again? Roy's going to have to eat out a long while. She'd had a cobbler planned for last night's dessert.

"You know. Gandhi."

Sure. Cerise knows about Gandhi. She saw the movie on video. What an amazing human being. "You could go by home when your father gets out?"

"I'm freezing meals for him already." Marie shows her teeth in a pretend smile.

Cerise wants to groan but holds it in. Marie's a terrible cook. She'll create some mess of a something from a magazine, something she won't even taste for flavor. Maybe that's it. Marie has no taste buds. And then, right then, Cerise's left hand feels worse than a thousand fire ants stinging it at once. She has no words for the sensation, doesn't know what to say. Childbirth pain is deep, womb and core deep, but her hand sends zings of pain all the way through all of her skin, like needles becoming liquid and stretching spiny tendrils up into her temples and down to her feet, and suddenly Cerise thinks she's going to vomit. She says nothing, tries to cling to the tiny raft of conversation, remember what they're talking about.

Marie says nothing. Laid on a table, Cerise's hands would ignite the surface. She swallows. She should sleep. Try to sleep. She closes her eyes.

"Mom," Marie prods. "Thomas and I have a proposal."

Cerise thinks about Roy, tries to picture his eyes. Her entire body feels dunked in boiling oil. The room swirls. She thinks she can smell the mess beneath the mittens. It's not what she would wish on anyone. But in the flash of memory, in those interminable seconds of searing, Cerise is more than happy, still, that Roy was spared.

Ariel stares. All day she's run from one near disaster to the next, but now—now she can't believe such a mistake like this could have happened. The presidential suite has been double-booked. A local hip-hop mogul, Greenback, and a touring lothario, some Somebody Important in the music world, have both been booked into the hotel's best suite for the same week.

"The Governor's Suite is perfectly lovely," Henry offers. He's the on-duty front desk worker with no connection to the grievous error that Ariel can detect whatsoever—and hence, possibly, Henry's obvious delight with the situation.

Henry's nasal gayness doesn't usually grate as badly as it is at the moment. "I thought the new computer program wouldn't allow this," Ariel says to him.

"It doesn't." Henry pulls the handwritten telephone log closer. For an apparent explanation, Henry taps the date the mistake was made. "This booking never made it into the computer. It's Bimbo's hand-writing."

Bimbo didn't last long. She worked the front desk for two weeks before she wormed her way into a touring band member's room. Late, late night, after the comptroller had set the bell out to be rung for service and retired to the back, Bimbo's unmistakable high-heeled totter, her sheath of waist-length hair, her careful scheming, all were captured on the security camera. The following afternoon, Ariel and the other managers watched the tape in disgusted fascination. Of course Bimbo had used La Belle Nouvelle to get to the bands. Of course her nickname stood to reason. And, of course, in the morning, Bimbo departed on a bus airbrushed with thorns and knives and bleeding hearts, never to be seen by the hotel staff again.

Yes, of course, it's Bimbo's fault, and now they have twenty-four

hours to fix the problem. They'd have zero if the hip-hop mogul's secretary hadn't called to reconfirm. She always does. Jawanda's got her act
together. Ariel's not sure why Greenback checks in and out of the hotel
when she's heard he has a mansion on that New Orleans golf course
where all the huge money lives. Women, Ariel supposes. Sex and music.
Sex and money. Last year, shortly after Ariel started, one of the bell-
hops brought a blacklight wand to work, the kind they use on crime
TV shows. Evidently ejaculate glows in the dark. Ariel lost two maids
from the kid's stunt, showing the housekeeping staff what they were
touching day in, day out. Sometimes, you just have to forget what's all
around you.

"Who's this other music guy?" Ariel asks Henry. "Give me a good
reason to piss off the regular."

"He used to be married to that actress," Henry says.

"What actress?"

"You know." He drums his fingers on the marble counter. "The
blonde."

If only Ariel had a nickel for every blond actress. "I have no patience
for this, Henry."

"You know. She's in that series. She sees dead people. Or maybe she
treats dead people. I mean, investigates them." Henry looks distract-
edly across the currently empty lobby. "Or whatever." He seems to
want to snap his fingers, Ariel thinks, to dismiss the gloom he's suddenly fallen into. The gloom of forgetting a blond actress' name. "So,
you let the kidlets watch TV?"

Ariel interprets: So, Ariel, are you at least letting your children stay
connected to current television culture so that they don't grow up to
be you?

She's not having a good day. She simply doesn't know who is more
important in the world of music, and so she doesn't know which one she
will need to call and apologize to. She worries the call will cost the hotel
tens of thousands. Risking losing a regular is bad enough, but if the
other is a major player, Ariel risks making the papers, something La
Belle Nouvelle doesn't need. Twice already the *Times-Picayune* has

mentioned the hotel in articles, once in a piece about suspicious liquor law adherence and once in a column about noise pollution. La Belle Nouvelle's continuing bad-boy reputation fuels business of the undesirable kind, and Ariel is, truly, at a loss as to how to stem the flow. The hotel needs guests if it's to survive, and the undesirables pay. But they also leave behind burned coffee tables and vomit-filled bathtubs, overflowing toilets stuffed with feminine napkins and beer bottles and styrofoam containers of red beans and rice. The lists never end. Ariel pays one housekeeping staff member time and a half each day for P 'n B duty. Puke and blood.

Ariel has to decide what to do.

She'll ask the sous chef. She'll ask him, ask Javier, under the guise of asking the entire kitchen staff. His shift started an hour ago.

Ariel allows the kitchen staff a radio. They'll know about the two music guys. They know a lot about music. "Man the fort," she tells Henry.

"Absolutely," he says. Henry's usually good for at least a smile, half the reason she hired him. That and he's proven to be a good snitch.

Ariel steps into the ladies' room and checks her reflection. Her face continues to hold up, something she is infinitely grateful for. She's very fair-skinned, pouty-lipped in a way she hated when she was a tomboy but appreciates now. She's thinned, too, since having Ella, her weight even lower than in high school. Ariel unbuttons another blouse button then rebuttons it. Javier, she hopes, might think she's a tease. She bends over for a quick flush, smoothes her hair, unbuttons the blouse button again, and walks to the back.

"Bimbo continues to haunt us, people," Ariel calls out as she pushes open the swinging door of the kitchen.

In the lull between the lunch and dinner crunches, the two guys washing dishes this month have settled onto plastic milk crates at the alley doorway. Cigarette smoke wafts in. Ariel has told them countless times to sit on the stoop fully outside rather than inside with the door open, but they never do. She suspects it's a shade issue. That or an authority issue. Everyone seems to like her alright, but there's a point, she knows. They tease her about her accent, and she teases back. For over a year, so far, she's made few enemies.

"What now?" Warren asks. La Belle Nouvelle's executive chef seems to squat under his own weight, his hips as broad as his stance. He is smart, acerbic, sometimes mean; he and Ariel have made a short but proud history of bitching at each other to their faces. She considers Warren her best friend at the hotel.

Nikki, on prep, chops onions. A mound the size of a small child waits at the side of her cutting board.

In her peripheral vision, Ariel takes in Javier. They ignore each other with precision. Her body warms in the unair-conditioned kitchen, a New Orleans norm she couldn't understand upon arrival, something as bad as not providing heat in the kitchens of Minneapolis in winter. She can't comprehend why the unions haven't gone nutty here. Javier cubes butter into a stainless container. He glances and nods at Ariel the way the rest of them do.

"Smoke outside or put 'em out," Ariel tells the dishwashers. They take a few last drags. "Bimbo double-booked the Prez," she says.

"Nimble Bimbo bounced best," Warren says to the salmon he dresses in long green stalks of something.

"Bimbo *bounced* awright," one of the dishwashers says.

Nikki points her knife at the ceiling. "To Bimbo!" she shouts, starting their chant.

"To Bimbo!" they answer Nikki. The kitchen staff stops what it's doing and downs imaginary shots.

"So I need your recommendation," Ariel says, tossing her imaginary shot glass over her shoulder.

Warren weaves green stalks. "Stop bothering us."

Ariel walks behind the line. "Your livelihood depends on righting Bimbo's wrongs."

Warren pinches the salmon's jaw and makes it say, "Me and Bimbo, we're both fish."

Ariel ignores him. "I need to know who's more important. I have to call one and deliver the bad news that he's getting the Gov's."

Javier says, "Not the Gobe-nor's." He looks at Ariel directly. Ariel thinks about meeting Javier in the safest of safe rooms they might have, the ones on the floors that the head of housekeeping has already cleared as clean. The ones with no other staff in sight.

Ariel meets Javier's gaze. Yes, it could be thrilling, but she wants to keep her job. Her family needs her job.

Outside the kitchen, when they've walked to the Canal streetcar line after shift, Javier talks almost dirty into her ear. Sometimes his language, sometimes hers. All she understands is his tone. He wouldn't crawl under the sheets and talk about making babies. He would talk about fucking, she knows, and that's what they would do. In the bathrooms, watching in the mirrors. Leaning over the bathtubs, her skirt lifted, fingers splayed on the tiled walls. He is what Ariel desires with a part of her body she has no control over. He is shallow, and he is beautiful. He is filthy and sexy and slick and wicked-tongued and poor. She couldn't become attached. Javier's not bright. And he is dangerous. Javier has admitted to stabbing somebody and not getting caught, and Ariel has no idea if he's telling the truth or not. Javier concocts sauces rich enough to kill old men. And Javier's skin, against her own, would make a beautiful contrast. He is new. And fresh. And so wrong she feels herself getting wet.

"Yes, the Gov," Ariel says, licking the corner of her mouth as though she's found some bit of remoulade there. "So who's more important: PhatCash guy, the regular, or Douglas-Michael Smithson?"

"Oooh," Nikki says and sniffs. "Too bad for you." She chops onions like a ninja.

"What do you mean?" Ariel asks.

Javier smiles a bright white smile at her. "No much choice," he says.

Ariel picks up a piece of cilantro and chews on it. "Chef, want to help me out here?"

"You?" He's back with the salmon voice. "You sentenced me to death. I can't help you now." The salmon has long green dreadlocks, maybe lemongrass, maybe chives.

"Nikki? Somebody help me out."

"I buy PhatCash," one of the dishwashers says. "Greenback my boy."

"Smithson *way* large, bro," the other dishwasher says. "My money on him."

"Awww!"

"Chef? Javier?" She has a flicker of a fantasy from last month, of Javier taking her from behind while she sucked his thumb. He reached around, moved his wet thumb down. She came fast. "Any advice you might offer would be helpful."

"It's a lose-lose, bosslady," Warren says. "Bimbo nailed you to the wall."

"To Bimbo!" Nikki yells again.

"To Bimbo!" they respond. All departed employees elicit the same toast. Ariel downs her shot. She wishes she had a real one at the moment. The dishwashers have told her all she needs to know. "So I'm screwed."

Lots of nods and mm-hmms.

"Give me a vote at least. Who's for putting Greenback in the Governor's Suite?"

No hands go up.

"So you're all voting to put Douglas-Michael Smithson in the Gov's?"

No hands go up.

Enough already. In a room upstairs, Ariel could force Javier to make a choice. Tell me or you're not going to get any of this, she could say to him. She could grab a breast for effect if she needed to, her ass, her crotch. Javier can't raise his hand alone in the kitchen, of course, but. Well, then.

She'll call Jawanda, Greenback's trusty secretary, and explain all about Bimbo. Jawanda might be able to help. If not, it's going to be a truly lovely day.

"Ain't no matter no ways," one of the dishwashers says. Ariel gave up trying to remember the dishwashers' names last winter. In a hotel with a staff of more than fifty, she has no patience for the people who come and go. It makes no difference to her their gender, their race, or their sexual orientation. Dishwashers are temporary in all of New Orleans, she has learned, and the less they feel singled out, the longer they actually stay. "Ivan gone get 'em both out town," he says.

"Who's Ivan?" Ariel asks.

Ed watches the swirling mass of orange and yellow out in the Gulf on the Weather Channel. It's called Ivan, and Ivan might just be the answer to the kids' prayers. All morning, Ed's nursed a serious backache from the events of the previous night, but now his brain bumps up against the threat of having to evacuate his family. He's never attempted such a thing. The Twin Cities don't pour out onto the highways and dissipate into the surrounding lake land at the first notice of, say, an impending snowstorm. He has no experience in such things.

A shopping spree is in order, from what he can gather. Ed pats his thigh, checking for his wallet. Most pickpockets won't try a man's front pocket, he learned years ago, and he feels his financial security to be better in New Orleans by implementing such a simple measure. Canned food. Batteries. He will even take one of the cars. There may be an emergency, after all, and emergencies warrant car use. Ed can't help but feel a bit excited, although he knows he shouldn't revel in potential disaster.

Checking on the Browns' house only makes sense. They may have mail that needs to be brought in. Or possibly something else he could do. He's never been inside Cerise and Roy's. With his decision to submit to his curiosity about the elderly couple, Ed immediately promises not to touch anything that doesn't need touching. Ed leaves, walks down the porch steps, turns around, walks back up the porch steps, and locks the door. Ariel would not be happy. They've already had one car keyed, the one she used to drive downtown. Or, rather, the CBD. Central Business District.

So much is different here. Everyone should be able to leave all their doors open. What a beautiful world it would be. Ed stops on his porch, watches an anole lizard bob on the railing, and gives thanks for what freedom already exists, for everything that is not threatened by crime. The little green lizard inflates the translucent sac beneath its chin, the skin glowing pink. A showy, brave thing, Ed thinks. He's reminded of the Harris boy.

Ed thinks he could have been a Michael in another life, or an anole. He understands their bravado at a gut level he can't analyze no matter how long he meditates on it. He crosses the street to that noisy, messy, chaotic house of the Harrises'. He hopes they'll give him news about the boy. If Ed were Michael, he might zoom around on a tiny motorcycle, too.

Something is not right with Ariel, Ed knows, once again, as he steps onto the Harrises' porch. He pulls open the screen door and knocks. Their window AC units blast in a line along the side of their house. Inside, one of the four grandchildren is crying. A My Little Pony missing its tail has been stuffed between the cushions of the old sofa propped up on cinder blocks on the porch. Inside, Klameisha, or maybe Debutanté, screams, "Somebody at the door!"

Ed waits. The baby continues crying. "The door!" one of the daughters yells again. Thinking about the universe, Ed waits. He sees a flattened cardboard paper towel roll, a fork, a sooty black pot missing the handle, three pizza boxes, bright plastic blocks. He waits. The baby's crying moves farther away.

Ed closes the screen door and leaves. He steps down to the sidewalk to go to the Browns' house next door. If any of the Harrises watch him through the windows, Ed wants them to see he respects their property, no matter how thin their lawn. He should volunteer to help them reseed it. If he bought seed for his own lawn, it would only be a friendly gesture to offer the extra to a neighbor.

Inside Cerise and Roy's, the air is warm but fresh-smelling. Ed picks up two flyers from the floor beneath the mail slot and lays them on the nearby table. The house surprises him. Spare, very clean. No clutter anywhere. He's not sure what he expected, but this isn't it. He moves to the mantel and looks at the lone black and white framed photograph resting in its center. Ed studies the grinning young couple, the woman thin and well dressed, the man handsome as Denzel Washington. It's Cerise and Roy, Ed realizes. And he realizes what the photo says. Volumes and volumes. Obviously Cerise would have risked her own life to save Roy. Obviously all Roy had wanted to do this morning when Ed and the Guptas visited was see Cerise.

Ed walks toward the back of the house, a double shotgun converted to a single home even before the Browns bought it, Philomenia told him once. An indulgent move, she said, considering the times. To absorb the half of a house that brought in rent, half that probably came near to paying the note each month, was a step very few people would make after the Depression.

Ed steps lightly. Again he's surprised by the order to the rooms, the sense of peace. Two covered pots sit on the cold stove. Under the lids, perfect greens and black-eyed peas wait. Who had the sense to turn off the burners? He opens the refrigerator door. Nothing in plastic. He grins at the old glass-lidded containers of leftovers. Those containers are collectible these days, he knows, expensive at garage sales and antique centers. He reaches inside and pulls one out. It's full of toma-toey corn and okra. Ed should know the name, but he can't remember it. He looks around for a microwave. Even cold, the food smells good.

On the countertop, Cerise and Roy have a stainless steel convection-microwave. A spectacular appliance, actually. The simplicity and qual-ity of what must be their lives again impress Ed. He removes the glass lid, cocks it at a forty-five-degree angle, and places the container inside the appliance. How does Cerise or Roy negotiate this thing? The but-tons seem almost cryptic, too simple to be simple. He pushes a couple. There. It's on. He can just open the door when the food's hot.

Ed goes back to the refrigerator. More containers. Everything seems to have the consistency of stew or thick soup, but each one intrigues him.

Half an hour later, Ed's full belly gurgles, the dregs of leftovers scat-tered around the counters and table. Good God, what amazing food. He's been to their neighborhood barbeques and knows that Cerise—or Roy?—can cook, but he had no idea what he's been missing on a day-to-day level. He needs some lessons. Or a better cookbook.

Ed looks around. What has he done? Now what? He feels spice in his stomach, wipes the sweat from his forehead. He'll do the dishes when he gets up from the table, tell them that he cleaned out their fridge to keep food from rotting, that he took care of the pots on the stove.

Ariel isn't right. He just knows it. He doesn't know what's wrong, something there that feels like lint. Or a fuzzy cable connection. His favorite channels hiding behind snow. She's not happy with him. But what can he do? Ed glances down at his distended belly.

He will try to visit Cerise again this afternoon after the grocery store. Or maybe he should go first and ask her for advice. Hurricane Ivan spins and spins and collects colors. Ed wonders how close to hot it will get. Red is the worst color, isn't it?

Save-A-Center crawls with people. The shelves have been scavenged. Ed pushes his cart to the soup aisle and finds what must be the least desirable ones left: lentil, vegetable broth, organic expensive options. He needs matches, candles, batteries, what else? He came here in a glucose-glutted panic after his feast, having skipped going to the hospital again, his original plan. In the car on the way, he discovered that all the radio stations had converted to coverage of the hurricane. No more classical music from the campus of the University of New Orleans.

If he knows one thing about this entity looming on the horizon, it's that he needs to show his family that he can lead them away from it. They will know he will keep them safe. He called the school this morning. The kids stay till the end of the regular day. Tomorrow is indefinite.

Ed scans the shelves and loads his cart with abandon. Smoked clams, an under-ripe pineapple. The toilet paper's gone but for a few stacks of individually wrapped rolls, over a dollar apiece. He takes six. What else, what else?

5

Philomenia Beauregard de Bruges stares at the door of her husband Joe's new bedroom. His care worker individual has departed for lunch. Now it is Philomenia's duty. Never did she guess she would be burdened with such a difficulty, with such a man under such terrible circumstances. She determines she will go into his room for a conversation. She owes him as much. Of course, he is not leaving for Hurricane Ivan. She has not decided if she will depart or not. Likely she will not be able to desert him when the time comes. She survived Camille. She will survive Ivan. Joe and she will make it through, although Joe unquestionably will not see next year.

She turns the knob. "Joe," Philomenia says from the doorway.

"Philomenia," he says. His mouth cracks into a weak smile. He amazes her with his continued show of out-of-character stoicism under duress. They have removed one-third of his colon so far. There seems to be little hope that the rest will survive intact. Prancie has prepared herself for his demise. She has determined she needs clarity.

"Hello," she says to the withering man. "How are you feeling today?" Joe has sustained three rounds of chemotherapy in quick succession. Philomenia does not believe the man who spent the bulk of his unencumbered life yabbering at long lunches in the French Quarter to be one to survive his trials. She imagines a life without him. She can smell it. *Prancie* can smell it.

"My mouth tastes like metal," Joe says. He lifts his hands into the air from the surface of his hospital bed.

"Yes," Philomenia says. It could taste like chalk, she guesses, or excrement, for that matter.

Joe looks at her as if she needs to give him a better answer, but how else can she respond to somebody telling her that his mouth tastes like metal? He makes less sense since his pain medication dosages have increased. Philomenia thinks about her journals, happy for the time his medication has afforded her.

"You're staring," Joe says.

Philomenia blinks. She had no idea.

"Will you be leaving for the hurricane?" he asks.

His predilection for CNN has not abated. He is staying abreast of the local situation. "Shall I?" she asks.

"The house withstood Camille," he tells her. They weathered the storm together as newlyweds. He knows this. She knows this. He tells her nothing new.

"What would you like me to do?" Philomenia does not relish the thought of driving alone to the airport. Flying to some city or another, to a random Hilton or an Intercontinental, brings a chill. She could make a proper trip of it and book a stay at a spa. Lord knows she is in dire need of some tender loving care. Prancie needs some time to herself. The home caregivers have provided such slim relief these last weeks that she has considered doing away with them altogether, but then she would be left bathing him, bathing Joe like his mother must have when he was a child, and this she could not manage.

She knows what Joe will say. She knows what he would have her do.

"You should evacuate," he says.

Of course. "I'll stay," she says. Of course. Philomenia wonders why they even choose to open their mouths for one another. They say exactly what the other already knows will be said. It is all so exhausting.

Joe smiles at her response, and Philomenia hides a cringe. A few days being massaged and attended to would be delightful. She steps to his bedside, determined to touch him somewhere. His hand? His arm? His hair looks far too unclean to finger. Philomenia makes a mental note to contact the service yet again about the inadequate treatment her husband is getting. His hair, what is left, should be washed regularly. She settles on his hand.

"Sit with me awhile," Joe says, and Philomenia cannot help but hear it as a command. Since his tribulations began, he has taken to commanding her. Philomenia feels like an emotional slave. If she refuses any of his commands, she is unsympathetic. If she refuses any of his commands, she is less than a proper wife.

There were years in the past when Philomenia resisted her husband in all the ways a proper Uptown wife might have. In turn, she carried his shirts to the cleaners without commenting on the unfamiliar perfume. She ignored his return to the gym, and she ignored his oddly timed showers. She dressed perfectly for the firm's biannual dinners and thanked him for each year's diamond. These concessions Philomenia chose for herself. Now, though, she has no means of determining protocol. What is she allowed? What must she tolerate?

Philomenia pats Joe's hand, sighs, and perches her skirted bottom on the edge of the mattress. Often in the last number of weeks she has been tempted to share a journal entry or two with him. Likely, however, he would not understand.

"May I turn up the television?" she asks.

Fearius stare at Muzzle in the hospital bed. His leg be in a cast, dangling like a big catfish on a line.

Alphonse pass Muzzle his take from the day. Muzzles eyes go big. "Baby bro play the game good," Alphonse say.

"When you can go home?" Fearius ask.

"Cant," Muzzle say. "You know Moms."

Pops be worse, Fearius think, but yeah, he know Moms. Fearius think maybe she gone get over it an let Muzzle come back after he done take his ride in the ambulance. "When you get out?" Fearius try.

Muzzle nod at his fish leg. "Leg got to stay up."

"We keep you, nigga," Alphonse say. "You say what you need, we get it."

"You get me some pussy you doin awright," Muzzle say and laugh his good ol laugh. They all laugh. Fearius know the not funny part be Muzzle get laid so much they aint no question he gone get pussy. He get it on his own or Alphonse buy him some. Fearius think about gettin some Westbank Vietnamese pussy some time soon. It aint cheap, he hear, but it tight. He quick think about cat pee help keep his dick down. He think about the banana truck junkie. He think about rotten meat.

Muzzle stop laughing and look at the curtain dividing the room. A white girl got her head wrapped up behind the curtain, her eyes wrapped up too, bulging like fly eyes. Muzzle dont know what wrong with her. He say he dont know if she awake or not, maybe she got her ears stuffed up too. Fearius imagine what it like not to see or hear. Maybe it be peaceful. Nice with everything soft and puffy. And then he think about a pillow, and smashing a pillow on his face, and then it not so peaceful. "We talk business," Muzzle say low.

Only Muzzle can get away with tellin Alphonse what they gone talk about, Fearius think.

"They toll me I strung up six weeks shortest," Muzzle say. "Could be up two three months."

Alphonse shake his head. "Damn, Shorty," he tell Muzzle. Muzzle no shorty. It just what they say.

Fearius excited by the news but have to pretend not. He gone work hard when Muzzle away and make hisself not disposable. What they say? Undisposable. He like the word. It sound like money. Undisposable. Fearius got a good chance he gone be better off than the normal wardie. That word around a long time now, a keeper. Wardie from what ward you come up in, like the Ninth Ward, whatever. Moms and Pops in the Sixteen now but theys both from the Seven. Fearius think he be good at new words, remind hisself to freestyle on some tomorrow when he workin. "Fo sho, Muzzle," Fearius say. "That be fucked up."

"Tell me true," Muzzle say to Alphonse. "How long you wait fore you cut me loose?"

Alphonse a good bossman. He and Muzzle be tight. Fearius jumpin outta his skin he so bad wanna hear what Alphonse gone say.

"We see," Alphonse say. "We see, nigga."

It be the fairest thing, Fearius understand. Fearius know patient, he remind hisself. He gone watch Alphonse and learn. Alphonse still alive, after all, and Alphonse still outside. It mean he be way smart. Alphonse turn and nod at Fearius, just a little. Fearius think he know what that nod mean.

Alphonse walk around the curtain then like he own the room and stare at the white girl. She skinny. "Hey," Alphonse say to her. "Hey, beanpole."

Fearius step up a few behind Alphonse. The white girl don't do nothing.

"Hey, slim," Alphonse say. "You awake?"

She still dont do nothing. Alphonse ask, "Think she ticklish?"

Fearius suck his teeth. He dont think they ought be bothering the girl, but he be way under Alphonse now, down by the bottom of the pyramid. He just a little block. He need to try not be a blockhead.

Fearius go up and look where he might could tickle the white girl with her head wrapped up. She sort of a mummy, only she breathing. She gots baby titties like his sisters back when they in junior high. He poke her in the stomach when Muzzle call out the other side the curtain, "Yo!"

A braided bitch in pink scrubs come in. Fearius pull his hand back.

"Hey," Alphonse say.

"Dont hey me," she say. "Get the hell outta here."

"What happen to her?" Alphonse ask.

"She not awake," Fearius say.

"You tell me how you got that bling round your neck," she say to Alphonse, "an maybe I tell you about her. Get. Now." She be a bitch with no patience, Fearius think. Cold and straight. She need to do time in juvey. That or get her smoke on, chill. She way too tight. And she old, but her ass high. Long legs make a nice ass. Cat pee, he think. Maggots.

"Fear," Alphonse say. He be the only one that don't call Fearius in full. But Fear aint a bad nickname. Alphonse backhand Fearius arm and nod they go back round the curtain. The nurse stare hard at them. She hold a bag with something clear in it. Maybe it liquid to keep the white girl out cold. Fearius guess she be burnt. He got burnt on his brain, what with old man Roy and the grill. Moms toll him. Moms hollered it at Fearius when he done come in last night, hollered bout what his brother do.

They go back and stare at Muzzle with his eyes close.

Fearius heard if you be burnt it better you stay unconscious. That or you wake up screaming, like your skin peeling off your body, like how it really done be with a fire, like no more skin left. It just gone. If you lucky, the skin kinda grow back, but different, or they patch it on like Moms did with their trouser knees when they little. Only skin dont make good patches. Him and Muzzles uncle on the Moms side, Uncle Terrence, he pulled down a pot a oil off the stove when he a baby, gots scars look like monster skin, like fake skin it so hard and not really move no more. When Fearius and Muzzle be kids, they gave Uncle Terrence a nickel and he took his shirt off and showed them the rest, monster skin all over his front. He done got but one nipple, the other one gone. And he gots just one place, Fearius remember, with three curls a hair on his chest. The monster skin stop right at his trouser line where Uncle Terrence diaper done be once. He lucky he lived, they say.

Now Uncle Terrence get hot real easy. His burnt up skin cant sweat no more. Uncle Terrence get drunk and sleep in his lawn chair at the reunions and make all the women worry if he too hot.

Muzzle start humming. He on the good meds. Alphonse toll him get scripts for more when he leave Charity. Their street worth be large. Alphonse say, "Shorty sho as shit celebratin in town."

"What?" Fearius ask.

"They be a hurricane party at Touro, yo."

Fearius nod. Their family aint going nowhere, but Moms hollered at all of em last night, inbetween when she hollered about what happen with old man Roy and Muzzle, that they gots to pack bags for the Hurricane Ivan. Fearius wanted to tell Moms it dont make no sense if they not going anywhere noways, but he know better. Fearius hangin on one spider thread, dont wanna hafta leave the house like Muzzle, go stay by some somebody all fucked up, stanky, sleep on the floor. So he keep his mouth shut and make a show of packing his bag. Klameisha shake her baby and shake her head at the same time, like Fearius a suck up, but what do he care what his sister think? He gone keep his bed for now.

A hurricane be great for the business. Fearius know he be breaking sale records when he get back out in the morning, all the peoples lining up. They gone have to stockpile if a hurricane coming.

Muzzle smile with his eyes closed. He dreamin about hospital pussy, Fearius think. That or Muzzle just fucked up on his meds. Doctors say he might could need a cane always, but Fearius cant see Muzzle with no cane. A limp maybe. Muzzle would go an play up a limp.

Alphonse give Muzzle a sign and go out the door. "Keep hangin," Fearius tell Muzzle and leave. Fearius happy he not in his bros place. And he happy Alphonse be his boss. Today, he just happy.

Breathing heavily, Ed stands in their living room holding his lower back, looking at his work. He's made five piles of his family's belongings, what he believes to be the most essential elements of their lives, one for each of them and one for the communal whole. Even at a quick glance, he can see that only some small portion of the piles will fit into either of their cars. Maybe they could evacuate with both cars. Actually, Ed realizes with a start, that's what they need to do. Why would they leave a car to be destroyed? Or stolen. Exactly. Ariel can drive one, and he'll man the other.

Ed thinks of the footage he's seen before. Flopping palm trees, huge breakers on the Gulf of Mexico. New Orleans has a few palm trees, some quite mature ones around the casino, a couple in neighbors' yards. Here-and-there palms. And then there's Lake Pontchartrain. When they debated whether or not to move here, Ed researched New Orleans. The big flat shallow lake, a pancake really, never struck him as a natural weapon, but that's what those in the know seem to deem it.

Okay. So the piles might fit into both of the cars. But he's not entirely sure that the portion of the communal pile comprised of groceries is supposed to come along. Don't you buy supplies for sticking it out, rather than evacuating? They can afford to stop at restaurants. Maybe snacks for the drive. But the drive to where? Ed's not supposed to call Ariel at work, but he did. She wasn't available, so he left the usual: Ask her to call home, please.

For the umpteenth time, he appraises the situation. He knows, at least, that Ella and Miles aren't back for another hour and a half. Ed decides he can celebrate his thorough preparation with a short trip to the river a few blocks away. He can go stand and stare at the water passing, some trillion gallons a second or whatever it is. He deserves the detour.

Marie walks in their hospital room door, and Cerise sighs. Here it comes again. Cerise is sure of it. Marie's going to push her proposal a second time, now to both of them, forcing what she wants.

"Mom, Daddy," Marie says, and Cerise knows she's right. Her daughter's playing to Roy's parental sympathies. The fact that a hurricane hangs out in the Gulf like some derelict on a corner doesn't help. The hospital's put out word that anyone who's able to leave, and would like to, should. Cerise would like to leave, regardless of the pain.

"Where's Lil Thomas?" Roy asks, sitting up, happy as a clam. You'd think he'd be sitting in a restaurant waiting on his filet mignon. "Bring on that boy."

Their daughter spreads her empty hands and scoffs. Like they should see she's the only one there, of course. Of course they can see Marie's by herself, but she shouldn't give her father flack for trying to greet his one and only. Lil Thomas is the apple of the old man's eye.

"Give your father a kiss," Cerise directs.

"Hi, Daddy." Marie leans in and kisses Roy by his ear.

Cerise is a third-round-to-leave hospital patient, one who's not supposed to go just yet. She can feel why. Her head sits on her neck like a basketball full of concrete. And then there are her hands. Sometimes the right feels more frozen than it does burned. She dreams they are big and heavy as cast-iron frying pans. Just about as useful stuck on the ends of her arms. In another dream they crumble away, her fingers burnt charcoal. In real life, Cerise is due for another debridement in two hours. They've already sliced open all her right-hand fingers because of how they turned into sausages. It's normal, they told her. It's called a digital release. The skin would just burst open, all irregular, otherwise.

"Mom," Marie says and steps to Cerise. Marie plants a kiss of gloopy lip gloss on Cerise's forehead. "So, Mom," Marie says again. "Have you made a decision?"

Cerise looks to Roy in the other single bed beside her. His eyes say, Don't look at me, but then his real voice says, "Seem like a good idea, Marie. I can help out in no time anyways."

Cerise knew she'd be outnumbered. She sighs a second time. Not like she was really gonna win this one though. "I wish . . ." Cerise says, "I wish I had a chance to meet this Keyshawn, Marie."

"His reviews are excellent. *Mother*. Trust me for once. I know what I'm doing."

Cerise knows she should trust her daughter, her over-forty daughter, but somehow she can't. There's something about Marie that's never sat right, and the fact shames Cerise. Who doesn't love her child more than anything in the world?

Keyshawn is a personal support worker, a PSW, a somebody to come to a house to help care for the folks with problems who live there. But Keyshawn is new to his job, still in classes even, and he's a friend of Thomas and Marie's, and they've worked it out that he's supposed to watch after Lil Thomas in the house at the same time he's looking after the two of them while Marie and Thomas are both away at work, all on Cerise and Roy's dime. Their own dime. Cerise can't figure out how it's any kind of deal at all. Supposedly Medicare covers a portion, but her headache springs all over again at the thought of negotiating through the maze.

"Roy?" Cerise asks. She wonders how Roy will react to a man helping around the house. To a man following her into the toilet. Cerise doubts Roy's even thought any of it through he's so damn giddy with his almost immediate recovery. If anything, the accident seems to have awakened a younger Roy who doesn't sleep much. Her Roy, her husband, actually wants to tell stories again.

"You already know what I have to say," Roy tells Cerise. "I said it. Keyshawn be fine if Marie say so."

Cerise sees what the future holds in a way that's different than she did a month ago. Than a week ago. She's known they've been loners, her and Roy, and she's known they've been lucky, most ways. Marie sure isn't a Harris child. But now comes the penance, huh? Here it comes. Keyshawn, Lil Thomas, Roy, her, the all of them, all in the house all day.

Cerise gets the skin graft when "a stable wound has been achieved." The doctors will be taking the skin from her backside. She's gonna have a brown palm. She's gonna have a piece of her ass on her claw hand.

What's she gonna do, have the Keyshawn boy follow her with a cart at Winn-Dixie to make groceries? Help her buy fiber pills at the Rite Aid with her white mitten hands? It doesn't make an ounce of sense, best Cerise can see, but she's at their mercy. At their mercy mercy mercy.

And who knows what the hell they'll all be doing about the hurricane.

Prancie admires her stacks of journals in the linen closet behind the towels. The neat rows and uniform bindings. Prancie prides herself on her daring. Her ability to hide her important observations and writings should be noted by at least one breathing person. And so the person is she. Herself. Prancie knows she has done a professional job. The hired help—whatever are those people called again?—are not allowed into private areas of the home, so they would never be aware of Prancie's work.

The daredevil neighbor has proven particularly vexing lately. Edgar Allan Flank. The stay-at-home father. He gave her his full name quite readily enough upon their meeting. Philomenia—for she was still Philomenia then—used all her life's training not to say, at his strange label, "Excuse me?" She heard him clearly enough, of course.

Now Prancie can see that Edgar purposefully assaulted her with his name. She must note as much in the two journals that document him thus far. Edgar Allan Flank uses his name as a weapon to shock individuals into silence or confusion, she thinks as she grabs for the journals. He has used this form of passive-aggressive communication for some time, if she surmises correctly.

As a child, the young Edgar surely suffered the small arrows of his classmates and peers. But unquestionably at a later stage he managed to turn the tide. Now he uses his name to his benefit. His adult approach, she thinks with acuity, is akin to walking across the avenue holding a machete: greet your neighbors and establish your undeniable presence.

Prancie carries the necessary journals into her private sanctuary of rooms. She will sit in the bay window. She takes her leisure flipping pages, perusing her work. Here. There he is. "Edgar Allan Flank," she writes, admiring her cursive, the curl at the bottom and top of the F, "has determined that he wields power with his name. It carries . . ." Prancie runs her pen over the word 'carries.' Carries? "Impact," she continues.

Her husband bathed once in the middle of a Saturday afternoon. Joe had done nothing but read the newspaper that morning. He purchased their Danishes early. He ate, read, pruned a total of three branches on the already pruned azaleas in the side yard and then stepped into their bathroom and turned on the shower. He left their house shortly afterwards. He smelled of cologne.

Philomenia did not ask. Philomenia did not think a thing of it then. But then again. She must have thought, for the half hour it took him to get ready that afternoon has since lodged itself in a nook of her brain. A cranny, really, but she does not take kindly to the word 'cranny.'

Prancie feels the need to tidy. Prancie would like to be rid of such memories. Cobwebs, the all of them. "Edgar Allan Flank has determined that he wields power with his name," she reads. "It carries impact—"

Joe smelled of cigarettes upon his return. He remarked on the moistness of her redfish. She used the same recipe she always had. Her grandmother's recipe. Philomenia began cooking full meals at eleven years of age.

"It carries impact—"

Edgar Allan Flank made such a preposterous show of himself, and yet he succeeded with the neighbors. The fiasco with the coconut cream flits across her peripheral memory.

"It carries impact—" she reads again. Her coconut cream was glorious. It sat better than a Chanel sweater draped over a— Lord, that bosom of Sharon Harris, that terrible, terrible bosom. Whatever reason would a woman have to display her assets in a less than favorable light? *Stand up straight, Philomenia. Present your assets with pride.*

One can easily remember when it is necessary to stand up straight.

"But the real problem," she continues in the more ruminant of the two journals, "is that he uses his name to manipulate his trusting neighbors. Orchid Street need not be inundated by such social climbers. Where, exactly—" To where indeed did Edgar Allan Flank hope to get?

And then the moths come in, bumping their way across her vision. Prancie knows better now than to swat at her face, though no one is watching her in her lovely and well-appointed bay window. The moths leave powder the texture of cornstarch in her hair. Invisible.

Joe often smelled of cigarettes. It was not his only flaw.

The distant whir of a hurricane with the quite sophisticated name of Ivan spins slowly somewhere over the Gulf. What might Prancie do with an opportunity to present her name to the world? Philomenia Beauregard de Bruges should rise to the weather. Rise to the challenge of another Betsy.

Prancie has assets. She should present them to the world. Prancie should assert herself and gain the power on the street she so rightly deserves. Prancie should give Edgar Allan Flank a run for his money. She might not have the physical prowess to lift heavy objects, but she has lived on Orchid Street as long as the Harrises, and she could ingratiate herself in other ways. Perhaps she could do some cleaning. They would never know it.

She could start at the barnacle, she realizes. She nods. If she understands his predilections, the stay-at-home father will be there often enough.

"I, too," she writes, careful with her penmanship, "can become an indispensable and essential element to the neighborhood." Philomenia never enacted change, Prancie realizes, but Prancie can make things happen. Prancie can take matters into her own hands. She need not phone the police at every turn.

The idea blossoms like a morning glory. She will begin by bringing treats to her neighbor while he pickles himself at Tokyo Rose. There is terribly much one can do with baking. So many ingredients. So many possibilities. Prancie writes faster. Oh yes, so much one can do.

6

Ivan. It sounds like a medieval horseman, and it's how Ariel pictures the thing, charging madly, cape flapping. Ariel has been told by La Belle Nouvelle's owners in no uncertain terms that she must stay at the hotel. Stay *with* the hotel, her stucco third child. The owners will allow her to move her family into a room if she needs to. Making her way from one cluster of employees to the next, Ariel contemplates the possibilities as she tries to take the temperature of her workers. Nobody's left yet. Nobody's quit, claiming an ill relative who needs evacuating, a dog that goes berserk with the telltale drop of barometric pressure. So far, so good. Ariel seems to be the only one with knee-buckling worry.

You're in charge, woman, Ariel tells herself. They look to you.

Warren, her executive chef, and a bevy of the housekeeping staff— actually, really, all the long-term employees, the ones born and raised in New Orleans—have begun acting as though they swallowed a bunch of ecstasy. Happy, happy. If Christmas knocked at the door, they'd be wearing Santa hats and jingle bells. Ariel doesn't get it. They're behaving as though some huge party sits on the horizon rather than the Grand Russian Death Czar.

"Tell him to order extra booze if you didn't already," Warren tells Ariel. He means her bar manager. Warren says there'll be a run on all things alcoholic. Ariel supposes she should listen to Warren. He hasn't steered her wrong yet.

"Anything more specific?" she asks him. She's happy Javier's on break.

"And you mean?" Warren sticks his finger into a pan of something rougey bubbling over a burner. The man can't have any nerve endings left in his hands.

He knows what she means. "Whiskey?" she tries. "Vodka?"

"Beer," Warren tells her. "All that they'll let you take, you take. And make 'em give it to you cold." He reaches for the olive oil. "And call Ice. Yesterday. You needed to call Ice yesterday."

Why would she call Ice? Oh, shit. Yeah. Ice. "On it," Ariel says and gives Warren a lame smile. He knows he's helping her out. She'll hit him up later again. For now, she needs to make sure her bar manager, who isn't due in yet for another hour, is ready for the hordes. Ariel pictures a scene her nightmares are made of, piles and piles of people cramming their way into the hotel.

In her dreams, she is the only one left. All the other employees are gone, and she must serve the hordes, pour drinks, book people into the rooms, make beds, cart luggage, cook, bring ice. Serve. For some reason the hordes wait for her, wait and huff and complain and wait. The chaos is barely contained.

But Ariel decides she must have a decent moral view of the world imprinted on her brain's hard drive; her nightmares are made of customers waiting for her service rather than customers running wild through the fields of her hotel, ravaging the pantries. They could be ravaging her in her dreams instead of tapping feet and rolling eyes.

"What's the special tonight?" she asks Warren.

He grins, something Ariel realizes he never does. They're all on E, she swears. Warren has braces-perfect teeth. "Everything fresh," he answers.

Her kids aren't back from school yet, she knows. Their house is a grand and spacious money pit. A big breath would knock down the entire block, for that matter. Do cars float? She tries to scan her disaster footage memory for why cars drive into rivers. That's what it always looks like, she thinks. People make the entirely irrational decision to drive directly into a river. Ariel knows better than to do that. She thinks she knows better. Maybe roads look like rivers when you've lost your mind. Or you forget the local landscape. Oh, *now* I remember, we turn left here into the rushing water then *right* at the next flotilla of debris.

"What?" she asks.

"Lady Ariel," Warren says, "we need to serve a goodly portion of our fresh produce, fowl, and fish, at the very least, lest the power go poof in the coming days."

Oh. That makes sense. "Got it," she says. "Make it special. Break our bottom line times three." Ariel has faith in the man. "Make it glorious."

She leaves for her office to call Ed again. This is it, she thinks, as their house line rings and rings. This is why he needs a cell phone. Environmentalist housedad or no, she needs to get in touch with him when necessary. Now is necessary.

Somebody knocks at her open door. Her always open door, a policy she started when she first arrived. It forces her to remain calm when she wants to yell at someone. It forces her to write letters when firing employees and pass the papers calmly across her desk.

It's Javier at her always open door.

And it forces her to keep her libido in check. "Yes?" she asks.

"Miss Ariel," he says in his thick accent. It took Ariel a full month to decide whether or not she'd accept the Southern formality as a term of respect from her employees. A first name is a first name, after all, preceded with a title or not. And the diminutive "Miss." Well. But it was a concession to local customs, finally, that Ed thought she should make. He convinced her that the staff would think no less of her. Ariel supposes he was right. Not that Ed could have had any idea what the words "Miss Ariel" would do to her coming out of the mouth of her sous chef.

"Hello, Javier."

"Miss Ariel, I talk to you."

"That's fine." She gestures for him to move past the door.

"With the door close."

"No. You know the policy."

Javier turns and closes Ariel's office door. "I am leaving."

Ariel can't help but stare at her closed door. Torn between standing

to open it and waiting to hear what it is he has to say, she falls somewhere in between, caught in a weird crouch behind her desk. Certainly
the position can't be a flattering one. "What?" It's a question she has
posed too often today. It's not one that she should be posing to Javier.

"Henny, she want to leave town," he says. "Ivan. She say it, we go."

Ariel likes to think of Javier's girlfriend as a chicken but knows the
young woman is far from it. Ariel saw the photo on the kitchen
employee bulletin board. The J for the H sound. Whatever. Really, Ariel
just dislikes the woman for the fact that she has Javier. Henny gets to
live with Ariel's full-blown crush. "What?" Ariel asks yet again.

"She wants for us to go," he repeats.

"All essential employees are required to stay right now." Ariel stops
herself from speaking too slowly, as if to a deaf person. Javier follows
just fine, she knows. Ariel stands straight, smoothing the front of her
skirt. "Please open my office door."

"Ariel," Javier almost whispers, "tell me what you need tell me."

What she needs tell him? When? She makes a move toward her door.

"I am going," he says.

"Why?" Ariel is caught between her desk and the door, between so
much. She considers grabbing Javier's face and kissing him. Or she
could swivel away and open her always open office door. Ariel can hear
the rest of the staff milling about outside, piles of them, the hordes,
dozens and dozens of employees watching her every move, listening to
her closed door with glasses pressed to their ears.

In the imaginary kiss, her paranoia is half subsumed. Nearly
usurped.

And Javier has stepped forward.

Ariel pushes him away when all her body says is to pull. Suck. "I'm
opening the door," she tells him.

"No."

What? "Yes, I am."

"Let me be with you," he says.

"Stay, then."

Javier steps even closer. "Tell me again. My boss say I stay, I stay. I
must, then."

"You need to stay with the hotel," Ariel directs and twists away from him. Her eyes see a desk less than tidy in her swivel, a desk stacked with work that means less than a great many other things. Less than her family, for one, she realizes with a start.

"I'm directing you," she says, knee-dipping in her heels just a little to get in and under his periphery. "You." She straightens her legs, holds Javier in his place with her gaze. "Are." She smells his smell of cheap Old Spice and his sauces of sin. "To." She crosses her arms. "Stay."

Will it work? She thinks it's what he wanted her to tell him. Order him.

"Henny," he says. "She . . . will call. You must tell her."

The possibilities of days with Javier loose in the hotel, the last bits of staff lost in some sort of dark and free place, a few guests here and there needing her attention—Miles, Ella, Ella, Miles. Her children should be at the forefront of her mind. She'd been calling home when Javier appeared.

Ed is a very good father, a very good househusband. That's an easy one. Henny, Henny, she can't please Javier as well as Ariel could. Age accounts often enough for skill. Ariel has skills. Great big whopping skills. And a killer mouth.

"Follow me," Javier says. Or maybe something else. She doesn't hear right.

Ariel takes her eyes off the lobe of his ear. "Excuse me?"

Javier only grins. He shrugs his shoulders as though he's said something innocuous.

It's the game they play, the advanced version of Power Struggle. It's addicting, really. When Javier asserts himself, she knows that he knows what he's doing. Ariel could fire him in an instant if she wanted to. "I'll tell her," Ariel says. "I'll tell Henny. You have to stay."

Javier takes Ariel's hand and stares at her hard. Ariel adores his clear want. He feels like all want, just body, heat, somebody she doesn't know and doesn't need to know. If they moved forward, stayed there for another ten minutes in her office, she would forget the city, the hotel, get lost. Javier fingers her wedding ring, and Ariel knows the forgetting is why everyone must do things with other people, the things that are wrong and hidden and taste like saffron and caviar and everything most people can never have much of, like liquid money.

Javier and she will continue the game another time. Ariel needs to get her door open. "Stop," she tells him, and he smiles. He doesn't stop. Javier's gotten braver lately. She should worry. Ariel pulls her hand away. "Let me know before, if you can, when Henny will be calling." She opens her door without giving Javier time to check himself, deflate some. It's a dangerous move on her part, but perfect strategically.

The hall is empty. Javier stands and frowns. "Miss Ariel," he says and leaves.

Jesus. Her whole body pulses.

Fearius get to Pigeontown by walking the levee. He see the big washed out part of sand, the river beach under the power lines. When the river not overflowing, it be where Fearius and his bros target practice. Well, when they young. Not so much no more. Once they shot at a dog skull, other times dead river rats. Rats all over. Garbage, beer cans on the beach. Logs and trees. Another time Muzzle tagged some big floating thing out in the water Fearius swore done be a dead body. They shot a junk .32, rusty, jamming, but they was happy it real. Cousin Limey stole ammo from their uncle.

Muzzle still be the best shot out of all them, Fearius gotta admit. Today, Fearius just gots a boxcutter in his pocket, but nobody gone bother him with Alphonse protection draped all over him. It feel like a magic cloak.

The dead body Muzzle shot done bob around in the garbage water and yellow foam between logs, out by the fence guardin the city water intake. A full-grown man might could stand up in that intake pipe it be so big, pushing out into the Mississippi and sucking it up. People say it be worse drinking the city water than booze. Fearius think they both bad, but they aint no thang. He drink em both, what the hell. All the bagged ice, cold drinks, hot sauce, sno-balls and what come from the same poison water, so they all be the same bad. The toilet of the world, or something like it, what they say. A photograph taken from halfway to the moon in a school book Fearius remember from third grade show the river lookin like a line of brown shit spilling out into the bluey-green Gulf water. New Orleans get they water from the American butthole.

Way he remember it, Fearius werent no more'n eleven when they shot at the body. Muzzle toll Fearius later that he crazy, aint no dead body, and he not gone tell Moms or Pops about no dead body neither. That day they done be hanging with Limey their cousin and his girl String. Fearius never know why they call String String, but she giving Limey head when he thirteen. Limey be all Mr. Knowin and say it aint no dead body too, but String, she look scared. Fearius could tell String knew it a body same as he knew. It look just like a fat white man in ripped up underwear. The face covered with leaves and hair and fucking goo, maybe chewed on. Muzzle tagged what Fearius think be the foot with the .32, but it hard to say.

Fearius dreamed about the dead body a long time. In real life, Moms and Pops done protect him and Muzzle and their sisters enough from dead bodies that it be the first real one he ever seen not in a coffin. Ones in coffins be hard as cold pie dough waiting in the refrigerator, but the floating one puffed up like a blowfish, and it done be a hot day.

Fearius dreamed about String too. She wear a big bra at thirteen. Maybe her name come from the string panties she wear showing out her blue jeans.

Now Fearius walk the levee and remember the body and think it funny how scared he done get. The body already dead, and he dint have nothing to do with it being dead, so it couldnt be no reason to worry. Yeah, they had the gun, and Muzzle gone to juvey for the first time after, but they still dint need to worry. A dead body a dead body, no ifs ands or buts, and a dead body dont care what the fuck all you do to it, ya heard.

Now Fearius walk the levee and look at the long neck white birds poking their long orange beaks in the dirt and little pools from the river. Lots of times he wished he could fly, but he think it gotta be hard to find a way to eat and rest much. It feel to him in his bones that birds have a hard time sleeping much more than three, four hours tops. They happy in the mornings, sad when the sun go down, dead in like, what, three years. Birds live fast, faster than a bro selling Avon.

Alphonse say he bringing Fearius a pager round noon, good for the loneliness. Not that Fearius really get lonely, but it just like a saying or whatever. The ward be way safe, aint no heat drivin round. Aint no heat care about Pigeontown never, no ways. A pager show Alphonse think Fearius can be trusted true now.

So Fearius hoof it over to the game, make his name, keep his bro up proper in the hospital, give Moms and Pops tight Christmas gifts and what all, surprise presents and shit soon. Today with the Ivan coming, Alphonse triple up the supply. It gone arrive six times during Fearius shift. Fearius pretend he never see when it get stuck into the hole over the back door, or if he see it coming, he walk away. It possible they might could be more careful with the Avon selling, but they never keep much cash money in pocket and just three cars worth a supplies on they bodies at a time. Alphonse, him and his people aint no idiots. Only add up to a short sentence max. And nobody forget Fearius a minor. Alphonse especially.

Fearius walk down his street, lift his chin at the lookout named Ali Abubu or whatever, Boo for short. He not so smart, maybe even slow. Eighteen, Boo never gone be but a lookout. He come up Muslim, so Fearius think it way weird he play the game.

Boo make a big sign, like it the best thing he get to do all day. Maybe it so, Fearius think, maybe it so.

The pink and peeling brown house seem funny today, and then Fearius realize the windows shutters be closed, the front door done up with a padlock. Aint no new For Rent sign, but Fearius guess that be coming next. He need to find a way to page Alphonse, right? Or maybe it a test. Maybe Alphonse already know about the house getting closed again.

Fearius think it a test, kind of, and he gone find a way to get in. Between the cat pee and chicken bones, he hope they leave his hole over the back door alone. He think it gone be the case.

He step around the side. He got his boxcutter, waitin until Alphonse give him something better. The walk over aint no different than any other day, but he know from his Moms and sisters the hurricane be a big deal today, lots of people thinkin on leaving. But nobody in Pigeontown seem any different, all the cars still sittin cold on the street, nobody much moving around their houses. It pretty much a junkie block Fearius work. Everybody sleep in. None of them leaving for no hurricane.

Fearius be stuck down between the houses in the narrow when he hear voices inside the chocolate and pink. Sound like straight up people, white or whiteified niggas. Fearius feel for the boxcutter then back out. He gone hafta wait outside till they leave, fuck up his game big time. Here come Ivan, and the only house on the block have anybody in it doing anything hafta be his work house. Motherfuckers. Maybe he wait. If they aint gone in ten minutes, he go in with the boxcutter and scare em out. He capable doing it, fo sho. He be Fearius, and his name mean something.

Fearius dont wanna rap with slow boy Boo, but it aint a good idea if he perch hisself on some neighbor stoop who actually be in there and take offense. A few folks still dont understand the economics right, get uptight about the Avon and what all. But Fearius know he best get a look at the niggas leaving. He decide they just whiteified niggas doing the owners work long distance, doing the whites work like they always done, always gone do.

Selling Avon, though, he be his own man, working for Alphonse, not answering to no Burger King faggot manager, not answering to no Yessir Nosir lawncare faggot. Fearius, yeah, that right, he be his own man.

Yes, yes he be. Know what? he think. Fuck those niggas in my house. Fearius got work to do. Fearius got sale records to break. Today gone be his day. What else he can use? There any crowbars or shit layin around? He see a rake and a metal garbage can lid. Make him laugh. He go in like a knight whacking it out on PlayStation, like a knight with a shield and a sword.

Aw, fuck them niggas messing with his work. It time they leave.

Fearius take the boxcutter and stick out the razor and walk back down the narrow. He gone show Alphonse what he made of. He gone rise up fast as lightning.

Everybody better watch, cause here come Fearius.

7

Ella starts up the chant on the walk home from school: "A beastie is coming for us. A beastie is coming for us." Ed doesn't know if he should join in with his kids or judiciously suppress it. Ella and Miles' mood is contagious, though. Walking in the middle, holding hands, Ed becomes one of the herd. He adds melody, as close to "Follow the Yellow Brick Road" as he can, and changes it up a bit. The kids get it in a couple of rounds, and they all skip down the sidewalk faster and faster. *"A beastie is coming for us, a beastie is coming for us, la la la la la la la la, a beastie is coming for us!"*

They skip around the corner and onto Orchid Street. Ed sees a Harris daughter, Angelique, leaning into the window of a Toyota. From the side, her stuck-out butt looks like a melon. He can't help the association and feels automatically guilty, but the young woman's hind end really is orb round. There's something otherworldly about it, Ed thinks, as his mouth continues its singing and his legs continue their skipping and his children stop before he does.

Angelique draws her body out of the car window and laughs at Ed. Not with Ed. Two dark boys sitting in the front seat of the Toyota laugh at Ed too. They even point.

Miles pulls his hand out of Ed's. Ed resists the urge to glance at Miles' face. No doubt the boy has turned the color of a berry smoothie, something that horrifies his fair-skinned son. Miles walks off the sidewalk and directly into the street. It's what they do, all the longtime locals. Walking in the street is where you walk. To use a sidewalk is somehow inappropriate, although Ed hasn't yet figured out why.

Ella, to Ed's small comfort, still hangs on to his hand. He can feel her dependence and utter unflinching faith through her sweaty little fingers. Her father is the man who saved the old couple across the street, after all. But who's now getting laughed at. Pointed at.

Ed watches his son put his hands into his pockets and shove his pants down. His son, oh, Miles, attempts a swagger on the asphalt. Ed can't believe it. Miles' hitch-leg limp is something Ed wouldn't be able to stop laughing at if Miles were putting on a post-dinner show in their living room. God, make him stop.

But Angelique calls out instead, "You go, lil' homey," and the car's two guys and she chuckle, but in a nice way.

Ed and Ella pass by on the sidewalk. "Hello, Angelique," Ed says as neighborly as he can. "Guys." One of the boys sucks noisily on his teeth in response. Neither says anything.

Ed feels for his neighbor and her melon bottom. All the Harris girls have one. He often hears where they've gotten Angelique's sisters, hears the babies in their house at all hours. Hears the raised voices. Hears the frustration. He wishes he could figure out a way to give parenting classes without offending anyone.

"Mister Ed," Angelique says, smiling, shaking her head.

"Mister Ed," the boys copy and then laugh again. How old can they be? They don't look old enough to drive.

Only at his front door does Ed realize why they laughed again. How would kids their age even know about the talking horse? Wouldn't the old television show be outside of their usual parameters of cultural reference?

On their porch, Miles fumes, his arms crossed across his thin chest. He taps his foot. His khaki uniform pants perch perilously low around his narrow hips.

No way can Ed say a thing. "What would you two like for dinner?" It's out of his mouth. He's the father. They need his guidance.

Miles stares at the siding by the front door as if it contains the answers of a universe.

"Pasta," Ella says.

Ed inserts the key into the lock. "You two need to double-check what I packed for the evacuation. I might have missed something."

"Yay!" Ella screeches. "Exacation!"

"What-*ever*," Miles says, but Ed can see he still has his son. An adventure looms on the horizon. Miles might get his subway ride yet.

Philomenia steps into her husband's room. Joe lies awake. He stares at the ceiling. "Joe," she says.

"Yes?"

"Joe—" He seems in need of something. "Would you like the television on?"

"What do you make of this ceiling?" he asks.

"What?"

"There's a certain inherent peace there."

"There is a piece of it where?"

"Philomenia. Stupidity doesn't become you. You heard me."

"What do you mean?"

"It's a ceiling," he says. "It does what it's supposed to do."

The nurse person has informed Philomenia that their care services will be suspended starting tomorrow due to Hurricane Ivan. This thing, her husband, then, constitutes what she must now tend. My, does Prancie need relief. "Baking!" she enthuses. "Baking is what Tokyo Rose needs." She must lay the groundwork now.

"Huh?"

"Eggs and what all," she tells him and adds a physical gesture with both hands to indicate what she means. To Philomenia's great relief, she sees that Joe understands she must bake off the perishables before the loss of power.

He returns to staring at the ceiling. "Imagine staring at a ceiling your whole life."

"Sorry?"

"Would you be able to see the ceiling change over the years?"

Philomenia supposes dying allows a person certain eccentricities.

But she has baking to do. Joe will have to be the sole ceiling gazer for the moment. "The freezer is full of peaches. Some are thawing now."

Joe begins humming a tune, then sings, *"Millions of peaches, peaches for free."*

Prancie knows that his end is near. He makes no sense whatsoever. And so he will never suspect.

Prancie has read the books she needed to read. Prancie has taken charge.

Apple seeds. Ground to a pulp, they are undetectable.

Joe puts his hands into the air and continues to sing. He appears to be feeling a large set of breasts.

Philomenia needs to be gracious. Philomenia needs to keep the bigger picture in mind. Prancie raises her hands to mimic her husband's. What is he singing? About peaches. *"Peaches for free,"* Prancie mimics. *"Peaches for free."* She rubs imaginary globes. She polishes fish bowls.

Peaches upon peaches and a number of days at the barnacle. She might make something of the opportunity yet, should Joe manage to hang on without significant care. "Back in a while," Philomenia informs him and steps out of the room.

A peach cobbler has been preordained. Prancie reaches into the stew pot in the lower cupboard and removes her baggie of secret ingredient. She made certain to purchase a new spice grinder for the task. Shall she wear a mask? Could aspiration of any airborne particles be a problem?

"Cheesecloth should suffice," Prancie says aloud, removing a roll from its drawer. She holds an end to the back of her head and begins to wrap the cheesecloth around and then around again. She is a kitchen bandit. "Pwew-pwew!" Prancie's voice ricochets off the kitchen walls, her gun finger pointing to the baggie, shooting. "Pwew-pwew-pwew." Prancie breaks out in peals of laughter. How delightfully fun. "Pwew-pwew!"

"No," Ed says. "Essential things. Things you couldn't live without."

Ella stands with her arms full of shoes. "Shoes are." She nods vigorously.

He can see she has several with no mates. He prays right there that Ella never becomes the kind of woman to whom shoes are an essential element of life. Air, clean water, shoes, food. "No, they're not. Amen."

A loud clump sounds from the ceiling overhead. Miles' room. The kids have gone mad with the prospect of Ivan. The living room floor teems, swaths cut through the new piles Ella and Miles have created. A garden hose, Miles' idea, slithers through the mess. A bin of action figure pieces has barfed out half its contents onto Ariel's old bathrobe, Ella's safety blanket.

When will Ed be able to clean up? When will Ariel come home? She left two frustrated messages but didn't say when she might get back.

Miles races down the stairs wearing his old hockey helmet and pads, the jock on the outside of his shorts, his stick clattering.

"No."

Miles spits out his mouthpiece and dances in a tough guy circle before growling, "I kick your muh fuckn ass, Ivan!" Miles crosschecks the air.

"Where did you hear that?"

Miles raises his stick over his head. "I kick *yo* ass!"

What?! Ed's deltoid contracts reflexively. His hand rises an inch from his thigh. Could the instinct to backhand a smaller being actually be innate? Ed repulses himself. He didn't do a damn thing. But his arm wanted to. How does that happen?

Now what? Parents have to react right away. Same as pet owners. You don't do anything about it right away and you might as well punish your underlings for finishing dinner or sleeping soundly for all the understanding they'll have concerning consequences of bad behavior.

Miles stands at the ready, proud in his old hockey uniform. In New Orleans. Ready to kick hurricane ass. "Miles," Ed attempts calmly. "Do you really know what you're saying?"

Ella whimpers and moves to Ed, pressing her load of shoes against his leg. "Ella, put them down. Just drop them."

She limps to a still-clear spot in the entryway directly behind the front door and unloads.

"Miles, answer me."

"Yeah," Miles says.

"Tell me what kicking ass means."

Ella turns and stands transfixed by the conversation.

"Ella, go upstairs and get your coloring books and crayons."

Ella shakes her head. Little eavesdropper.

"Go."

"Okay." Ed listens to her take the five steps necessary to put her out of his line of vision, then stop. Well, so be it.

"Miles Davis May, tell me what the words you just said mean."

Miles inserts his mouth guard. "Kitchkin bupt," he shushes, spitty, through his mouth guard.

That's it. Ed grabs Miles' arm, his bicep more sinew than muscle under his skin. "Enough! I mean it! I want some straight talk from you. Take that thing out of your mouth."

Miles pokes out the mouth guard with his tongue so that it dangles from its strap off the front of the helmet's cage. There is no remorse in his steady gaze. "Kickin' butt," he repeats.

"So you're going to kick *my* butt?"

"Maybe," Miles says.

"I beg your pardon?"

"I *said*, 'Maybe.' "

Ed closes his eyes, breathes again. It's not working. He wants to spank Miles. Ed really, really wants to spank his son. Ed squats down on his haunches and grabs both of Miles' arms. "You're being disrespectful. I know you're excited about school closing for the hurricane, but I won't allow you to swear or to disrespect me. Do you understand what I'm saying to you?"

"But Dad," Miles says, "more, I want to kick *Ivan*'s muh fuckn ass."

Ed shakes Miles. Hard. Hard enough that Miles' little head stuck in its big hockey helmet jiggles back and forth. Ed can't believe what he's doing as he does it.

He stops. "I don't care what you hear on this street, Miles! It's not to be repeated in this house!" Ed pulls the helmet off to find Miles staring, unmistakable fear in his teary eyes.

Now Ed wants to hug his bad son, but he can't. Ed has to be respected or nothing else will work.

Shit, of course Miles wants to be tough like the neighborhood thugs and the bullies at school. Who wants to be the wimp? No way, though, that Miles has any true idea what 'motherfucker' really means. Or that's what Ed chooses to believe at the moment.

Ed gives up. He's so damn weary. His abdomen whines with gas from all the food he ate at the Browns'. A fart now, and he'll lose Miles for good.

Ed stands and clenches. "Go to your room. I want you to think about where you went wrong today. I'm going to come up in half an hour, and you'll tell me what you've learned."

"Dad—"

Ed raises his index finger and points up the stairs.

Miles doesn't budge.

"I'll carry you up there if I need to."

Miles takes his stick and clacks his shin guards. Clacks as if he's won the fistfight out on the ice. Unspeaking, he heads up the stairs. Ed hears Ella's smaller footsteps race up in front of Miles'.

Where, in hell, is Ariel?

Roy, he's off at his second-to-last bandage change before home. He said he felt like walking himself over to the other floor rather than letting some nurse do it in the room. He doesn't have much faith in them, the nurses, but Cerise thinks they're safe to talk to. Seems to her the nurses would rather socialize anyways.

He's faking his pain now to get to stay with Cerise another night. He's better than fine.

Cerise lies there and wanders in her head, back a long ways.

When Cerise went through high school, she ran the dash. Faster than any other black girl in Louisiana for her last two years. She never got to race any white girls though, so she never knew if she ran the fastest ever. Her times said she did, but then who knows what white girls coulda' done if they'd seen Cerise's dark legs kicking down the cinder in front of them. Can't ever underestimate the white ladies. Cerise bets that her lady neighbor Philomenia, in her day, made a good showing. Cerise has never figured out exactly what Philomenia mighta' done—something like gymnastics, Cerise guesses—but the lady carries her body in that way. The way how you know a man could hurt you something fierce, and you know it just from the way he holds his shoulders. That's the way Cerise knows Philomenia had something.

Cerise would love to see the white lady run. Run to save her life. No. Not that, really. Cerise wouldn't ever wish that on a soul. She'd mighta' liked to see the young Philomenia give it her all, though, around a track loop back when. Take a hurdle or ten of 'em, maybe the triple jump.

Cerise bets Philomenia could be good in the sack but chooses not to. It's something you can just see in a body. A body's potential. But the white lady would have to want to be good when she's bedding her man. There's a difference.

Cerise hasn't found any surfing on TV for days, although she might have dozed off before finding it. She's taken to surveying the nurses about what they like to watch best on television. Cerise has been mightily disappointed so far. The bachelor show. And the other one that sits a contestant under the spotlight to answer questions or ask the audience for help. Or the person can call a friend. Cerise has noticed that the friends rarely seem to come through for the people sitting under the spotlight. It wouldn't be an easy place to be. Likely they're supposed to be the friends with the quickest internet, the ones to Google the right answer before thirty seconds run out. Marie, Cerise's own daughter, would be a terrible phone call contact person. Cerise wonders if Marie would even answer the phone.

Roy, he's never given a damn what he watches on the TV. Cerise sometimes thinks he waits for the commercials. He laughs at the crazy ones they all invent now. The things don't make a bit of sense, but Roy laughs and laughs. The gum commercials from England—or maybe they make them here?—crack him up especially.

Today, after the last debridement, they told Cerise the necrosis isn't under control. It means, in no goddamn uncertain terms, that she's dying from her right hand up. The flesh on her palm is dead, but they have to get it under control. How the hell do you control dying flesh? She's gotten so she's allergic to some of the pain medications they're giving her, throwing up, and they don't like putting her seventy-plus years out cold each time because of the long recovery coming up from under. So it works like so: they don't but poke her with a needle all over her hands to try to numb her. The middle's nothing on the right. The nerves died with the flesh. But the edges, where the second-degree burns are, the shots don't do a thing. Neither on the left. Not one thing. Pain with no words for it.

She asked if it was like gangrene. They told her not exactly.

Lady doctors, men nurses, everything's changed.

Cerise hasn't seen the same doctor more than twice since she woke up in her mittens. Charity Hospital is what it is. Once you're stayin' alive, they don't care so much anymore. The tired doctors treat her as what they see, she knows. A black woman old as cane dirt. How much can that be worth?

"Yo," a boy says, sticking his near-shaved head in the door. "Yo, ma'am. You Missus Brown?"

She's never seen the person before. He looks like he has no real want in the world to be there. "I'm a Yo or I'm a Ma'am?"

"That'd be a ma'am, fo' sho'," he says.

Cerise nods. "Come in where I can see you full."

The boy puts his head out into the hallway and looks around. "Aiight." He walks in like a teeter-totter, tipping side to side. A gold medallion swings back and forth across his Saints football jersey, and the child has to hold his trousers up with his hand in his pocket.

"So who's visitin' me?" Cerise asks him.

"My name Alphonse."

"An' why're you visitin' me, Alphonse?"

"The Ivan's coming. I checking up, yo. Seein' if you needs anythin'."

"It's kind of you to call, but I don't know why it'd be you're here in my room. You know my husband?"

"That be ol' man Roy?"

She takes no offense. She's lucky as hell to have a real ol' man. Makes her smile, even. Luckier than ever. "Age don't make a man, Alphonse."

He gives her a head jerk up, a little one, a sign of acknowledgment. "True."

What in the world is this child doing in her room? If she could think straighter, she might recognize why or how. She's certain he doesn't come from Orchid, though. He doesn't want to be here, no question. He looks up at the sliding ceiling rail that holds the dividing curtain that she and Roy have pushed out of the way. Some of the metal clip things have come out and dangle from the curtain in rusty blops. Cerise sees what they all know. Charity is the best place to be if you're dying fast, but soon as you're not, get out fast as you can.

Alphonse steps a weird shuffle. Cerise watches him doing something in his oversized trouser pocket. "What you doin', boy?"

"Yo, don' worry, lil' ma'am." The boy draws a roll of cash out of his pocket. It's rubberbanded loose into an O, fat as a mirliton squash. On the outside is a twenty.

Her days behind the register help her see what it adds up to if it's all twenties, in the range of thirty-five hundred to four thousand dollars. Cerise, suddenly, thinks she knows who the boy is in the grand scheme of the accident. She can't take drug money no matter how kind the boy's gesture.

"Don't think it," she tells him.

"Why you say that? Fear say you gone say that."

Cerise doesn't really understand what the child says, but she knows he's trying to give her money for something. He has something to do with being the boss of the cause of the accident. There's always a chain. Always an above-person, somebody higher, somebody making a bigger cut, somebody taking the risk of going to prison for longer than the lower-downs. Cerise looks down at her mitten hands resting on the thin Charity blanket. That PSW Keyshawn could eat up their savings something fierce. "No, but thank you."

"Muzzle gone make it right when he can."

"Alphonse, I appreciate your— No. But I thank, I thank . . ." Lord, they could use the money now. But the drugs kill their people. And how old can this boy be? He's the boss? He couldn't be more than nineteen. Cerise, she knows on the spot, will be crying for her city tonight. How terrible.

The boy tosses the roll of twenty-dollar bills onto Cerise's bed. "Let your ol' man do away wid it, den." Alphonse nods a little nod at Cerise. "Missus Brown." He goes out the door.

Cerise squints at the roll of money. It lies between her knees.

Prancie twinkles around her kitchen on her toes. Peach cobbler and peach upside-down cake cool on the counter. Prancie has never felt so light and happy. She never understood what taking true action could feel like. To be in control of others' destinies is a wonderful and freeing sensation.

Joe, when checked earlier, said that the new mayor, Ray Nagin, has announced that those who can leave should leave. The city is evacuating in earnest now. Joe predicted that tomorrow could prove quite difficult on the highways. He said that Philomenia should change her mind about staying. He made reference to her lack of common sense.

But she will do no such thing. She has good work to do at the barnacle. If only the mayor came to visit! Imagine, the new mayor eating her treats! He took office over two years ago, but Prancie cannot help thinking of the bald man in such a manner, as somebody new. He has risen up in their fair city from a strange and new place, from a fresh land of contemporary finance and business savvy. His shiny head seems to her like the toe of a new patent leather shoe. New! New!

Former Mayor Marc Morial left more than something to be desired. How contemptible he was to attempt to change the city charter so that he might reign for yet a third time! Philomenia, repulsed by that police chief Pennington, stepped into the voting booth and made her choice gladly. Prancie could be proud. And certainly, now, here, her new mayor chooses to inform his constituents wisely and with full candor. Make an exodus! Depart!

In the middle of a particularly long twirl, Prancie stops and stares at her creations. No. What could she be thinking? Of course she could not have the new mayor indulge in her treats. Maybe she had been caught up in the notion of meeting the man, of touching his head. Prancie would so love to just once feel his scalp. Nothing could be so intimate. The sensation might be akin to touching a newly birthed baby, she thinks, although not likely so wet.

Tomorrow, then, Prancie will take her treats to the bar. She can easily assume a hurricane party from the place. She will make her presence known. She will take control.

Prancie steps to her sink and opens the window over it. *Room temperature out of the oven, Philomenia.*

And there. Good Lord. The stench will destroy her gifts. The wafting scent of something curried and cloved and rose perfumed and foreign floats into her kitchen. Its exact identification proves impossible. Into her own home.

Philomenia closes the window. Peaches must taste like peaches.

"Where the hell?" Roy demands.

"He's Michael's boss," Cerise answers. "I'm for sure."

Roy has unrolled the money, and it's what Cerise suspected. All twenties. But her memory of the thickness of bills has failed her. Maybe they used to be more crumpled, or more valued, in her time. The child has given them two hundred and fifty thin twenty-dollar bills. A dirty five thousand dollars.

Roy stands and drags a chair over to the door of their room. He props it under the knob and returns to his bed, spread out in little piles of money. "Aw, Cherry, this is somethin'."

"Roy."

"This," he says pointing at the buffet of cash, "*this* can help us."

"It comes from the wrong place, an' you know it."

Roy looks at all the money, and Cerise thinks he could really drool, make spit come out of his mouth right there over it. She sure as hell doesn't want some drug-dealing thug thinkin' he's done his penance for her getting a claw hand. Her right hand might not tap out at much other than peppers on a cutting board ever till she's done, but.

But Alphonse feeling good about paying off young Michael's mistake can't be part of the deal. It just can't. Right? It can't.

"Cherry, you got a graft you gone get through. An' then we got a care person stayin' with us. Whatever situation Marie tell us about. How nice this be?"

Cerise just gives her husband a look he knows.

"It ain't traceable," he explains.

"You don't say."

Roy tries to go at it a different way. Cerise can see so in the way he shifts his body. He presses his hand to his bandages under his shirt in a cheap trick to get her sympathy. "What about we put it away for Lil Thomas?"

She'd thought about that already. Into a trust. Something the boy's parents couldn't ever touch. "No."

Roy's eyes search out hers till she gives him them. "Baby," he says. "*No.*"

"What you want me to do with this?" He's sort of massaging the piles of money, mushing them all together and across his sheet.

"Best you roll in it, husband."

He checks her eye. Cerise wonders how hard he'll fight. "Yeah?" he asks.

"How much you think a burnt-up hand is worth?"

"Whatever you say," he tells her.

She holds up her mitten hands.

"Whatever you say," he says again.

8

Yesterday Fearius thought he gone teach them a lesson. But right when he went down the narrow, he could hear the whiteifieds leaving, just preppin the house for whatever the Florida peoples pay em to do. Fearius backed up the narrow and gave em their ten minutes to get out.

But now, here, his best sale day possible, they back, draggin out bags of garbage and makin noise inside at straight up eight in the morning. Fearius walk slow down the block and think on things. Alphonse gave him a pager, but if Fearius decide to disturb Alphonse in the AM, Fearius best have a important code to send. Likely indeed, Alphonse just send back something saying for Fearius to take care of it himself. Fearius cant look like no baby with his thumb in his mouth.

Juvey showed him how to stand up. Troy from Arabi who been in for over a year showed Fearius how to sharpen his toothbrush into a point on the cinderblock and where the one hitter be hidden in the showers and who to buy from for what smoke goes in it. How you dont ever get yourself into a place with no move, like with chess, get sneaked up on from behind. Keep your back to the wall. Eat meals at the corner tables an face the whole dining room.

Hell, a boxcutter way sharper than a pointy toothbrush.

And two against one aint bad odds. They sure gotta be a couple of slow bros yessiring, wont have any desire to take Fearius on. They have families and whatall to feed. Potbellied pigs in the house and ol ladies lyin on couches eatin candies.

Look out, whiteifieds, Fearius say in his head, turning around. He step faster, leanin back more, and the tunnel start comin on the way it does, all the edges disappearing, almost like Fearius be walkin into a movie and get zoomed at triple speed to where he need to get to.

Fearius push on the button for the blade in his pocket and turn down the narrow, same as it feel like he done a thousand times already now. He take the boxcutter out and drag it along the house, peels of chocolate paint flaking onto the ground. Voices leak out the rotten wood.

And *zoom*, he be in through the back door.

One whiteified nigga from yesterday stand in the kitchen shaking his head at the mess, dissing crackheads and unclean habits. He shut up when he see Fearius. The other voice still come out another room: "They's just a worthless lot. Don't work, don't do nothing but poke needles into they veins and spread the HIV."

Fearius tap the boxcutter against his thigh, tip his head at the shut upped one in the kitchen. Fearius put on his cornerstore Chinese motherfucker face. "Best you wrap up yo shit now," he tell the man and squints.

The man raise his hands. "Whoa, whoa," he say. He got on pink dishwashing gloves like some woman.

Fearius laugh. "You done wif the pots an pans yet?"

"I don't know what you doin' here, son," the man say quiet at Fearius, "but I don't have no troubles with nobody." He keep holding his gloves up in the air.

"It time you pack up and evacuate," Fearius say, and in come the one from the other room.

"What the devil?" This one have a surgeon mask droopin round his neck, wearing full ass zipped up coveralls. What they think, that they gone get AIDS from picking up garbage? Come to think on it, maybe if the garbage end up being needles an all, it possible.

"Don't mean y'all doin' bad work, but it time you go now. They's a *hurr-a-cane*." He tip his head on the beats.

Coveralls aint quite as accommodating as Gloves. His face start twisting up, and Fearius know it gone become a toothbrush situation from the past. Funny thing, Fearius teeth be white as rice now for all his carrying his brush through his juvey days. Coveralls look at Gloves who just stare.

"Now," Coveralls say, "this ain't right." He run his eyes up and down Fearius, and Fearius feel it like the man using his fingers, like the man deciding if he gone take Fearius or not, testing if Fearius skinny enough or soft enough in his heart to break. "Boy, get your crackhead shit out here now before it's too late. What, you like ten years old?" Coveralls start walking forward. He has a old cold drink can in his hand, one turned into a pipe with a hole cut in the side, and a full garbage bag in the other. All a sudden, Coveralls throw the can at Fearius and swing the garbage bag then let it go. It whomp Fearius in the chest but it dont take him down.

Coveralls come in.

Fearius step back and get stuck against the counter. Coveralls sort of wind up a old school swing from down low by his hip, telegraphing his punch, and Fearius see he gone get hit hard if he dont move faster than the old fuck.

It always about training, same as anybody fighting in a ring. Fearius just do what he practiced more than ten thousand times in Baby Angola. Fearius crouch and slap Coveralls punch out the way then flick his boxcutter light on the mans thigh.

Coveralls grab onto his leg right away. "What the *fuck* you do, child?!"

Gloves still have his hands in the air. Fearius watch the blood startin to darken Coveralls leg.

Got to step up. Stand tall. "Likes I said," Fearius drawl, standing straight again. "Time to evacuate."

Gloves nod and walk sideways like a crab over to the door.

Coveralls be breathing hard through his mouth. Flies gone lay eggs in his teeth he making it so easy. "I see you," he tell Fearius. "I *see* you." He poke a finger in the air at Fearius face.

Fearius squint up his eyes at Coveralls and say, "Can't see nothin'." Fearius wipe the boxcutter on his jeans. "And Nothin' gone leave my house, ya heard?"

The bleeder seem like he want to spit but change his mind. That or maybe he gone be sick to his stomach.

Fearius raise his chin in the direction of the door and push out his lips.

Coveralls look at his leg and back up at Fearius face. "Ain't too young to go away for a while," Coveralls say.

Fearius shakes his head. "Naw. Ain't nobody sending me away today. They's a hurricane comin." He steps aside for the men to get past him with less worry. "Time to pack up your womens and they bon bons."

Ariel carries bags of nonperishable groceries to the better of their two cars. "So you all can call me from the road?"

"Did you just say 'y'all'?" Ed asks.

Please, she thinks. Get the hell out of Dodge so I can go to work. "I said whatever you heard, evidently," she answers.

"I heard 'y'all,' A."

"Then that's what I said."

Miles and Elizabeth Gupta heft his bulging hockey bag to the curb. The girl has eyes the color of fake jade, lighter than clear green. Behind giant black lashes, the shade is sort of surreal, a color Ariel would normally attribute to contact lenses should she see it in the irises of some guest. But Elizabeth is seven. And she has educated parents.

Indira rolls a suitcase down their front walk and waves at Ariel with her free hand, ducking her head at the clatter of her suitcase over brick.

"So you two have cell phones, right?" Ariel calls out to Indira.

"Yes," Indira says and nods. "And we have a charger for the cigarette lighter, so we will have all the power we need."

Ariel watches Miles interact with Elizabeth and once again knows what the future holds for her son. Miles, she thinks, will be raffish. An Errol Flynn. The girls will call incessantly.

Ariel wishes she could concentrate on the exodus of her family and the nice neighbors, but she has to get to the Belle. She probably should have spent the night there last night already. Ed simply couldn't comprehend her late-night return home even after her explanation of what she had to accomplish, of what needed to be done for a hotel in the French Quarter before a hurricane made landfall. His inability to understand her position, or more seriously, her importance at La Belle Nouvelle, feels purposeful and unkind. Watching Ella schlump her Barbie-pink backpack across their small patch of grass, Ariel winces with parental guilt.

Can she do this? Can she really stay?

She kissed the kids good night last night at three-thirty in the morning. She set her alarm for seven. She and Ed argued till five. And Ariel is as awake and energized as she's ever felt in her adult life. She walks over to Indira. "Let me help you," she tells the woman. Indira wears a sari the color of mashed sweet potato.

"Oh, stop," Indira says good-naturedly.

Ariel wants to hug the woman and ask her to watch over her children like they were her own.

"If I can't carry my own luggage," Indira continues, "what will I do when faced with carrying children on my back through floodwaters?"

"Swim like a dolphin," Ariel says. She would like to ask the woman to be her new best friend in New Orleans. They continue down the sidewalk. Ariel stares at her own shoes as they click on concrete. She wears good shoes. Impractical, sexy shoes. Today's cocoa three-and-a-half-inch heels gleam in the morning sun.

Indira rolls her suitcase up to their minivan and lets go. The handle of the suitcase slaps against the fender. "Oops," she says. "I could be the dolphin nanny. Or the swimming babysitter."

Ariel laughs. The woman is odd.

"Will I be responsible for fetching fish meals?" Indira asks.

"I think we could negotiate duties."

Indira looks at her daughter and Miles beginning a tug-of-war on the Guptas' front lawn.

Ariel gives Indira a smile and says, "You know, college freshmen, soon, won't have known a Cold War world."

"That's one of the better reflections of hope we might have that I've heard about these days."

"So," Ariel says. Miles yanks his hockey helmet from Elizabeth's hands. "As my kids' new adopted guardian and the securer of all things children in Breaux Bridge, Louisiana, you must promise me that our husbands will not ordain potato chip dinners and beef jerky breakfasts."

Indira presses on the mound of luggage already piled into the open back of the minivan. "My sister's sister-in-law and her husband will not allow any such dietary lapses. Well, I don't think. They will likely be vegetarians still."

Ariel thinks Indira is glorious in orange. Saris would be easy to pack, flat and thin. And the wrinkles would wear out in an hour or whatever.

Indira looks at the minivan and sighs. "I suppose the automotive industry is working on the self-loading vehicle already, don't you think?" She pushes on the mound of luggage again. It doesn't move. Ariel likes this woman. "If the hurricane hits New Orleans," Indira asks, "will your hotel be safe?"

"La Belle's all cinder block under the stucco. A 747 couldn't do it much damage. Ooh. Sorry. Bad taste." Ariel's forgotten how to talk to people outside of the hotel.

"Good," Indira says. "We can use that information to reassure Miles and Ella if they worry about your staying in town."

Ariel looks at her kids. They're readying to go to Disneyland. Their glee is palpable. Worry?

Sharon Harris comes out on her porch bitching at somebody still inside. Her metal screen door slams shut, the hydraulic thingy obviously broken. "Get it done, Klameisha. I'm not takin' sass from you and your sorry behind on *this* day." Sharon looks out to the street and waves at Ariel and Indira. "Hey, ladies!" she says warmly. She turns back to the screen door. "Formula, diapers, wipes, and water. You get that baby daddy to find them in this city and bring them by, and you best tell him to do it before my shift done or he can answer to me. Come here and shut the door."

Sharon turns and walks across the street. "How you two managing this hot mornin'? You scared?"

"Are you staying, Sharon?" Indira asks.

"Likely. I made 'em pack bags, but Nate and me, we got through Camille when we was babies ourselves. We probably gone stay. But you got any questions? You got water and batteries?"

"I'm staying too," Ariel says.

Sharon's eyes go wide. "Miss Minnesota's stayin'?" Sharon laughs. "Well, good for you. You come over if you need anything. My schedule's a lucky one this week. I'm off the next three days after pulling ten in a row. Just in time to sit in the dark with no television and no air-conditioning, forced to cook up everything in the house." Sharon shakes her head. "Think I'ma stop at Tokyo Rose when I get home tonight an' have me a Corona with lime."

"I'd join you," Ariel says, "but they've got me in a room at the hotel for the next couple of nights. Holding down the fort and all." Ariel shrugs. "It's weird. Everybody keeps acting like it's a big party."

"Well, girl, it *is* a big party," Sharon says. "Where you off to, Miss Indira?"

"My sister's sister-in-law and her husband own a motel in Breaux Bridge. We have adjoining rooms with the Mays, minus Ariel."

Ariel thinks about telling the women that only her last name is May, not Ed's, but decides against it. He'll have enough to contend with on the road. On their road trip.

"I suppose that's inland enough," Sharon says. "You all have fun. Miss Ariel, you want my cell number?"

The woman is so foreign to Ariel, strange and funny and forward and generous. "That's a good idea," Ariel tells her. "Let me go get mine, and I'll punch it in."

La Belle Nouvelle's staff has lost it. Not really, but Ariel's amazed. She's absolutely sure many of them are gobbling up drugs. Which kinds, she's not even certain. Far more than their usual, in any case.

But everybody's still functioning, so for now she's not going to come down on a single one of the loyal crew. She's short only three staff total. The rest have signed on for the full cruise. Beyond Douglas-Michael Smithson's people calling last night to say he would not be making it to

New Orleans because they were uncertain as to his abilities to get out—woo hoo!—Ivan's fixing all sorts of other things as well. Henny's going and Javier's staying. And the Belle's stocked with booze. To the tits, as Warren would say.

Ariel stands in the kitchen near the load-in dock as the guys from French Quarter Ice dolly three hundred bags into the walk-in freezer. The Belle's ice-makers could do all the work, but that little matter of a potential power outage screws everything up.

The kitchen radio's tuned to WWNO, and everybody nods and responds to what the announcers say: "If you're just now getting onto the I-10, you will be in for a wait. Please make sure you have your gas tanks full, folks. It's gridlock here at the 610/I-10 juncture, and it's only expected to get worse."

One of the ice guys whistles at the news.

Ariel wonders about I-90, the highway the Guptas and Ed took to get to Breaux Bridge, then wonders about how gridlock goes away. If nobody moves, then how does gridlock get fixed? How long can gridlock hold out against a hurricane? Ariel would just drive on the shoulder, she decides. Or maybe everybody else would have the same idea. Ariel sees the parents with kids about to piss their pants, the people with crappy cars running into the red temp zones, all of them driving on the shoulder and picking up pieces of metal and highway garbage. They'd get flat tires and kick up roadkill onto other cars . . .

She could walk to the corner store and buy condoms.

"I-90 looks to be no better," the woman on the radio says. "The mayor urges anyone evacuating to consider alternative routes."

"People, west is not best today," her radio partner chimes in. The man sounds like he sings the blues in his spare time.

"Ain't that the truth," a new dishwasher hollers out.

"Fo sho."

"I hear ya."

"To Ivan!" Javier calls out suddenly. He holds an imaginary shot glass aloft. *"Arriba,"* he says.

"Arriba!" The pretend glasses go up, including Ariel's, as per tradition.

"Abajo." He moves his hand low.

"Abajo!"

"A centro." Javier pokes his hand away from him.

"A centro!"

"A dentro." And in it goes.

"A dentro!"

Ariel tosses hers over her shoulder as always. She thinks she can remember the toast. It's sort of a play on words. She had one quarter of Spanish in junior high before she switched to German, the popular language back home. Pretty much, they just sang songs and sat on dirty handwoven carpets in the hippie Spanish teacher's classroom. Ariel still knows the lyrics, phonetically, to the one about the cockroach.

Javier leans into the stainless steel countertop in front of him. His teeth show white against his skin. Ariel can feel the shape of his hips from a distance.

"Now to Brett Abernathy for an update," the blues-singer-in-disguise says.

Another bluesman comes on to describe Ivan, the numbers, the longitude and latitude and speed and direction, but Ariel doesn't listen, or not exactly. She tries, but she has trouble picturing the thing in time and space without a meteorologist's hand gestures moving over a map.

"We can get us a lil' TV in here maybe?" It's the new dishwasher again. "It don't make no sense on the radio."

"True enough, friend," Warren agrees. He looks up from the bowl of dry rub he's concocting. "Whaddya say, Miss Ariel? Mighten we get a TV for the hurricane's arrival?"

Ariel doesn't see why not. But it's her immediate leverage. "Lots of No Rezes today so far," she tells them. The hotel is filling up with people coming in off the streets. "Maybe. Keep prepping."

"A Nazi boss," one of the passing ice guys says, tossing a smile at Ariel.

Javier catches Ariel's eye. The bad word seems to entice him somehow. He could be into bondage secretly. Ariel supposes she could tie him up and kiss him all over his back while he ground his beautiful hips into the sheets. "Damn straight," she says loudly.

Warren shoots her a look like, You're learning, girlfriend.

Best Ariel leave the kitchen without much more said and stay on their good side.

Another round of dollies, and the ice is finally in. "Sign, Chef?"

"Yup."

It's the first time she'll have spent the night in the hotel since her interview.

She's going home at some point soon. She has a house to finish securing. And a bag to pack. Rite Aid sits at the corner of St. Charles and Louisiana for what she might not have already.

9

Elizabeth's thin brown arm pokes out the side window of the Guptas' minivan in front of them. She waves and waves back at Ed, Miles, and Ella, her pink palm fluttering. Ed taps out a greeting on his horn.

Their cars sit, unmoving as stones, in gridlock. Most of the people around them, Ed included, have turned off their engines. Better for the environment. And the car. And gas. Not more than an eighth of a mile ago, when they still crawled along, they passed a red-haired man holding a handwritten sign over his head on the highway's shoulder, leaning on the back of an old Lincoln: `gas please name your price`.

"*Da*-ad," Miles says in the coveted passenger seat beside Ed.

Whatever Miles might be berating Ed for now, he doesn't know. The horn beeping?

"Pleasepleasepleasepleaseplease?"

What does his son want? "What. Miles."

Miles says something back, but Ed can't hear him with their windows rolled down. An enormous black SUV the size of a small school bus idles menacingly beside them to their right. What could that thing get—seven, eight miles to the gallon? The vehicles disgust Ed normally, but this one blares rap music loud enough to deafen the people who lounge inside, the engine running, the blackened windows all up. He can't hear his own son sitting beside him over the din.

Ella rhythmically pushes her feet into Ed's kidneys from her car seat behind him. She's long known the spot for maximum impact. "Yes. Ella."

"Me too!" Ella screams.

"You too what?"

A back, darkened window of the SUV whirs down slowly. The music has to be doing damage to the passengers' ears. A man with strange teeth—are they gold?—grins at Miles and bobs his head. Miles begins bobbing in imitation immediately.

Ed leans forward and twiddles his fingers at the man. Ed's attempting a French assassin's calm demeanor, but really he wants to try to hear what the rap is saying.

As if he reads Ed's mind, the man in the SUV says over the noise, "Lil Wayne." The window goes up again, but the rap is perfectly audible, if Ed could actually understand it. He strains to listen carefully and thinks he catches some of it:

"... drop your knees ... won't be long ... I don't use rubbers ..."

What an absolutely asinine thing to rap about! All young people should be using condoms. Every single time. Why would somebody brag about that? He might as well be rapping about how brave he is to play Russian roulette!

Miles picks up on the refrain, belting out, "Drop it like it's hot, drop, drop it like it's hot!"

Deflect. Redirect. "Miles. Miles! What did you want to do? The pleasepleaseplease thing?"

Miles keeps up with his own refrain, falling out of sync with the one coming from the SUV. "Drop drop drop it when it's hot, drop it drop it when it's hot, drop it when it's hot."

Three teenage black girls saunter up, two carrying a cooler and the other the biggest bag of potato chips Ed has ever seen. They dance along the white line between the SUV and Ed's car. They stop and gyrate next to Miles, who stops his singsonging and stares. All three girls wear very, very short shorts. Potato chip girl suddenly flops over in time with the rap and bends herself in half. She jiggles her raised butt in rhythm to the refrain. Ed's stomach flips when he realizes he is staring at the outline of the large girl's vulva.

And then they're off. The girls stop at the back of a weird SUV–pickup truck hybrid ahead of the SUV by another two cars.

A row of police vehicles speeds by in the opposite direction, heading towards New Orleans.

Miles starts to bob his head again.

The girls wriggle and dance. They elicit honks and hollers.

"Cool," Miles says.

"What part?" Ed asks.

"You know."

Ed doesn't know. Not at all. He has no idea what part of anything Miles has just witnessed is cool. It could all be, or none of it could be. Cool. Ed's concerned that this is something he should be able to discern without asking.

"Daddy?" Ella asks.

"Yes, love?"

"How come they did that?"

Ed thinks he knows right away what his daughter is after but doesn't want to address it. "What do you mean, Ella?"

Up ahead, an old fat beige man exits his car. He holds a beige poodle in his arms. The man could be of any heritage on earth for all Ed knows. Beige is beige. He's just a human. Holding a dog.

The beige man puts the beige dog on the ground. It's old and shaky and clearly not doing so well.

"A dog!" Ella calls out, and Ed thanks Buddha for the diversion. Ella will work her way back around to her question, maybe tonight, maybe tomorrow, maybe a month from now when she witnesses some other impromptu bit of booty-grinding, but for now she's happy enough to watch an old dog on the side of an old highway full of parked cars.

The dog sniffs the owner's car tire and lifts its leg.

Twisting in his privileged front seat position, Miles tells Ella, "It's a boy dog."

"It's *pee*ing on the tire!" Ella yells.

Ed can't ignore the shuddering SUV. Certainly what he thinks he hears can't be what he really hears: *"stuffed you in the ass—"* How can a highway have turned into a tailgating party? What wonderful phrases will Miles learn today if they're forced to remain here? And Ella . . . if Ella starts talking about slappin' a ho, Ed's going to lose it.

"—*dick like a python*—"

Ed rubs his hand over his greasy face. He can feel a rivulet of sweat find his crack.

"Like a *python*!" Miles bobs his head till it looks like he could fling it off his neck. "That's—a—snake!" Miles informs Ella.

"Ewww!" Ella squeals, stomping Ed's kidneys.

The beige man watches his dog piss on the rear tire of his own car, and Ed glances up at the three girls by the fender of the hybrid. Two teenage boys have come out to join Potato Chip and the Coolers. The boys snap their fingers over their heads and nod while they look up and down the rows of stuck cars. It seems, clearly, that they're the best thing going for all the visible gridlock around.

The back window of the SUV whirs down again. The smell of marijuana wafts Ed's way. Gold Teeth nods with squinty eyes at Miles. "A lil' solja," he says. "Dap." The man extends his muscled arm and tight dark fist far out his window toward Miles.

Ed doesn't understand what's going on. Maybe the man's passing Miles a joint. A seven-year-old boy. "Hey," Ed says, "do what you want in your own car, but that's not for my son," just as Miles makes his own fist and butts it into Gold Teeth's.

The man smiles and nods at Miles. "Dat's right." He pulls his arm back in his window and frowns at Ed. "What you think I'ma do?" The window goes up.

Ed's certain he can hear laughter beneath the thump of the eardrum-bursting rap. Lil Wayne, the guy said. Ed'll have to look him up on the internet.

"So can I?" Miles asks.

"Can you what?"

"Me too," Ella says.

"What?"

"Go to the Guptas' car."

Ed realizes they've seen more than just the girl trio and dog man get out of their cars and move around. The cars have been stopped for nearly half an hour. The stretching, the standing accompanied by neck-craning, began at least twenty minutes ago.

"Pleasepleaseplease—" Miles begs, his brain turning to jello in his bouncing skull.

"Miles, stop that."

He stops. "Please?"

"What if the cars start moving again. Then what will we do?" Ed can see they wouldn't be the only ones needing to regroup. He's just not sure he should bother the Guptas right now. It's nice enough of them to extend the offer to stay at the motel in Breaux Bridge, making sure that their in-laws saved an extra room for Ed and the kids. He's happy, at this point, that the black SUV isn't stopped next to the Guptas' minivan.

"We could ride with them," Miles answers.

"William pulled my hair," Ella says.

"Nuh-uh." Miles twists in his seat.

"Yeah-huh," Ella says.

"He did not." Miles unbuckles his seat belt. "You're making that up because you *wanted* William to pull your hair."

"He did so!"

Ed reaches to turn on the radio. He'd sworn he wouldn't turn it on, afraid the kids would feel his anxiety. His fingers rest on the button. "You want music?" he asks.

"Nuh-uh!" Miles says again and lunges between the seats at his sister.

"Daddy!" Ella kicks at Miles and manages to catch his chin with a hard one.

Miles bites his lip and goes at Ella again. Ed blocks him with a fast arm. "You keep up this sort of behavior, and you can both stay in your seats till kingdom come." Kingdom come? Where the hell did he pull that one from? Confirmation class? "Alright. Let's take a break."

In the rearview, Ella sticks her tongue out at her brother, and Ed sees Ariel in the gesture, through and through. He's so completely disgusted with his wife's place of employment right now he can hardly think it all through logically. Who in the world separates a woman from her family during a hurricane evacuation? "Miles, be careful getting out your side."

Miles swings open his door wide and is out of the car. Ed grabs ineffectually at his shirt, missing any piece of Miles at all.

"Daddy!" Ella whomps on Ed's kidneys for the umpteenth time. Ed has sworn he will never, ever call her on it. It's her sole means of exerting any kind of power, trapped in a child seat in a vehicle she doesn't drive.

"Hang on, Fitzy."

Ed opens his door and steps out while Miles beelines it to the Guptas' minivan.

Heading back toward New Orleans, an ambulance races past on the other side of the highway. Ed really wants to listen to the news. Maybe he can have an adult conversation with Ganesh and Indira while the kids play. On the highway. Or in the tall median grass where snakes and used needles hide.

It's so, so hot.

By the time Ed opens Ella's door, she's unbuckled herself. She reaches out to Ed, the gesture that always turns up some daddy dial inside him, some inherent protective knob that gets cranked to high when Ella's little hands come at him to help her or hold her.

If he had to, Ed would kill the men in the SUV for Ella. And for Miles too, of course.

"Let's take a break, hey?" he says to his daughter.

"Let's take a break," she says back.

Indira gets out of the driver's seat. "Good idea," she says to Ed as he approaches with Ella. Miles opens the sliding door to the minivan and crawls inside.

Ganesh steps out. "Well, we might be in for it."

"Might?" Ed asks, and the three of them laugh.

"Ella, there are games inside," Indira says, and Ella crawls into the car over the Guptas' driver seat.

"Sorry," Ed says.

"Whatever for?" Indira says, passing her upturned palm around to indicate the state of things around them.

Ed smiles. "Thanks. You hear the SUV next to us?"

"Baton Rouge hears it," Ganesh says.

They all nod with the unspoken. They are, the three of them, Ed decides on the spot, sensitive and wise people. Louisiana has a reputation that perpetuates itself for good reason. We choose diversity, Ed thinks. We choose a European approach to living. We care about more than money, and our communal culture stems from an acceptance of everyone's differences.

One of the male friends of the girl trio stands up in the back of the hybrid truck bed and then steps onto the roof of the cab. Ed waits to hear the metal *oomp* of the cab top bending inward, but he can't over the rest of the noise. The kid seems to be legitimately trying to check out the traffic. Ed wouldn't mind a little feedback.

The boy must feel eyes on him. He hitches up his sagging pants, then pushes them half the way back down again. He raises a hand to his brow and scans the road behind everyone then turns a hundred eighty degrees and looks ahead. The road goes quieter for the boy's report.

He wears a pick in his afro, one of a few Ed's noticed the last few months. Maybe the natural look really is taking hold, even in New Orleans.

The boy shakes his head exaggeratedly. He turns around and runs his own flat hand across his throat, then gives the finger.

They're all dead-screwed.

A communal groan sounds out from the road.

Ed gives the boy a thumbs-up thank-you. "You know," he says to Indira and Ganesh, "one of my biggest worries with all of this is getting stuck on the road when the hurricane hits."

"I know," Ganesh says. "I want to go for it and drive in the median."

Ed is surprised by the admission. He nods. "Better still, why don't we all just get over there?" Ed points to the deserted other side of the highway. Except for emergency vehicles, it's been empty for hours already. "I'm dying to get going."

Indira nods in agreement. "So much road wasted."

The minivan waggles with the movement of children inside. "It does seem," Ganesh says, "that there's a better plan here somewhere."

"You'd think so," Ed says, looking around, the heat turning the infinite line of cars ahead into a swimmy mirage. "You'd really think so."

The SUV goes mercifully silent for a few seconds before another rap begins: *". . . you workin' with some ass . . . make a nigga—"*

Ed feels his face warm with a blush. How can a person pretend he doesn't hear that? He can't imagine ignoring the noise, those lyrics, indefinitely.

They really need to get moving.

Four hours later, they have driven twenty-seven miles, with a hundred-plus to go. Ed glances at the speedometer. They go so slowly their speed doesn't register.

Miles has peed into a flip-topped Tupperware pitcher packed expressly for just such a purpose. Carrying a spare sari—or fabric that looked pretty enough to be one—Indira took both the girls into the grass a couple hours ago, setting up a little latrine, blocking the view creeps might have had from the road.

Now Ella sleeps in her car seat, and Miles' fascination with the pitcher of piss has finally waned. It sloshes quietly, tucked in on the floor behind Miles. Pouring it out while everyone inches along simply isn't an option.

They have escaped the black SUV for the time being. When Ed drove past the broken-down car in the lane ahead of the SUV, he sent out his second prayer of thanks for the day.

Miles stares into the credit-card-sized screen of a handheld computerized game Elizabeth has loaned him. The repetitive music that plays over and over has Miles in its hypnotic grip. The boy's mouth hangs open as he stabs with his thumbs.

Ed wants nothing more than to crush the thing in his bare hands. Certainly the batteries can last only so long.

He sighs loudly. His minimal Buddhism training is wilting further with each passing month in Louisiana. He can't remember the wording of the lesson he wants right now, the one about why we tend to be afraid of what we don't understand. He doesn't have the proper headspace to even try. He should at least reconnect with his son. Since the swearing last night, Miles has felt far away. The SUV didn't help today.

"Why does the music stop and start over like that?" Ed asks.

Miles doesn't respond.

"Miles?"

"Just a minute!"

They roll past an obese man in a plaid shirt driving a '50s Caddy. His backseat is full to bursting with life belongings. Ed hopes they've not made a dire mistake by not packing photos, by not having gone to their safety deposit box for important papers. And then his insides contract. He very much hopes they have not made the most irreversible and pre-ventable mistake by not getting Ariel in the car too. What would his life be without her? What would Ella's or Miles'?

Ed suddenly wants to sob. He should have fought harder. She could find another job. Or he could go back to work. This year, with Ella being gone at school a full day too, he has significant time on his hands. Or they both could work, but work less. Spend more time together.

The tinny tune on the game starts over again.

"What are you trying to do on that?" Ed tries again.

"Errr!" Miles growls, and the music begins fresh immediately. "Col-lect mushrooms!"

"Shh. Your sister's sleeping. But I know that one. It's retro. Do you know that expression? Retro. On Ms. Pac-Man I bet I could *kick your butt* when we get to the hotel."

"Daddy," Ella says, very awake. "Daddy, I gotta go."

"Loser," Miles said. "It's Super Mario Brothers."

What did Miles just call him?

"Daddy. Right now."

10

A banner slouches from the barnacle's front roof gutter. It advertises a hurricane party. Philomenia knew to count on predictable behavior.

Through the ginger leaves, she watches the bartender, Thurman, carry boxes printed with the distinguishable bat wings of a hard liquor company from his car. Why he has decided to give himself an alias, Philomenia has no idea. Who decides to call oneself Pedro? It is a name best suited for a plumber, or possibly an immigrant roofer, not for a young man studying medicine. He sets the boxes on the stoop. Philomenia can see that they contain food. White bread bun packages sprout from one. Baguettes, no doubt the worst the city has to offer, shoot from another.

Philomenia knew Thurman's father, Thurman Junior. He and she were both much younger and decidedly more impulsive when they interacted. This offspring Thurman, unfortunately, lacks his father's magnetism and has the exaggerated features that so many of the younger generation seem to sport. Such large lips and eyes. Many Tulane students resemble dolls, and far too many of the young men seem purposefully effeminate as opposed to dapper and self-possessed.

The barnacle opens its dark and ugly door at noon.

Prancie paces and smiles, now in front of her bedroom bay window. She has prepared to make an appearance at two PM, and she has prepared herself to truly become another person. She will need to be warmly personable and possibly be touched by near strangers. Normally, her scalp would prickle at the thought, but Prancie has come to realize that sacrifice is part of a mission.

She might, too, find herself in the position of needing to drink alcohol. This she can justify only by knowing she will come ever closer to her objective. She must don sheep's clothing, and if it comes stitched in the form of a fuzzy navel or a kir royale, she will don what she must.

"I thought I would share some of the baking across the street," Philomenia twitters, her head inserted only slightly into Joe's door.

He sleeps.

"For your party," Prancie says, as light and lively as she is able.

Thurman III looks at her five-pie carrier, full of treats. It takes her a bit of effort to raise it onto the bar. The young man looks back to Prancie's face. "Hi," he says.

"Hello," she says, ready for just such a reaction. "A peace offering." Still, Prancie's hand goes to her throat in an instinctive gesture she had not anticipated.

A modicum of Thurman Junior glints behind the eyes of this rogue. "Really?" His groomed eyebrows rise.

Well, of course. She would not choose to joke in such an unpredictable situation. "Yes," she says. "Yeah." The word feels so false from between her teeth she wants to inhale it back inside her lungs.

Be Prancie, she breathes into her head. It is a hurricane party. "Please," she tells him. "Really. We are—we're—all invested in the neighborhood."

"You going to pull barbeque duty out front later, too? Flip some burgers for me?"

Fair enough. The young man has reason to believe her intentions might be less than selflessly generous. She would prefer nothing more than to see Tokyo Rose obliterated, but she must remain a stealthy warrior on her mission. "Didn't you partake in—" Proper grammar and diction are harder to lose than she believed they would be. One only needs to listen to the hotel heiress who so shamelessly promotes herself to understand the lack of language skills the younger generation possesses.

Try again, Philomenia.

"I am sorry for being a thorn. But these," she says, attempting false modesty, "might pass muster. And I can tend, man, a grill with the best of 'um."

"Let the lady feed us, for fuck's sake," the blond, bearded man Philomenia recognizes as one of the regulars says. He sits on a barstool in a shirt that should be buttoned but is not. She sees the light hair that grows on his tan stomach. He must like to pretend that he lives on the beach in Florida rather than inland Louisiana. She knows his walk before and after his visits to the barnacle as well as she knows her own shorthand. He has been coming to the place since it opened. Still, Philomenia does not know the man's name.

She steps away from her creations and extends her hand. "Prancie," she says and smiles as wide as she is able.

"Shane Geautreaux. A pleasure." He raises Prancie's hand to his lips.

She carries antibacterial gel in her handbag. To touch the bathroom door would likely be worse than sitting on a barstool. She could remove the gel under the cover of the dark bar without too many people seeing. "Are you hungry?" Prancie asks Shane.

"Well," he says, giving Prancie an eyeing, "I haven't filled up this hollow leg yet."

Prancie shows her teeth again. "Be adequately warned. It's dangerous food." And then Prancie feels her face spread out into a smile she cannot help. She tells the truth! And she stands inside the enemy's lair, undetected.

"What'd you bring, pretty lady?" Shane asks Philomenia's bosom.

Oh, my. "I have sweets and salties," she says. "Peach cobbler. Some, well, you might call it party mix. Pretzels mixed with whatnots."

Thurman III laughs. "I think I'm allergic to whatnots."

"Well, of course," Prancie counters. "You're not old enough to have acquired a taste."

Shane laughs.

Two very young women bend together like flower heads at the other end of the bar. They grip beer bottles as though they pull on goat teats. This newest generation of girls represents all that is wrong with Uptown New Orleans. Why would they choose not to leave the city? They have entire lives to live, and they decide instead to come to the party of some reprehensible bar a few blocks away from their university while their classes are canceled and their parents undoubtedly worry for their welfare. These young women, oh, Philomenia could so easily tell them where they need to go.

So Prancie will begin with them. She hoists her five-pie carrier off the bar top and walks it towards the girls. Assuming they are not regulars, a singular visit to her treat trays will not hurt them all that much. Besides, both pad themselves with plenty of flesh. A few pieces of cobbler will only make them believe the barnacle is unclean, that the glassware has been improperly washed. With luck, they will decide their digestive woes constitute reason enough to choose another venue in which to imbibe.

"Hey," Shane says, "where you going with that?"

Prancie turns with all the charm she can emote and says, "I'm coming back. Ladies first."

Shane Geautreaux holds his glass aloft. "Too true," he says. "I heard ya."

Prancie approaches the milkmaids. "Some hurricane treats to go with your beverages, ladies?"

"Ooh, yeah," the smaller of the two says.

"There are napkins on the—yes, there." Prancie places the carrier on the bar in front of the young women. "Take some. Those are mini quiches. Savory quiches."

"I *love* quiche," the larger says. "Wow, these look great! Thanks so much."

They pile several of Philomenia's hand-stenciled paper napkins with treats.

They must be hungry.

"What about us poor sops down here?" Shane calls out.

It is very nice to feel wanted, Prancie thinks. "Coming," she says and smiles again. Who knew this would prove perfectly delightful? To maneuver inside the walls of her nemesis should not feel so enjoyable. Or, possibly, it should.

She'll make certain Shane takes seconds.

The process will be a lengthy one, Prancie believes, a matter of months, but the end result will be ever so satisfying.

Shane grabs a handful of her party mix and stuffs it into his maw. Some of the patrons, Prancie determines, will be easier than others.

"Mother, Keyshawn is prepared to go to work tonight. He's willing to stay in town during a hurricane to care for you in your own home. What more could you possibly want from a PSW?"

How 'bout the fact that Cerise could possibly want to *not* have a personal support worker at all? She doesn't answer her daughter.

"I don't know," Marie continues, barely stopping to take a breath, "I mean, they say you *can* leave if you insist—which is exactly what I think you should do, insist, that is—and I just think it'd be better to be in your own home with your family than by yourself in a hospital. Your and Daddy's place made it through Betsy and Camille, so you know it'll be safe. And Lil Thomas, Thomas, and me will all be there, so you'd have lots of company and we can help with anything else that's needed."

"What about my treatments?"

"Well, see, now, that's exactly what Keyshawn is for."

"You said he wasn't a doctor, Marie. Now he is?"

"No." Marie puts her fists on her hips. She's got three different looks that say frustrated. She wears one of them now. "He has a specially equipped van for all sorts of people, and it'd be part of his job to take you back and forth to the hospital for your treatments."

Such a hassle. Why can't Cerise just stay here so everybody doesn't have to know each and every time she needs to use the facilities? "I think I could sit in a normal car. The rest of my body's still fine, Marie."

"I'm just *saying* . . ." Marie stops and huffs. "You're not going to try to tell me that you'd really rather lie up here in this nasty old hospital room during a hurricane than be surrounded by loved ones at home. You're really not going to tell me that, right?"

"So you're the boss of me now, are you?"

"I just meant that Keyshawn is a real professional. He has the van because he wants to be the best at what he does. And he will be. But you do what you want. You always have. And you always will. Go ahead and be alone. I don't care." Marie picks up her handbag off the floor then walks to the big bouquet from the neighbors. The nurses have kept it looking pretty, plucking out the droopy flowers. One of them said it was good feng shui to only keep flowers that are completely alive. Cerise wonders if she has bad feng shui since she's not all completely alive. She has a crumpling leaf for a hand.

"It's getting smaller," Marie says about the bouquet, frowning. "Are people stealing your flowers? See, this is exactly the sort of reason why you should get out of Charity Hospital."

"Nobody's stealing my flowers! It's feng shui."

"What is? That makes no sense, Mother. Making bouquets smaller is feng shui? Somebody told you that to get you to let them take your flowers."

Good Lord, her child has no sense at all. How did this person come from her own body? It seems such an impossibility at the moment that Cerise smiles.

"What's funny?"

"Nothing," Cerise says.

"Well, I'm going. The boys are waiting on an afternoon snack. You decide what you want and we'll do whatever. Keyshawn needs to know, though, by three. Otherwise, he's evacuating."

"The boys? As in more than one?"

"You know what I mean. Daddy, Thomas, Lil Thomas."

Marie will put Roy back in the hospital with her cooking. *Her boys.* Cerise has had just about enough of that. Cerise is the person to care for Roy. "Go get whoever we need in here. I'll tell 'em I wanna go."

"Really? Oh, it's going to be so much better." Marie bends over

Cerise and hugs her, clonking her in the arm with her hard handbag. "It might even be fun, you know? All of us playing games by candlelight with the rain on the roof."

And what's Cerise going to hold her playing cards with? Her toes? "Ask the nurse at the station what forms need to get signed. You'll have to do it for me. I'll give them my permission."

"Aren't you even a little excited?"

I can hardly wait, Cerise thinks. She can just start asking who's ever nearest to follow her to the facilities and help hold up her robe. But, then, that would mean the air-conditioning is still working for her to be wearing a proper robe. That the electricity's still on during a hurricane. Exactly. Why wouldn't she be excited?

"Hi, Sharon," Ariel says into her cell as she drives back to Orchid Street, the driving itself, as opposed to riding the streetcar, feeling like a luxury. She passes workers nailing plywood over the windows of a restaurant, but otherwise, the streets feel nearly deserted. "Am I bothering you at work?"

"Hell no," Sharon says. "I'm glad for the excuse. Rolanda, I gotta take this. What's up, Miss Minnesota?"

Ariel can hear Sharon moving through noise. "You know, I don't even know what you do at Touro. I'm sorry."

"Ain't no thang. I'm the blood collector. I'll poke you sometime. Nobody ever even feels my needles."

"You're an RN?"

"Naw. Not yet. Still over at Delgado Westbank inchin' along. How you doin'?"

"Good. Lots of people at the hotel have done this before, so I have help."

"Oh yeah, we all done this before."

Ariel clicks on her right turn signal. She refuses to adhere to the local custom of not using it at all. "Well, I was really hoping you might tell me what to do to get the house ready."

"By your slim lil' self?"

"It's just me now."

Sharon laughs big, and then Ariel hears street noise. Sharon must have gone outside. The click of a cigarette lighter sounds, then an exhale. "Your house have real working shutters on it?"

Ariel should know this. "How do you mean 'working'?"

"They actually open and close up an' they the right size for your windows."

"I don't know."

"Well, that's the first thing. They not just for decoration. If yours close, close 'em. An' pick up the yard. Anything that can fly, you know, lawn furniture and plants in pots and shit. Fill your bathtub up with water, case that goes. You have a gas stove?"

Potted plants can fly? Ed always cooks. What do they have? "Yeah. Gas. Is that bad?"

"No," Sharon says, "that's what you want. It's gone still work when the power goes out."

"You know it's going out?"

"Girlfriend, it always do."

"The power's going to go out?"

"My accent that hard for you?"

Ariel has no idea how to take this. She doesn't know Sharon well enough. "No. Not at all. I understand you."

"They all like you up in Minnesota, lady?" Sharon laughs again, and Ariel knows the woman's just joking now. She wasn't sure.

"Uh," Ariel says, "maybe? No. Hell no." She pulls up in front of their house. She looks at it objectively for a second, wondering if it will still be there in twenty-four hours. It's a pretty house. She looks across the street at Sharon's house and feels stupidly guilty for something. What, she's not exactly sure.

Sharon exhales again, probably making her cell phone smell like cigarettes. "The power always go out, but it's possible just for an hour or whatever. You free to leave the hotel if you need to?"

"I don't know," Ariel has to say again and steps out into the heat of the afternoon. "If I had to go, I guess I'd just go."

"Well, if the power go out much more than a day, you best deal with your fridge. They can grow things. It's too late to board up your windows if the shutters don't work, but you need to take your breakables you care about off the sills. If it's just you, likely your food supply's okay, right? I don't think you'll be trimmin' any tree branches by yourself either, so take a look around your yard. You see a big branch hangin' over your dining room, an' you have nice things in the dining room, you might want to pull the old table or china or whatever into another room. I'll be keeping an eye out, but make sure you lock all your locks and get it secure. Bike locks on the shed and whatever."

Ariel had no idea. Maybe she just didn't want to have any idea. Really, if Ed's going to leave her here alone, what, actually, could she do by herself? "Wow. And here I was just going to pack a suitcase."

"You can most certainly just do that too, Miss Ariel."

"So, you and Nate are staying with the kids?"

"Well, whichever ones decide they gonna be by home for the night. But, yeah, we're stayin'."

"The news shows it's a Category Four right now." Ariel walks up her porch steps and looks around at what might fly: potted plants, a skateboard, their porch swing.

"You scared yet?"

"Yes," Ariel admits.

"Good. You need to be. Don't get so drunk you can't think on your feet."

Ariel hadn't even been thinking about getting drunk, but she can see the logical progression. She actually feels like having a drink now. "When do you get off?"

"Not till seven, hon'."

"Oh. I did feel like having a drink. It's weird."

"No. It's *serious* tradition."

Ariel walks to the shutters that hang on the outside of the living room windows. She pulls on one. "It's stuck on," she tells Sharon.

"What's that?"

"The shutter's stuck onto the house."

"Make sure they's no hook-n-eyes on the back before you give up."

"I don't know what you mean."

"Run your hand up behind the shutter, see that they's no clip thing to hold it open."

Ariel does as she's told. She feels something. "I think there's something."

"Good. See if you can spring it."

Ariel fiddles and the shutter pops free. "Oh, hey. It's off the wall."

"It still on its hinges?"

Ariel swings the shutter. "Yeah, it works."

"Well, then, you have working shutters. That's good. They can save windows."

"Thank you so much, Sharon. Will you take a rain check on the beer?"

"Whatever you do, don't leave beers on my porch for a present. Kids'll pretend they never saw 'em."

Ariel can imagine. "When this is all over, maybe we can go have a drink at Tokyo Rose or something."

"That'd be nice," Sharon says, but she says it like suddenly she doesn't believe what she says at all, words just leaving her mouth like so much smoke.

"Really," Ariel tells her.

"Alright, Miss Minnesota."

Ariel feels almost dismissed and strangely sad. Sharon seems to be a good person when it comes down to it. It'd probably suck to have a bunch of crappy kids. "Be safe and all," Ariel tells her. "Is there an expression I'm supposed to know before a hurricane?"

"Huh?"

"Like, 'Till the wind blows us back together' or something?"

Sharon laughs again. Ariel really likes her laugh. "Woman, you say some funny things. I guess you can tell me good luck. Then again, you could tell me that any day of any ol' week."

Ariel smiles and watches a green lizard skitter across her porch railing. She guesses she could. "Good luck, and I'll see you in a couple of days."

"Nice talking with you, Miss Ariel."

"Bye." Ariel waits for Sharon to say good bye too but just hears the connection quit. Southerners seem to do that more often, Ariel's come to realize. They don't give proper good byes. Maybe it's a more optimistic approach. Or something.

Ariel unlocks her door. She'll ready the house best she can and squeeze in a second shower.

11

"Philomenia," Joe calls out from his parlor bedroom.

Prancie looks for her filé in the spice cupboard.

"Philomenia."

Can she not even have a moment? Prancie removes the thawed lump crabmeat from the microwave. The urchins across the street have no idea how good her gumbo is yet, but they will. She has promised to return with dinnertime food on schedule.

"Take a look at this thing," Joe says when Prancie enters in her apron. He points at the swirling mass on television.

"Yes?" She tries to hide the annoyance in her voice. Shane Geautreaux promised to wait for her return. She could not resist his challenge for her to make a gumbo from scratch.

"Look at this thing!" Joe is so strangely animated. His hair has begun to fall out in earnest from the chemotherapy. It seems the objective is to shrink the remaining tumors if possible before excising so much more of his colon that he will not have enough left. A shame, really. His hair was always one of his best features.

Philomenia vaguely remembers a childhood dog, an Irish terrier, that needed to be plucked in the spring. Its coarse winter coat came away from its back in handfuls. Now Prancie must consciously fight the urge to do the same to Joe's head. "Where will it make landfall?" she asks.

"They say to our east, but none of them seem to know exactly. It's back to a strong Category Four." Joe inhales. "Hope I get some of that gumbo."

"How did you know?"

Joe was always such an eater. "How did I know?"

"I suppose that might be a silly question." They both know he is not allowed gumbo to eat at this juncture.

She could walk over and just rub his head, imitating an affectionate gesture, and see what happens. He is not the sort of man who would look better bald. She entertains the notion of buying him a wig and giggles.

"What's funny?" Joe's eyes dart to her. Clearly his faculties fire on all cylinders today. 'Fire on all cylinders' is an expression Shane used often this afternoon. Prancie had to listen carefully numerous times for the context in order to discern his meaning. Now she thinks it to be a fine way to put some things.

"My apologies. I just, well, I was imagining you in a wig." She should not have said it. She need not be cruel at this point.

Joe bursts out in laughter. He still has so many stitches that Philomenia worries. She does not desire to address his bleeding this evening or any other. Her duties at this point in their marriage are very clearly defined, such that she has to do next to nothing for him should she not want to. She is quite happy he manages in the facilities without her, thank you very much. "What do you think," he asks, "maybe a long red one?"

Prancie suddenly has no idea what Joe is saying. "Sorry?"

"Or a 'fro. I could wear a rainbow afro." He makes himself laugh more.

"Joe," Philomenia warns, "be careful of the stitches."

"Oh, they're fine. I want some of that gumbo, woman!" Again, the strange buoyancy to his speech. "We'll need some hot food for what's to come. Look at that thing!" He points again to the TV screen as if it suddenly shows something new.

"You're repeating yourself."

"But *look* at it! It engulfs the Gulf!"

"We will be fine." It is out of her mouth before she knows it. Of course Joe will not be fine.

"You're a shallow woman, Philomenia." He shakes his head. "What an act of nature! Of God! The raw power, and here man is, yet again, at its mercy."

"And women," Prancie says.

"What?"

"You said, 'And here *man* is.' I added 'women.' "

Joe blinks. Which of the three usual dismissals will it be: the head shake, the hand wave off, or the scowl? Joe scowls.

Prancie makes a tally mark in the air.

"What are you doing?"

"Joe, I'm going to get back to the stove. Did you need something?"

"You have no idea the magnitude of this storm."

"But I do," she says and leaves the room. Of course she does. Fortunately the regulars at the barnacle do not.

Fearius so busy he dont have time to wash his hands between cars like he like. The whiteified pussies done left, drippling blood dots down the narrow, made Fearius think of bread crumbs that gone disappear soon in the rain comin from the Ivan. But Fearius so busy he just dont stop. Even Ali Abubu be raised up to a runner today.

The Tulane peoples come sometimes two, three cars in a row. The college fucks be pretty stupid to trust their connections the way they do. Maybe Fearius should be lettin Alphonse know bout the lineup they creating on the street, but if Fearius so busy, Alphonse only gone be ten times more.

Fearius done worked hours and hours, wishing he had a weather report, when a car roll to a stop make his skin go tickly by his ears an on his neck. Something aint right about the car, not neither the two niggas in it. They *too* right. All their bling hangin perfect, the car real clean an dope, but it dont smell like a niggas car. Smell like it been parked a long time, like nobody drive it. An they something else Fearius cant put his finger on top of an squash down just yet. Hafta read em fast and make a decision like Alphonse trust him to do.

"Yo," the driver say.

Leaning on a parked car, Fearius give him the littlest head jerk he got. He duck to see the other one better in the passenger seat. Dude look straight ahead, almost like he scared. And right then, Fearius think he goin down, oh fuck, an all he gots be the boxcutter, and Alphonses protection aint nowhere suddenly in Fearius lifetime, maybe afterwards in revenge, but Alphonses protection aint here right the fuck now, not *no* fucking *where.*

Fearius put his hand in the back his pants like his training tell him. Make em think he has Alphonses Glock. Might get Fearius one second more.

"Hey, hey," the driver say, and his accent aint right. The nigga hold up both his hands off the steering wheel and say it again. "Hey, hey. Just lookin to score, bro."

And there it be. Stupid motherfucking police. The 5-0 undercover. Fearius wonder where they come from first before New Orleans with the accents. And then he wonder why they wasting their time here in Pigeontown. And then he wonder which of the whiteifieds talked. Fall-out. The whiteifieds got brave and took it too far. Even they know it always better to stay away from the law.

Fearius guess he done make a mistake, but right now he cant do nothing about it. He gotta keep selling Avon and hope these two ghosts dont come back round the block and watch.

"What you think?" Fearius ask. "I aint stupid. *Bro.* You in the wrong place."

"Not what I heard," the driver say.

"You heard wrong." Fearius take his hand out from behind his back.

"Course it true, nigga," the one in the other seat say.

Fearius duck an look hard at the pussy. Cant be no moren twenty, twenty and one. A dog trying to move up or a somebody trying to stay outside. Doing his duty. Yeah, sure. That be it. He goin down otherwise, just a somebody done got caught already and made a agreement. Gotta do his duty.

"You aint no friend a Alphonse, maybe?" Fearius ask the passenger. "That where I recognize you, friend?"

"Who?" The nigga wont look but forward, wont let Fearius see his full face.

Damn if Fearius dont feel like hootin. Fearius spot them both, and fast. No chance they be coming back with the lookouts crawling all over Pigeontown today.

Fearius draw a lil line in the air. Another favor for Alphonse mean one coming back his own way. Fearius fake a laugh. "We done see you, niggas. Try another day." He slap the top of the car he be leaning on and look at theirs, so clean he could lick it if he had to. Dumb fuckers, huh?

The drivers shoulders kinda sink. He know Fearius aint gone shoot him and he know he fucked up.

"Show me yo slugs," Fearius say, "an I get you what you want." Fearius want to see some 24 carat teeth.

"What?"

"Dats what I thought," Fearius tell him. The drivers mouth be slugged up about as much as Fearius gone get all As this year in school. Driver dont got no grill, not one lil speck of gold in his mouth. "Go on now. Theys a hurricane comin."

The driver look like he wanna eat Fearius with giant wolverine fangs. Too bad. Gots to get going now. We all see your car, *bro.* Go try under-cover workin across the bridge, *yo.*

Fearius waggle one finger at em. Aint no guessing which finger.

It may not be a well-oiled machine, but La Belle Nouvelle seems to be handling the influx of mucho-mega guests perfectly well. The hotel's booked to the gills, including Greenback in the President. It's happy hour, and room after room calls down for champagne and booze and ice buckets of beer, so much so that Ariel moves two trusted housekeepers over to room service, prompting them to tell the guests immediately when they deliver the food or drinks that they "are only substitutes and thank you for understanding, considering the circumstances."

As Ariel oversees check-in, a waitress approaches the front desk. "Miss Ariel," she says.

A family of five stands at the marble counter, the youngest son hanging off the marble lip and banging his tennis shoes on the glass front.

"Excuse me," Ariel says to Bimbo's sure successor, Falana, and the ever-trustworthy Henry.

Ariel directs the waitress to the edge of the lobby. "What is it?"

"Greenback, um, is in the restaurant. People just keep joining. The table's up to twenty-five."

"Shit."

The poor girl stands there, the messenger, wringing her little ring-covered hands. Ariel makes a mental note to control the hand jewelry on employees when Ivan's all over.

"Everybody," the girl tries further, "I'm sorry—they're saying . . . everybody says that he—"

"I appreciate directness," Ariel tells her. What is her name? Denise. Deborah. No. The weird Irish D name.

"He's going to have a huge party in the Presidential Suite. That's what, um, what people are saying."

Der-ba-lah. That's it. But the girl spells it strangely. Ariel had never seen it before she approved the hire. Something like Dearbhla. "Der-blah," Ariel says, "you're fine. Thank you for telling me. How's the kitchen? Are they ordering food?"

"Not really. Um, not yet. But people keep coming in. We, I, don't know if they're guests or not or if they're staying or, or . . ."

Okay. "Okay." Think it through. "Have you all at least alerted the kitchen as to what might be coming down the chute?" Ariel takes Dearbhla's arm and gets her moving back towards the restaurant.

"We keep telling them when more people sit down at the table."

"Good. Just stay loose or whatever. Take it easy. We have a pretty good excuse today, you know?"

"Yes. Sure, alright. Thanks, Miss Ariel." The Irish girl lopes away at a good pace, her fluffy strawberry blond hair holding its shape as she goes.

Yes. Sure, alright then. What can Ariel do to help the situation? She supposes she'd best go make the gesture of attending to Greenback and his hangers-on personally. Last Ariel heard, the hurricane wouldn't be hitting New Orleans directly, but then a bellboy said it would still blow the city apart if it came close enough. She's waiting for Indira's call; Ariel's set her cell to vibrate as her personal example of professionalism-under-fire.

Please let Greenback and his crew be sitting in smoking, she wishes, and please let them be smoking plain cigarettes. Please let Greenback be in a wonderful mood. Please let Greenback keep his people in control well enough that she doesn't need to play hardball. Twenty-five. He's never had twenty-five along for the Greenback ride before. Ariel's worried the number's not topped off yet. Hey, yo, she thinks, there's a *hurricane* on its way. Greenback can have what he wants with a hurricane coming, she guesses. She knows so.

As long as the hos don't misbehave enough for her to have to call them out. And as long as the boys keep their thangs in their droopy pants in the public places. And as long as nobody breaks more than what Greenback's willing to pay for.

Deep breath. In she goes.

Ariel walks into the restaurant as casually as her Minnesotan legs will allow. She smiles, of course, the best version of Nice-n-Pretty-n-Cool she can do.

They sit in piles, sort of, something out of a film the Rat Pack might've been in, skimpily dressed women draping themselves around men wearing jewelry. Or one of those paintings from an art museum where black people dance and grind and sit and take up space in a better and more colorful way than white people do.

"Look it heah!" Greenback shouts in his smoke-scratchy bass of a voice. "It the general manager. Forgive me, lady, but you doin' the best impression of Tomb Raider I seen in a long time." He raises a flute of champagne Ariel's way.

The whole six joined tables of them, twenty-five and growing, bust up as if they'll all die laughing.

"Boob Raider one my faves," a guy says.

If Ariel weren't so flattered, she might counter. But hell, she'll take Angelina Jolie any day. Thank you, thank you. "Dearest sir," she says flirtily. She's the general manager. She can flirt if she wants to. "Might I help you in making this evening any better than you've already planned?" She needs to see if she can't get a total head count out of him, figure out what he's stacked up.

"Come an' sit your pretty—ahem—Ms. May, I think you should join us unless the hotel be about to fall apart, you think?"

Ariel wouldn't mind sitting down, but she's more interested in knowing what Greenback wants to do for the next forty-eight hours. If her stores of champagne and towels will hold up. How many she'll need on P 'n B duty tomorrow and the next day, dragging out piles of dirty sheets nobody in her right mind would want to touch.

"A GM—" Be casual. He's just flattered you. "Well, on the eve of a hurricane, a GM has things to do," she tells him. Ariel practices the best open body language she has in her repertoire.

She sneaks a glance at Greenback's guests. She sees a lot of skin, some of it better left covered. The women have buckets of confidence. Bras full of confidence. Or no bras, just boobs overflowing with confidence. Ariel will give the ladies credit for that, for sure. Southern black women don't seem to have much problem showing a lot of what they have. Or it's part of the cultural world of the recording industry of New Orleans. Either way, these people hanging on to Greenback live in the moment. Ariel supposes there's no better moment.

"Iffin' I have extra peoples stayin' in my suite for the Ivan, Ms. May, you best charge me for 'em, hey?"

"I think we're speaking the same language, sir." Ariel turns on her heel and hopes her ass still looks as good as she thought it did when she tried on the skirt. She looks back over her shoulder for effect with a purse of her big lips and a little rump jut. Hey, she's the GM of a hotel staying open the night of a hurricane. Whether or not the owners would say so, Ariel's decided she's allowed to do whatever makes the most sense. Flirting with Greenback more directly than she has in the past makes perfect sense.

"Dat's what I'm talkin' about!"

"Oooh! Fine thang, lady manager!"

In her turning around, Ariel catches one of the hangers-on sucking her teeth at Ariel. The woman isn't much to look at except for her bumps and lumps, but clearly she doesn't like Ariel.

Or maybe it's all just an act. Ariel has other things to worry about.

It like it cant get no worse. First the 5-0 come up all transparent, like Fearius could see through them a mile away in their car an hour ago or whatever. But fuck no. Of course it gone get worse after. Aint like the ghosts drift away and just not tell nobody about what they find.

Selling Avon might could be easier, fo sho. But Fearius, he put a lot of paper in Alphonses pocket today. Not a bad piece in Muzzles neither.

Banana Truck come up an has a order like she picking up burgers and fries for a whole office or something, and Fearius have to tell her she need to get it under control.

"Come on, Fearius," she say, and that all Fearius need to turn around and walk away. He dont care how much a regular she be. She saying his street name make his stomach burn. Aw, naw. Go away, banana woman.

She know his name, which means it getting out there. Good and bad though, right? Rock and a hard place.

She honk her horn at him like some mess, maybe like the mess she be, her hair gettin worse with each day passing. Theys little worse for a woman than to show her lack of self management with her hair. A woman done lost her self respect when her hair out there all whacked.

Or that how most think on it. Fearius have too much cash money sittin where it shouldnt be right this moment, and he got Banana Truck tryin to buy him out. Even if he manage to get another runner up fast with more supplies, it probably just one those days. What's the word? Chaotic.

"Go round the block," he say to Banana Truck. "Come back in ten, I see what you gone get."

"Ten minutes? Muzzle never made me drive around the block and come back."

The woman gots her head screwed on wrong. How many times he have to tell her he not Muzzle? That and Fearius bet Muzzle never had no day like this one. "Ten," Fearius repeat and step away. He make the signs for how much at Ali Abubu hangin on the corner.

"This is bullshit," Banana Truck say loud enough for Fearius to hear, but he know she gone come back right on time.

Damn, Alphonse getting rich today. A hurricane be the best thing out there for business, Fearius gotta admit. Maybe not the best for trees and roofs and shit, but a hurricane make the Avon business boom, no lie.

Ali Abubu hoof it around the corner and Fearius take one deep breath before another car roll up, a motherfuckin Escalade. Fearius done seen it before, and then he realize things aint right again. It be *so* not good. Aint no reason to have Alphonse escorted over right now on this day. On *this* day. Whoa na.

The blacked out driver window go down real steady, hardly making any noise.

The lieutenant named Brick driving. Fuck. "Wardie," he say. He run his tongue under his top lip like he got some chicken left in his teeth. Fearius know aint nothing there.

Fearius raise his chin at the lieutenant and give a side tip to Alphonse in the passenger. "Pickin up?" Fearius try. "You rollin in it today, boss."

"Yo, Fear. You know why Ima here?"

"You visitin?" Fearius try and fake a laugh. He stuff his fists in his trousers to show Alphonse he the Delta dog or whatever his roll be at the minute. Like, Here be my belly.

"No, I aint," Alphonse say, not returning a laugh.

Brick run his tongue across his bottom teeth, and Fearius know it aint no good, whatever it be. And then it hit him.

"Got word the 5-0 on it, Fear. What you do, lil man?"

Where do Fearius start? Begin by telling about how he keep Alphonses best interests in mind always, how he dont bother Alphonse with the small shit? "Thinkin where I stand, like you said."

Alphonse sit and wait.

"Couple of whiteified niggas messin wif da house for hurricane prep and what," Fearius say. "They done kept at it."

"You think you gone show them a *lesson*?!" Alphonse yell.

Fearius fucked. He got a sharpened toothbrush in his fist, yo. Not. What that could do against whatever Brick got? "I know. Jus tryin to think where I stand."

"I called in favors, hear?"

Fearius nod, his fists in his pockets still. He heard, he done heard.

"Muzzle gone be paying," Alphonse say. "And you gone be paying. Your mistake cost you an arm. Maybe a leg."

Fearius think he gone get shot then, but the window go smooth back up, and the Escalade roll away. Fearius heart tickin like a bomb under his ribs.

Shit, his brother gone have to pay for whatever mess Alphonse fix? The day just pulled a big dark fucking cloud across like a curtain, a fat fucking hurricane kind of curtain, straight across Fearius day.

The whole party of them gets Cerise home by dinnertime in a kind of convoy, Roy, Marie, Thomas, Lil Thomas, and the person. The PSW Keyshawn. His touch and his questions and his fake caring feel thick as corn syrup poured all over Cerise.

Ivan's turning towards Mississippi. They can only hope the state of Louisiana will stay lucky. Seeing her house again for the first time, Cerise is happy as a clam, but damn if she's gonna tell this dog pack how she feels, the way they're all sniffin' at her butt to see where she's at, where she's been.

"We thought you'd like to be in the living room, Mom," Marie says as they bunch through the front door.

A hospital bed imposes itself suddenly, shoving all her other furniture against the walls. The chrome and height of it hurts her eyes. "I don't need that," Cerise tells everyone.

"Of course you don't," Thomas confirms. "But wouldn't it be easier?"

Cerise doesn't answer, and not two seconds pass before Marie says,

"See, I told you," to everybody but Cerise. "I knew she wouldn't want to be out here."

And right this instant, Cerise thinks, for once in Marie's forty-plus years, her daughter is absolutely and completely and one hundred percent right in her understanding of what Cerise might want. Cerise does not want to sleep in the living room, and she's not going to either. She will sleep in her proper bed with her husband. "Thank you, Marie," Cerise says. "You knew right."

Keyshawn holds a couple of suitcases. He turns his head around. Cerise has no idea what the bags have in them. Supplies to rewrap her hands? His clothes? It's a guessing game. Cans of condensed milk? Pieces of a body? What the hell did Cerise do to allow a stranger into her home, much less to help her with regular functions?

"But the bed is part of the setup," Marie tells everybody. She glances over at Thomas like he holds all the cards.

Cerise hates that more than anything. She didn't raise Marie to have to check on her husband's opinion every other minute. Last Cerise knew, Marie was out-earning Thomas anyways, even with them both working part-time.

"Whatever the setup is, it's going in the bedroom," Cerise says, making sure they all hear the decision in her voice.

Lil Thomas fusses in his car seat. Thomas starts to swing the boy real high and swoopy.

"Do I have to sleep in the hospital bed?" Cerise asks, and everybody turns altogether to Keyshawn.

"It's recommended," he says, and Cerise notices right away that he's deflecting, turning it around away from him and *his* opinion. Maybe it's good talking skills, or maybe it's the way he's going to be for days and days on end, interminable.

Still, Cerise does like his dreadlocks. They're pulled back into a cluster that makes her think of an alien that starred against Arnold Schwarzenegger in a movie she saw on cable. She has to wonder about the hygiene of the big ropy things, but they look interesting.

"It's recommended," Keyshawn repeats, "but I don't know that it's completely necessary if you're hell-bent against it."

"I'm feeling pretty hell-bent against it," Cerise says. She catches a glance from Marie to Thomas. Well, Marie did get it right. "Why'd I need one anyways?" Cerise asks. "I'm mobile an' all."

"Circulatory recommendations," Keyshawn says. "To keep your torso and, well, you've been dealin' with it all at the hospital already."

"Pillows in a normal bed alright with you, Keyshawn?" Cerise asks.

"If you can deal with them and not move around too much, I'm cool."

Cerise watches Marie give Keyshawn some big bug eyes. Cerise can only guess the eyes are for what the two of them have talked about already. About Cerise. Who cares.

Cerise steps to Roy and puts her arm around his middle real gentle. They're both still here, miracle of miracles. Who cares if she can't work her hand perfectly in the future.

They still got a future.

By eight o'clock, after everybody's decided where they'll sleep and where to put their things, Cerise blinks at the television version of the hurricane. There's some wind and rain on its way, to be sure, and they could lose power, and the city won't be working in a real way for a day or two, but it's hard to believe that nothing much more is coming. After following a path that finger-pointed right at New Orleans, why did the storm suddenly change its mind and start moving someplace else?

Cerise and Roy have extra space in their house they're happy to have, but she's not sure it's enough under the circumstances. Marie, Thomas, and Lil Thomas are sleeping in Marie's old room. Cerise and Roy converted it into a proper guest space since Marie left behind her Earth, Wind, and Fire posters on the wall decades ago. The dining room that they never use for just the two of them will service Keyshawn fine enough, with the rolled-in hospital bed for his very own.

Keyshawn explained the bathroom process to Cerise beforehand at Charity, and when it came down to it, he did well enough. He used a lot of toilet tissue, which is likely better than the opposite, but Cerise made a mental note to buy more fast.

Out in the living room, Cerise sits next to Roy on the sofa. He pats her leg incessantly as they watch the television. Cerise is pretty sure he feels happy for the opportunity to do so. Her Tylenol 3s help her hands a little bit.

Lil Thomas lies on a blanket by the television. Cerise hasn't said anything about his placement yet even though she wants to. He kicks and punches his arms when the volume goes up, the news cutting to another reporter.

"Did your people leave?" Roy asks Keyshawn.

On TV, a woman in a red slicker stands in front of a dark parking lot. Cerise wonders why she doesn't take the hood off since it's not raining yet.

"My mother's at my sister's place in Jackson," Keyshawn says. "There's just us two kids." Cerise figures Keyshawn doesn't care to talk about his father one way or the other.

"Keyshawn's sister is in law school," Marie tells her parents.

Cerise thinks Marie wants them to believe Keyshawn comes from a good family, but Cerise has always known the truth. Good children can come up in bad houses, under bad parents, and bad kids can come up with parents good as saints. It hardly matters. Look at Marie, Cerise thinks and suddenly feels shameful. Look at Nate and Sharon, then, she thinks to herself. Look what they got themselves, despite them both putting in hard days at work nearly every day of their lives, at least as long as Cerise has been knowing them. Sometimes, Cerise has to think, the city of New Orleans isn't such a good babysitter.

"What sort of law she interested in?" Cerise asks.

"Well, she just switched to urban planning," Keyshawn says, sticking his finger into his dreadlocks somewhere and scratching. "She said because she wanted to do something more valuable for society."

"I didn't know that," Marie says, frowning. "When did she switch?"

"What exactly they do in urban planning?" Roy asks.

"They plan civic spaces," Marie says.

"This semester," Keyshawn says.

"Like parks?" Roy asks.

Lil Thomas wriggles again when the news cuts back to Angela Hill in her anchor seat. Would Angela ever evacuate?

"Well, urban planning can run the gamut," Keyshawn says. "Beyond civic issues—"

"I'm having a beer," Thomas says, standing. "Roy?"

"Now you're talkin'," Roy answers.

Cerise would like one too. She could have one with a straw, maybe hold it between her knees. Better still, Keyshawn should have to help her with her beer. It's what he's getting paid for.

Cerise looks at her daughter. When did the shift happen? She raised a daughter to be a strong woman in all ways, not one to let a husband offer only a man in the room a drink. Handsome men are some real problems when they're younger. Cerise remembers. "I'll have one," Cerise says.

"I don't think—" Keyshawn starts.

"A Budweiser'll kill me?"

"Mother."

"A Budweiser'll *kill* me?" Cerise holds up her mittens. "I don't deserve a beer too? On the night of a hurricane?" Cerise is sick of all this already.

Lil Thomas gurgles happily at the sound of Cerise's voice over the noise of the television.

Again everybody turns and looks at Keyshawn. He shrugs. "I guess it'd be fine. I was goin' to say, 'I don't think it'll hurt any,' but honestly, I don't know. My dietary class is next semester."

Just how long does a person have to study to learn how to keep somebody comfortable? "Good," Cerise declares. "Raise your hand if you want a beer." She sticks her mitten in the air. Roy and Thomas raise their hands too. Marie and Keyshawn keep theirs down. "Keyshawn, you don't like beer?" Roy asks.

"He's *working*," Marie reminds her parents, "and I'm nursing."

Just like trained robots, they all turn their heads and look at Lil

Thomas. He raises two chubby fists in the air like he's voting, and then they all get to laugh together.

Cerise thinks the night's going to get long with them all waiting and staring at the television. No matter what, Marie'll be making a terrible mess of breakfast in the morning, whether or not a single one of them gets a decent night's sleep. "Well, then," Cerise says, trying to get Thomas into the kitchen after the beers.

"More when we return, New Orleans," Angela Hill says on the TV.

Cerise nods at the blond lady's timing.

La Belle Nouvelle's bar staff rocks, Ariel thinks, at least at the moment. Look at Carrie and Harold go. Her Harry-Carrie team could damn well work with Cirque du Soleil. The bar is packed to the tits, to the balls, to the walls, and the two of them move like dancers.

Ariel watches and swings her crossed leg, dangling her shoe off her toe, sitting next to Greenback's business partner Phatty, *the* Phatty of PhatCash Records. Phatty says he's going home, but he has yet to make any move to leave. Ariel entertains the notion he has a little crush on her, the white girl, for all the attention he's lavishing.

She reminds herself that she's doing almost exactly what is required of her at the moment. She should be mindful of her surroundings, but she should most certainly socialize with the VIPs.

So that's what she's doing.

Ariel sips at her Cristal. Phatty, who's anything but fat, bends and touches the arch of her foot. "I like your curves."

Ariel wants to call him on his brazenness, but then again, he's Phatty. He can do pretty much what he wants. Best Ariel guesses, he's maybe a year or two younger than she is. She's been trying for a childhood cultural reference here and there, but she already knows that what she brings with her from the North doesn't always work here in New Orleans. He acts like he's her age, in any case.

Every last one of the rooms is checked in. Housekeeping is staying on top of the roll-away beds and extra pillows, and the kitchen is closed. Closed, closed, closed as of ten minutes ago. She told the kitchen, minus the dishwashers, they could hang out with the patrons if they changed into decent street clothes. There's a hurricane, after all. She's guessing most will come out for their two-drink allowance and sit a bit rather than taking drinks to go. They always order double-size styrofoam cups of the strongest mixed drinks they can get for their allowance, generic white Russians and rum punches and, huh, hurricanes.

Ariel looks at Phatty and wonders for the tenth or hundredth time tonight what he might be like. What would it feel like to abandon her married-and-mother life for a single night and watch a thug roll a condom on his hard cock in anticipation of fucking her?

He has nice ears, tight to his head but not too small, not too big. Phatty also has great shoulders, evident beneath what she guesses is a Ralph Lauren dress shirt.

Javier, well, where the hell he be, yo? Best he get his fine ass out here soon; or, or he's going to have competition. Ariel can hang with the gangstas, ya heard. Or she can try. She doesn't say too much, which seems to serve her pretty well. She couldn't try to talk the same language, but she can be a foreigner who understands and knows when to nod.

Phatty raises his jaw to the bartenders. "They good."

"I know how to hire," Ariel tells him. She keeps swinging her shoe off her toe. She can't tell if he has the kind of brain in his head that she likes or if he's just good at what he does.

Ariel thinks for a second about when she watched Snoop Dogg in some interview. Behind the façade of a dopey rap artist resided an acutely smart human being. Ariel was blown away at how he'd both memorized all sorts of factual information and thought on his feet at the same time. Go figure. She sure didn't expect it from a stoner rapper. She considers whether or not Phatty is anything like Snoop Dogg, whether either of them has killed another human being. Why she's become obsessed with murder since she's moved here, she thinks as she sips her champagne, is anybody's guess.

Harold makes a lot of noise with a martini shaker behind the bar, shaking and tossing and making people applaud.

"You like tricks, Miss Ariel?" Phatty asks.

Ariel looks around for Greenback, her real client and the Somebody she trusts. She takes another drink of champagne. They've missed a hurricane. Or a hurricane has missed them. She has reason to celebrate, right? Does she like tricks, Phatty has asked her. Ariel really doesn't know how to answer. "What'd Greenback tell you?" she asks.

"Why you bring him into this? I'm askin' you."

"I guess not so much," she tells him. "Or, more, I don't like *being* tricked. I prefer directness."

"So iffin' I told you some of my direct thoughts, you'd appreciate that?"

A woman sprouting out of her halter top leans over Phatty from behind and tips his head back for a long kiss. When the woman is done, she stares directly at Ariel, then walks away.

"Who was that?" Ariel asks.

"Ol' flame," he says directly.

"And she wants you back?"

"Naw. She be hitched."

"You kiss married women?"

"Now, Miss Ariel, you saw she kissed me first, didn't you?"

Yes, Ariel saw that.

Javier sits at the bar with Warren, a terrible combo for Ariel. And, well, Ariel's decided at the very moment to remain with the Greenback contingency, meaning, only, really, Phatty. Two more slender flutes of champagne into her stomach, and she's fully in his court. Ariel feels the "ladies' " eyes on her, or, more realistically, burning through her for the fierceness behind the stares. Phatty's not married, she's discovered, but he is a Playah through and through. He told her as much. And Ariel likes as much at this juncture. She is, after all, free from all familial obligations tonight.

She's beginning to feel a tug of worry at not hearing from Ed or the Guptas, but she has faith that all is fine. They'd have called already if there was an emergency. Indira seems like a very responsible person.

Javier sits at the bar in a good starched white button-down. It fits him well through his narrow waist. Maybe he's had it tailored, or Henny knows how to sew. He looks nearly as good as Phatty does in his shirt. From the set of Javier's shoulders, she wonders if he isn't jealous. The thought makes Ariel point her toes. Her shoe falls to the floor.

Phatty bends and picks up her shoe. "Good shoe," he says, giving his stamp of approval on yet another item or entity under Ariel's control. Unregulated, free-for-all finances—being rich as hell—might have such an effect on a person, she supposes. You'd just go around the world determining what was good and not good. Quality or just not worth it.

Ariel glances up from Phatty looking out the top of his eyes, his face level with her lap. Her groin warms.

Javier glances her direction. Warren's eyes follow Javier's.

"Jimmy Choo," she tells Phatty, putting her shoe back on. "A little too much *Sex and the City*, but what's a lady to do, you know?" Ariel downs the rest of her champagne. "Sir, it's been a true pleasure." She stands and smooths her skirt, making sure not to teeter.

"You leaving," he states.

"For now. But I'm sleeping here." The information is out of her mouth before she can cut it off. "Can't go far," she attaches as a weird addendum.

They both stand. "An' if the Ivan doubles back?" Phatty steps into Ariel's personal space. He smells good. He gets so close she swears she can feel heat coming off of him.

"Then I'm here longer than I thought," Ariel tells him. Could she sleep with somebody she'd not even entertained before tonight? She's married. Hell. Some part of her has gone wrong, drifted away in the last few months, a house pet gone wandering for lack of the right attention. Ariel wants another drink. She doesn't have to stand on the street waiting for public transportation, and she doesn't have to drive. She can drink more if she wants to.

Carrie gives a come-over-here gesture to Ariel.

"Miss Ariel," Phatty says into her neck, "you're fine, an' you know it. But that's cool. You got my number."

His card on file. Yes, she does have Phatty's number. Ariel raises her hand in recognition to Carrie. "Thank you for the champagne," she says to Phatty, "and the company. And the shoe retrieving."

"A sincere pleasure," he states.

"Yes," she states back. She looks into his eyes and tries to see what might be there in all different ways. She knows they could sleep together. That's an easy one. Unfortunately, she wants something more than sex, if she has to admit as much. She wants somebody to *want* her and somebody to want *her*. It's sort of a whatever about sex, like a yeah, big deal, sex, but of course not—Jesus, she's not had sex with anybody besides Ed for years. She's so terribly horny for somebody else.

Maybe it's genetic.

Ed's a good father.

Ariel walks over to the bar. Carrie's half-swamped. "What's up?"

"We need music," Carrie says.

"It's playing," Ariel answers.

"No." Carrie fills five rocks glasses with ice. "We need way good music. Can we play something besides cable radio?"

Ariel never liked cable radio, but it's easy to turn on and just forget about. She looks around the room. "You think you can find music for this room that won't cause a riot?" The mix of patrons runs from the local ghetto rich to European tourists. Ariel has no idea what would please everyone.

"Stay on the radio," Javier says a few barstools away. "Play salsa. Everybody like salsa. Happy music, party music."

"The sous speaks the truth," Warren says. He raises his traditional bottle of Boston-made beer in acknowledgment.

"And we can play it loud!" Carrie says, pouring Absolut into three glasses of ice. She's a good bartender. A good hire, Ariel thinks.

"Go for it," Ariel tells Carrie.

"Cool."

"We short anything yet for a full breakfast tomorrow?" Ariel asks

Warren. He's also ensconced in a room for the next two nights. A round bachelor, Warren can't mind it too much.

"Champagne for mimosas," he says. "Didn't know Greenback would be carryin' so many friends."

"But they're drinking Cristal," Ariel says.

"Aw, Minnesota, they won't be by the end of the night when it's all gone. Use your pretty flirtin' head."

"What?" Ariel can feel her face flush in embarrassment. Warren always calls it like it is. "I wasn't flirting," she says.

"And I'm not fat," Warren says.

"Husky is all," she tries.

Javier, Carrie, and Warren all laugh at her blatant euphemism.

"Fine," Ariel says. "You call yourself whatever you want. I'll call you husky."

"And I'll call you a flirt, Miss Ariel."

Javier sits entirely still, like he's a deer trying not to call attention to itself in the wilderness. Trying not to give himself away.

"Carrie, give me a glass of something sparkling that's open. Prosecco, cava, California, they're fine. Save the official stuff for the paying customers. When you have a chance."

Javier moves his glass to his lips.

"What're you drinking, Javier?" Ariel asks.

"*Ron,*" he says. "Rum with coke."

They've just started carrying Louisiana high-end rums. "Cane?"

"Bacardi," he answers. "Gold."

Ariel wants to taste it on his tongue. She wants to press herself up against him, push him onto a wall, and suck his tongue into her mouth. When else will she have the opportunity? How can she make Warren go to his room earlier than later?

"Spunk," Warren says, "gold or not."

"Want to fight?" Javier asks Warren, smiling. Warren has clearly trained Javier in all foul words. Ariel doesn't think she learned 'spunk' till she was twenty-five. And English is her first language.

"Beer?" Javier continues. "A chef drinks beer?" Javier uses his hands when he talks, and they're moving around now. Ariel watches his fingers, the smooth skin of his wrists. She will kiss there, right there. "Where is your wine, Mr. Executive Chef?" Javier asks. "Open your palate. Your *palais*." *Palais* he says with what sounds to Ariel a perfect French accent. He's figured out that Ariel, having grown up in the language-arid Midwest, gulps any foreign language. Javier knows a smattering of Portuguese, some French. It will be her undoing, straight from his lips.

"Wine, schmine," Warren says. "Been there and done that, friend. And you're drinking rum for what reason?"

Jesus. Ariel senses Warren's not going to give up the night easily. He'll see Javier as a bar companion.

She is beginning to think she will take what she can get, yo.

Some Greenback women dance between bar tables. Three in particular attempt salsa, bumping and grinding all wrong next to a man who looks as though he's visiting from Indiana and has never had such a show in his life.

More than two hours have passed, and Warren won't leave for his room upstairs. If Ariel were honest with herself, she'd admit to Warren being a guardian of hers, but she's not in the mood to be honest with herself. She's in the mood to do whatever the hell she feels like.

At 1:03, her phone vibrates from her hip like a new wound, a reminder from a different part of her life. Ariel excuses herself from Warren, Javier, and a cluster of patrons. Greenback's people still go at it strong, just down the bar. The place is stuffed full, the loud Spanish and Mexican *musica* making everybody happy.

Ariel stands, sticks a finger into her ear and holds her cell phone to the other. "Hello?!"

"Ariel?"

"Hello?"

"Ariel, it's Indira. Can you hear me?"

"Hang on."

Ariel heads out into the lobby.

"Hello?" Ariel says again.

"Hello, Ariel. It's Indira. We've finally arrived."

"Just now?"

"One hundred and thirty-one miles," Indira says. "Fifteen hours and twenty minutes since we spoke last."

"Oh, my god."

"Yes. Ed is here. I'll pass the phone to him, alright?"

"Thank you so much, Indira. Thank you."

"Hello?" Ed's voice on the phone, Ariel had half hoped, might drag her—kicking and screaming?—into reality. Just the tenor of his voice itself would be a slap across the face.

Or not.

"You would not believe the drive, Ariel. Unbelievable. Really crazy. Unbelievable. The people—Ella had to pee—"

"Are you all okay? Everything's safe?"

"Didn't you hear? The hurricane's going to hit east."

No. She had no fucking idea. She's only in charge of an entire New Orleans hotel. She never thought to get news updates. "Yeah, Ed. I heard. In an hour or so."

"Are you okay?"

That's a loaded question. Sure, she's okay. "Of course. We're booked solid, and we're going to run out of booze, but yeah, we're fine. If the gangstas don't turn on some quiet sad sack in the corner, we'll be just fine. Are the kids asleep?" She wanted to say hello.

"It's one in the morning."

"How's the room?"

"Honestly, A?" he says, starting to half-whisper. "Straight out of *Mississippi Masala*! It's like the producers modeled the movie on this actual place. They have drawls but with East Indian accents."

"Who's 'they'?" Ariel watches as Phatty strides into the lobby with two of his entourage she suspects are actually his bodyguards. She hasn't seen him for the last hour and then some. She thought he'd gone home. She finds it ironic that she would move to New Orleans only to encounter people who need to go about their daily lives with bodyguards. Or an entourage.

" 'They' are the owners of the motel, and trust me, it's really a *mo*-tel."

Phatty says something to his guys and then starts walking in Ariel's direction. "What?" Ariel asks.

"So." Ed sounds suddenly loud and fake. "We'll give you a call in the morning when we can. I don't want to use up the Guptas' cell phone time."

"The kids were okay?"

"What do you think? They were—hi. Yes. Of course. Indira sends her best. I'll call tomorrow."

"I'm glad somebody else had a cell," Ariel says.

"Love you too," Ed says and hangs up.

He did not, Ariel thinks—and Phatty is on top of her, his smell and shirt and ears and shoulders and his everything else. He takes her by the back of the neck and then brings in his beautiful lips, prettier than Ariel thinks a gangster should have, and presses them soft but, oh. She's gone.

When Ariel opens her eyes she sees Phatty's stepped away from her. Two people stand at the perimeter of the lobby.

She glances at the front desk. Empty.

Javier stares.

Warren runs his meaty hand over his face and shakes his head.

"You can choose a night you don't forget, Miss General Manager," Phatty says. "I be in the limo for ten minutes before it just whisk me away from the ball."

Ariel has no words.

12

In the motel room, the Guptas' gracious in-laws have left extra soaps, plastic-wrapped toothbrushes and combs, and a stack of kids' videos. A VCR blinks beneath the television, the time unset. The video boxes look well worn. Ed is exhausted and grateful.

He takes off his shoes and removes the orange and brown bedspread from his double bed. He pours two fingers of Scotch into a plastic motel cup, glances at his sleeping children in the bed beside his own, and flips on the television. Finally, he lies back against the headboard.

Never, in all his years on earth, has he had a day like today. He cannot believe that the cars simply sat like so many planes on the tarmac, only the waiting went on and on, everybody trapped. The panting dogs, the cat carriers, the shrunken elderly in backseats staring forlornly, the music, the dancing in pickup truck beds, the public urinating, the eating, good god, the eating as if there would never be any food again, people gobbling mindlessly, zombies with their mouths moving, the highway shoulders filling up with everything cast off, beer cans and popped-open dirty diapers and tabloids and chicken bones.

"Call today," a woman in a camisole and panties says on TV. She sticks her finger in her mouth and twists side to side as she holds a cordless phone to her head. She kneels, her shins disappearing into a sheepskin rug. "We'll talk." Somebody has directed her to try to sound smoky, Ed thinks. She sounds like a ten-year-old with a sore throat. A 900 number appears across the bottom of the screen.

Humans, right now, disgust him. He changes the channel. Tanks grind across the screen in black and white. He searches for the weather. Find the bigger entity, Ed, he thinks. You can do it.

Ella pushes on Ed's chest. "Daddy, where's the beastie?"

Ed wakes up entirely disoriented. The television runs an infomercial of some cooking gadget. The clock on the VCR still blinks at noon, or midnight, one or the other. The window behind the curtains looks black.

"Come here, sweetie. It's okay."

Ella crawls into Ed's arms. "I had a dream," she says. "You went flying away in the air and didn't come back and I couldn't find Mommy."

"Where was Miles?" Ed asks quietly, trying not to wake the boy. "Your brother would always protect you, even in a dream."

"He pretended he couldn't hear me. I yelled and kicked on him. He dint turn around."

"Aw, Ella, you know about dreams, right? They're not real. We're all here."

"Mommy's not here."

"Mommy has to work."

In the blue gloaming of the TV, Ella frowns. "No she doesn't."

"You know how it goes. We talked about this. Mommy is responsible for many people, and a lot of those people are guests from far away who are very scared. Mommy's the boss, and she's keeping the guests comfortable and not afraid."

"Why can't we stay with Mommy?"

Ah ha. Tricky little girl, his Ella. They're safer here? No. That puts Mommy in danger. They could have stayed with her in the hotel? Too dangerous not to evacuate. Hmm. Ed hugs his daughter nestled into the crook of his arm. "Because we're free to go on an adventure to Breaux Bridge."

"I'm hungry. Miles is mean."

"Well, let's see what time it is and maybe we can go for pancakes."

"I'm tired."

"Are you hungry or are you tired?"

"I'm hungry tired."

Ed laughs. The kids munched on all sorts of snacks in the car for hours, as did Elizabeth and William, Indira said. The two of them voted to veto dinner, but who knew the prolonged driving would eliminate the choice for everybody? By the time they drove into Breaux Bridge, Ed didn't see a single place open. They rumbled over the metal bridge spanning Bayou Teche and into a closed town. Too late for anything other than what they brought with them. "Do you want a snack?" Ed asks Ella.

She shakes her head and snuggles into his ribs.

He wants another child so badly he can feel it right there, there in his ribs and in the pit of his stomach. He can bring another good human being into this world. Somebody who might appreciate rap but wouldn't make a living shooting videos with women who misrepresent their own sex. If his children were to become musicians, Ed hopes they'd employ women who did not bend over in the middle of traffic in shorts no longer than underwear.

It's still dark. They'll get breakfast later.

By the time everyone is ready to go out to breakfast, Miles and Ella have already eaten a thousand mini cheese crackers and an entire bag of beef jerky Ed bought at the gas station at six AM. Ed has only, in the last twenty-four hours, begun to appreciate the necessity for the regimentation of the military. He feels almost stupid for never having understood the need for command and immediate response before. He believed everyone could, well, get along. But going through the last day, night, and this morning, he has come to one of the quickest and surest realizations he has ever had. Somebody must, indeed, lead. Somebody must take control, and do it, as they say, swiftly.

What a bunch of moles they all are, they, the gazillion evacuees, bumping around blindly. What a fucking mess.

Ed needs to readjust his attitude, he thinks, as he, Miles, Ella,

Ganesh, Indira, William, and Elizabeth wait in line outside of some well-reviewed brunch restaurant in the historical and charming town of Breaux Bridge, Louisiana.

And it is charming, this town. An old-school old town. The Guptas' in-laws, the managers and owners of the Bayou View Motel and RV Park, have been absolutely kind, and the hostess here at the restaurant who took their names in line thanked them for coming.

Ed has been awake, more or less, since four when Ella woke him. He values sleep, and he has gotten little. He also values, he decides on the spot, a Northern dialect.

The family of large Southerners immediately behind him punctuates their conversation with swearing and absurdly loud laughter. One of the older women in the cluster continues to find Ed's aching back with her elbow as she pontificates about hurricanes of yore.

Who cares, Ed thinks. Hurricanes are completely bogus. They should try a good old tornado ripping across central Illinois and see what stories they have to tell.

Jab goes her elbow again straight into his spine. Ed turns around to see that it's a hard-cornered handbag that's doing the jabbing. It's only remotely possible she's utterly unaware of her surroundings. "Excuse me," Ed says and holds his ground.

" 'Scuse," the handbag woman says without looking at him. Ed can't help but notice she is even darker than either Ganesh or Indira. The woman wears what looks like Sunday best, including a red felt hat. It's a hot Louisiana September Thursday morning. What's the occasion? "And I toll him back," the woman continues, "get that thang away from me unless you want to be contributin' it to the boudin."

The rest of her group shrieks.

"Whooooooooo," a wheezy man sighs.

Ed can guess what the purse jabber wants to make sausage out of; context is everything.

The Bayou View never even lost power last night. And New Orleans evidently took the wispy tailwinds of Ivan perfectly fine. Ed had already decided that they would turn around and leave immediately after break-

fast when Ganesh said the mayor had advised that evacuees not return
for another day.

Miles and Elizabeth play tic-tac-toe on the sidewalk with chalk. Elizabeth has clearly discovered the foolproof double-corner-diagonal-
followed-by-a-third-corner win, something that's eluding Ed's son.
Each and every game, Miles is getting creamed. Still, he perseveres,
trying to cheat, making half Os and then changing his mind when Elizabeth gives away her coming win with a smile and chalky lurch.

He has to learn, Ed reminds himself.

Ella, on the other hand, sulks against the painted brick wall of the
restaurant in the sun, her pale scalp showing pink through her blond
hair. William Gupta, ignoring children and adults alike, makes distended shapes with his entwined fingers and sings a made-up song,
something about waffles, waffles, waffles, waffles.

Sporting a Rorschach of sweat on the back of his cheap gray dress
shirt, a fat man from the group behind Ed steps up to Miles on the sidewalk. "She gone beat you again," he says. "Look how she settin' it up.
Look, boy." The man points a shiny shoe toe at the game on the ground.
"See? You can't never let her take kitty-corners without a built-in
block."

Miles stares openmouthed up at the stranger. He looks back down at
the grid on the sidewalk and then back up again at the man. So this
black Jerry Falwell has come to instruct Ed's son in the strategy of tic-
tac-toe. With his shoe. No, Ed doesn't think so. Not today.

"They're just playing," Ed tells the man.

"It all the fundamentals," the man says to Miles more than he does to
Ed. "Next you be playing checkers and not see what coming. Dominoes. Risk. This a building block. Look, see." The sweating man uses
his shoe toe again and taps at the sidewalk.

Ed grits his teeth. Quit with the toe, asshole. Inhale, exhale. Ed walks
to Miles and kneels. "See how Elizabeth is tricking you here?" Ed
points out the diagonal Xs. Miles has already lost if she plays it the same
way she has for the last five minutes.

"Yeah," the fat man says and tries to erase Miles' last O with his
shoe. "You need to go here or here," he directs.

"Is it fair to give away movements?" Indira asks plainly.

The man chuckles. "Give away the girl's move? Oh, come on. The boy needs a fightin' chance, don't he?"

The blubber contingency behind them bursts into new laughter. Ed stands and wipes sweat off his forehead. Both parties watch everybody's moves now.

"I don't want to play," Miles mumbles under the scrutiny of stares. He plops his chalk onto the sidewalk.

"I win again," Elizabeth says, quickly drawing how the rest of the game would have played out on the pavement.

"Aw," the woman in the red hat says, "he a quitter." She laughs a big belly laugh.

"Don't be no quitter, boy," the fat man says.

"He's my boy," Ed says.

The man makes a face Ed has no idea how to interpret. "Yes," the man says and pauses, seeming to decide how he wants to react, "he sho' is." And then the man does something horrible, to Ed's mind. The man raises his hands in the air in a surrendering gesture, shrugs his hefty shoulders, turns, and steps back to his group.

The man says something to them under his breath, and they all snicker.

Miles crosses his arms and scoots around on the sidewalk to face the street.

Philomenia wakes with a start. She rights herself and steps from her tall bed. She does not know why she has been awakened. She walks to the bay window and looks outside. Strangely, and not as she predicted, the barnacle is silent and seemingly closed.

Joe.

She should be sleeping beside him in an additional bed down in the parlor, but she refuses on numerous grounds.

Yes, Joe could be dead. There. She has thought the words again. It is likely part of the standard transition process for those left behind. She considers the possibility once more. While she slept, Joe might well have expired. She listens, but she hears nothing downstairs, as usual.

Philomenia moves through dim moonlight to the hall. The linen closet beckons. If this is the night to change her future forever after, she will record her thoughts before descending the stairs. She retrieves the top journal and returns to her sanctuary.

Prancie tucks her feet up beneath her bottom like a girl while she sits in the bay window overlooking her block. She finds the new, fresh white sheet of paper, sets her pen to it, and begins.

Firstly, she finishes the supplements and postscripts documenting issues that arose this afternoon and evening with Shane Geautreaux. The man has disturbing tendencies, most especially considering his alcoholism. His compliments perplex Prancie without question, as does his seeming intelligence. The equation does not make sense best Prancie is able to decipher. His compliments are astute, to her mind, but how is it possible for him to formulate them clearly? He appears, on first encounter, to be a sane and observant individual, yet he imbibes throughout the day, ingesting no other liquid besides alcoholic beverages. "That he could be right about my personal, physical appeal but wrong in so many other ways," she writes, "displays the absolute complexity of human beings." What else explains a person such as Shane?

On the other hand, Ed Flank's disappearance from the block for Hurricane Ivan proves nothing short of divine intervention. Prancie fully believed he would loll around on his front porch until he drank himself into a stupor, holding down his fort, as it were, while his wife brought in the bacon to support the family unit. Ha! Prancie will record it. She still feels rather buoyant from her day at the barnacle. Unusual phrasing is coming easier to her for all the banter time she . . . she 'put in.'

"While his wife brings in the bacon," she inscribes, "Ed slothfully lounges about the home. He would likely be indigent without her. I pity the children their father's lack of gumption."

Still, Prancie is displeased by the fact that Ed Flank persuaded the Gupta unit to evacuate with him. Prancie had high hopes of making . . .

how would Shane put it? Headway. Yes, headway. The pen goes to paper. "I had high hopes of making headway where the cooking scents are concerned. Unfortunately, the party has departed for grounds no less secure than that on which I now sit."

Prancie pauses and stares out the window at the darkened barnacle. Sometimes, on the odd night, its eternal Christmas lights have felt almost festive. They help her to believe that other individuals were still awake at the same time as she.

Tomorrow she will feed more of the patrons who have plagued her for countless nights with their screeching laughter and their car smashing and their sobbing on her front steps, unaware that an actual person might reside within the home, might worry for the young Tulane woman with hair the color of a canary crying and crying on an actual person's stoop.

Prancie wishes only to be free of her burdens. *Philomenia, stop. Self-pity is unbecoming.*

Prancie wishes to become her new name fully, to embrace the sound and feel and scent of it. Her new name might be a perfume, it smells so fresh. Prancie is spring grass. Prancie is the mint in sweet tea.

She will accomplish what she has set out to then. She puts pen to paper. "Ed Flank will be heartily sorry for his mismanagement of his position in this neighborhood." Prancie pauses. "I will, with conviction, gravity, and fairness, cleanse the street of all that must go."

Shane Geautreaux told Prancie that she had the most beautiful clavicles he had ever seen. Honestly, who knew he would even know such a word?

Philomenia awakes with her cheek pressed against the glass of the bay window. The milky light of a September morning seeps into her vision. The air is so thick these days, she thinks.

The journal rests, splayed, across her nightgowned lap.

Has Joe seen it? Yesterday he managed to wheel his intravenous device back and forth to the rear door to gaze at the cloud formations in the sky. He might take it upon himself to come and visit her in his final hours. He might struggle up the stairs. The journal on her lap would not be what Joe would likely find comforting in his last minutes.

She revisits her pages and thinks momentarily that her handwriting seems less her own in the most recent paragraphs. One might surmise she had fought sleep before succumbing. It would explain the change in the cursive.

Prancie carries the best she has to offer toward the establishment of Tokyo Rose. Her husband Joe still lives and breathes, surprisingly quite happily, with his cable television. Prancie must unquestionably continue to curb her worrying about him. Doing so gave her so much peace yesterday she can hardly define the sensation.

This new offering of food is extraordinary, she admits. Indeed, she holds in her hands a gift the likes of which the barnacle patrons have never tasted before.

Philomenia plucks the screen door open with the pointed toe of her sling back and calls out, "Come and get it!" She has not heard her own voice as loud as it is now in years. "Come and get it!" Oh, but it feels so good to holler. "Come and get it!" Prancie roars.

"I heard ya', Miss P," Thurman III says. "Hang on."

When he walks over to help Prancie with her bags, Thurman III does not seem the same person she came to know yesterday. "How many do you have?" he asks with a good degree of disgruntlement.

"I do have more food across the street. Thurman, are you all right?"

"I'm not feeling so hot." He blinks slowly. "A late night." He sets the bags on a cocktail table.

"It seems to me you closed earlier than usual last night."

"Yeah? Huh. Too many shots then. Aspirin, aspirin, where are you . . ." The young man sets out on a search behind the bar.

Maybe Thurman will be less hungry today. If he would only leave his position here, he would undoubtedly become a moderately acceptable physician eventually. He is not serving his own best interests by working in a bar so often when there is serious studying to be done. Prancie stays attuned to her case study's symptoms. "Is your stomach bothering you?" she asks.

"Drive-through Taco Hell late night has its repercussions, Miss P, if you know what I mean."

A smile tugs at Prancie's lips. Her treats are working. "I'll be back in a moment with more."

Thurman shakes a medicine bottle. "What's for lunch, anyway?" The loose rattle suggests few pills remain.

"These are just the *accoutrements*." Prancie flutters her hands over the bags. "The crock pot comes over next."

Prancie returns with her étouffée. "Here, Thurman, take this."

"Miss P, you call me that one more time and I'm banning you for life."

Prancie shakes her head. "I simply can't call you Pedro. It maligns your father."

"Shows how well you know him then. He can't stand 'Thurman' either."

She is momentarily astonished. "Well, then, why in the world did he choose to name you the same?"

"If you want the truth, it was a stipulation of the will."

"Your grandfather?" Philomenia never liked the man. When Thurman Junior escorted Philomenia to her cotillion, his father did not bow as properly as he should have, as if he thought her own father had not attained the necessary social status to earn her the right of coming out. "Well, that is highly unfair. Highly."

"Pedro's cool then, okay?"

She simply cannot bring herself to look at this young man and call him by such a misnomer. "Please, I need another choice. What is your middle name?"

He plugs the crock pot in at the end of the bar where he has created a buffet of sorts with her various side dishes. "Pedro's my middle name," he says. Prancie believes she is being teased.

"And if I were to make up a new name for you? Something only I called you?" Prancie quite likes the idea.

"Keep cooking as good as you do and you can call me Dick, all I care. Just lay off the Thurman." Well, now, she has just been complimented again. Who would have guessed that the barnacle could produce so much praise?

"This is what I call a spread!" a familiar voice says behind Prancie. She turns with a smile on her face to see Shane Geautreaux in silhouette, backlit in the frame of the doorway, his arms outstretched. She believes he looks, momentarily, like the savior.

Do not expect any man to save you, Philomenia. You will be gravely disappointed.

13

By noon, Lil Thomas' crying has taken over the house. Cerise wants to know, in about ten minutes flat and counting, why Marie and Thomas don't just go home and take their boy with them. Cerise can only guess it's 'cause she's now officially disabled and her daughter's friend is supposed to be her official caretaker, only nobody knows if Keyshawn knows what he's actually doing.

Today, Cerise's left hand itches as fierce as the time, decades ago, she had a pH imbalance in her privates. Cerise bangs her mitten, subtly as she can, on her chair armrest. She doesn't care if her behavior is normal or not. She absolutely cannot stop what she does. It itches and itches. The hyenas on the Animal Planet scootch their bottoms against anything they can find. Everything walking on some kind of legs has gotta scratch an itch now and again.

Marie bounces wailing Lil Thomas on her hip and blocks Cerise's view of the television. He sees Cerise and holds out his arms to her to be taken. It breaks Cerise's heart. She wants nothing more than to be able to hold him, hold Roy, hell, even hold Marie in a hug, but it's against doctor's orders, and she can understand why. She wouldn't be able to help herself. She'd use her hands, curl them around a baby bottom or a shoulder and bust open everything, maybe make the right hand just plain fall off. "Move out the way, Marie," Cerise says. "Let me see these poor Alabama folks. Look it. They lost everything. The tree squashed their car *and* their house."

Marie turns around to look but stays right in the way. Lil Thomas swivels to try to keep reaching at Cerise. Just breaks her heart. Lil Thomas' crying goes up another notch. "This not gonna work," Cerise says.

"You think they have good insurance?" Marie asks.

"No, Marie. This."

"What?"

"Turn that off. Turn the damn TV off. You're gonna deafen your boy before he's walking."

Marie takes the remote from the coffee table and aims it at the screen. Lil Thomas turns off his crying with the television, and the room goes blessedly quiet for a moment. Cerise can hear all three men out on the porch conversing. Roy and Thomas took a walk around the neighborhood this morning like two boys exploring a just-found ghost town. Now they all talk and talk on it, about luck and Camille and the pumping stations and the Mississippi River and the cushion of the wetlands getting eaten up. Talk and talk. It's all Cerise can do now, and it's the last thing she feels like doing whatsoever. Talk.

Marie looks down at the silenced child in her arms, then looks back at Cerise, a surprised look on Marie's face.

"Sensory overload," Cerise says, not even wanting to explain more. "Babies need a break."

"Normally he loves the TV on," Marie says, fluffing Lil Thomas' silky curls. His cheeks are pink, his upper lip covered in snot.

"At your house, where he knows everything," Cerise says, "an' things are normal. Here it's all new, with other people and strangeness. Use your head. You're a smart woman. Just use your smarts and apply them to your baby. It's not so hard."

Marie looks indignant first, and then she looks just plain hurt. Cerise doesn't care. She's sick of it all. Marie pulls a tissue from her brassiere and wipes Lil Thomas' nose, which gets him crying all over again.

Cerise finds Marie's tissue storage in her brassiere old-timey enough to want to say something about it, but she bites her tongue. "Why don't you three go home?" Cerise asks. "Get him back into his environment. He'll be better there."

"You're kicking us out?"

"The hurricane done passed us by, case you didn't notice."

Marie stands with her mouth open. She closes it with a clack of teeth. "Right now, Mother," Marie says, her voice so over-calm that Cerise knows she's in for a lecture, "I know you're in pain, and so I know not everything you say is always going to be sensitive or even pertinent. But, yes, sure, we can leave. I hope all goes well with Keyshawn. He has our numbers if there's an emergency." Marie gives Lil Thomas' nose a final quick swipe. The boy twists his face away and then head-butts his mother in the chest.

Cerise taps her left hand on the armrest. Tap, tap. How much is she supposed to put up with? And then she feels like crying. She will not. She will not give in. Tomorrow's another debridement. Another time to see if death's still creeping out of her right hand towards everyplace worse. "I love you," Cerise manages. "All of you. Very much."

Marie isn't even looking at Cerise anymore. She's moving around the room picking up Lil Thomas' toys and baby teething cookie messes and the men's scraps with her one free hand. "I'll go get Thomas to help pack up our bags," Marie says and heads to the front door.

Cerise hears Marie say through the screen door, "Mom says it's time for us to go."

"Naw," Roy says. "You stay tonight too. We have some dominoes to play."

"We should give you some peace," Marie says.

"But I don't want you to go," Roy says, and Cerise thinks he sounds like a child.

"Come on, Thomas. Help me pack up. Daddy, we'll leave the leftovers. You and Keyshawn should be able to heat them up easily enough."

Cerise rolls her eyes and stares at the black television screen. It gives back a bowed reflection of her sitting in the room alone, a skinny little dark person curved at the edge in a chair. Cerise raises her mittens and stares at the screen. When she moves her arms toward the middle of the room, the mittens get ever so much bigger.

During the brunch crunch, the biggest they've ever had, Ariel finds Javier in the walk-in cooler. She closes the door behind her and blocks him from leaving. "*He* kissed *me*," she says quietly.

Javier won't even look at her face. He seems very angry, as she suspected.

"I went to bed alone," she continues, "as I think you know." He and Warren walked Ariel to her door. She picks up a case of Freixenet.

"And you leave after to meet the black man," Javier almost hisses.

"I did no such thing."

"How do I know?"

"Javier, why would I bother talking to you now with the door closed? Do you know what risks I'm taking?"

"Nobody sees us."

"I did not leave the hotel. I wanted you to come to my room."

Javier lifts his head from his metal pan of collected ingredients, his pounds of butter and quarts of cream. His eyes. Hmm. Ariel backs up, taps the safety release, and spins out into the kitchen. "So, please, you'll have to be more aware of sodium," Ariel says, hauling the case of cava.

She tries to imagine salvaging anything after last night. Her orgasm came hard as a ton of rocks, alone in her room, her head full of two men. It could have been better, she thinks, lugging the case to the bar. Could've been better. Where's her manager-on-duty? Ariel shouldn't have to heft anything in heels like these.

In her office, Ariel's cell rings at two in the afternoon. Everyone at the hotel has heard the news about the mayor's request to give the city another day before returning. Seeing the Gupta phone number pop up on her caller ID, Ariel stands and paces. She still might have a chance. "Hello," she answers.

"Ariel," Ed says, "oh, save me. I'm dying to get out of here."

"Why? What's the matter?"

"It's . . . there's . . . I don't know. It's chaos. All the people."

"What?"

"I'm not sure I can explain right now." He sighs heavily. "We're okay. It's just not great times, if you know what I mean."

"When are you coming back?"

"You're okay with our staying another night?"

"What?" Ariel paces faster, watching the indentations her heels leave in the tasteful patterned carpeting of her office.

"You didn't hear?" Ed asks. "The mayor wants us to stay away if we can for another day. Fear of the highways getting blocked again. This is abysmal, Ariel."

"What's so horrible?" she asks before she wishes to take it back. Of course, as a sympathetic mother and wife, she would know exactly what's not so much fun about an evacuation road trip.

"I'll tell you when I see you," he says. "I don't want to be a glutton with the Guptas' phone. Anyway." He pauses. "I miss you."

"I miss you too," Ariel says. She doesn't even want to consider the potential truth of her statement. She hopes, only, that it comes from a decent place in her little black heart. "Are the kids nearby?"

"They're swimming," Ed says. "Somebody has a pool. It has a giant mosquito net around it. It's the craziest thing I've ever seen."

"You can see them from where you are?"

"The Guptas are watching. I'm in the front yard."

"Give Miles and Ella big kisses for me. Make me out to be a super-hero, right?"

"Right."

There's another pause. "Ariel?"

She sucks in a breath. "Yeah?"

"I love you."

"I love you too." She presses the on/off button with her thumb.

Jolly, buzzed Chef Warren soaks in the praise of employees and patrons alike at the bar. Were he to accept all the offers to buy him drinks, he'd land himself in the hospital. Still, he's taken advantage of more than a few so far. Ariel admits he saved the day with his perfect orchestration of every meal for the entire hurricane scare. Tomorrow's breakfast will be difficult with relatively meager supplies, but Ariel has complete faith in her friend now.

Whether or not he truly has any faith in her, she doesn't know. Possibly. He's at least pretending he believes that Ariel didn't initiate the kiss with Phatty. She told Warren about her talk with Greenback today and how he apologized for Phatty's indiscretion. She told Warren about how it seems Phatty's reputation for just such 'attacks' has landed him two sexual harassment suits to date. She wishes she might somehow get Warren to share the information with Javier, but that's not something she could ever ask. Imagine: "Oh, and can you tell Javier too?"

Javier, Warren's officially anointed right-hand man as of the toast half an hour ago, remains in the hotel after his double shift, a glimmer of hope for Ariel in the gesture. At the moment, Javier flirts openly with a Greenback hanger-on, a woman who scowled at Ariel the night before. The woman has set her two-thousand-dollar handbag prominently on the bar. With ostentatiously long fingernails painted gold, she pets the Italian leather of it now and again as though to keep it from barking. She needs a leash.

Come on, Javier, you can do better than that.

Ariel believes it's for show. He's still here, which means Henny's still away. They need to get rid of Warren. Well, get him drunk enough that he'll have no suspicions at all.

And nobody else's inklings either. Keep the prying eyes off Ariel's room.

It's possible.

Ariel makes the GM rounds, moving from one cocktail table to another asking patrons about their stays, making small talk. She catches herself saying the same things over and over again: "Yes, we were lucky." "Oh, no kidding!" "Let's hope it's not practice for the real thing." As she goes, she keeps a steady eye on her surroundings. She'll check with the front desk in a little while. Last she heard, they have over 80 percent checking out in the morning, some requests for late checkouts, and Greenback still hangin' around till further notice. House-keeping's collecting overtime, so none of them are bitching too loudly yet. Tomorrow might prove different with the masses leaving, but for now it's all copasetic. Except for Javier and Ariel.

She's a GM. If she can't string this thing together, she's worthless.

It's the last night. Time to take what she wants.

He knocks, and she opens her door. He walks in.

She's not been up here long, long enough only to use the bidet. He closes the door behind him.

She steps backwards till her ass, in its skirt, finds the wall closest to the bathroom. She has decided how this will happen. Slowly. Languorously. In all the rooms.

He seems to think otherwise. He seems to think she is someone deserving of a sauce, or a spanking, or a blindfold.

Her husband will be a cuckold in minutes. She will be something else. She doesn't know the word for it yet.

This light brown man takes her hand and leads her away from the wall and into the bedroom of her suite. Wait.

He holds her hand aloft, near her shoulder, as if they were beginning a dance. He kisses the very tips of her fingers and breathes in. She believes he kisses to test for what he wants. Her fingers are rosemary and orange flower water and goose fat and his grandmother's tamales. If he licks them she will use them, wet, to feel his earlobes. She will run them up the sides of his neck.

He only kisses. She warms anyway.

It has to be enough to block out the noise of everything else, the names of her children.

He kneels. Standing, she stares at the top of his head. His hair, so short, shows his scalp. He rounds his shoulders to remove her shoes.

She grabs the back of his collar and pulls him off the floor. His fingers graze the insides of her thighs as he rises.

They kiss. She likes to kiss, very much. She likes to spend time on mouths.

He kisses and moves his mouth over her neck. He stops and sucks, and she has to push him off for the mark he seems wanting to leave on her throat.

As his answer, he pushes her down on the bedspread. She props up on her elbows and watches as he unbuttons his shirt. He exposes a tattoo, of what she cannot exactly discern. There is a heart, maybe, a knife or thorns. He tucks his hands around behind her where she lies, unzips her skirt, and pulls it off. He unbuttons and unzips his pants, bends, pushes her knees together, and straddles her own with his. He crouches and runs his hands over her silk blouse in a motion of reverence. She is Mary in blue. He will move up to her mouth and take her tongue into his mouth and next take her, pushing her underwear to the side.

But he hovers over her breasts still contained in their blouse and bra. He rubs on them. He will conjure a genie soon. His erection, having escaped his shorts, pokes through the slit.

He is hard, and he is not her husband, and he wants to be here or he would not be here at all with his girlfriend away and his boss boozily installed in another suite, and she decides now is the time to reach for the condom under the pillow. She pushes down his boxers. She rolls it on.

He drags her underwear down her legs. They catch at her ankles.

She still in her blouse and bra and heels and he in his gold chain and scent of grease, of just plain kitchen grease, fuck hard on top of the bedspread.

He stares straight into her eyes as if he might find something to kill in her pupils. She, in turn, reaches down to cup his testicles. She knows he understands what she holds in her hand.

It's a game they play.

Last night, Fearius let himself be trapped up with his own family for exactly four hours before it came clear aint nothing making its way to New Orleans gone kill him or his people.

Today he hoofed it something fierce, pullin numbers like Alphonse maybe never seen for the lil old shit Pigeontown street Fearius work, and still. Fearius know he got stomped down to the bottom of the latrine. You step up and win or you step up and lose. Fearius got the second.

And how many days now he have to prove himself? Ten or ten times ten? Who know. He just fucked. Fifteen years of age and fucked till he die or till he make nice again with Alphonse. Time for nothing but to work and work overtime, ya heard.

Right now he lie in the front room while all the babies sleep, all the family besides him sleeping in the back rooms. Muzzle still hangin up in Touro.

The last while, the Moms and Pops not so stupid they think Fearius goin to school, but they still pretend with the hours he keeps. Fearius rise same as them and his cryin nieces and nephews, and they eat some something, and then on her shift days she work the morning, his Moms say good bye and love you and all three of them leave the house. Maybe half the days Angelique make it outside the house and visit some classes. If she keep up with high school and the grades she earn, she be done when she make 25. But she stayed out of babies so far.

So Alphonse get all Fearius dollars, all, for the day, the biggest day the firm probably ever have, and Fearius, he still be in the shithole. But he aint expired. He lie watching a movie starring a white vigilante on his Moms and Pops TV in the middle the night.

It aint bad always. One, one thirty in the AM. Least he dont have no broken leg and be hung up in a hospital, yo.

And at least Fearius still breathing.

14

Something rises. An escalator in Prancie's head has opened a square hole into which she can ascend, and she will follow it. It is a mechanism to the skies. Freedom.

"It had to come sooner or later," Joe says. He breathes deeply. Prancie sits beside him on their back porch. Leaves will not change color in New Orleans, and the earth will not harden with frost, but a dry wind has finally brought with it the season of autumn.

Shane Geautreaux would say, 'It ain't perfect, but I'll take what I can get.' Prancie can hear him clearly.

It is October 20th, and Joe is still here. Despite Prancie's preparations, he seems to have no intentions of going elsewhere.

"When's the last time you saw these?" Joe asks and lifts his shirt. His scar remains below his belt. Prancie does not know to what he refers. The meager hairs of his chest?

"I don't know what you mean."

"Look," he says. "My ribs." For over a month now, Joe has remained effervescently happy despite his treatments. Philomenia cannot comprehend his state of mind nor its source. He is neither a man of great faith nor a man of bravery. And now he is a man of very little hair. The day Prancie returned from the Tokyo Rose to find Joe shaved bald by his careperson, she gasped. Now, however, she has grown used to the sight of his naked pate. She finds it smooth to the touch. In turn, she no longer fancies the mayor whatsoever.

Her daily kindness to Joe comes in the evenings when she touches his head, her fingers light as feathers. He closes his eyes and groans. His reactions do not appeal to Prancie. She creates new horoscope signs on the dome of his skull, connecting freckles.

It is true. Joe has lost a goodly amount of weight. The cancer has served him well in terms of his physique. "I believe I saw those last when we only dated," Philomenia says of Joe's ribs. She should find his improved form appealing, she tells herself. It should spark some form of appreciation in her.

Joe nods, smiles, and pats his shrunken stomach. "Looks better too, don't you think?"

Prancie does not want to think about Joe's stomach. The cool breeze comes on, and Joe lowers his shirt, raises his nose to the air, and inhales loudly once again. "It's wonderful," he says.

"Yes," Prancie says, wishing instead to inhale the dank perfume of the Tokyo Rose. She has promised Joe three nights a week. Tonight she must attend to him, but Prancie senses Shane across the street. Shane Geautreaux sits, of course, in his usual seat and compliments other women less deserving than Prancie.

What will Shane eat today? He has come to depend on her cooking. He has spurred Prancie to new heights of culinary expertise. But on these nights that she remains chained to Joe, Shane resorts to fast food, he has told her. Such a pathetic option! Prancie has often suggested he try some of the local restaurant fare. They live in New Orleans, for goodness' sake. He says that dining alone is no dinner at all. She supposes she knows what he means.

Some weeks back, niggled with something she could not clearly identify, Prancie started creating special plates for Shane in order to spare him from her usual fare. She set aside a portion of food before mixing her special ingredient into the larger whole. Alas, she found the man such a devotee to her cooking that he nearly always took seconds and sometimes even thirds from the communal pots and warming trays.

She no longer adds her special ingredient. Prancie will find a way to address the other patrons soon enough. For now, however, she cannot endanger an intelligent and thoughtful man.

Tonight, dinner in her house will no doubt prove to be equally as distasteful as Shane's fast food. Chemotherapy and a colostomy add up to nothing delicious when it comes to dinner. Yogurt or creamed soup.

Joe pretends that he wishes Philomenia to eat regular fare without him, but she remains true. She has always remained true to him despite her desire to do otherwise.

Staring out at the blue sky of the October afternoon, she thinks yet again about What Might Have Been, what might have been had she not ignored the signs of that day, the first day of these last several decades. Her brain returns to it like a tongue to a canker sore after having eaten too much sour. She has thought too much sour as well.

It's all good, she tries to remind herself at the advice of Tokyo Rose friends.

That first day, when they were still only engaged, Joe's hair was disheveled. His mouth seemed irritated, his lips enlarged.

"You ate something spicy at lunch?" Philomenia asked.

He laughed and then said, "You could say that."

She wore her yellow sundress. They sat on the balcony of his family's home on St. Charles Avenue in the wide shade of the old live oak. She had absolutely no idea what he told her whatsoever. Philomenia felt herself blush with the teasing she believed directed at her.

Why she thought it would be flattering to carry a hand fan like some Spanish flamenco dancer, Prancie has no idea. Philomenia switched it open with a snap of her wrist. She considered herself to be beautiful. What man would not wait for such a flower?

She remembers the streetcar passing noisily on the tracks. She remembers she said, "Must they squeal so much?"

She remembers Joe becoming sullen as the martinis he said he had at lunch wore off.

She remembers thinking her pedicure looked perfect.

The watching hour approaches. Prancie relishes it above all others. Her porch is quite obscured, tastefully, by variegated ginger. While she can see out, when the overhead light is switched off, none can see her.

Philomenia carefully rinses and loads their two bowls and two spoons into the dishwasher and stares out the window over the sink. She has opened all the windows in the house this evening, letting in the air. Next door, the Guptas prepare something that begins with garlic and onions and turmeric. Since Prancie began cooking for the Tokyo Rose, she has found foreign odors less offensive, although she cannot imagine why. It is possible they will carry her into her new future. Prancie inhales, readies herself, and returns to Joe in his room.

He laughs at a commercial. He laughs out loud, shaking his head. Philomenia sees nothing funny about it. Most of television these days perplexes her, as though it has moved away from her somehow or begun to employ a new language.

"Come sit!" Joe commands and pats the hospital bed.

"You are wide awake tonight," she says, perching her bottom on the mattress' edge.

"I feel wonderful, Phil. I really do."

He teases her as well. They have long agreed that he cannot shorten her name. He does not know her new one. She has determined he never will. "I am glad you are feeling well tonight."

"I can feel them shrinking," he says. "Really."

She supposes he refers to the multiple tumors. He speaks of an impossibility, but she can play along for the time being. He has always put a well-appointed roof over her head, if nothing else. "I am happy," she tells him.

"Are you?"

How does he intend the question? Lately he joshes so much she does not know how to interpret what he says.

"Are you?" he repeats.

"Am I happy that you feel good tonight?" she asks.

"No. Are you happy?"

She did not anticipate such a deliberate question from her husband. They have moved through separate corridors for so many years of their married life that she has learned to expect nothing from him but inane banter. Small talk, as they say. After some contemplation, she tells him, "I think for you to ask me such a question when you attend chemotherapy appointments is unfair. Would you believe me to be happy right now?"

"You should be," he says, seeming to have hardly heard her at all. "There's no time like the present. Live your life, Philomenia. Come here and give me a kiss."

What? "I beg your pardon?"

"Come on. Your mother didn't make it to sixty, Phil. Live it up. Live!"

Her mother is not an allowable topic of discussion. This, too, Joe knows. The break in weather has provoked him towards impertinence. Philomenia frowns.

"I know I'm not supposed to talk about it, but hell, you might well inherit what she had. Time is short, don't you understand? Live life! There's beauty in everything!"

She has had enough of listening to the man who has lived a disrespectful life. She will not live life as he has, nor will she entertain his hollering any longer.

"I am going to clean," she says, standing.

"I'll help," Joe says, sitting straight up.

"You will not," Philomenia says, righting the seams of her skirt.

"I could if you let me."

She will not let him. Her watching hour approaches.

Ed Flank exits his front door carrying both a glass and a bottle, Prancie sees. He has altered his pattern of behavior since returning from his evacuation with his children and the neighbors. Numerous times in the last weeks, she has seen him drink two and sometimes three glasses of his dark liquor on his porch at night. He does not seem to be enjoying his life in the same way he did before the threat of Ivan. His wife, Ariel, on the other hand, seems very light on her feet these days.

Now Ed pours himself a drink and sighs loudly. Some months ago, Prancie carried one of the back garden's Asian stools to the front porch. She can swivel on its ceramic top to view any of the neighbors without being heard. A number of times lately Ed has stared directly at her position for great lengths of time. In such circumstances, Prancie reminds herself that she cannot be seen and studies the man's face for what must be occurring, or not occurring, inside his brain. She senses that he is having troubles. She could have predicted as much. She *has* predicted as much.

Joe will be having surgery to remove an additional portion of his intestine and must enter the hospital the evening before the procedure. The timing means that Prancie is allowed the happiest of Thanksgiving meals with her friends at the Tokyo Rose. She deposits Joe early, mid-afternoon, promising to return the next morning. Aware that Philomenia wanted to share her cooking with others, Joe approved her budget for a full dinner.

She has cooked since dawn. Her work will culminate shortly with the exodus of the bird from the oven. Twenty-five pounds will go quickly across the street, but she has other dishes. Pies, dressing, yams, mirliton casserole. She has decided to invite Shane to help her carry her fare when the time comes. She will not invite him into her home, since that might be perceived as improper, but she can place the covered dishes at the ready on her porch.

She has chosen a casual dress that exposes her clavicles as well as her calves and knees.

Cover your knees, Philomenia.

"Cover your knees, Philomenia," her mother told her.

"Pardon?" Philomenia asked. She and her party guests celebrated her seventh birthday.

"Place your napkin not only in your lap," her mother instructed, "but cover your knees when you wear a short lower garment. It blocks any untoward viewing."

Philomenia looked around at her party guests in the backyard. Some girls had yet to come to the table, happier instead to make giant dish-liquid bubbles with the large wire Os the housekeeper's husband had fashioned for the day. Why, on this of all days, did she need to behave properly?

"Do as I say."

"Yes, ma'am." She never knew to respond otherwise.

Indeed, she still does not, although her visits across the street are beginning to arrest some of what has been unkindly described as her 'unflinching formality.' Those words came directly from Thirsty's very own mouth. It is what she has decided to name Thurman. And shame on him for saying them. Still.

In all her days since her seventh birthday, Philomenia has yet to expose herself to any untoward viewing while wearing a short garment.

She allows Shane the pleasure of carrying over the bird under its foil hood.

"It's a thing of beauty," he says for the second time. "Honestly, Miss P, this is the finest damn bird I've seen in years."

Prancie feels herself glowing. As they carry food across the street, Roy Brown waves to them from behind his oil barrel grill. The man must have strength the stores of which she cannot imagine to cook on the apparatus again.

Sharon Harris deep-fried a turkey in her crawfish pot earlier. Prancie had been on her way to checking with Thirsty about utensils. Sharon said that she and Nate were going to attend the opening day at the race-track. She proclaimed the appropriation of a most spectacular hat for the occasion from her sister-in-law. "It got a peacock feather," Sharon said, and Prancie nodded and then smiled.

Sharon would not quiet, however. "You been nice to those Tokyo people lately," she said. "That nice."

Fortunately, Prancie had anticipated the day she would be confronted with her actions. "There is that adage about joining them if you cannot beat them," Prancie said.

"They's that," Sharon said. "How's Joe?"

"Tomorrow is the second surgery."

"He's in my prayers."

"Thank you." Prancie walked on, stopped, started, decided to change her path, and returned to Sharon. "Thank you. I will tell him."

"Hey," Sharon said. "I know a lot about blood. You get me his numbers, I can tell you what's goin' on under his skin."

Prancie nodded, not immediately knowing why she had returned to speak with Sharon. Suddenly, Sharon's suggestion made sense. Why not deliver blood test results to her neighbor? Joe's doctors so often spoke in terms absolutely indeterminate. Sharon could help Prancie know just how many days they had before the inevitable.

"White cells and what," Sharon continued. "I know how to read 'em even if I'm still over at Delgado."

"That would be very helpful," Prancie said. "Thank you. And happy Thanksgiving."

"Ain't it about helpin'?"

"Most certainly," Prancie agreed even as she realized that what the woman offered was likely nothing more than a neighborly pleasantry.

Now Prancie decides to find out how Cerise is faring since her skin graft. For to be social on Thanksgiving, as she has been reminded by Sharon Harris, is what the holiday calls for. "Happy Thanksgiving, Mr. Roy," she says, gesturing with her shoulder to Shane to continue carrying the turkey into the Tokyo Rose.

"Back atcha, Miss Philomenia," he says. "Back atcha. Happy Thanksgiving for sure. We have plenty to give thanks for."

"That we do," she says. "Tell me, how is Cerise managing?"

"Well, she doin' alright. She doin' alright. Making her fingers work normal ain't the easiest, but she has two hands again without no bandages."

"Then it is a real Thanksgiving."

"An' Joe?"

"The second surgery is tomorrow."

"Bless his soul."

Prancie has no intention, but she need not tell kind old Roy that. "Is your family coming over?"

"Any minute, Miss Philomenia. How you know? Any minute."

She shifts her large bowl of dressing to rest on the other hip. "And what goes on the grill today?"

"Cherry making me do things fancy. She can't stop watchin' that

FoodTV or what's it called. I think she just trying to fuss with my cholesterol in secret. We got oysters she wants me put on the grill. On the grill! They get topped with something vinegary. And the shrimps, but she have me stickin' 'em on skewers with no butter. And corn. She says it tastes best grilled. But the best part? She got some ostrich meat from Mandeville. Ostrich steaks! A teeny bitty ol' thing of a turkey in the oven on purpose 'cause we got ostrich meat on the grill! How crazy that is, huh?"

Prancie has long suspected that Cerise's cooking would likely rival her own. Now she knows as much. Someday they should exchange recipes. Before they die, Prancie thinks suddenly. "It sounds delicious," she says.

She feels a presence approach from behind her. "Hello," a man says. Prancie knows his voice before she turns.

"Sorry to interrupt," Ed Flank says.

"You? You kidding? You interrupt me the rest of your life, young man."

"I'm on the prowl for poultry seasoning. Do either of you have any left?"

"Oooh! You don't got your bird in the oven by now, you eatin' at midnight, Rescue Man!"

Prancie surveys the man from the side. He is still fit. He appears sober. "Hello, Ed," she says.

"Happy Thanksgiving," he replies. "No. It's for the basting butter. I ran out. I have more butter but no more poultry seasoning."

"An' why I think you's a vegetarian? You making a bird today like everybody else."

Prancie says nothing.

"I try," Ed says, "but I lapse on holidays. Sometimes purposely."

No doubt he lapses in other areas as well.

"Sure. Cherry done got every spice known to man. And then some not known to no man." Roy laughs hard at his own joke.

Ed seems to find it equally funny.

Prancie stands and smiles because she is expected to. She does not understand Roy's joke. "Well, I am off to feed the masses." She tosses her hand in the air to indicate the Tokyo Rose. "They would eat hot dogs, otherwise," she adds.

"That's incredibly generous of you," Ed says. "I'm sure they're grateful."

Are they? Prancie cannot say, but it has become a thing more about her, as it were. This much she recognizes. She dances in her kitchen now four days a week. And, too, because they are not drinking on empty stomachs, fewer patrons have vomited on her yard in recent months. "Good bye," she says.

15

Ariel and Ed wrap presents on their bedroom floor. Ariel can't remember when she last attempted the task. Ed has his practical uses. A tube of green foil paper in his hand, he straddles a box not far away. They have maybe four hours tops before the kids wake up.

"Miles has got to know," Ariel says.

"He does," Ed says, the wrapping paper obscuring his face.

"He knows there's no Santa Claus?"

"I had to tell him a couple of weeks ago."

"You didn't think the subject was important enough to tell me?"

Ed keeps wrapping. "When would I have done that?"

"What? Has he promised to keep it a secret?"

"Well, he's Miles. We'll see."

A cardboard wheel of ribbon escapes Ariel, rolling under the bed. "Don't tell me some . . . some *nothing*, Ed. You're here every day. I'm not. Do you think Miles has ruined Ella's Christmas?"

Ed shrugs and goes after the wheel. "Can either one of us stop him if that's his intention? I asked him not to tell. But he's his own person." He hands the ribbon back to Ariel.

Ariel is so sick of Ed's Buddhist parenting she would like to cram a candy cane down his platitude-spouting throat. "Has she said anything?"

"Who?"

How can he not even know who she means? "Ella, Ed. Ella."

"She's all about the Grinch this year. The Jim Carrey one, not the animated one."

And so? "What do the Grinch and Santa Claus have to do with one another?"

Ed stops wrapping. "Are you asking me that question seriously? In a five-year-old's mind, what do the Grinch and Santa Claus have to do with one another?"

It's in her contract that Ariel takes off both Christmas Eve and Christmas Day. She wishes she had some work emergency, but even that wouldn't alleviate her agitation. Henny has brought her family in for the holidays. Javier isn't possibly available till the 27th, not that he's even the actual diversion Ariel's interested in. Life just comes at you, she thinks. At the moment, she has no idea what she wants. Maybe only that Miles has not told his sister that there's no Santa Claus.

Ariel feels her nostalgia for the holidays dissipating. She used to love them. Since she graduated from college, until they moved here, she collected glass ornaments, no permanent home in sight. Her long-term monogamous relationships, her hippies and her brokers and her lawyers and her musicians, none of them understood the boxes of ornaments. Ariel's not sure she understood them herself. Boxes of Christmas tree decorations take up a lot of space in the back of a Volkswagen van no matter what. In a BMW trunk, almost nothing else will fit.

Buddhists have a strange sort of appeal. Ed wooed her without wooing her. They, Buddhists, somehow make her think of vegans, although you can choose to eat meat if you want to when you're a Buddhist. They're not actually the same thing. Best Ariel understands it, when you're a vegan, you lop off both extreme ends of the eating spectrum. Nothing animal, obviously, nothing processed or messed-with. She forgets, exactly, what's on the other end of the spectrum. Sugar? Alcohol? She always wants to compare it to the color spectrum, but she never remembers what comes after purple on the wheel or after starchy vegetables on the lineup of food. The forbidden you don't even know is forbidden.

Ed was just, solidly, in the middle. Accepting of anything. Or accepting with an overriding conscience: do the least harm.

Objectively, Ed is a score. Really. He's attentive, procreating, a cook. Liberal. Tallish. He follows Ariel where she needs to go for her work. But, too, it's as if the extremes of his personality have been sanded away on purpose. He has purposely sat his own ass under a gigantic sander and allowed his furious anger and crying joy to be abraded away. Where is his passion? Has she ever seen it? He was a Buddhist when they met, and when they met, nothing felt more necessary, more comfortable, more easy than dating a Buddhist. Still, she knows his beliefs have never been as simple as 'Hey, whatever.'

These days, though, she's beginning to feel from Ed that it's a 'Hey, whatever, glad you're home, and now I'm going to have a drink out on the porch away from you.' He never really drank before.

Ariel pulls off a length of ribbon. "Ella might not have a great Christmas if she finds out there's no Santa Claus."

"Of course there's a Santa Claus." His optimism is not contagious.

"Would Miles be so deliberately cruel? He knows how old his sister is."

"Oh, *Christ*, Ariel. Wait. Excuse me. How about 'shit'? Does 'shit' work? Shit, Ariel, where have you been? You're gone for more than work."

"So, we're going to fight on Christmas Eve?" She gestures with the scissors. "I really don't want to fight."

Ed scoffs. "We'll make love then, not war. Right, Ariel? Isn't that right?" His pointedness is ungainly, she thinks.

They've had sex a couple of times lately. It sucked, but Ariel believed Ed forced her to acknowledge the intimacy of the act, something she found stupidly difficult. After all this time—and *he doesn't know*—why would it suddenly feel so hard to fuck her husband?

"I just hope Ella gets to enjoy Christmas morning a few more years," she says.

"Nice deflection there, Ariel."

"You *really* want to fight on Christmas Eve?"

"What'd you get me this year?" Ed asks.

She's had next to no time to shop, and he knows it. She got him a couple of shirts. They're in a bag on the floor of her closet. "Why would I tell you that?"

He rests the green foil roll on his lap. "Do you want to know what I want for Christmas? You didn't ask."

She will not be sad tonight. She doesn't have it in her. Why the hell is he pushing her? "What do you want for Christmas, Ed?"

"You. I want you back."

"I'm right here."

"No, you're not."

Ariel sighs and looks at the box she's wrapping, an encased-behind-plastic hoochie fur Barbie coat with white go-go boots and a lavender glitter dress. When did Barbie go ghetto? When did Ed find the time away from the kids to buy this box of shit she knows he doesn't believe in but bought out of love for their daughter, this box of shit Ariel knows Ella's going to go nuts for?

Ariel understands exactly what Ed means. She won't acknowledge it in the slightest. She just can't. She is her own person too. She doesn't have to be only wife-mother, only mother-wife. She's allowed to be an independent human. "Whatever," she says.

The lavender glitter dress makes her want to cry.

Fearius, he the man in this group, no question. He and Taliqwa been banging what, five days now, but on New Years Eve, when Fearius hold whatever anybody need for smoking on top of holding Taliqwas ass in his hand, he the man. He wearin a new down coat with a hood trimmed out in real fur. A fat bottle of cognac in his pocket, advertising he set for the night.

They there for the Mid City bonfires on the boulevard that get set blazing at midnight. The firecrackers going mad already, peoples everywhere, way more than a thousand, maybe like two, three thousand. Taliqwa and Fearius, and her four friends matched up in couples two n two, came over together in one of the moms borrowed Camrys. Taliqwas girlfriend pull a roller cooler with cold drinks in it. Taliqwa say she dont want to stay too long case she has to pee cause she dont like peeing in no grass.

Fearius spent his whole life coming to one bonfire or the other for the holidays. Tradition in the N.O. aint no joke. He has some warm memories of Moms and Pops bringing them when they kids. It always so crazy to see the big piles go up in flames, people gathering and drinking, everybody happy, snackin, dragging they dried up Christmas trees and throwing em on top a the piles like those spears they throw at the Olympics. This year, the Mid City pile big as a house, almost. It got couches and chairs in it, including a whole damn regular tree, a oak or whatever.

"How you gone make this New Years my best ever, Fearius?" Taliqwa ask over her shoulder, backing up into him.

"Girl, I show you five times in one day what makin your year the best ever." He come around her front and suck on her mouth. She taste like vanilla ice cream.

"Stop," she say, pushin on him and smiling. "You messin up my gloss."

"Gimme some more that," he tell her. She come back at him and he grab her neck when they kiss. He like how she tug his tongue in and breathe around it, makin a slurpy noise, the same way she do his dick. Taliqwa aint shy, and Fearius aint stupid enough to ask her where she learned her tricks. He might could fuck her for months and not get tired of it.

"Hey," Taliqwas girlfriend say, "get a room." Taliqwas friends all a little stiff, one of em going to private school, but they awright. The two dudes visitin from Baton Rouge. Fearius already know they scared of him, which make it a great New Years Eve, one where Fearius dont have to fight his way up to whatever place he hafta fight up to normally. Top dog, even for just one night, feel nice.

"Really," Taliqwa say and slap Fearius on his chest. "Cut it." He been working out, doing push ups and sit ups and what in his room at night. His physique lookin fine these days. An he got Taliqwa to prove it, yo.

Fearius pull the bottle of Hennessy from his inside pocket. "Girl," he tell Taliqwa, "get those cold drinks out the cooler."

"Can mine be weak?" one the other girls ask.

"Whatever you want. It New Years Eve." Fearius way outside his normal grounds, so he need to look for bangers and other wardies, but he think he gone be fine here in Mid City. No dying for two years at the New Years bonfires over this way, which be a little surprising considering what all people throw into the flames when it heat up. Fearius seen people toss in all kind a shit. Never mind the gasoline, a bottle rocket take your eye out if you dont see it comin. He wonder on if those tsunami people in Indonesia and wherever, if they knew what hit them. He think it way better to not know, not see it comin at all, but he aint worried tonight in no way.

Fearius like to think he know the difference between a gunshot sound and a fucking firecracker, but maybe he dont when some go off right behind them. In his coat, he dont flinch big enough for the rest of em to notice and call him out.

He got his Jericho in his pocket now, a 9mm, so Fearius aint afraid of shit besides maybe Alphonses wrath. Son a bitch have a noose around Fearius neck so tight he can hardly breathe. That and whats done happened to Muzzle. He out his leg cast but now he hooked on the painkillers and got his sorry motherfucking ass fired from the firm. His bros plain ol stupidity sure dont put Fearius in a better position with Alphonse. Muzzle livin somewhere off the Claiborne with a slut, last Fearius heard. She keep him in his meds.

But it New Years Eve, and Fearius allowed to have some fun. Even Alphonse give his blessing for it today, toll Fearius to find him some pussy for the holiday. Fearius dint bother telling him he already had some.

They sip on Hennessy and cokes. Fearius let Taliqwa hang on him some more. They watch the hippies run around playing with hoola hoops and ribbons on sticks. All the hippies high on E, Fearius think. Ecstasy out the roof on cost, not even worth it for the firm to take it on, last way too long. Hours and hours. Just a dopey drug, make everybody want to kiss on everybody the way Fearius hear it. Sort of the way he feel right now with Taliqwa being so nice.

She not the sharpest knife in the drawer. He like that saying. And it just fine with Fearius. He have all kinds of street smarts, but he not so big on schooling neither. Fearius like her happy approach to the world. He needed him some happy approach. Each and every single time he come around, she pounce all over him like she aint seen him in a year.

The bass come at them first before Fearius see the car moving slow as a shark fin down the one side the boulevard still open to traffic. Best Fearius can see, they crammed inside like sardines. Like a initiation.

Fearius take Taliqwas arm and pull her behind him then tell the rest of em to move back behind him too.

Granted, they deep into the crowd. Lots of hippies and white drunks would be goin down first, but Fearius sure as hell dont like what he see. His hand go in his pocket.

16

"Daddy," Ella says, walking down the steps of her school, waving a piece of paper, "I got the baby."

"What?"

"I got the baby."

Ed has no idea what his child is saying. "What do you mean, Ella?"

"I ate the baby in my cake." She nods her blond head on her skinny little neck. "The cake is a big doughnut with purple sprinkles and with frosting."

Ed is scrambling. "You had a treat at school today?"

"It's called . . ." Ella holds out her backpack for Ed to take. She nods her thank-you. "It's called . . . a . . . it's called a, a . . . I bited the baby. Miss Morgan says I bring the next one." Ella shoves the piece of paper into Ed's hands.

"You're supposed to bring a baby to school?" Ed has no idea what's going on. Maybe a premature training day with the girls to make sure they don't want to get pregnant early?

"In the Mahdi Gra cake," Ella says, and there they are. The magic words. It's all about Mardi Gras. Has it started already? Ella got the little plastic baby in the, hell, what's it called? He looks down at the teacher's photocopied instructions. In the king cake. It means Ella has to provide the next cake to continue the utterly incomprehensible tradition. The coffee cake ring, decorated in acid-bright Mardi Gras–colored sugar crystals, has a baby baked into it somewhere. If you get the piece of cake that contains the baby, you get to host the next king cake party. Last year, Ed was beyond confused. Baking small hard plastic things into food eaten by young children at school struck him as a lawsuit in the making.

Now he recognizes that the seasonal chaos has begun again. He's not ready.

"The king cake," Ed says.

Ella bobbles her head in a nod once more. "Ya-huh, the king cake," she repeats. "I got a purple piece. With frosting."

"Sounds good," Ed fakes.

Where they live in the city isn't necessarily terrible as far as the parades and traffic and tourists are concerned, but Mardi Gras makes Ariel's trip to work in the Quarter almost impossible on the streetcar. She'll have to start driving to the CBD again till Ash Wednesday. Not so hot for their carbon footprint.

Ed holds Ella's hand as they walk up to the corner where they always wait for Miles to come running out the school's south door, and Ed realizes anew that he doesn't trust Ariel anymore. He has the distinct sense she's been doing something stupid for months. Still, he refuses to take the extra measures. He will not plant tape recorders or buy spyware to check her e-mails and internet usage. He can't bring himself to do it. He hopes only that she will stop whatever it is on her own. His passive approach seems the wrong one, even to the Buddhist side of him, but Ed no longer knows how else to be.

Lately he's had the desire for some company in his misery. He's decided that today he will walk across the street when Ariel returns home from work and have a pre-dinner cocktail at Tokyo Rose. The bartender who helped with the Cerise and Roy Brown accident seemed to be a nice young guy, someone who might lift Ed's spirits.

Miles bounds down the school's steps and hurdles a bush. He runs as though he's being chased by a fire-breathing dragon, or a giant mechanical monster, or a gang of flying monkeys. It will be something or other.

"We have to go!" Miles screams. "The zombies are coming!"

Today, the zombies attack.

"Right now?" Ariel asks as she walks in the front door.

"Yup," Ed tells her. "You had your time away. Now it's my time."

"Well—" she says, and Ed is past her.

"I won't be too long," he says on the porch. "Dinner's in the oven. Ready at seven. You can set the table, right? Salad's in the fridge." Ed heads straight across the street. For all he can tell, it's a perfectly fine place.

Ed opens the front door and, in the dim light, sees a number of people on stools around the bar. He has glanced inside before to simply see what it contained, but, to date, he has never had a drink in Tokyo Rose. That's about to change.

He steps in. His eyes adjust. It's a little place. And there's a naked guy at the bar, right in the middle of the bar, sitting by himself. The guy has tucked himself in, but his ass is bare on the vinyl seat. He's drinking a pint of something. Ed sees a pile of clothes beside his stool. Ed looks towards the door he just entered then back at the naked man.

"A free drink of your choice when you're naked," a blond, bearded man seated at the bar tells Ed. He vaguely recognizes the man.

"Really?"

"That's seriously with a capital S," the man tells Ed.

Ed hesitates then takes a seat around the bar corner from him.

"How you doin', Rescue Man? Nice to see you." The guy smiles. "Shane. Originally we were hopin' that women would be taking off their clothes." He shakes his head as if he remembers something funny. "Pedro wrote it on the board one Mardi Gras night two years ago. It stuck. Now it's our Mardi Gras special. The bar figured out they can make way more from the gawkers coming to check out the nakeds than they lose on the free drinks. Usually the ones takin' off their clothes start out confident and end up not nearly so much. Naked people can get pretty uncomfortable fast in a bar full of clothed people." The man's ready to launch into a nonstop lecture. He's clearly used to talking to strangers.

"Guess that's true," Ed says about being stared at naked. He feels like he hasn't spoken to an adult for a very long time. Ariel doesn't count for a number of reasons. "It's Shane?"

"Yup. We met at the accident, but I wouldn't expect you to remember me."

Ed looks at the young naked man down the way. He seems like a college student, maybe a fraternity brother working up his courage before a hazing. A couple of black guys talk loudly at the far end, not paying any attention to the naked man.

"Almost always, only guys take their clothes off, we found out," Shane says. "Their tits don't catch the light, you know what I mean."

A woman might feel awkward drinking a drink, sitting at a regular bar without a shirt or bra on, Ed supposes. Or pants or underwear. A man can hide his genitals in his lap, but breasts grow from a different part of the torso.

Ed looks for a bartender and glances at the naked man again. The guy gulps his beer as though he can't wait to get his clothes back on.

Why wouldn't the French Quarter strippers flock to the place to—how has he heard the Harrises say it lately?—get their drink on, before heading off to work for the night? And then Ed has another slow-brained realization. Strippers work for way more than drinks. Probably most of them, anyway. The professionals just wouldn't bother.

"Our very own Tokyo Rose was in *Gentlemen's Quarterly* magazine," Shane says. "They wrote about the Mardi Gras special. You may or may not be surprised by how many people have taken their clothes off in here since they ran the article." Shane pauses. "Rescue Man."

"Sorry. Ed," Ed says and stands, leaning to extend his hand. Something has just occurred to him. "Do you, would you know—is my neighbor hanging out here sometimes? Philomenia?" Ed has wondered about her dignified traipsing across the street for a while.

"Who?" The blond man stands and shakes Ed's hand.

"The lady," Ed says, and the good pre-med bartender comes out from a back room and over to Ed. What's his name? José? "How you doing," Ed says and extends his hand again. "Good to see you under different circumstances."

"Yeah, hey, good to see you."

"Ed," Shane tells the bartender. "And that's the man who invented the naked drink, Pedro. Pedro, Ed, Ed, Pedro. All right then. Pedro, put Ed's drink on my tab."

"What'll you have?"

What do people drink in bars? "Whatever the naked guy's having," Ed says loudly enough so that the naked man turns and raises his glass in a toast.

"Good call," Pedro says. "Pilsner Urquell ain't cheap. Way to stick it to Shane." Pedro flips a pint glass up from a low shelf and moves to the taps.

"The little shit has a surly bartender act," Shane says.

"Hey, Shane. Did I tell you Urquell's gone up? Twenty bucks a pint."

"Well, Rescue Man deserves a drink, whatever it costs."

The naked man, the bearded man, and Rescue Man. When Ed gets his drink, the three hold theirs up. "Cheers," Ed says.

The naked man finishes his and grabs his clothes off the floor.

Ed decides he wants to know badly enough. When the young man's put on his boxers, Ed asks, "Why?"

"Why not?"

Huh. Why not. Ed could have two free drinks in a row if he took his clothes off for the next one. When's the last time he took off his clothes in public? Has he ever? Sure he did. Years ago. They had the protest at Reed. Ed smiles at the memory. Over two hundred of them, a mad, penis-and-breast-slapping dash across campus.

Why not a naked drink?

Because he has dinner later. The kids would know things weren't right if he didn't come home on time. He's always home. He's the constant. Ariel's schedule sure doesn't let her be any kind of constant. That and Ariel herself. What time is it? He could have a second pint. He'll buy it, though.

"So, have you had your naked drink already?" Ed asks Shane. The beer tastes great, Ed thinks.

"I take my freebie as late as I can. When it's the darkest."

"That's the truth," Pedro says from the bar sink. "The man might look like he's drinking in Margaritaville, but trust me, you don't want to see the rest."

"I'd never let Miss P see me naked," Shane says. "I'll have mine after she leaves. She is a lady, after all."

"Philomenia, the neighbor, you mean?"

"Is that her real name?"

The naked drinker, finished dressing, raises his hand. "Hasta mañana, Pedro. I'm bringin' the boys."

"Bring the ladies, would ya?" Pedro says. Ed is aware of the television-style banter of their talk. He can understand why men would want to leave the house for a drink in the evening.

The door tinkles with the sound of rusty jingle bells on a string as the man goes out. "Has Philomenia seen any naked people yet?" Ed asks. He practically guzzles his beer. It's delicious. "Does she even drink?"

"She's had three drinks in three months," Shane says, "and I bought her all three. She's turned down thirty times as many."

The entire scenario blows Ed's mind. Why is Philomenia, of all the neighbors, hanging out at Tokyo Rose? Ed was certain she thought the place despicable.

"She cooks the pants off everybody I know," Pedro says, washing glasses.

"Really?" Ed asks. What's the deal, they moved onto a block of amateur chefs? "She brings food over? When naked people sit at the bar?"

"It's the first day of the season," Shane says. "She doesn't, well . . ." He looks at Pedro. They both start laughing. "Likely Miss P doesn't know about the Mardi Gras special."

Oh, to be a fly on that wall! Ed thinks.

"Look," Pedro says. He walks over and puts his hands on the bar, leaning into his shoulders. He's a good-looking kid, Ed notices. "We love Miss P's cooking, and she's been real nice to us lately. But she'd been after the owners, the manager—everybody—for fuck, what, five years? Since we opened. Calling the cops every other night till the cops themselves told her she had to stop or she'd get charged with something."

"I can't say I'm all that surprised." Ed drains his beer.

"You know it, Rescue Man," Pedro says. "Next one's on me."

Well, if Ed's offered two free beers in quick succession, why should he turn them down? The zombies haven't come to get him yet.

Cerise sits in her director's chair on the front porch and watches the block. She hasn't been out in a while, but it's Mardi Gras season, something that used to make her feel happy. Even back when she filled her days up behind the register checking out lines and lines of drunks buying canned beer to take to the parades, she still liked the season. Always seemed to her the days welcomed the upcoming year.

Today, though, just isn't provin' to be the same. She lifts her claw out of instinct to say hello to passersby but then puts it back down quick. Cerise might as well have a wooden hook on the end of her arm. A damn shame. It's all contained now, something she never used to think about, that skin contains the rest of your body.

She can't hardly move the claw, and she can't stop thinking she's waving her backside at the passing people, considering from where they took the graft. Cerise turns both her hands over in her lap and looks down at the palms. The left one is colored right, but the right hand— the right looks like something she might've patched on Marie's trousers when she was little. It don't work good, but she massages her fingers like she's told.

Funny, getting to be a left-hander in old age has changed her whole life. Never mind she can't use her right hand. It's like her whole head's been made to shift to the other side like the Discovery Channel says.

Cerise has come to see that a lot of, well, she guesses it'd be North American ways of being, from doorknobs to car controls to television remotes, are all made for right-handers. She's been practicing trying to write with her left hand, but she thinks it's useless. No way in hell is Cerise going to learn how to hold a pen properly enough at this point to let people decipher her message on the other end of a note card. Best she learn how to use a keyboard one-handed better than she can right now. The hen pecking's going to be her demise.

She scratches her left hand on everything, including the director's chair armrest. She comes back around, over and over, to all the animals on this globe that itch themselves. Some things everyone just has in common. She thought maybe she'd stop itching by now. Go figure. Maybe she's made it a habit.

Can't be much past eight when the Harrises, only the three of them, leave their house, the parents going to real jobs, the son Daniel going to a street job. Used to be they had a daughter with them sometimes going to school. "Sharon, Nate," Cerise says, raising her left hand. "Daniel."

"Miss Cerise," Daniel says first like he's tryin' to beat his parents to the punch. It makes Cerise smile.

"Daniel, you eat yourself a healthy lunch."

The child heads off towards the Bend, towards Pigeontown where she knows he works, same as where his older brother did before the accident.

It's hard for Cerise to think about the accident sometimes, but then her brain just does its thing. Maybe she could've used a broom handle or something to try to lift the grill, but she wasn't sweeping the damn porch when it all occurred. She was heading to make groceries, and Roy wasn't going to stop burning and wait for her to go back inside and look for a mop or some piece of wood layin' around.

In a dream, Cerise made the boy Michael get up on his broken leg and come drape over on the grill on top of Roy. It was to get the heat to cook him rather than Roy. It was sort of working, but Roy kept on with his groaning, and Michael's broken leg started bleeding, and the blood cooked up like the inside of a sausage, and then Cerise laid her hands on anyway.

The way Cerise tries to see it, you can't undo one damn thing. You wish you could, but you can't. The older she gets, the more she realizes that fact. You just can't undo what's already happened. And the older she gets, the more damn regrets she has about her past actions no matter what understanding she's come to.

She wishes, for example, that when she'd gotten pregnant with Marie, she'd not eaten so much seafood all the time. All she wanted was oyster po-boys with extra tomatoes. Now she keeps reading about how pregnant ladies shouldn't eat anything much out of the water at all. And she wishes that she'd told her sister how much she loved her when she was alive. They just never said the words coming up in their family, and now she can't ever say them to Desiree but in a prayer. Cerise wishes she'd been kinder to her sister the night she went on the date with that boy in that car. So many years ago, she thinks. Fifty-six last month. She wishes the Harris boy hadn't gotten on that motorcycle. Lord, she wishes he hadn't. But where can it stop? She wishes Michael's friend hadn't loaned it to the boy in the first place. She wishes Roy hadn't decided to grill. She wishes they had bought a regular-size grill rather than that damn barrel.

She will kill herself with wishes, Cerise thinks. Maybe that's how so many her age go.

She needs to find a way to get over her right hand.

Cerise opens her nutritional shake with her left hand and takes a sip. She tries her normal ways of helping her mood. She thinks about being legless in a wheelchair. She thinks about Roy having died. She thinks about Lil Thomas dying. She thinks about a hurricane actually hitting New Orleans again. She thinks about being alone. It's just a hand. It's just a hand. And it's still connected to her arm. Get over it, woman. Move forward. You don't got one other choice in the matter. You ain't going to lay down and die just yet, damn it.

Ed is spoiling Ella and Miles tonight, exactly his goal. They need some good attention. Ariel's working later than late. She can't object when she's not around.

Ed and the kids rode the streetcar to the corner of St. Charles and Napoleon where it stopped, as far as it goes during Mardi Gras when an Uptown parade route is cordoned off. They walked down St. Charles a number of blocks to the corner of Marengo.

Every single week without fail, Saturday evening makes Ed think about date night. For years, he's spent the night alone—not including the kids. He can't remember when Ariel had one off.

This Saturday evening, Ed looks around at the crowd of parade-goers near him. Many are coupled up. A teenaged boy tucks his hand into a chubby girl's back pocket. A pickup truck parked on the cross street with its tailgate down hosts a keg party, no less than ten young people dancing in the truck bed to music blaring from a porch nearby.

Ed keeps an eye on Miles, who runs around with other kids on the grassy middle of the shut-down boulevard. Miles and another boy chase the rest with cans of silly string. Ed bought Miles the stuff off one of the trolling pushcarts loaded down with a thousand different pieces of junk, all of them made in China or Mexico. Miles chose silly string and two boxes of snap 'n pops to throw on the pavement. Ella chose a plastic jeweled tiara, a glowing purple necklace, and a bag of penny candy.

The Sparta parade, followed by Pegasus, is supposed to roll at six. People and their ladders glut the curbs, children sitting in homemade box seats on top of the ladders, sitting on This Is Not a Step, waiting for the parades.

Ed would swear there are more ladders tonight than at any parade last year. He doesn't see black people with ladders, only white subur-banites, the ones who drive their behemoth SUVs into the city for a few hours and leave mounds of garbage behind. Sure, the ladder contrap-tions might let children see better, but, lined up, they create walls, expanses of ladders that people can't really see past or move around. Ed thinks the city needs to ban ladders too close to the curb.

Ella holds his hand and watches her wild-child brother. Sugared to near hyperglycemia, she bounces in place. Ed knows she'll be awake hours past her normal bedtime. Oh well. Kids should have treat days. New Orleans has a lot of special days. Ed is beginning to under-stand why.

Maybe he should have more himself. Adults deserve treat days too, don't they? He's raising children, providing everyone with a clean and habitable home, cooking nutritionally sound food. He should be allowed to spend time at Tokyo Rose when he wants to. Well, when he's able. A few treat hours here and there.

The other boy with silly string, a black boy, catches another black boy without anything for a counterweapon but a corndog. The little kid's been running around with it, making Ed nervous for well over a minute. Running and eating food on a pointed stick never go together very well.

Ed can't really tell which kids belong to which adults. The grown-ups stand drinking or sit in lawn chairs, socializing, not minding the children.

The one black boy sprays a wad of silly string all over the other black boy's corndog. The second screams to high hell. Miles stops running and watches. The boy with the corndog loses it. He smacks his mess-on-a-stick over the head of his aggressor. Ketchup and silly string splatter.

The bigger kid, the one with silly string, shoves on the other one, and suddenly they're scrapping on the matted grass and streetcar tracks.

A nearby white woman exposing too much cleavage says, "Hey, hey!" She holds a plastic cup of beer and wears a green feather boa around her neck. "Stop that!" The boys roll onto the woman's feet. "Hey!" Ed can see the decision playing across her drunken features: Should she pour her drink on the boys?

Ed waits and watches for the boys' parents to break it up. Miles seems to be waiting for the same thing, but nobody really intervenes. Ed's son remains frozen when the boy he's been chasing, a white boy with a buzz cut, figures out he's no longer in danger. He races at Miles, his arms extended, and, with the force of a small bulldozer, shoves Miles to the ground as well. Aggression has taken hold of the children.

Ed rushes out and breaks apart the tussle between Miles and his attacker. He looks to the other two boys still fighting. Nobody does anything. The boys continue to roll around. Ed drags Miles by his upper arm to the scuffle of the other boys and picks up the kid on top. "Cut it out!" Ed hollers. "That's enough! Go on. Get back to your families."

A couple adults nearby applaud Ed.

The black boy he has by the shirt collar, the one who had the corn-dog, stares directly in Ed's eyes. He can't be more than six years old, max. Ed expects the boy to swear at him, but instead, he starts to cry. The kid cowers, hanging in his loose shirt in Ed's hand like he's slung in a hammock. "Stand up," Ed tells the boy. "I'm not going to hurt you."

The boy still on the ground stares wide-eyed up at Ed. "It's okay," Ed says. "Just get up. It's okay."

The boy stands and stares at Ed as though he's a principal.

"Are you okay?" Ed asks.

The boy just stares. Ed realizes he still grips the other boy's shirt in his fist. Ed lets go.

"He my brother," the bigger one says suddenly.

"You two are brothers?" Ed asks.

The beat-up one nods.

"You shouldn't fight," Ed says, not knowing another piece of advice to offer just then.

They both take off down the boulevard, racing on for more than a block. Where are they going? Where's their family?

Miles twists out of Ed's grip and immediately shoves his way into the crowd. Ed stands alone, a schmo just trying to do the right thing. He looks at the tens of people suddenly watching the Ed show.

Ed raises his hands and shrugs. His Rescue Man cape is stuck up the crack of his ass. Maybe he really just doesn't understand this city. Probably not at all. Everybody else just stood around letting the boys work it out. Is that what you're supposed to do? Is that how life works, as long as nobody gets seriously hurt?

Ed looks to where he left Ella. He doesn't see her. He looks left and right from the spot where he's sure they just were. No Ella. He looks back to the spot in the crowd where Miles disappeared. No son.

Don't panic. Hang in there.

Panic sets in almost immediately. Ed feels the absolute necessity to yell. He doesn't even think about it. The urge comes from a primordial source. Ed holds his hands to his mouth and shouts into the crowd, "Ella! Miles!"

"Jesus, buddy," somebody says back. Ed looks at the person, a white man holding a styrofoam bowl in his hand, shoveling a plastic fork of something into his mouth.

Ed shoves his way into the crowd. "Miles! Ella!" Ed bumps around between folding chairs and people who've marked their patch of ground with picnic blankets. Ed will clear the entire block in one fell swoop if he cannot find his children in five seconds flat.

Ed spies something glowing purple in the crowd. It's a necklace.

"Hi, Daddy," Ella says. She holds out her bag of candies to an elderly black woman in a lawn chair. Sharing, like a good girl.

"No, thank you," the woman says to Ella.

"Where's your brother?" Ed asks.

The black woman pours bottled water into her hand and rubs it on Ella's sticky face. "There you go. And see? Yo daddy's here right fast." The woman wipes at Ella's face with a napkin next, saying to Ed without looking at him, "Beautiful child."

Ella knows she's being talked about, showing her teeth in a grin, when the sirens on the police cars clearing the way for the parades sound out in the street. What is Miles wearing? How can Ed see him in this fucking bedlam? "Thank you," Ed says to the woman. "Come on, we have to find Miles." He picks Ella up.

"You lose more'n one child? Mmm mmm." The woman shakes her head.

Ed gets out of the crowd and walks the streetcar tracks back and forth, scanning. It's the wrong place. Everyone has turned towards the boulevard to watch for the start of the parade. Ed needs to get to the street. Miles would head for the front, no question.

On horseback, black men in cowboy hats and fringed chaps clop down the street. The horses take fancy steps. People applaud. Ed works his way through the crowd as the horses move away. "Horses!" Ella exclaims.

"Ella, what's Miles wearing today? What do his clothes look like, sweetie?"

Ella shrugs in Ed's arms, fingering her glowing necklace, chin on chest. She's picking up Ed's vibe.

"Help me remember," Ed almost pleads. The horses dance away

down the avenue, but a random popping remains. Ed knows. He just
knows. He heads directly to the sound.

And there the little shit stands, throwing his snap 'n pops into the
street during a parade gap. Another older boy across the way has a box
too, and they wing the tiny gunpowder spitballs towards each other's
feet as hard as they can. "Miles," Ed says sternly a few people away
from his son, "come here right now."

"Just a minute," Miles says, not even looking at Ed, digging through
the sawdust of his box for another mini bomb.

Ed steps out into the gap. Coming his way, white-hooded white men
on horseback beneficently anoint parade-goers with odd pope gestures.
Ed grabs Miles' wrist and pulls him away from the street through the
crowds, apologizing to people as they bump their way to an open space.

Ed squats on the streetcar tracks and puts Ella down. She rests one
small hand on Ed's shoulder as she shakes her candy bag in her other
tight fist, looking intently at what's left. Swedish fish flop. A distant
marching band's music drifts their way. Ed squares Miles' shoulders to
face him. "Miles, what you did is unacceptable. Absolutely and completely wrong. You can never, ever do that again. Do not ever leave me
or your mother and walk into a crowd. Do you hear me?"

Ella stops her bag shaking and stares at her brother.

"What?" Miles asks in a Pee-wee Herman voice. "I can't hear you."
Miles takes a snap 'n pop and throws it at the streetcar track. It misses,
landing unexploded in the dust beside the metal rail.

Ed stands, spins Miles around, and spanks him.

17

All the housekeeping staff get to leave after turndown service, as Ariel insists, unless there's extraordinary P 'n B work to do. Most of them have some form of family to get back to in the evenings, or more often a second job.

The Belle feels better at night, a little more room to breathe. Fewer people Ariel needs to govern. Most days she's a woman covered in ticks.

When Warren's big back is turned, Ariel gives Javier the eye, her nod.

The parade lumbering down Canal will keep her on-site for hours still. The guests have made their communal way out to the boulevard in their clanking attire of plastic beads. The kitchen is prepped for the late-night menu.

Usually it goes like this: Ariel makes herself scarce for a while. Javier takes his break or finishes his shift. She flashes the room number with her fingers at him when she can or, when she has no other option, leaves it written on a slip of paper slid under the edge of his employee locker. She's vaguely aware of the fact that her handwritten numbers could be used against her.

Through room 341's window, Ariel watches tourists ooze down the street, everyone moving towards Canal.

Ariel doesn't understand the Mardi Gras holiday, but she's happy for the excuse to stay away from home. Life around Ed has proven next to impossible. The kids have been monsters since Christmas.

The knock sounds.

Ariel closes the curtains. She answers the door.

Javier shoves past. He says something in Spanish she can't understand, but it makes no difference. It's the quality of the foreign that tamps down her reservations, quashes her higher reason. He smiles, his teeth pretty against his dark skin. He lusts after me, Ariel thinks. He has never used the Spanish word she recognizes for dirty female anatomy, so he must be saying something complimentary.

She has melted slowly over the course of his shift today, started thinking about the finish by midmorning. One direct look from him in the kitchen, and the burner gets lit. Lately, when she's sitting at her desk in her office and decides to go to the kitchen for something or other, her nipples harden. He could ring a bell and she'd start salivating.

Javier pulls an accordioned strand of wrapped condoms from his pocket and tosses it on the bed. Ariel can't get caught buying them with Ed in town. She wears an IUD.

"Wanna fuck the boss?" Ariel says. She raises her skirt.

"Díme más, guapita sucia."

She will never let them make a mess. Climbing between hotel sheets is off limits. Since Ivan, they've spent no more than fifteen minutes together in a room.

But she has lost count of the number of times. She wonders what that means. Do other people keep track? Men would. Javier probably knows exactly. The conquest of a GM would be worth a count, or so she thinks. Or maybe she hopes.

Ariel believes Javier now asks her to raise her skirt further, which she does.

She's come to learn he's a leg and ass man. Javier gives props to her tits, but only because he seems to think he should. She's never cared all that much about her own breasts, so she's fine with his predilection. Once, on his knees above her as she lay on her back, he straddled her face. She licked him wet and then pushed him towards her chest, squeezing her breasts together with her arms so he could slide inside the cleavage. It seemed to work for Javier. Anytime he gets away without wearing a condom is good for him. He moved between her tits while she called him names, puckered her lips, and stuck out her tongue. She worked her fingers between her legs, but still he came far quicker, long before she ever might have.

If Ed ever leaves town again without her, Ariel will let Javier into other places, do things that will make him want her every moment of every day. But some things take time, tenderness, commodities they have little of tonight.

Ariel and Javier kiss. She wears lipstick that doesn't transfer. They take off their clothes, Ariel quite carefully. They place their clothes on the two double beds, then couple in the narrow, carpeted space between.

It is never amazing, and still, beforehand, it is often all Ariel thinks about. As soon as it is over, though, she wants nothing more than to secure her job and leave the room unscathed.

Javier flushes the latex evidence away.

She attempts small talk as she dresses. "Are you going to catch any of Mardi Gras this year?"

"Where is the time?" He pulls his knit boxers up his legs.

"Exactly."

He nods. "Exactly."

They finish dressing. Ariel picks up the packages of condoms. "You want to take these or should I?" In the past, he has sometimes taken them. Other times, she has carried them back with her inside her bra to her office, where she stashes them in her locked file cabinet. Since she and Javier have started what they have, Ariel wonders if there wouldn't be a photo book opportunity based on locked file cabinets. Imagine what would appear. Open the drawer and line up the contents. Bottles of booze. Drugs. A dildo in the drawer of a banker, an incriminating Polaroid in an executive secretary's. A strand of condoms in a hotel general manager's. Look at what we keep locked up at work.

Javier only lifts his jaw, indicating to Ariel that she take them. So she will.

She always checks the hallway first, as casually as she can, then sends Javier on his way if it's all clear. So far, it's always been all clear. He grabs her ass on the way out. She'll follow in another couple of minutes.

Cribs be one of Fearius favorite shows, fo sho. It his planning show, give
him ideas how he gone deck out his house when he earn it. The cars
themselfs be worth studying, Fearius think. All the music artists he
hate, alongside the ones he love, they all show they bedrooms and
refrigerators to the world. Usually they finish up the show with the
rides. Some them have what, like a dozen cars and motorcycles and
ATVs and shit. Boats. The pimp on the screen now have all his cars in
the same color, the color of his hometown football team, a ugly motherfuckin green.

Taliqwa funny these days, so Fearius, he been hangin at home during
his down time. He and Taliqwa talk, but it aint like they *talk*. She distracted. School proving difficult. She said her Baton Rouge friend worryin about being pregnant. Fearius saw a pregnant girl today, probably
made only thirteen, fourteen years of age. She waitin at the streetcar
stop. Her bellybutton poking forward under her sweater. She dint look
like so much in the face, but her little ol legs. They just sticks. Made
Fearius a bit sick in the stomach, if he had to make his feelings known.

That and he be worried Taliqwa displacing her friend pregnancy. He
understand the word displacing all the way through.

"Daniel!" Moms yell from the kitchen. "Now!"

Why the fuck he hafta have dinner, Fearius dont know. He buy his
food outside the house, dont ever eat much at the table. Still, sometime
he like to sit with the family and chat. It a ritual and whatever. They
bust up laughing most nights less Pops get angry about Muzzle or hisself. Usually, they just pretend, same as in the mornings, that Fearius in
school but maybe failing or some such. It easiest, make the day easier.
Pops, he just want him some peace, he always say. Want a little peace
under the sun be his expression. Dont want to mess with nothing but
making a honest day wage.

It the problem with Pops. Aint no such thing in the honest world.
Aint no peace and aint no day wage worth how much he be toiling. No
way Fearius gone become his old man.

Fearius never even really know the man he call Pops. The ol man dint never touch any of them kids in a nice way coming up, just looked at em, smacked somebody when he think it necessary. Sometimes his Pops make Fearius imagine a lion out in Africa, a animal that make babies but could eat em an not care if he decided he hungry. Usually, the old man happy enough to have the company to growl at and roll around in for a hour or whatever before he go to sleep. More often though, he go out, stay away for the night, come back before sunup. Whatever. He and Moms have a arrangement or something. It always been that way. Least they keep a house. Least they keep a roof for over the nephews and nieces heads.

Cribs flashing through one more time what the pimp done show in his house. Theys way too much green color everyplace, but Fearius like the idea of the Jacuzzi in the bedroom. How great that be to bang and then go sit in a Jacuzzi? It spell relief like Rolaids.

Klameisha walk in the room holding Kymika. "Danny, you dont get your ass up you know what gone happen." She step a little closer and say low, "Give us a good night, lil bro. I needs it fierce. Just a little peace."

Why everybody in the house want peace when all they make is the opposite? Still, Fearius oughten to listen to his sister. Not no Alphonse or nobody else gone know if Fearius decide he want to obey a woman who not his own moms right now. Fearius, he dont want a bad night neither.

Fearius stand up. "Heard ya, K."

Klameisha hold out her hand like Fearius should dap. She so white-ified, he think. She got her two babies, a terrible burden, but otherwise, she just a nerd. When he earn his own crib, Fearius gone buy K a year at the university. Not at no Delgado neither. He gone buy her a year at UNO. She too book smart for her be wastin her life sittin at home with babies. Maybe he help her out with tuition before he have his own house. Life be short.

"Whatever," he say and pass her by.

Moms insist they all sit in the same room, includin the babies. The adults get the table, the babies the floor iffin they in a car seat. Usually they go in the playpen in the corner. Stuff em all in with some juice bottles, shut em up for a meal. Arlet been protesting lately though, gettin trapped in there. Fearius plunk down at the table and wonder what Muzzle be eatin these days, iffin he eatin any food. Fearius aint even hear from his own blood brother since he in the hospital.

Dude on Cribs has him a snowmobile. Fearius love to ride one some-time in his life, go racin over snow. You can eat snow, Fearius under-stand. He wonder on what it taste like. Plain, likely, like a sno-ball with no syrup.

"Daniel," Pops say at the table, "pass the mustard."

"Cut the mustard?" Fearius say. "But I dont got to."

The table bust up laughin, Fearius gift. He can always make em laugh if nothing more. The kids in the corner make noises like they tryin to laugh with the table too. Moms reach over and grab his ear an twist it, same she always done, but she do it nice. Always. Even when she know she suppose to discipline or whatever, she never hurt Fearius really. She careful not to twist off his ear.

"Not what I hear comin outta you at night," Debutanté say, an every-body laugh again, pretending Fearius pass gas when he sleep.

What the expression? Tooshay? "Tooshay," Fearius say.

They all dig into the fried chicken from up on Louisiana Avenue. Moms made a special trip, even heated up corn an baked biscuits from the bust open roll you whack on the counter edge, Fearius favorite. He been slippin cash into the Moms wallet the last weeks. He bein rewarded, maybe. Maybe she give up her hard position seein what hap-pen to Muzzle. Nobody talk about him no more. Moms and Pops both make it the law in the house. It like he dead when he not even. Fearius wonder when they gone get the word about him make it true.

"Angelique AWOL again," Pops say, not ask.

"You find her, Nate, you let me know," Moms say. "Go walk around the parade route, please. Or, know what? She been enjoying text mes-saging lately. Why you dont go text message her, tell her to join her family for dinner."

Pops roll his eyes. The white part show yellow. Fearius dont remem-ber when they a different color. "She cant throw our money away no better?"

"She gone text back say save her some wings," Fearius say.

"Yeah," Debutanté says, standin to tend to Trevor who done tipped over in the playpen, not big enough to right hisself. "I eat her wings. Put em on my plate, thanks very much."

Everybody chuckle for Debutanté, cuttin up, tryin to keep the dinner time nice. Good for D. She not always very funny.

The new maid that Ariel didn't want to hire but the head of housekeeping hired anyway appears as the elevator doors part. "What are you doing up here, Miss Ariel?" the woman asks.

Ariel steps into the elevator, thinking as fast as she can. This new woman—Ronda? Rhoda?—was too brash for Ariel right away. Too much attitude, not enough respect. Now Ariel's certain her initial read was right. Who asks the GM such a question? "Tell me your name again?" Ariel asks and pushes the ground-floor button.

"Rhoda," the woman says.

"How are you enjoying the Belle?"

"It's easy compared to the Hilton."

Well, no shit. "How's that?" The elevator doors refuse to close. Ariel hits the button again. "The Hilton's bigger, of course," Ariel says. The newbies get the crappiest shifts. Rhoda would have to stay the latest tonight. Any Mardi Gras night, the long-timers are pretty scarce. As long as the Belle has an adequate staff count across the board, Ariel lets the other managers determine scheduling in their respective departments. The elevator door finally closes.

"I just saw Mr. Javier up here too," Rhoda says. "Just a minute ago." The woman stares straight ahead at the elevator doors, praying mantis jaws closing down on a suspicion.

Is this a joke? Blackmail straight out of the chute? Rhoda's been here maybe a month, and it's already time to try for something bigger than crap housekeeping, is it? Oh, not tonight, sweetie. Get your redneck flat ass back to Chalmette. "You're from Chalmette if I'm remembering correctly, right, Rhoda?" Ariel's heart beats a crazy beat beneath her shirt. She's bothered by her own nervousness.

"No," Rhoda says. "We stay over in Violet."

Ariel checks out this brazen housekeeper. Her hair, what must have been a dark brown to begin with, didn't make it all the way through a bleaching. It's now a funny orange. She has saddlebags, and her uniform tugs across her crotch, making the mathematical signs that indicate lesser than or greater than, those sideways Vs, right at her groin. She wants something, something more than what she has. Ariel has no choice but to put her in her place.

"So a dishwasher told me a few weeks ago," Ariel starts and waits till Rhoda actually looks at her face. It's a test. "You know how they call the young women from Chalmette 'Chalmations'?" Ariel stands to her full height and faces the maid straight on.

"I heard it," Rhoda says.

The elevator dings the ground floor. "Don't they call all of you from Violet Violations?"

The doors open, and Ariel walks out. It was stupid to jab at the girl, but what could happen? Rhoda's going to sue? Well. Maybe Ariel will fire her first. Ariel has kids to feed.

When Ariel pulls into their driveway, she sees Ed on the porch, waiting. She's happy they have a driveway, considering all the parked cars on the street, there for the crap bar, Ed's new hangout. The multitudes of Tulane and Loyola parking stickers on their block give the kids away. Maybe her husband's got his eye on a girl gone wild.

Ed raises his hand in greeting. Ariel raises hers in response. Jesus, he's so damn dejected lately. And still, she simply can't muster the sympathy she needs to help improve his mood. There's something about self-pity that prompts the exact opposite reaction than the desired one in Ariel. The more Ed wallows, the less sorry she feels for him and the less she regrets her actions.

The spanking incident essentially cinched the deal for her. He sobbed about it, telling her the blow-by-blow details. But there's simply no excuse for spanking, especially when Miles is such a decent kid. None whatsoever. She doesn't care how bad Ed feels.

As Ariel gathers her briefcase and water bottle and purse, Ed approaches her car door. "They're watching the boob tube," he says, leaning in to give her a peck on the cheek. "I'm off to the Rose."

He's shortened the name of it even? "Nice to see ya," she says.

"Don't worry. Not that you would. I'll be back." Ariel watches him in the rearview. He walks down the driveway and across the street. He doesn't look back.

He just sat there on the porch waiting for her to get home so he could leave? Unbelievable. Ariel slams her car door and locks it. At least she won't have to look at his hangdog eyes. Go get drunk again, Ed. Just go.

Inside, Ariel hollers her hello to the kids. The TV blasts something she doesn't like the sound of. East Coast accents. Neither Miles nor Ella acknowledges Ariel's hello. She almost runs into the room.

Tony Soprano fucks a woman who's missing a leg.

Ariel grabs the remote from Miles' hand and turns off the television. Both her kids gawk at the blank screen. Ed and she have a bunch of channels blocked on the downstairs TV. Did Ed watch something earlier in the day and forget to reset it? "*Hello*, I said," Ariel says to the both of them, moving to stand in front of the screen. "Hello!"

"Hello, Mommy!" Ella yells back. She stands and hops on one foot towards Ariel. "The naked lady," Ella says as she hops, "has a plastic leg that comes off." Ella's mouth is stained green.

"Some people have accidents—what did you eat for dinner?"

Miles does his caught-in-the-act act. He goes effusive. He leaps up and races to wrap his arms around Ariel's waist. "I love you, Mommy," he says, trying out the sound of the word he gave up at the start of this last school year.

"Show me your tongue," Ariel says, holding her son's chin in her hand.

Miles sticks out his tongue. It's neon green.

"What did you eat for dinner?"

Ella wraps her arms around Ariel too. "Noodles," her daughter says.

"Noodles and what?"

"Just noodles," Miles says and reaches up to try to pet Ariel's hair, his toddler habit that got him to sleep.

"Miles," Ariel says.

"And butter," Ella says. "I love you too, Mommy."

"I love you both very much." She rubs their backs and runs her hands over their heads. Buttered noodles are Ella's favorite, but they're not any kind of dinner alone. Ariel kicks off her heels. "Okay, okay. Let your *mommy* get changed." Ariel gives Miles the look that says, I know what you're up to, and I'm going to let you off the hook for now. She sees he understands perfectly.

Ariel takes the remote control with her. "No TV till I get back down," she says, and Miles nods vigorously. Both the kids have adopted that frantic nodding. She'd like to squelch it soon.

Ariel's skull fills with gunk as she changes as fast as she can. She can smell Javier on her skin. What is Ed doing? What the hell is he doing? It's Mardi Gras, and he's across the street partying with college kids. He's serving their own children buttered noodles for dinner—and what else? She'll search the trash. Ariel's guessing green popsicles or candy. He's unlocked HBO.

Her panties are damp from earlier. She puts them in her bathroom sink and runs water over them. Miles didn't seem as confused as she would have hoped watching Tony Soprano and his mistress. He seemed very, very interested. Miles has yet to turn eight, never mind Ella. Ariel pulls on a pair of old jeans worn through at the knees. Would Ed have purposely left the lock off the cable to try to teach her a lesson? Ariel, despite her anger, can't imagine it. He loves the kids above all else. He wouldn't let them see what they shouldn't. She puts on an old T shirt.

If she can smell Javier, can Ed? Not that she ever really gives him a chance to sniff. Warren says men have a more consistent sense of smell.

"Is it time for popcorn?" Ariel asks, heading down the stairs. She wants some. She could use some bolstering for the talk she gets to give, helping Miles and Ella to understand what can happen between adults.

Alphonse ring Fearius new cell when he already asleep. His hours different than the bossmans. Fearius scramble for his phone. "Yo." Not one other soul have the number yet, so it gotta be Alphonse.

"The time here, solja."

"How that?" Fearius ask.

"We get there. First, Fear, yo bro motha fuckin sick, I swear. He sick in the head an sick in the body. He just fuckin gone. I stepped out on some tree limbs to check his whereabouts and what all, ya heard? Took me some work cause I a person who care. Yo bro, he a twig with a limp, friend. You best tell your moms or whatever you need."

What Fearius suppose to say? "That fucked up, A."

"Dont think you know the half of it, lil man."

An now what Fearius suppose to say? He dont wanna know what all Muzzle done. Fearius his own person. He aint just a lil brother.

Alphonse sit and wait, dont say nothing more on the other side the phone. Fearius sit and wait too. Eventually Alphonse say, "Never mind yo bro. Time to step up. You got yo first job."

Whoa na. Sellin Avon and doin jobs dont have one thing in the common. It aint right. "How that?" Fearius ask.

"You due."

How the fuck Fearius due? He dint buy into no fuckin killin game. Whoa na. Fuck him fuck him fuck him. "How you see that, A?"

Alphonse laugh so loud on the other end Fearius hold his phone away from his ear. And then, like of course, Alphonse done laughing completely. He go silent. "It your turn. You steppin up."

Fearius dont have a answer but the one Alphonse make him give. "Bring it."

18

Prancie dresses for a night out during Carnival season. She has no certain recollection of when she did this last. She would venture a guess of fifteen years at the very least.

Only half an hour ago tonight, she rose from their marital bed beside her sleeping husband and entered her closet to change into something appropriate for the outing.

This morning, Joe's overseeing physician claimed that all preexisting tumors have been successfully removed with no additional signs of new polyps. Prancie cannot 'wrap her head around' such a notion. She holds on to the hope that the scourge has simply moved to a new and more lethal place of residence in Joe's body that the doctors have yet to detect.

Tonight, Prancie will leave their home at eleven and make her way across the street carrying nothing more than her handbag. She will bring no offerings of food. She will be the person she is and see if she is welcomed. This afternoon when she delivered the barbequed miniature sausages in sauce that Thirsty requested, Shane said he would keep a fire burning for her, so Prancie must believe that at least one person in the establishment will be kind.

Prancie considers a number of shawls. She determines the golden yellow one provides the necessary flair required for the season. With the air of a person deserving of an entrance, Prancie flings the end of the pashmina across her shoulder and descends the stairs, Joe be damned.

The sight from her very own front door prohibits Prancie from leaving the house. She is nervous. Where is her fortitude? *Without self-reliance, Philomenia, you will go only where a leaf floats. Listen to me.*

Suddenly Prancie does not care about her personal credo pertaining to alcohol in the slightest respect. She will find some fortitude in a bottle of cognac. She steps over the creaking floorboards and into the parlor. She removes the key to the cabinet from its hiding place and turns the lock. Inside she finds what might usually be found in any fully appointed Southern home, a number of pistols and a goodly amount of alcohol, along with photocopies of deeds, trusts, and the rest.

Prancie settles on a bottle of Hennessy. Its color and shape both call to her. She knows that a snifter is required, withdraws one from the shelf, and removes the corked top from the bottle. Decidedly, Prancie thinks as she pours, her life has made a number of turns these last months. She will continue forward on her new path. If such a principle as justice exists in this world, she will receive hers.

It is not, as they say, smooth. The liquor moves from the top of her palate and straight into her sinuses. She stifles a cough. Prancie remembers Humphrey Bogart and Lauren Bacall and Cary Grant. They seemed always to have a snifter of something in hand, functioning perfectly well while drinking alcohol. She thinks of her own Joe. She is stronger than he. Prancie swallows a goodly amount in three gulps, what she imagines to be approximately a quarter cup.

She quietly rinses the snifter in the kitchen sink, dries it with a cotton towel, and returns it to its original place. She does not expect Joe to notice. She does, however, need to sit awhile and consider the results of the Hennessy.

Or quite possibly, she should do no such thing. Likely, while Joe sleeps, Prancie should leave the house.

After rechecking her reflection in the entryway mirror, Prancie departs.

The Tokyo Rose glows like a Parisian bistro across the street as Prancie steps off her porch. In no way does it prove to be a quiet place as she approaches, but she welcomes a bit of noise. As she closes in on her beckoning oasis, she sees that a large man on a barstool sits outside the open door. He must be what they call a doorman. Prancie straightens her spine, presents her assets, and approaches.

The very large man's thighs hang partially over the edges of his stool. It would likely be an uncomfortable position for him. "Hello," Prancie says.

"ID," the large man says.

"Sorry?"

"ID."

"I am not sure, pardon, I—"

The man squints his small eyes at Prancie and only then seems able to see her for the first time. He flings his bald head at the mayhem inside. Prancie assumes she has been allowed admittance. "Would you care for a water or a cold drink?" she asks the man before passing.

"Ma'am?" He raises his eyebrows as though she has spoken Chinese.

"Would you like a beverage from inside?"

"I'm cool, thanks."

"Not a problem," Prancie has learned to say.

Inside, young people slither between one another and crush against the bar. Many hold bills in front of them or over their heads, attempting to obtain drinks. Still many others already drink from large plastic cups, certainly full of copious amounts of alcoholic beverages, Carnival punches and whatnot.

Prancie feels quite light despite the close crowd and the distinct heat. She removes her pashmina immediately, folding it carefully over her forearm. She feels a touch like a matador, or a senorita.

Thirsty, behind the bar with two other workers, likely cannot even see her. One of his employees pushes his dripping finger on a few buttons of a stereo system, and a new song begins. The throngs of young people respond to it almost immediately, many of the young women beginning to dance in a distinct manner.

Prancie looks surreptitiously around the room for Shane. It is very dark.

Some of the lyrics of the song playing become clear, but as Prancie deciphers them, she grows uncertain as to the accuracy of her hearing. She believes she hears an African American singing, *"Is that your ass or*

your mama have reindeer . . ." The young women farther into the bar-
room begin not to dance so much as to pump their behinds up and
down. Certainly Prancie is not understanding the lyrics clearly. What
do female bottoms and reindeer have to do with one another? Prancie
tries for a minute but cannot find a common denominator. She very
much wants to find Shane and make this outing worthwhile.

The young people encroach and jostle. Prancie decides to move in
the general direction of the dear and delightful Shane and his usual
perch. She will figure a way to accidentally touch his bare chest once
more. Oh, what an escapade that was! How much fun to be able to purposefully play with another adult! Prancie should pat her own shoulder
for taking the walk across the street at such a time tonight. She will find
Shane and enjoy her visit here, the very place that in years past has filled
so many a journal. This month the Tokyo Rose has also taken up numerous journals, but now for different reasons.

Prancie makes very little headway towards Shane's regular seat. The
young people shove quite relentlessly on those who do not shove back.

The bar is dark as ink and musky, and, at the moment, quite luscious.
Prancie's entire front feels warm, as though heat has begun to radiate
from her stomach and out towards her skin. She lays her hand against
her sternum. The music seems suddenly louder as now both the young
women and the men become more active in their dancing. Prancie hears
the distinct lyrics above the din, *"shake your tailfeather."* That! That is
what the young people are doing, shaking their tailfeathers!

She pushes through now, confident in her ability to find Shane and
to procure a drink from Thirsty. Prancie does not even see the small
half circle of coeds gathered densely around the bar. She sees no more
than the modicum of breathing room beyond them. Only when she
bursts through does she realize the others are cordoning off the region
for a purpose.

From behind, she sees two men sitting at the bar. But something is
amiss. Neither wears any clothing.

Has she entered the dream state in a public place? Such an occur-
rence would be unfortunate. She has no knowledge of her behavior
when she goes to that place. She has no memories. She must leave.

Prancie looks quickly to the front door and the circled young people around her. They seem highly animated, the young women's makeup suddenly garish and bright, even in the low light.

Prancie clutches her pashmina to her chest now. Why are naked men sitting at the bar? Why does nobody acknowledge this fact?

Something makes her glance again at the men, at their freckled backs and moderately fuzzy buttocks. Why, how should they come to be here like this? Prancie feels she is suddenly part of the attention as the others assemble around her now as well as the two men. She looks to the bartenders. Thirsty is clothed and very busy. Carnival season taxes all bartenders without question. Thirsty, Thurman, seems very real. She waves hello to him, but he does not see her.

And then one of the naked men does the unconscionable. He spins on his own barstool, stands, and exposes himself to the rest of the room. The music continues, and Prancie is certain the moths that flap across her vision during emotional moments have followed her across the street to this terrible place.

"We can even do it slow, we can even do it slow, take it where . . . just take that ass to the floor."

The coeds scream and hoot. Prancie sees only a penis that does not resemble Joe's in almost any way.

"Grab it!" a young man says to Prancie. He pushes her towards the man. She stumbles in her heels. Women shriek gleefully.

Suddenly, Prancie collides with a naked chest. She knows this chest. So much laughter. Laughter fills her ears.

Prancie lifts her head from the bare chest to look at the face of the dream place's naked man.

Shane Geautreaux stares back.

From the vinyl barstool beside the one from which Shane has risen, Ed Flank stands. In so doing, he produces an audible fleshy sound as his buttocks come away from the cushion. He is the second naked man.

Prancie cannot establish the veracity of the situation in the slightest.

"I like them thick with their mind right . . ."

The chest, the chest she knows. Prancie rights her twisted feet and fumbles with her pashmina. So much noise erupts from the young people around her, she cannot hear her own thoughts. She corrects her posture.

This world cannot be real. In front of her stand, in slim order, a naked Shane Geautreaux and a naked Ed Flank. Each wears a single strand of plastic beads around his neck.

Prancie raises her hand to her mouth. She feels, vaguely, like a silent film actress beneath all the noise. She is frozen.

The laughter deafens her. It mutes her. It excises her.

Shane reaches his bare arm out in her direction, and Ed covers himself.

It is undone. It is all undone.

Sobbing, Philomenia closes her front door. The plain strangeness of their act, their, their *exposure* . . . What could they have been thinking? She is humiliated beyond measure. Philomenia's breath hitches as she steps out of her shoes and crumples on the parlor's chaise. Why? For what purpose? Why, why?

She wets the upholstery with tears until she can produce no more. Only then does she realize that an acquaintance beyond Ed, Shane, and Thurman could have seen her collapsing toward a nude male in a public arena. Her reputation could be ruined for eternity. The rumors. The destruction. She can just hear Sharon Harris asking about Carnival season with that look on her face. The woman would ask as casually as chatting about the weather. Philomenia begins to cry once again.

Philomenia regains her faculties and does not know where she lies. She feels constrained in clothing. She blinks in the dark until the reality of her own parlor solidifies. Why would she be here? And then the memory of earlier events rushes into her. They slam into her breastbone with such a force she feels physically injured.

A black silhouette of a figure stands in the doorway. Philomenia stares. What is happening?

"Philomenia," a voice whispers.

Has someone arrived to take her? She does not move, a hare sniffing upwind.

"Philomenia." She knows the voice. It belongs to her husband. He turns on the chandelier. She sees it needs a cleaning.

"Joe," she says, sitting upright, attempting to untwist her skirt, the zipper of which has made its way nearly around to the front.

"I've come to an important realization tonight," he says.

She runs her hands over her hair. She can feel the puffiness of her eyes without needing to see them in a mirror. "What is that?" She stands, then bends to retrieve her pashmina from the floor beside the chaise.

"Stand up."

Please, she thinks, let me be. Tonight is not the night. She stands again but cannot muster the reserves to square her shoulders properly. "Yes?"

"I want a divorce."

"Dudes! Well done!"

Ed and Shane have enjoyed the attention of young college people for hours now. The episode with Philomenia couldn't have been choreographed better.

A young drunk guy, likely underage considering his enthusiasm, has fastened his hand on Ed's shoulder, now in its T shirt again. "That was the, like, the best! No fucking joke. You two." The guy shakes his head and whips his index finger back and forth between Ed and Shane. "You two are my heroes, dudes." He takes a gulp from his cup. Whatever's in there, it's left a fuchsia, curling mustache of a stain on his upper lip.

Ed's superhero cape has come unstuck from the crack of his ass, and he feels fine. He leans in towards Shane and says to his new friend, "Do her face again."

Shane laughs before going stony. He widens his eyes, then blinks theatrically, raising his ungraceful hand to his throat. His open mouth makes no noise that Ed can detect. Ed laughs crazily, drunk. Shane is one of the best mimics Ed's seen in years.

Shane cracks up again. "You'd think the woman had never seen a—aw, hell, who are we foolin'? We knew she wasn't going to take the naked drink lightly." Ed's new friend lifts his glass, his eyes going almost sad. "We just didn't know it'd be the two of us."

Ed has had so many free pints on other guys in the bar, along with two young women, that he's lost count. And he finds himself feeling more welcomed than he has since he moved here. No man should be only a husband and father. There's room for an in-between person, a, well, just a man. Ed can be a man and not feel guilty about it.

A terribly pretty young woman talked to him half an hour ago about the happening. She still stands with her friends, her head showing now and again through the weaving crowd. She has the biggest beads of all of them. As they made small talk, she glanced at his ring finger. After a good ten minutes, she took a matchbook from the napkin holder on the bar and a pen from her purse. She gave Ed her number. She gave him her number!

Damn if Ariel shouldn't be a fly on the wall in here. Damn. Should he have another pint? "Shane." Ed clunks his glass against Shane's. "What time is it? Time for another drink?"

Shane raises his bare wrist to his face. "Half past a hair."

"Yo, Pedro," Ed yells. "What time it be?" Ed's practicing his new local dialect. Or is it idiom? He doesn't know and he doesn't care. He's trying to sound like a black thug. What time it is. What time it be. It's one or the other, he thinks, or that's how Ed hears it.

"Two-thirty," Pedro says without stopping his mixology. The guy's a master. Ed's going to tell him he needs to enter those contests on cable for the best bartender.

"Two-thirty," Ed repeats. The numbers don't register, until all of a sudden they do. It's two-thirty in the morning, and he's got a matchbook in his pocket from a college woman. It's two-thirty in the morning, and he has a family across the street. The one with the kids he gets to get up with in the morning. Damn. He's screwed.

"Shane, Shane," Ed says, grabbing the man's arm with both hands. In the action, Ed recognizes he's truly drunk. "Shane, I gotta go. Thanks for the fun. See you tomorrow."

"Hasta luego," Shane says. There's a singer Shane reminds Ed of, kinda, but he can't remember his name.

"Yeah," Ed says. "Loogie loogie." They both laugh, and Ed gets out the door somehow.

Fresh air hits him cold in the face. God, and Buddha, that feels good. Fresh air is a blessed thing. Everybody should give thanks for fresh air. Ariel might actually be asleep. She knows where he's been. Been there all night.

How is he going to face his neighbor in daylight? Ed takes a couple of steps down the sidewalk. He sees glistening slug paths, a roach. His body feels heavy. He'll sleep. Philomenia, he supposes, might be a decent person underneath all the pretense. Shane seems to think so.

Ed moves his hand to his back pocket for the matchbook. It makes him so damn happy. Ha ha, Ariel. He passes the Browns' house, all tucked in for the night. He wants to be them. Or him. He wants to be Roy. They're so good.

Ed tries to keep his course straight on the sidewalk and realizes he can't quite. He's actually weaving and noticing he's weaving. Wow. He looks down at his clumsy feet. They seem to belong to somebody else. He's almost staggering. Ed laughs.

He looks up at the sound of some weird swishing. A black man in a huge hooded coat has appeared. He is just steps away from Ed, coming at him with one arm swinging, rubbing nylon against nylon, the other arm tucked across his chest and inside his coat. The part of Ed's brain that's working snaps to attention. Is he about to be mugged?

Ed won't change his path for the man. He will just walk straight ahead. He's seen interviews about how bad black men can feel when whites cross the street at the mere sight of them.

Ed's feet don't cooperate with his intentions though. The black man comes on, and Ed walks straight into him, slamming shoulder against shoulder.

The hooded black man is very fast. He twists and ropes his free arm around Ed's neck from behind. Before Ed has even thought to struggle, the man has a handgun smashed into Ed's cheek.

The man yanks on Ed's neck, forcing him to arch his back, his knees to bend. He struggles to stay standing. "You fuckin' with me, cock-sucker?" the black man says straight into Ed's ear.

Ed can only barely shake his head no against the gun. Jesus, Ella, Mom, Ariel, Miles, God, Buddha, please. Ella, Ella. Who will take care of her?

"You fuckin' with me, cracker? You think yo color save you?"

"No," Ed says. "I—I live here. There." He attempts to point.

The hooded black man doesn't say anything. Ed racks his addled brain for the teachings when facing death. The metal of the gun is warmer than the air. Ed has the crystal-clear understanding that it has been warmed by body heat, close to the black man's flesh beneath his coat. For all the studying, Ed has never lived more in the moment than now. He understands something essential.

The black man lets go, and Ed staggers, then falls to the sidewalk. "You the motherfucker saved ol' man Roy."

Ed looks up at an eclipse, the man's hood blocking out the moon. "I lifted the grill," Ed says. Ella, Ella, Miles, Ella.

"Rescue Man, don' fuck wit me 'n mine, hear?" The man steps over Ed's legs and turns his body sideways, lowering his gun against his thigh, surveying the street.

Ed sits like a child. He stares up at shadow. "Who are you?"

"I Fearius."

"I know you?"

"Fuck you, cracker. You all the same." The man winds up to deliver a Timberland boot kick straight to Ed's ribs. Ed knows he needs to protect his head. He curls into a ball, tucking up his knees, covering his skull with his arms. He clenches his teeth for what comes next.

But nothing more comes. He waits for a kick. He waits for a bullet. There's nothing. Footsteps down a sidewalk. Nothing more.

19

Roy has Cerise set up nice in her lawn chair on the neutral ground side of the parade route, their cooler right beside her. They're trying to be neighborly again these days, having the Guptas up with them to the Babylon and Chaos parades. The Indian family doesn't have one slim idea about the how and what all to do during Mardi Gras. "You excited 'bout the parades, William?" Cerise asks the little dark boy standing in front of her.

The child shrugs, moving his fingers weird, like he's playing a flute that's invisible. He's just plain odd for his age. "A real unique boy," Cerise says to Indira, sitting next to her in one of their extra chairs.

"From birth," Indira says. "Answer Miss Cerise's question, William. Are you excited?"

"It's possible," the child sings in a cartoon voice. He hitches up his little pants with his fists and swings his hips to one side and then the other.

"You ever seen one?" Cerise asks.

William shakes his head and drops to his haunches, picking up a dirty strand of broken beads. He smiles and starts wrapping it around his skinny wrist like a bracelet.

"No, no, wait for the whole ones," Cerise tells him. "There's good ones comin', trust me."

William looks at Cerise, then unwinds the beads, flings them to the ground, and starts grinding them into the dirt. He takes a squashed paper cup, sticks his hand in it to open it up, and puts it on top of the dirty beads ground down into the earth. It makes Cerise think of him making a tombstone. A strange creature, that one.

Roy talks with Ganesh behind them, guarding their small Weber grill. He doesn't have any food on it yet, but they lost so many sausages in years past to drunk white people grabbing and dashing, he got in the habit. Cerise knows Roy's happy to have something to do and a new person to talk up. The Guptas eat chicken dogs just fine, even brought their own. Cerise knew it.

She scans the crowd for Marie, Thomas, and Lil Thomas. They know where everybody always gathers. Cerise thinks it's a good idea the three of them meet people from another country. Expand their horizons and their brains. Babylon rolls at 5:45, the paper said, Chaos at 6. Her offspring just need to find a parking space and get over here before the route gets closed off and they can't cross anymore.

"So Elizabeth at her first slumber party," Cerise says to Indira about the lady's daughter. Talking about nothing takes a little practice. Fortunately Cerise has more than half a century of practice.

"Is that what you call them here?"

"Or a sleepover, maybe."

"Yes. She was so excited she could not sleep last night. I cannot imagine how she'll fare this evening."

Cerise smiles. "Remember how much fun those are? You never know how they tax the parents when you're a kid." Cerise keeps her right hand down in her lap like she's learned to do. The fingers move a little with the memory of pillow fighting with her sister a very long time ago.

"And you return home the next morning utterly distraught," Indira says. "Sleep-deprived, of course, but you don't know it at that age. You only question why it is you should be forced to leave your new soul mates ever again."

Cerise knows it. "Ain't it the truth." Ain't it the truth. She thinks she sees her own child and her family workin' their way up Milan across the boulevard. Cerise doesn't have a lot of time before they descend. "So I been thinkin'," she says to Indira, "I have me a little windfall, and I'm a new left-hander and all." She lifts her claw. "You're up at the university and Ganesh, he, he's at the zoo. I need to get outside the house, and I don't mean babysittin' my grandson, even considering the ladykiller he gone be someday. He too cute." Cerise catches herself tapping her left hand on the aluminum armrest. "I'm thinkin' classes or the like. Right Brain Drawing for Seniors, maybe, or Feed the Big Cats Some Fingers Day." Cerise has been coming up with class names and outing adventures in her head for the last couple months, looking at catalogs from the local colleges, all of 'em recruiting seniors something fierce.

If laughing but not making a noise counts, Indira seems to think Cerise is funny.

"Lady, don't you make noise when you laugh?"

Indira snorts then, and Cerise gets her neighbor through and through. "You're a snorky laugher," Cerise says, and Indira bounces, giggling and not makin' a sound. Her weird son, William, begins to imitate his mother, shaking and sort of dancing around their space. The child gonna benefit from stem cell research.

"Excuse us, excuse us." It's Marie along with Lil Thomas and his father.

Cerise feels happy to see 'em despite the real luggage they roll up. They're using suitcases to tote their parade things, sort of like how the white people use wheels on everything, on their ladders and coolers and wagons piled with tents and blankets and what. Only Marie and Thomas ain't white. Lil Thomas might never know his heritage at this rate.

"We can talk about my possibilities later, right?" Cerise asks Indira.

"Sorry?"

"Classes or something. You know, Cooking the Elderly," Cerise says, making herself snicker too. But she's got an even better one all ready to go: "Penguins Versus Septuagenarians: A Study of Ground Speed."

Indira just shakes, then snorts. How's that laugh not contagious? Cerise wants more. It makes her feel a whole lot better. She's got a long list of classes in her head. Cerise stands up to do the introductions. Marie sets Lil Thomas down, and he toddles at Cerise and hugs her legs. The boy's growing faster than a banana tree. Cerise reaches down and rubs his soft head sandwiched between her knees. He's a loving child who's always going to know his grandma as a left-hander. That's fine, she tells herself. She's finally in her right brain.

Messin with the dumb ass Rescue Man done teach Fearius everything. It all about surprise. Cant be no slinkin along slow, like how the niggas done in the car at New Years Eve, no announcin yourself. Fearius pace his room, get ready to do this thing.

It be about this, Fearius think: How he might want to go down? Make it quick. Do it right and dont let fear get into the hit first. Whoever get popped gotta go down not afraid of nothing, fast, not knowin. Just do it fuckin right so the Moms and Pops get the news there werent no suffering. That be important, Fearius think. Some people gone be left livin still afterwards. You gots to be a tsunami when the hit have his back turned to the ocean. Lethal.

How many times Fearius walk around they block lookin for practice? He werent gone shoot nobody, but it about learning a new thing. Fearius gotta practice somehow. Poor mo fo Rescue Man, made Fearius feel like shit the last while. The man a good person. It the same as old man Roy. They only in the wrong place at the wrong time. Honest, Fearius dint mean nothing by it. He just hafta practice. He gots a job to do.

He dont do his job, he dont got but numbered days hisself. The Moms need her a good birthday, ya heard. And Taliqwa, she might be needin a treatment if she ever fill Fearius in on what goin on for real. He aint gone be no baby daddy no how.

Alphonse only done need to say the hit name, and Fearius know why Alphonse want him gone. Nigga been encroachin like a roach into Alphonse territory for what, two months. Everybody know the upstart a fool.

And now the fool be Fearius responsibility. Fearius wish he could feel the power in hisself, but he only keep feelin Rescue Man breathin so hard. It obvious, Fearius learnt, that it dont take nothing to get drunks down on the ground or to get em dead. They so slow they down before they even know it. Oh, hey, Im down on the ground, damn. How I get here?

Sorry, Rescue Man. He a easy target, but Fearius dint mean to hurt the dude. Fearius hope he okay.

Awright. Fuck the pity game. Fearius got work to do or he gone become work for somebody else. He pace in his room, hold the Jericho and feel the weight for the twenty something time. They aint light, he figuring out. He shoot it up over by the levee, but he still dont have no plan, dont feel so much confidence yet.

Fearius know where the fool at tonight. He advertisin it for weeks, got him a party out on the boulevard, showin off his snake money while the parades roll.

If Fearius do his job right, nobody ever see him. Nobody remember a thing about him. Not a thing. Fearius gone be invisible. He gotta be. He hope the hit drunk as fuck.

Marie and Thomas and Lil Thomas scooch in and everybody gets comfortable in their canvas chairs and what, Thomas with the men, Lil Thomas on the ground in front on a yellow fuzzy blanket Marie lay down. Cerise wanted to tell her it's gonna get filthy with just a couple adult-size footsteps and that it's way too nice for a parade, but Marie cares about what everybody thinks, so the thing's just seein' its last outing is all. These past months Cerise is learnin' when it's worth it to speak up and when she shouldn't bother.

That Keyshawn, for example. He turned out nice enough, but soon as they took off Cerise's left hand bandages, he had to go. And bye bye babysitter for Lil Thomas. Wasn't more than two days with that foolish setup before Cerise knew it had to stop. Good thing Keyshawn came at a bargain. Good thing he's nicer than Marie and didn't demand more money. Tonight's the first night Marie's bringin' her family around since Cerise quit Keyshawn. Come to find out, Marie told Keyshawn he'd have three months' work, not three weeks. Nice of her daughter to spend her mother's money, huh?

Marie had candy dreams of getting rid of Lil Thomas for days on end or some such. Cerise could've told her that new mothers don't get any rest, but Marie wouldn't have heard it. After all, Cerise don't know one damn thing at her age, right? Cerise told Keyshawn he wasn't needed any longer in the morning, and that evening when Marie came over, Cerise just half-listened. The surfers on the muted television stunned the judges and the folks on the beach while Marie yackety-yacked away.

So it's a peacemaking visit during Carnival. Life is short. Cerise can do this, no problem. The men start readying the grill. They're talking politics, but nicely, what they think the mayor's doing wrong and right. Everybody can talk on a mayor, especially a bald black used-to-be busi-nessman mayor, and have an opinion without getting deep into the big party differences and what. Marie sort of twists around in her canvas chair to participate with the men. Her whole life she's been a daddy's girl. She prefers men. It's fine by Cerise. She knew it when the child was a month old.

"Might I see your palms?" Indira asks.

Cerise doesn't know how to react. Her trees? She just looks at Indira.

"I'm curious about the lines," Indira keeps on. "To Indians, pardon, to East Indians, palmistry is significant."

"My hands?" Cerise looks down at the things tucked into her lap. Well, why not?

Indira smiles with so much kindness in her eyes, Cerise feels like she's being attended by the best doctor in the world. "Please," Indira says.

As Cerise presents her hands to her neighbor, some young Italian-looking man on the boulevard with a bullhorn says, beeping and announcing into the crowd, "And now Miss Sarah Kay! Twirk it! Binks has a stiffy." A white woman dances, working her behind. She's pretty and has long legs but not a lot of backside. The Italian grunts into the bullhorn in time to something. Cerise isn't sure what the folks are after, but they're fun enough to watch.

Indira takes Cerise's hands in her own.

One guy in the bullhorn group across the way is tall as a basketball player and shaved bald. He has crazy eyes and a loud voice. He keeps shouting about cats. He holds the rubbery hose end of a keg tap in his hands and pours it directly into his mouth. Young women by him wear butterfly wings and short skirts.

"Were—or—are you right-handed?" Indira asks.

"Now I'm a left-hander," Cerise says for what feels like the tenth time in so many weeks. "But I used to be a righty." Suddenly Cerise feels happy for her lefty status. What did the History Channel say about the statistics when they showed those horrible machine-gunning errors? Lefties make up just over 10 percent of the world. So now Cerise is a black, seventy-plus, left-handed minority with a—say it, girl— disability.

Indira gently kneads Cerise's stiff right hand. "Depending on the tradition, I would read one or the both, comparing one to the other." Indira tries to flex Cerise's claw fingers. Cerise sees the lady nod. "Can you make a fist at all?"

"Watch this," Cerise tells her and tries to make a fist. Her fingers go in all of about an inch and stay in the same shape.

Indira smiles. She presses on the graft. "May I be honest?"

"Don't know why not," Cerise says.

Marie's entire attention has gone to the men. She's not listening at all. Only Cerise'll hear what Indira's gonna predict. "I have wanted to see your palms since the accident. It does not happen so much that people become children again."

"Look," Cerise says, smiling, a little embarrassed despite not wanting to be, "you can see I don't match, and you can pretty much guess where the skin on this one came from. How that makes me a child, I can't truly say, but—"

"You have only your beginning lines, or how they begin again, more accurately. You have the ability to understand distinctly where you have come from and where you are going."

The bullhorn group across the way sends two of its women into the boulevard turning cartwheels. One wears an afro wig and a hat she holds on her head with one hand as she turns. Other white people on either side of the group stare, standing around their ladders, frowning and folding their arms. The bullhorn group doesn't have any ladders.

Lighten up, Cerise thinks about the frowners. Why most white people from the suburbs don't know how to have any fun is beyond her. Maybe they think they get to live for two hundred years and have time for everything. Fools. Best take it while you can. All those fat folks ought to be considering turning some cartwheels too. For that matter, Marie should go dance for Lil Thomas and show him how to have fun. Buy him something that blinks and put him up on her shoulders.

Indira still cups Cerise's hand like it's a piece of dinosaur eggshell. She runs her finger in there, a place where Cerise can hardly feel at all. Watching Indira rub and press, it's more like she can imagine feeling the woman's touch. "Babies are born into this world with just these lines on each palm," she says. "Essentially it is the balance of these few along with what the rest of your hand does in relation to these lines that reflects your life."

"Tell me when I'm going to die," Cerise says all of a sudden, and she doesn't even know the place it came from. She didn't think she wanted to know such a thing.

"That is a common but mistaken perception," Indira says. "You cannot exactly read the future from a palm. You can only see what an individual might have currently and how that could affect a future."

"So you can't see the hardwiring."

"Actually, you can, to some degree. The hand that is not your dominant hand better predicts what you have inherited genetically."

Cerise laughs. "Then what do we do with me and my backwards hands?"

"My dear," Indira says and lays her warm hand inside the permanent cup of Cerise's right claw, "you are blessed."

The bullhorn honks. Cerise thinks she has not heard right. "I am what?"

"A wise person. Maybe a seer. Do you know the word?"

"Age earns rights, I guess," Cerise says, clucking.

"See here?" Indira runs her finger along two lines in Cerise's hand. "You use both your heart and your head equally and greatly. It is what you were given at birth."

Cerise glances over at Marie, who's now gotten up and out of her seat to stand with the men. Cerise isn't so sure about her own great gifts, considering her daughter and such. "Hmm," Cerise says and takes her hand away from Indira. "Thank you, darlin'."

"You would be surprised by the thousands of years of documents behind the study," Indira tries.

Cerise lifts her eyes towards her daughter and her husband. "I don't think either one of 'em would call me wise."

"Others' perceptions do not make a bit of difference if they do not make an appearance in the lines. As they say, Miss Cerise, stand tall."

Cerise realizes all of a sudden she's been given a pep talk. The lady's nice. "What you plannin' on puttin' on that grill, Roy?" Cerise asks, although she knows full well what's coming. Dogs. She wonders if they accidentally mixed up all the different kinds of hot dogs whether the Guptas would get sick from eating the sacred cow.

Beliefs are some of the strangest things on the planet. Maybe Cerise'll decide down the road to read up on palmistry. Go to a library.

The bullhorn group gets bullied by their ladder neighbors into being quiet. Shame. They had something goin'.

It fucked up over this way. Fearius never completely comfortable on this side, most always during Mardi Gras. Theys too many people. It hard to move around everybody, hard to go by so many white folk parkin while he tryin to be invisible even when they all *pretend* he completely invisible. Fearius have a license plate on his ass, and you know every last cracker memorize his letters and numbers, thinkin, The Negro who keyed my car! I saw him!

Fearius walk Danneel Street most the way from his ward. He almost there now. The air good tonight, cool, and Danneel run parallel to St. Charles but off, what they say, the beating track. It off the beating track by three, four streets at the least. Fearius gotta keep hisself safe for the time. Ha! Shit. Safe for the next five minutes? Least the niggas chargin fifteen a pop for they Section 8 subsidized parkin spots not pay him no mind when he pass.

He need to get a little chant up in his head, Here I go, here I go, here I go. Step up, bro. Get it right. Keep yo life. Get to feel Taliqwa again, over and over, yo. Keep yo life. Keep yo own life. Keep yo life. He done feel a little sick in his stomach back when he cross Napoleon Boulevard and look down to where the parades make the big slow turn onto St. Charles.

Babylon rolling, the marchin bands drummin and the girls clackin in they cowboy boots with the taps on em. The girls in front the marching bands wave flags or only dance, all of em with no pants on. Just leotards. And they wear nylon stockings in the color of they skin, even the dark girls. They must make them getups custom, like car interiors on Cribs. First time Fearius remember growin hard and linkin it up with something he see be when he five or six, watching the high school dancers in leotards.

This day he up here for another reason. Fearius walk slow on Carondelet now, glancin down the one short block to St. Charles at the cross streets, seein all the 5-0 standin in the middle of everything, scoutin the crowds. Guns hangin huge on hips, clubs unsnapped, ready to beat some nigga down. Two of em at every intersection, some standing full on in the middle the boulevard. The marchin bands hafta bend they straight lines to go round em, like the police fucks made of stone. What that they say about a unmovable object?

He got to screw his head on straight now, stop gettin distracted.

From a balcony bout ready to fall off the side a ghetto house, a old white dude shake his finger at Fearius, actually shake his finger. The man too old to care about. Fearius keep walkin. Funny what one motherfuckin block can do. St. Charles full of mansions and right behind it be shit squares, crumblin down.

Last word Alphonse get, the party up over by Delachaise, one street off Louisiana, the mo fo busy intersection with the gas station and pharmacy and the corndog stands and the quick shop and Fearius stomach in his throat. No question they be people everywhere, no question why the nigga choose it for his party spot in the first place.

This thing Fearius have to do aint easy. He got three blocks to go and not one real plan. He hopin his gut tell him what to do. What the chances be he gone get taken out hisself by a solja after he shoot the hit? His legs feel like he been smokin, like noodles. Fuck, he so scared his hands prickly.

He kinda go out his head then, floaty, thinkin on what he shoulda put in a letter in his room for Moms.

And then he almost there, and the fog clear out his head like the ghost of Jesus or somebody blow it out with a big breath. Poof. Fearius know what he hafta do. Pass once and make sure the hit at his own party then go hang on the other side the parade, watch behind lots other people, wait and see if the nigga leave to buy popcorn or somethin. Fearius have only as long as two parades of marchin bands. If Chaos start rolling and Fearius still dont have it clear, one on one, he gone hafta go into all of em, pretend he a friend. He gone get shot if he hafta go in.

Here come Delachaise. Fearius walk down it and see one huge fuckin pile of brothers an they bitches. The hit done make em all a stage from boards and scaffold things. They dancing an drinkin, and worse, theys a empty circle round them all like a lieutenant piss out they territory.

Fearius think on it a thousandth time. What if he just tell Alphonse there werent no opportunity? Same as always, any way he figure it, Fearius fucked iffin he dont try. Likely dead he dont try. Maybe he just leave town now, disappear.

Naw. He aint no coward. Cant be a coward no matter what else. Fearius is *fearius*, motherfuckers. Fearius invisible. Nobody gone see him.

He look for the hit, remember he have that blockhead. He got a square skull. Fearius know him from the third grade when the idiot not readin still even when he held back two years. The kids laugh when Blockhead get called on and he read words backwards or just make em up. After a while, the kid finally only look at the book pictures and tell a story. Fearius never figure out why Miss Franklin let him go on an on with everybody bustin a gut. Guess she needed her a laugh. Fearius remember the teach puttin her head on her desk and slappin it, her shoulders jigglin with her laughin. Fearius know Blockheads birthname but aint gone think it. He only the hit.

Fearius walk along casual on the far side St. Charles with his hood up. So many niggas out during Mardi Gras the hit an his guests aint gone single Fearius out right away. Fearius step casual, just turn his head a inch.

There he be. There the hit stand. He in among everybody, but theys no mistakin the skull shape of a person cant read.

Fearius keep going towards the crowd around Louisiana ahead. He gone cross the route where the bros not lookin and come back up the other side. He feel all a sudden like he could run a race an win, his muscles so ready.

He wonder if Blockhead ever learned him any writing at all.

Fearius glance back over his shoulder, make sure the hit still hangin, and he see something he not sure he see right. The hit leavin everybody and headin over to the dead side St. Charles. Fearius stop an turn. It true.

Walkin slow as his legs let him, Fearius go back in Delachaise direction. His hand go in his coat. He gots to get a round in the chamber, but he need two hands.

And it like somebody watchin over, decidin the cheetah get to catch the zebra tonight, cause right then a marching band start up with a blastin loud number, got a dude in his tall hat and tails out front, liftin his knees proud with his baton, and not nobody lookin Fearius direction suddenly.

Fearius take out the Jericho and pull the top hard to get a round in, keep it close to his leg on the away side the parade. The band a blessin. Nobody see Fearius.

Fearius, he surviving. He the fittest of them two. He gone be the eater, not the dinner, too bad for Blockhead.

The hit head up Delachaise. When Fearius take the corner, the nigga gone. Fearius stop an squint up the dark street. The band play, and Fearius skin crawl. He hear drippin somewhere.

It somebody pissin.

Fearius try hear around the blood pulsin in his own ears. He follow the piss noise, steppin with no sound.

The snares start passin on the boulevard, rat tat tat, rrrrrrrrratt tat, and there the dumb mo fo blockhead be by hisself, pissin in a bush by a stranger door. How dumb you gots to be, nigga?

Do it right, Fear, do it right.

Blockhead maybe sense Fearius cause he turn and look with his dick in his hand. His motherfuckin dick in his hand.

Fearius raise and point.

"Who dat?" Blockhead say, laughin, and Fearius realize the nigga cant see Fearius at all. It hafta be Fearius luckiest day ever. He gone get to live.

The snares keep goin.

Blockhead never had shit in his lunchbox, never sat with nobody. He took food off all of them younger kids, stuffed his mouth up like he jammin it with words he need to read out later.

Fearius aim and try to shoot in time with the drums. Rat tat tat.

He run and run. He dont even hear no sirens. He run some more and pant and run, cutting in and out, tryin not to go in any straight line. Finally, he understand he in the clear. Best he stop and stroll.

His coat slippery with sweat on the inside, stink like gunpowder. Him or me, him or me, him or me. It the chant back home. Him or me.

Blockhead. Him or me. Ronald Walters ate Fearius sandwich once, even with two bites gone. Left Fearius warm milk and a soft apple.

20

Philomenia rests her pen atop her journal. She does not know what to write.

Outside the bay window, the live oak dips its branches toward the lawn. She realizes she could not bear living in a place where every tree shed its leaves each year. This particular New Orleans March is bleak enough without deciduous influence.

Soon it will be buck moth caterpillar season. They have overrun the city in recent decades, stinging all manner of warm-blooded beings, although she cannot remember large barbed caterpillars inhabiting her youth. Likely they arrived on a ship from a poor and foreign place, similar to the nutria, those bloated rodents plaguing the waterways. She stares out the glass panes that need washing. Certainly, it seems, Louisiana is the receptacle of all manner of biological offal. The barnacle across the street provides testament to the fact.

She must not collapse. She must regain something of her former strength. Something.

The greatest luxury a man can offer a wife is to allow her to remain in the home. Choose wisely. To marry an impoverished man for love is to destroy your future, Philomenia. The working world is not your place.

Joe claims that he will not work another day in his life. "Not one more fucking day in that office," he actually said indelicately. He has escaped hellfire, somehow, and he remains resolute in his decision to escape Philomenia. After her years of service, she cannot, still, fathom his request. He insists that she come to an understanding about his choice. They cannot continue to live in the house together indefinitely, he has said. He has said that he does not know exactly how to explain why he has made his decision, only that he will see it through to its end.

He has said that they will need to sell the house since he will be neither working nor dying. "Sorry about that, Philly Phil Phil," he said. "Bet you're pretty bummed out, huh?"

Along with his new hair, Joe's coarseness has grown with each passing week since the unspeakable night of Carnival. He sleeps in the guest bedroom. She carries on with her cooking and cleaning, proffering her skills in what she acknowledges is an ungainly attempt to sway him.

Philomenia will not leave this house. She is deserving of this house. She has earned this house, has she not? She has spent the majority of her years on Orchid Street.

She lifts her pen and opens her journal to a fresh page. "I have guarded this block," she writes, "since I was a newlywed. That I am told I must leave against my will is incomprehensible."

A mouse has begun appearing. It chews, now, on her spinal cord. Its actions prove far more substantial and difficult to ignore than those of the moths. "That I . . ."

Joe's recent words about her health have embedded themselves, syphilitically, in Philomenia's brain. He has willed her the future she cannot have. She cannot.

She is able to recall the exact circumstances with great precision.

He stood at the kitchen island as Philomenia, after baking, prepared a marinade for the evening's roast. He chose a warm blueberry muffin from the cake plate. He lifted the domed top of the butter keeper by its button of glass, looked into it, and then licked its edge with a long and whitish tongue. He rubbed the muffin along the stick of butter, embedding crumbs. He opened his mouth as wide as it could be opened and inserted the muffin. He bit off half. He smiled.

"Delicious," Joe said. He spoke with his mouth full, she knew, because he no longer cared what she thought. No, more accurately, he spoke with his mouth full because he knew she would not care for his doing so.

Salvation, the mouse says. You know where it lies.

He seemed never happier in his life. "You know, Philomenia," he said, wiping the melted grease from his face with his forearm, "you still have time for love. A year or two, at least. How old was your mother when it did her in?"

Philomenia added cayenne to the marinade. "Sorry?" She could not have heard correctly.

"Stare at a ceiling for months, Phil Philly. Philly Philly Philly." He pushed the rest of the muffin into his mouth and rubbed his stomach. He closed his eyes. "You are a very good cook," he said, again with food still in his mouth. "Milk." He pointed to the refrigerator.

Philomenia obeyed. She took his favorite glass from the cupboard and filled it. She passed it to him. He gulped greedily. She can still see his Adam's apple moving under his skin. Are they extricable entities? Can an Adam's apple be removed and held in a hand like a marble?

"Really, Phil, you should go hog wild before you don't know what you're doing." He took another muffin and rubbed its top across the stick of butter.

Philomenia mismeasured the cumin. "What do you mean?"

"*You* lie sick while I go across the street night after night, is what I mean."

"I made food for those people. I shared—"

"You really don't know, do you." He looked down to the muffin in his hand and then up to her face. "You're sick with what your mother had."

Philomenia turned to the cupboard. She needed a dish. She needed something from the cupboard.

"I'm guessing under those clothes somewhere is a nice little package even now. Good Lord, Phil, go get yourself something while you still know what you're doing." He laughed. He took yet another bite of blueberry muffin. "Fuck somebody else besides me before you die. It's coming on."

"Your maladroit language, Joe, is beyond—"

"My God!!" Joe's yelling filled the room. He threw what remained of the muffin across the kitchen. It burst against the pantry door. "Wake up!! Listen to me!!" His neck colored angrily.

Philomenia placed her fingertips on the lip of the countertop. She looked at the bowl of marinade, an oily red. Joe, she realized with startling clarity, had always been exactly and only what her mother required Philomenia find for a husband. She could not say she had ever loved him. She raised her face. "Yes?"

"You're sick." He squeezed his face into a rumple of aging skin. He closed his eyes and shook his head. "I'm sorry, Philomenia. I've been a, I have not . . ." Joe began to cry. "Please." He ground his fists into his temples. A tear came from his right eye. "You're sick."

She clearly remembers him standing and picking up the piece of muffin from the floor. He took a sheet of paper towel and wet it. He wiped down the pantry door before the blueberries had a chance to stain the white paint. He went to the sink. He bent his shoulders along with his head. "How can I make you hate me?" he asked into the garbage disposal.

Salvation lies in your skills, the mouse says, and the moths come in en masse. Wings beat across the view to the barnacle, for how long, Philomenia does not know.

When they leave, Prancie retrieves her pen from the floor. Joe, she realizes, still consumes her food with gusto. The solution has been there from the start.

Ariel can't believe it's April. Here in this soggy city, the months escape through her hands, fish back into water.

She paces a path through rooms she shouldn't be in, thinking what she's thought from the very first: Javier will never go down on her. Maybe it's a cultural thing. Maybe he's afraid of Henny catching the scent. Funny. When Ed tries, he can make Ariel come with his mouth in a couple minutes. His mouth and a finger or two.

It's something about Javier's desire to *have* her. Everybody wants to be wanted, right? She can't analyze her poor choice. Actually, that's not true. Ariel could break it down to the minutiae as to why she's taken on Javier. She just doesn't want to look at the pieces.

Stopping for her reflection in one of the Governor's Suite's bathroom mirrors, Ariel remembers the lost opportunity of Phatty with the smallest twinge of regret.

Isn't the grass always greener in memory? She slaps her own cheek. Ariel gets a nice pink blush on her pale skin. She slaps the other side. She feels moderately mentally ill, although she knows she remains rational and cognizant and enough of whatever all else is required for work and mothering. It's the wife-ing that's giving her pause. She hikes up her skirt, takes off her underwear, and lays it neatly on the vanity.

She's here, and waiting, and her body's switched on before her brain. She does not like herself. How, though, how in hell do people stay satisfied with a tiny sliver of life like it's the best cake they'll ever have? Javier, at least, is something other than cake.

His knock sounds. When Ariel lets him in, he comes straight at her. Lately he seems to want to fuck as fast as she will allow. She allows it. There's something impious about it that she relishes, something very not right.

Javier takes Ariel by the upper arms and pushes her backwards into the living room of the suite. Staring at her mouth, he shoves her down to sit on the arm of a love seat, grabs her hair and yanks on it, forcing her head back. He mashes his lips on hers. Javier opens her jaw. She sucks his tongue to the back of her throat, filling up her hollow.

He pulls her to her feet. She takes a wrapped condom from her bra and tears it open. He does not step out of his dropped pants, only watches as Ariel rolls it on.

She is his doll. By her hair, Javier turns her away from him, his free hand running up under her skirt, and then he is inside her quick and hard.

Ariel inhales sharply. He pounds against her ass, and she grunts, and she sees the black man with his arm around Ed's neck suddenly, the way he described it, the gun, and her stomach tightens like a fist. She is going to stop this, she thinks, all of this, and then the door to the suite opens.

Ariel swings her head over her shoulder. Javier's head follows. The prep cook Nikki is balancing an elaborate fruit tray. She seems intent on

242

AMANDA BOYDEN

not dropping it, looking down. Javier's cock is thrust as deep as it goes. He turns back to Ariel, finds her eyes, and smiles. He keeps fucking. She knows he is only a few strokes away. Hair rips from her scalp. He shudders into her as Nikki looks up.

Fearius walkin his normal morning route, starin out at the river from the levee. It gone be hot soon. Theys a gap by the power lines with no trees where the river shows good, even from a distance. It so damn brown. Water aint suppose to be that color, he dont think. He always wonder what it do in a glass bowl. Do the mud settle at the bottom finally like a science project?

Then he think on swimmin and how he aint been in so long. Moms use to sign em up for summer swim at the pool down on Tchoupitoulas. Muzzle push him off the high dive once an lost his privileges and then done blame Fearius. His bro beat on Fearius for a week.

Then he think on where Muzzle be now. Word on him be bad, worse than bad. Make Fearius feel somethin not coming clear yet, maybe like how he next in line for taking care the family, like what the bible stories talk about brothers and all. Fearius cant exactly touch on what eat him about Muzzle and him, how they twined together. He only know he not no Muzzle. Fearius not even smoke no weed for a month. He suppose Muzzle have a reason why he stay away from his family. Fearius still cant figure why Muzzle not come at him with a gun, rob him naked. It not like he dont know where the work go down.

How much Muzzle love his lil bro? Fearius not sure. The not knowin make him sleep bad every night.

Two of those long neck white birds fly right over Fearius then, and he think some more on Muzzle. Another hundred something steps an he thinkin on Blockhead. Alphonse done send another solja that night down to Charity get the official report.

Alphonse tell Fearius it not his fault Blockhead dont die. He say Fearius back in honorable standin.

Blockhead in a wheelchair droolin, cant even talk. Lyin in bed some nights, Fearius think he go sneak into Blockheads house and finish him off for his moms and pops. It take everything Fearius got not to think on it 24/7. It like Blockhead more a lump a meat than he ever be before. Make Fearius sick.

His own Moms ask back a month ago if Fearius losin weight. No possibility he tell the Moms how the world be so heavy it eatin him. Hoofin it alongside the bike path on top the levee, he shake his head. He look up and see lil ol Miss Cerise hoofin her own skinny ass up the levee from near the water intake. Fearius gots to go down that way over to work. He like her. They be knowin each other since he born. Miss Cerise dont call him out, just let him be, though she never catch him before goin into Pigeontown in the mornin.

The ol lady study her feet goin up the grassy slope, steppin carefully. Even from where he at, Fearius see her one hand hang kinda funny off her arm. His stomach twist watchin her go slow up the hill. It like sittin in a class knowin he cant answer one fuckin question the teach put out, an sooner or later he gone get called on, only the class be the world now. Somehow you hafta answer some way. He dint think this gone be how it goes. Not no how. Blockhead figure it out a long time ago. You gotta answer. Look at the pictures and make up a story. Fill up the time till you off the hook.

Miss Cerise stop and rest, her face tiltin to the sky. Fearius keep goin and catch her attention. He the one wave first.

She do a funny thing, lift one arm part way and then switch to the other arm. She wave like a Miss America then, little but real big at the same time. Fearius get this weird idea to quick squint his eyes. Miss Cerise goes blurry, and he can see her when she young. He punch her dance card any day, ya heard. He like that sayin.

Fearius open his eyes wide to the sun and think maybe he not right in his head no more. He make sixteen soon. Miss Cerise a hundred. Fearius wish Taliqwa let him come round. He don't care she getting fat like she say. He just miss her. Her company and pussy both.

He walk up to Miss Cerise and hold out his hand, pull her up the last couple steps. "Mornin, Miss Cerise," he say.

"Hoooo! Thats the biggest hill in town," she say, stompin her feet. "How you doin, Daniel?"

"Awright," he say, wishin he be able to tell her his true name. "How you?" How you since my big brother wreck yo life?

"Im a left hander now," she say. She raise her left hand there on top the levee, and Fearius not *fearius* one drop no more. Somethin wrong with him. He want to lay down and let a big ball roll him over, press him into the ground down to China where nobody know him but he can get the news to Moms that he okay, Pops maybe too. Not Alphonse or nobody else find him in Chinkland, hey.

"Why you up this way?" he ask.

"Took a walk down Oak. Been a while. Lots of new stores and restaurants."

"Yeah?" Fearius never go in neither. If he shop clothes, it down in Canal Place where he buy what show his money.

"I thought your schools in the other direction," the old woman say.

Salright. He knew it coming first thing he see her. Fearius just shrug, stuff a hand in his pocket hold up his trousers. He know Miss Cerise aint no fan a showin drawers.

"Pigeontown has some real troubles, Daniel. I worry about you."

"I be fine." It make him feel better somehow knowin Miss Cerise care about him a touch.

"Schools not always a complete waste," she say. "You might could go an not care about the grades. Just go for something to do. Maybe youll enjoy history or mechanics or something."

Now Fearius gotta laugh. "Bout all I enjoy be the—" How he say it proper to Miss Cerise? "The young ladies the best part bout any school."

Miss Cerise laugh too. "Your sister, now shes a student, right?"

"She a nerd, right. Not in no classes with the babies though."

Miss Cerise dont say nothin about it, just smush up her mouth.

They walk on a little ways. Fearius gone double back to work. He respect his elders usually.

"They got daycare scholarships and things for young mothers who wanna study," Miss Cerise say all a sudden.

"That a good idea," Fearius say, an mean it.

"It is, isnt it?"

"Sho is. For real." Klameisha need to be back at school. Comin up, Fearius always think she gone marry the president or be Oprah she so smart. Now she change diapers. "I like that idea," he say. "Klameisha and the babies both be more happy she go to college."

The lil ol Miss Cerise walkin alongside him smile an try clap her hands, only they dont make no clapping noise.

This day, Fearius be the kid got coal in his stockin. Everywhere he turn, he feel sad. Maybe it time tonight he go visit the hens in the Channel, go get him somethin make him feel good. "I best be gettin on," he say and stop walkin.

"You find yourself some nutrition for lunch," Miss Cerise say, "or take a break and come to my house."

Right. Lunchtime the busy part the day with the hospital workers on break an the Tulanes between they classes. "Awright," he say. "Thank you."

"You know I still cook."

"I know it," he say. "It smell good every night, yo." He start gettin on.

"Daniel," she call out. He stop and turn round. "You an your brother aint the same. You can do whatever you want, you hear me?"

How he can tell it to a ol lady that he dont have no choice? "Yes, maam." Fearius head off to work.

On the sofa, Ed eats toast spread with peanut butter. He looks down at his dirty white T shirt with a strange sense of pride. Never would he have believed he could manage to produce such a spectacle, the stains and the belly both. Granted, he might be all of three months pregnant for its size, but still. Alcohol, sloth, and gut-wrenching fear at gunpoint can change a man.

He has two hours still before the kids get out of school. Ed aims the remote control at the television and flips through, not really looking. The TV turns into a sort of kaleidoscope when you click it fast enough, he's learned. He pauses momentarily at *America's Funniest Videos*, these days shortened into the strange acronym AFV, as though it's something masculine and motorized. On the screen, there's a medley of accidents arranged to classical music, tree swings snapping and skiers crashing and babies tipping upside down, the sights so disturbing that Ed nearly gags. How can any of this be perceived as funny? It's all horrifying. It's disgusting. Any of those accidents could have resulted in tragedy. Broken necks and premature death.

He turns off the TV and stands, tossing his toast onto the coffee table, where it lands, satisfyingly, peanut butter side down. Crumbs pitter from his dirty shirt onto the floor. Bravo. Everybody should notice when he doesn't clean.

Ed moves to the foyer and peers at the house across the street through the narrow window flanking the front door. Ariel desperately wanted to call the police that night. Ed wasn't about to ever, but he told her he'd go into the station in the morning when he sobered up.

He lay wide awake. As the sun finally rose and Ariel breathed evenly beside him, he solved the riddle. Of course. It had been the younger Harris boy, Daniel. Ed had just never seen his face. He lied to Ariel the next day about filing a report. Being a snitch in New Orleans doesn't really fly, he'd heard numerous times in the Rose.

Ed suffered, to be sure, but he's not interested in sending the kid back to juvenile. After all, Daniel only helped Ed to understand his own lowly position in the world. Brilliantly, actually.

Through the window, the Harris house gives up nothing at the moment. A plastic shopping bag flutters, snagged on a curl of their porch ironwork.

Gandhi tried never to kill a living entity, although he confessed to having trouble with scorpions. Ed isn't any Gandhi, but he has some determination. He won't ever tell Ariel about the identity of the attacker. Instead, Ed's developed what he could only call an obsession with Daniel Harris.

Last night, Ariel crept into bed so late he had to pretend to be asleep. She'll approach him when she's ready, he guesses. Or maybe not. He doesn't know her at all anymore. He's married to a stranger.

Their kids need a mother. He's willing to continue the sacrifice for now. He'll never forget his mantra at gunpoint. Never. Being a father is tantamount to nothing else.

The plastic bag sags on the iron railing. Winds at the end of April must not be much. He feels it, feels the same way: not much. Ed puts his cheek against the glass of the window. It's cool. He wants more. He lifts his shirt and presses his belly onto the glass too. Raising his arms over his head, he fits them into the rectangle. He closes his eyes against the cool.

Can she even do this? Ariel's not sure. She drives in the general direction of home.

Javier kept his back to her when she entered the kitchen at lunch. Warren disappeared into the walk-in. No question the rest of them know now, down to the dishwashers. Nobody uttered a word. The kitchen had never been so quiet.

She informed her managers to call her only if they were incapable of solving a dire problem on their own, and then she left.

Ariel detours towards the place on the river everybody calls The Fly, a big, manicured, grassy expanse of public land alongside the river, near the zoo. It qualifies as a sufficiently calm place to go before telling her husband about fucking her sous chef for months and then getting caught by the prep cook on hotel property.

Again she considers not telling Ed. How much easier would that be?

She has to. She runs the risk of him finding out another way otherwise, although it's a risk she feels almost willing to take. Ed hasn't been doing well since the attack. Since before the attack.

Ariel knows it's her fault. All of it is.

She pulls into a parking space and gets out of her car. The Mississippi roils an ugly brown. On the other side of the watery expanse, processing plants of some kind rise like giant smoking toilets equipped with blinking chimneys. Behind her, a slow-rolling car passes blasting shit rap. She doesn't turn to look, doesn't care who drives with his wrist on top of his steering wheel.

The moment, or the living in it, has trumped her. How could she have let this happen? And now she's going to go home and destroy the tenuous peace. Oh, God. But he has to hear it from her. She may well lose her job. He needs to know about the possibility beforehand.

Ariel turns away from the river and walks to the car. College-age students wing a frisbee around in the grass.

Ed must have had twenty women pining after him when they met in college. Ariel felt like she'd won the lottery when she got his attention. She heaves a hard breath into her lungs and unlocks her car door. She's locked everything since the attack, even if she's going to unlock it immediately after, even if everything seems perfectly safe.

The drive home is ridiculously short. Ariel thinks about driving some more, maybe going around the block and taking off again, but she knows there's limited time before the kids get out of school. And Ed might not be sober tonight. She doesn't know when else to get it over with.

Pulling up to the house, she's taken aback. What is that? What the hell? She slows on the street before turning into the driveway. Ed—is that Ed?—has squeezed his half-naked body into one of the front windows by the door. Is she seeing right? What is he doing? His stomach distends against the glass, his cheek flattened into a pale pancake. What in—what is he doing? She can see his eyes are closed.

Is he dead? What has happened? Ariel's hand moves to her horn before her brain knows what her hand is doing. She honks loudly.

Ed jolts alive. Her husband in the window is alive. He twists away without looking outside, gone into the interior of the house.

The voice of the dishwasher from the Belle is the one that comes to her with imaginary words: "Ain't gone be easy, Miss Ariel."

She turns off the engine. More than most men, Ed has feelings. She wraps her hand around the leather handle of her briefcase. Ed cooks. Ed listens to NPR. She will not cry. She will not. Ed just pressed his half-naked body into one of their front windows. Ed stays out late drinking across the street.

Fortitude, Ariel. You have to tell him.

She puts the key in the door. "Hello," she calls out.

Nothing comes back.

"Hello. Ed. Where are you?" She sets her briefcase on the foyer table.

Ed descends the stairs, pulling on a Chicago Blackhawks T shirt. "Hi," he says. "Why are you home?" He does that, gets to the point so fast he yanks the rug out from under her.

"Were you just pressed into the front window?"

"It felt cool," he says. He comes down the last step and kisses her cheek in greeting. He's started the habit since they've been here.

"It's really weird, Ed." She tries to catch his eye. He won't give it. "You looked like an exhibitionist."

He barely tilts his head in acknowledgment, walking into the family room. "So you're home for what reason?"

Ariel follows. "Can we talk?"

Ed stops in his tracks. His shoulders relax. "Yes."

The family room is filthy. She feels like she's going to collapse. "I need to sit down."

"Alright." Ed sits in a chair.

Ariel brushes crumbs off the sofa and sits. She looks at the man she married. He looks very sad. He knows. He's known in his gut from day one. She's sure. He carefully rests both of his forearms on top of the chair arms. Ariel's reminded of an execution. She only knows her opening words. Time to get them out. "I fucked up," she says. Ariel can actually see the impact of her blow. Ed pulls in his stomach.

"How so?" he asks, and just then she notices for the first time in years how absolutely beautiful his green eyes are. What has she done?

"I—"

"Since Ivan, right?" he asks.

She's struck silent.

"Right?"

She can only nod.

"I knew it," he says. "Who?"

"Somebody at work."

He blinks as though he's a person in a movie who's been slapped but remains stoic. "Who?"

"A, a cook."

Somehow these words affect Ed more than the others she's uttered so far. He grips the armrests. "Are you fucking kidding?"

Ariel is certain she will cough up her heart in a second. "It's over."

Ed tips his head down and rubs his face. "When?" He looks up and places his arms on the chair again.

"What?"

"When did it end?"

She'll be honest. "Yesterday."

"What color is he?" he asks quietly.

She can't be hearing him right. Why would he ask that? "Why would that matter?"

"What color is he?"

"I don't see why that matters at all, Ed. It's over."

"Is he chocolate or mocha or café con leche?" He's strapped into the electric chair.

"Ed—"

"What color is his cock?" He clears his throat and spits on the coffee table.

She looks and sees grimy plates, a piece of toast, candy wrappers. A glob of spit. So this is what she's earned for working seventy-hour weeks, she guesses. It's what she gets for Javier. Ariel fingers the hem of her skirt. She wore it when she and Javier fucked at some point. She's never had it dry-cleaned. "Brown," she says.

Ed is on his feet. He grabs a plate and slams it on the floor, shattering it. *"Fucking fuuuuuuck!!!"*

Ariel hunches on the sofa. Her heart can't fit up her throat. It's stuck. She retches.

Ed's changed.

So has she.

21

Cerise walks the park. Audubon's prettier than she even remembers. She doesn't know who started it, if it's private or public in its money and what, but there's a golf course and a bike path and pavilions where people can have birthday parties and family reunions. She's even seen wedding receptions, mostly pretty white ladies having their pictures taken under the live oaks drippin' Spanish moss.

Tradition is tradition, she supposes, no matter what it makes her feel like. In her right head, Cerise knows those white brides have nothing to do with her history or why Cerise was born and raised in Louisiana. But in her wrong head, those white brides still make her life harder in this year of their Catholic lord or however it goes.

Most ways, though, Uptown is a fine place. She wishes her daughter thought the same. Ain't no changing Marie. Cerise could put Roy on the task of getting their daughter and her family to come back this side of town, but he'd come in afterwards just sayin' what Cerise already knows. Marie aspires to oatmeal. She wants new, bland, beige, soft porridge.

At least a dozen geese on their way from someplace else in the world waddle around by the big pond, fixin' to go another place else soon as they can work it. They fatten themselves up on the green green grass. Cerise gets a kick out of 'em. They'll eat every speck of bread and then chase away the little kids who throw it. Dropped onto the paved path, their green turds are big as a child's. Guess the geese take in more grass than bread, considering the color of what they leave behind.

Cerise keeps walking, passing the geese and the other birds visiting the pond, ducks with funny red lumps on their heads and the snowy egrets nesting in the trees and the long-necked gray fishing birds perched out on bare branches, staring at the water. Cerise forgot how nice the park can be. She's real happy she made the effort to come by.

She gets halfway around the path when she sees the sari-wrapped shape of Indira Gupta coming at her. They meet up in the middle. "Hello there," Cerise says.

Indira has a big smile on. "Dear," Indira says. She takes Cerise's left hand and gives a squeeze. "It's nice to see you."

"I forget how nice the park is. A good place for walkin'."

"Indeed, yes. I walk every Tuesday and Thursday between classes."

Cerise nods. "We can go around the loop together?"

"Surprise company is a blessing," Indira says. She hangs on to Cerise's hand like they're schoolgirls, swinging it a little as they go along the path. They giggle at an orange puppy waggin' its tail, the young man from Tulane or Loyola smiling at the other end of the leash.

They get to the far side and begin the royal walk down the corridor under the canopy of the live oak trees, all of them planted hundreds of years ago in two lines. Every day in her life that Cerise has come here, the views knock her out. People who never knew air-conditioning must've walked through here. People who died of malaria must've walked through here. Slaves had to've walked these exact steps, carryin' umbrellas for the people they served. The place ain't no Hawaii, that's for sure. Sometimes history can sit like a brick, huh.

A browny turtle the size of an Oreo cookie scootches across the path. Cerise bends and picks it up with her left hand. "Ain't it beautiful," she says. She puts it into the cage of her right hand. "Look at that."

Indira steps close to see. "How wonderful." She rubs her finger over its shell, and the feet and head tuck in even further.

"We should put it by the pond," Cerise says. She points at the neat circle of water nearby on the golf course.

"Are we allowed to walk there?" Indira asks.

"I'm too old to care if we can or can't," Cerise answers and starts walking off the path and onto the golf course.

Indira doesn't follow immediately. Cerise turns and looks. Indira stands at the edge of the path like she's stopped at the ocean. "Oh, come on," Cerise says. "They're not going to evict us."

The lady in the sari tiptoes her way to Cerise. Those getups don't allow a woman to move very freely, but they sure are pretty. Today, Indira wears one that reminds Cerise of a butternut squash, all yellowy and rich. Maybe Indira could do Cerise up in one sometime. She'd like that.

They both go to the pond, where Cerise bends down and tips the turtle out onto the mud by the edge. Accidentally, she tips it onto its back. She puts it right with her left hand. She and Indira watch the tiny thing for a while till it pokes out its head and quick claws down into the water. Cerise smiles.

"What do turtles eat?" Indira asks.

"I think maybe they're vegetarians." Cerise dips her hands into the pond water and carefully washes them. "They can carry salmonella, though."

"You're kidding."

"No, but I don't think our lil' shelled friend was hangin' on to anything but fear up on that path."

"Is there salmonella in the pond?"

"That's a good question. Maybe I'm just washin' on the diseases." Cerise stands and wipes her hands best she can on her blue jeans. They head back to the paved path. Three bicyclers whiz by on the bike side. A squirrel barks in a tree.

Indira's sari swishes as she goes. After a while Indira says, "I overheard something terrible yesterday."

"What's that?" The green canopy overhead makes an arch for what looks like a mile.

"Ed and Ariel," Indira says. "They're having difficulties."

Well. "It happens."

"I heard a dish break."

Cerise looks to the lady. A dish ain't nothing to worry about in their neighborhood, certainly nothing to worry about in their city. Indira's a touch oversensitive, likely. "Hmm. That doesn't mean people parts got broken too. Married folks can get mad at each other."

"She, Ariel, she's been unfaithful, with a coworker."

Cerise doesn't know what to make of this. She's first struck that their very own Rescue Ed has been hurt by his wife. But then she's struck second by the fact that Indira would listen to her neighbors' business so close. Any marriage that makes it has horrible times. It's just a fact. Cerise has always found it funny nobody wants to talk about those times to warn other couples. For better or worse means for better or *worse*. No joke. It will happen. One or both people in the marriage. Now it's Cerise's time to be old and wise and impart some knowledge to the naïve lady in her squash-pretty sari. "I'm sorry to hear it," Cerise says. "Ed's a brave man, but, to be honest, we don't know him well other than him being able to lift up a big grill."

"How do you mean?" Indira asks.

"Well, I guess I think it takes two people to make a mess, and I've had a hand in making a couple in my life."

Indira stops in her tracks. "That is an enormously generous approach to infidelity."

Cerise stops too. "It's a real one."

"Ganesh would never be unfaithful," Indira says.

The woman doesn't really want to see with open eyes. Or maybe Ganesh is a saint. Or a monk. Or from Mars. Maybe Indira's been sitting up in the academic towers too long to know the truth of flesh and marriage. Cerise should say what she's supposed to say. "Of course not," she tells Indira. The woman's a little plain in the face, a little tight around the mouth. Maybe Ganesh is the perfect husband of all time, though Cerise is guessing not, even if Indira doesn't know it. Everybody wants more, and everybody should, what . . . should strive for being the best human being she can be. Or he can be. That people make mistakes is part of the sad side of living, along with dying and maiming and all the rest.

"I just find it unseemly," Indira says. "The shouting and the breaking of things . . ."

Cerise doesn't know how to tell a lady who lives in a different world of her own how to take a look at the rest of 'em. There's always something more underneath. It's the privilege or the curse of old age to be able to see clearly. You finally know it's not all as it appears. You can find the carny mirror, if you want, and stand there and stare and say, 'That's the true thing,' but, of course, it's not. Cerise thinks Miss Ariel has a hard life. She's never home more than eight hours a day. The woman's sleep-deprived, likely, for starters.

"Life can be so hard," Cerise says and realizes what she wants to say from her heart will probably fall wrong. Still, she needs to say something to Indira. "I saw a show on cable about refugees. The parents passed their children to the camera people to take so maybe they could have a better—"

"Miss Cerise," Indira says as they continue walking along the loop, "I do believe you are the most tolerant person I have ever known."

"Maybe you just don't know very many tolerant people, then."

"That is possible."

They walk under the spread of live oak branches. "I'm sorry you had to hear that," Cerise says.

"Hear what?"

The woman's not so forthright, Cerise thinks. "The arguing and all between Ariel and Ed," Cerise says. "That's never what you want next door."

"No. It was difficult."

Cerise lets it lie. They finish passing through the corridor of trees, and Cerise asks, "So, any ideas about me taking classes or doing something at the zoo?"

"I'm not sure," the woman says. "Loyola is rather inordinately expensive, although there are community-based courses. I do not— actually, I'll get you a catalog."

Huh. Cerise could have done that on her own. "Thank you," she says.

They walk most of the way around the loop being quiet, looking at nature and other people. This park couldn't be much better, with or without a trip that includes a neighbor, a turtle, and plenty of squirrels and birds. "I think my legs have only so many steps in them today," Cerise tells Indira. "Best I carry the rest of me home."

"I'm so happy we met here," Indira says.

"Me too." They wave at each other and go. They're not really kissers or huggers at this point, which is fine by Cerise.

Indira heads back to Loyola and Cerise starts zigzaggin' a path to Orchid Street. Seems Indira forgot about Cerise taking any classes. That's fine. The lady's surely busy. As she goes along, Cerise thinks about a documentary she saw on cable about a woman in a wheelchair whose arms didn't work either. A quadriplegic rather than a paraplegic. The lady painted with her mouth. She gripped a paintbrush in her teeth and worked her head to make a painting.

On the way home, it's what Cerise decides to do. Not necessarily paint with her mouth, but just to paint with her new hand. If a lady can do it with a brush in her teeth, Cerise can do it with a paintbrush in her opposite hand, that's for sure. And what better to try to paint than sights in Audubon Park? Some of the birds sit still a long time. Even if they don't, the trees sure do.

Yes, that's exactly what Cerise will do. Left-handers are good at art, aren't they? She'll paint her some leafs and sticks, maybe put a person in there sometimes.

The Jazzfest crowd did Ariel in. The aging music lovers in their straw hats and coconut sunscreen overtook the Belle. They're good-natured enough, she supposes, but yesterday, the last day of the festival, couldn't come soon enough. P 'n B housekeeping has their work cut out for them today.

Mondays depress Ariel beyond reason. But she's never been more depressed than today. Ed has barely spoken to her in three weeks, and only in front of the kids. The instant Miles and Ella are down for the count, he's gone. Tokyo Rose across the street gives him what he craves, she guesses.

Ariel sits in her car in the French Quarter lot and cries. She needs to talk to somebody who'll cheer her up. Anybody.

The entire hotel knows, down to the last busboy. She feels the stares, catches the smirks. Nobody's yet disobeyed her, but the onus seems to have been clamped on her as sure as a stockade. How it is that Javier gets off scot-free, Ariel can't wrap her head around, although it sort of figures in the sickest way. Latino cook lands the white bosslady. Who do you vote for?

Ariel flips down her visor in the car and, there in the mini mirror, stares into one of the most pathetic faces she's seen in ages. She wipes away mascara and snot. She can't understand how she got here, making the leap across that enormous divide. Something other than sanity must have coursed through her veins that night she did what she did for the first time. Ariel the Other. And still, *still,* she feels sorry for herself at least as much as she does for Ed. Work is now utter and complete torture. To maintain her authority, hell, her posture, pains Ariel beyond belief.

And Javier. He's cut off all communication with Ariel. She never guessed he'd be such a prick. Objectively, she might have seen it, but getting to know him, she really never thought he'd flip like a switch. Shouldn't he shoulder some of this? Ariel takes makeup from her purse and tries to fix her eyes. She couldn't say Javier had ever been gentle, but he was reverent enough for Ariel to assume she'd won his respect. Stupid her. Stupid, stupid her.

Just for Ed, Ariel sits in her car with the motor running, cranking the air-conditioning. And because it's hot in May in New Orleans, and because she wants to, fuck it all.

She scrolls through her cell phone list of contacts, trying to find somebody to talk to. When you aspire to run a place, and you're a woman, you don't really end up with a ton of friends. Ariel pauses on the few names from Minneapolis she'd consider calling, but on a Monday, midday, none of them will answer.

The thought that she has no real friends makes Ariel cry again. She drips tears onto her cell. How entirely pathetic.

She's just so damn lonely.

Okay. Oh. There's somebody she could call. Sharon Harris. She might make Ariel feel better with her laugh alone. Ariel dials and waits as the phone rings.

"Yeah, Miss Ariel," Sharon says.

Ariel is suddenly so stunned to reach somebody on the other end who seems genuinely happy to hear from her that she starts sobbing.

"Oh, hey, whatever it is, talk it out. Catch yo' breath. Talk it out."

Ariel cries out loud. "I—I screwed up," she says, not knowing she was going to talk about it at all, and only then, confessing to Sharon Harris, does Ariel realize that's exactly what she really did do. She really and truly screwed up. "Oh, my God."

"It gone be alright," Sharon says. "Just keep breathin', lady." Ariel can hear Sharon tell somebody in the backround that she's going to take a break. "You just breathe and I'm gonna find a quiet stairway or somethin'."

Ariel looks for tissue in the glove box. She can't find anything. She puts her cell to her chest and sniffs as big as she can. "Hi," she says to Sharon eventually.

"Hi there, Miss Ariel."

"Thank you for answering."

"Why wouldn't I?"

"I . . . I don't have any friends here."

"Ain't you an' Indira friends?"

"I don't think she likes me," Ariel says. "She's pretty much—" Indira's siding with Ed, Ariel understands. "I made a mistake with another man," Ariel blurts.

"Aw. An it makes you sad?"

It gets a little laugh out of Ariel. She guesses sleeping with another man should make her *happy,* shouldn't it? "Yeah, I guess so," Ariel says. "I really hurt my husband."

"He want a divorce?"

"He hasn't asked for one yet."

"You want a divorce?"

Does she want a divorce? She hadn't even considered one. No. A resounding no. Wow. No. She wants what she, they, have built. "I don't think so. No. I want my family back."

"You breathin' okay yet?"

"Thanks. Yeah."

"You think he gone do somethin' foolish now too? Get some vengeance?"

"I don't think he's like that. I just think—I think maybe he's broken."

Sharon doesn't say anything for a bit. She lets breath out of her mouth. "I hear you. Let me go get my smokes."

"Sure." Ariel listens to the woman move around and then hears street noise, the click of a lighter.

"I'm here," Sharon says.

"I know I don't deserve any sympathy. It's my fault, but . . ."

"There's the thing," Sharon says. "It may be your mistake, but if you heartily sorry, you should be allowed some forgiveness. It just gone take others more time to give it, usually. It'll come if you work on it. You don't work on it, likely it won't."

"You're being so nice, and you don't even know what all happened," Ariel says.

"Oh, I know well enough."

"Really?" Ariel wipes dust from her dashboard.

"I know all about it. Not yours, mind you." Sharon laughs. "Life ain't perfect." Ariel hears a cigarette drag. "I know about hard times though."

"Tell me," Ariel says, as straight as she's ever spoken.

"I got three dead family, premature by violence, an' a husband with a girlfriend I answer the phone to, Miss Ariel, an' that's not the worst of it. We can talk on my children if you in the mood to feel good about yoself today."

Is she being mean? Ariel doesn't know, once again, exactly how to take Sharon. What she says, though, is horrible. "I don't mean to—"

" 'Salright. I not being vengeful. Some my children don't do the right things, though, you mighta noticed. And I thought I teach 'em. Ha!" Sharon coughs into her phone. "I even can get the girls free birth control with a connection here. Ain't that beatin' the band?"

Ariel has no idea what to say. She listens to Sharon smoke. "I think—
I don't know what to say." What does she want to say most? "Really,
thank you for talking to me like a human being. Everybody else makes
me feel like a monster."

"Come on, Miss Minnesota, you ain't no monster. You just a human
being like the rest of us. I stand by you if you need a friend. You in that
place you could need a friend, I think."

Ariel starts crying in her car again. When did life get so hard?

Prancie prepares. While the recipes might not have exacted what she
intended at the barnacle, likely due to the fact that the food was so
widely dispersed, there can be no question her meals will be more effec-
tive at home. She will double, or triple, her secret ingredient. Joe will
eat her food, and he will love it, as he always has. Chopping green peppers, Prancie smiles.

His intentions to leave her, or rather, to have Philomenia depart their
home, will never materialize. Never.

From the kitchen, Prancie hears the front doorbell ring. They do not
allow solicitors, nor is she expecting a package. Prancie wipes her hands
on her apron and goes to the foyer, where Joe has opened their door to
the neighbor Ed, the local drunk. "Hi, Joe," Ed says. "Listen. It was
nice talking to you yesterday. I wondered if you wanted to grab a drink
across the street."

"Sure," Joe says. He turns to glance at Prancie and then steps
through the screen door. "Love to."

"Joe, the doctor said—"

Her husband waves her off. How is it he has become friends with one
of the enemy? When did they speak yesterday? Prancie needs to know
how this connection was made and, more importantly, consider how to
sever it.

Philomenia fights the urge to call after him or to press her hands
against the screen. He will return, and her meal will be ready. She will
say she has already eaten. Afternoon drinking should make him even
hungrier.

Everything a wife must do lies in the planning. If you are prepared for every situation, you will always be able to hold your head high.

One thousand eight hundred and sixty-six. It is the number of days she has collected apple seeds. Indeed, she had been planning all this time without even knowing the reason why.

22

Taliqwa call. Fearius aint heard from her fo like a month. She way off his radar, even if she carryin his baby. Fearius think it not his. She run around plenty. Way he hear it, she fuckin one them Baton Rouge boys at the same time she with Fearius right along side two *other* wardies. He try not think on how stupid he musta look, bein all lovin with her like she his when she bangin anything with legs.

He hangin at work when she call. "Hey, Fearius," she say kinda rushed. "You okay? You out still?"

"I outside, if that what you mean. What up?" She gone ask him for money or somethin.

"You dint hear yet? Your brother Michael."

What happen to Muzzle? "What?"

"He roll over on Alphonse."

Whoa na. But Muzzle not like that, not even if he high. "He aint like that."

"They haul Alphonse in. My cousins sister friend see the whole thing."

"How they know it my bro do it?"

"I dont know." Taliqwa sound frustrated on the phone. "It the word, Fearius. I just call see if you okay, but whatever. You go on with your life."

"Why you have to get like that? I just ask a question."

"Your brother a snitch, Fearius. You gone have some times. I just
wanna see you okay is all. I carryin your baby an what."

"Girl, dont even go there. You know it not mine."

"I can sense it," she say.

"Whatever." All Fearius want to do get off the damn phone with
Taliqwa and make some calls. "You awright?" The words come out an
he wanna suck em back in. He just seem weak.

"Whatever back atcha, big man," she say. "Just tryin do my deed fo
the day. I call you when I get the baby blood test."

"Go on an do that, Miss T." He hang up.

Fearius pace the narrow back and forth fast. What happen now?
What the fuck happen now? First he need to find out it true. If it true,
his world gone change again. If it true, Taliqwa right. He gone have
some times.

Fearius put in a call to the lieutenant. His voice mailbox full. It aint a
good sign, yo. Not no way. Fearius hold his post till somebody tell him
what all else to do. It the only thing he know. Much he want to, Fearius
cant be callin the Moms right now, showin he on the inside. Who else
might know bout Muzzle?

Lieutenant finally swing by late, makin rounds in the Escalade. "Get
in," Brick say. Fearius go to the empty passenger side and step up.

"You hear, huh?" Brick ask. He a giant. He make Alphonse feel protected. No wonder why Brick be a lieutenant. He got three bullet scars,
one on the side his head in a line where no hair grow, like he stuck in the
80s with a do from MC Hammer hisself. Brick old, like twenty.

"I hear all kind things," Fearius say, tryin. "Boo say the 5-0 beat
Muzzle into talkin."

"Boo a retard." Brick dont say nothin more. He drivin around somewhere, nowhere.

Fearius wanna ask where they goin but know better. He not Muzzle,
but he connected by blood. Fearius got somethin comin one way the
other.

Brick not sayin nothin. He turn an drive up by The Fly. The sun goin down. Fearius got his cell, got his Jericho, got his pager. He try and see what Brick carryin. What the fuck goin on? Fearius pretend he worse off, pretend he just have a sharpen toothbrush. He take it and stick it in Bricks neck right now, surprise the lunkhead. Get out and run to Mexico. Texas not far enough. What up here on The Fly but a fast way a puttin a body into the river?

Fearius not make sixteen yet. He some young fish food, hey. His scalp crawlin. Fuck, he dont want give Moms a Blockhead.

Brick pull into like three parking spots sideways. He turn off the engine, a good thing. If he want make it quick, he leave the car runnin. "Muzzle a snitch," Brick say, and Fearius feel his words like a punch.

"I not Muzzle," Fearius say, the first words out his mouth to try an earn him time save his life.

Brick look down on Fearius. "Alphonse gone pay fierce fo what yo bro do." Brick slide his hand down the side his seat. "Like Angola fierce, not gettin out but bein carried feet first."

Fearius try get at the front his boxers without Brick seein, and there it be. Brick lift up a Uzi Fearius see once before and put it in his lap aimin at Fearius sideways. "Yo blood fuck up," Brick say. "Muzzle gone."

"I not Muzzle," Fearius say and know he cant get the Jericho in time. He lift up both his hands like he bein bank robbed. "I swear I not no Muzzle."

"Here how Alphonse arrange it," Brick say. "You gets to prove you not Muzzle o you get yo coins."

Fearius dont want him no coins on his eyes. "I hear."

"It come from Alphonse," the lieutenant say, an Fearius believe him. Fearius sure he hearing the truth. Brick look sad. He an Muzzle come up together, Muzzle hangin with the older kids when he just a runt. It a small world they all busy in.

When you little, when they ask you what you wanna be when you grow up, Fearius answer he want be a builder. He wanna build things, bridges an skyscrapers and what. Fearius remember what Michael— what Muzzle—done say one day when he come home for dinner. Muz-

zle say he got a friend who a boy wanna be a dancer. It Brick. Over the
years it come clear that Brick mean like second line dancing, not like
wearin tights for ballet. But back when he say the words, everybody
think he gone be a ballet dancer and prance around in a tutu, laugh and
laugh. Now he big as a house. Nobody make fun a Brick no more any
day the week.

"It come from Alphonse," Brick repeat, "not me."

Fearius look at Bricks finger on the trigger. "Say."

"Make him his bail an take him out," Brick say.

Fearius look at the Uzi an look at Brick. He hear right? "You want me
kill my brother?"

"Alphonse say it. We raisin funding fo Muzzle bail. No choice,
lil man."

Fearius gone save his own life first, work on Muzzle second. "He my
brother," Fearius say again, like for a exclamation point.

"I been knowin Muzzle years," Brick say all sad, holdin the Uzi.
"But he fucked up now."

"He done fuck up, yeah," Fearius say, his arms gettin tired from
holdin em up. "I put my arms down?"

Brick nod.

Fearius put his hands on his legs, stare at em an dont recognize em.
It like they connected to somebody elses arms. "When?"

"It yo call after he out, but Alphonse not takin no less. Alphonse say
it all start goin bad when you come in, Fearius. It yo fault." Brick stare
out the front window his Escalade, look down the road winding by the
river, not even at the water.

It not Fearius fault, not nohow.

Muzzle beat the shit out Fearius when he little. Fearius bet Muzzle
beat the shit out Brick too when they kids, even with Muzzle bein
younger. Funny how everything get goin backwards. Now Fearius got to
kill Muzzle or he be killed hisself. He take his orders an think about the
rest when he have breathin room. The Escalade not the right place, not
when it full with a Uzi. "When I get the bail?" Fearius ask.

"I call you."

"You drop me by Camellia Grill maybe?"

"You an yo fuckin horse balls, lil man. No wonder he say it start with you. Get the fuck out, nigga."

The walk back from The Fly long. Fearius dont know what he gone get when he make it home. The Moms and Pops likely fightin, assumin Pops there, over what they do about Muzzle. The sisters gone be real quiet. Hey, Fearius, all he hafta do be commit murder. On his brother. Aint no thang. Fearius stop in the middle the levee and puke up what left his lunch along with the grape cold drink he have after. Fuck if the mess dont stink.

After some days, Fearius come to think on why Muzzle not be free if he turn state witness. OPP down at Broad an Tulane Avenues pretend they cant help Fearius. His bro lost in the system. Maybe Muzzle go into the Witness Protection and Fearius never see him another day the rest a they lives. Fearius wish. His bro just rotting somewhere inside the Orleans Parish Prison guts, got his sign in name backwards or somethin.

Five days in, the supply start gettin sketchy. Ali Abubu come tell Fearius Boo not got no work after today. "I sorry," Boo say. "I like lookin out fo you."

"You a good look out," Fearius tell the retard, tryin to be nice. It like kickin a dog bein mean to Boo. What the point? "What you gone do?" Fearius ask him.

"I gone work," he say.

Duh. "Yeah," Fearius say, an that all.

On day seven, they find Muzzle in the OPP with the help a Moms bitchin up to the ceilings. Both Moms and Fearius get in for a sittin after they fill out papers an Fearius lie about his time spent in juvey.

Behind the plexiglass, Muzzle look bad. Worsen bad. Fearius feel Moms go real sad next to him, but she hold up. Moms the strongest lady Fearius know. She put her hand on the plexi and say, "I love you, Michael."

Muzzle look like he think on smiling but his bottom lip split so bad and only half scabbed up he cant. He too much a man stick his hand up against the Moms. She take it down eventually.

Fearius see Muzzle done lost twenty five, thirty pounds easy. Mo fo on the product. Son a bitch. Muzzle sittin on his hands an chewin on his cheek, swingin his jaw back an forth like Banana Truck. What the hell happen in nine months?

An this the fucker Fearius get to off. This sad sack a shit be his blood brother. When Muzzle open his mouth to talk, Fearius see his bro missin a front tooth. That gotta hurt. "Moms and baby bro," he say, noddin.

Moms clamp her hand on Fearius leg where Muzzle cant see and squeeze hard. Man, Moms deserve better. It pain Fearius bad, real bad.

Fearius lift his jaw at Muzzle, ask, "What you need?"

Muzzle laugh like he lost his brain, show em instead he lost two teeth. "How Witness Protection sound?" So it true. It all true. Muzzle roll on Alphonse. Do NOPD even do Witness Protection? Fearius not hear about it yet. Likely not.

Muzzle suck at the hole in his teeth. "Yeah," he say, noddin, "ate me some teeth for lunch last week."

Moms lose it. She just go on an lose it.

The pink an chocolate house not be touched since the, ha, what they call, the episode Fearius have with the cleaners, but now he not feel very safe no matter what.

It make sense. It the middle days a June, an Fearius get Muzzle sprung yesterday with the Moms help. Fifteen g down payment. She know it not honest money, but who care, right? The Moms first baby boy out, hooray.

But then Muzzle gone back fast to where he get his fix, barely say the thank yous.

Fearius start countin days. He know they his to count. Not nobody else with brains gone take Muzzle out. Everybody know it Fearius test. It his job. Straight out the bible, yo.

Alphonse probably gone down forever. The 5-0 done find they supplies in the kilos. Guess Muzzle know where the big haul always be cause he the one rat it out. That an word by Muzzle talk on the jobs he know bout. Muzzle name the enforcer Alphonse sometimes use. The killer nigga on the run now, they say.

The Alphonse machine still workin, but with a lot less. Everybody conserve some, get rid the Boos where they can, runners doublin up.

None them in Fearius whole family, not the Moms or Pops or none them kids, been outside town past Grand Isle. If Muzzle try an run, he not gone know where the hell to go. He never even be to Florida, an Fearius hear it a quick drive. Hell, skinny missin teeth Muzzle gone be lucky if he dont OD. It Fearius biggest wish. He dream it all the time. He step up with the Jericho an aim it at Muzzle an see his bro already dead, a needle stickin out his arm. The rush of happiness crazy. Then Fearius wake up.

Most the time he occupy down time from work with video games. He like John Madden an San Andreas. Fearius a little embarrass Debutanté win every time, but whatever. The games keep his head off what he dont wanna think on.

Fearius learn a word in school before he step out. It a great word, one he always wanna use somehow, never had the place. Now he do. The word extrapolate.

From this day on, he able to extrapolate where it all go. Oh yeah.

23

The lowdown is just nuts. The way Ed hears it from Joe, Philomenia and Ariel ought to join forces. They'd wipe out their husbands in one sweep of their brooms.

Joe says Philomenia has a genetic disease, fatal familial insomnia, which sounds like it has everything to do with not sleeping but most of it has to do with losing your mind. Apparently she's inherited it from her mother. Joe says he never thought he'd survive his cancer, but he has, and now he has a life again. He's alive! The man's energy is truly contagious and exactly what Ed needs. With the kids at day camp and Ed pretty much relinquishing all of his household duties, Ariel's left having to pick Miles and Ella up, and his days are free.

He and Joe have been coming to the Rose most days for a month now. Now Ed and Joe have the perfect toast every afternoon: "Fuck the wives!" and then one more time, "Fuck the wives!" They raise their glasses along with whoever might be along for the ride. Shane's around sometimes, and he'll join in, although Ed notices Shane doesn't actually say the toast, only raises his glass. Ed's never been big on swearing, but somehow this feels about right.

Joe knows all about what Ariel did, as do most of the other regular patrons in the Rose. The thing is, though, they all stare out the dirty window now when she comes home with the kids. Somebody almost always whistles. They say things like, "Hell, who cares what she did. She come home to me, *I* take her back." Or, "Now *that's* worth forgivin."

Ariel is beautiful. It's something Ed had forgotten. He admits it with a twinge of regret and a big swallow of beer.

Ed can't get over the broken trust. He has no idea if Ariel's sleeping with a different hotel guest every other shift now. Having once believed she'd never be unfaithful, he now keeps thinking she will be at every turn. The logical portion of his psyche says Ariel lives with great regret these days, a chaste and routine subsistence, but some other part of him, a bitter troll of a part, trots out from under the bridge and throws temper tantrums about her continued infidelity. She has made a fool of him.

Ed wishes he could cast spells. He would return Ariel to the state of mind when they first fell in love at college and keep her there the rest of her life. That'd be a great spell.

"My best guess is that she has maybe six months, a year tops," Joe says, wrapping his big mitt of a hand around his pint glass. "I really thought that since she'd made it to this age she was in the free and clear."

Now that's some painful realizing. Joe doesn't love Philomenia though. He claims he never has. How's that for an ugly arrangement? "But if you never loved her, whadda you really care?" Ed's trying to be callous and funny, but he's not sure he's pulling it off. What hard, dried little piece of Buddhism Ed has left hurts to know Philomenia has never been loved by her husband in the thirty-two years they've been married. She seems very lonely.

"She'll tell you the same thing, like I said," Joe says. "It's comfortable. She's been a good friend most of the time. Wrap up housekeeper and personal chef into one, for decades, and that's what I've got with Philly Philster. Why wouldn't you want to keep that kind of friend around?" Joe lays his hand on his stomach. "Man, have I had some cramps the last while. Excuse me. The new and improved guts are still healing, I guess." He goes to the front door. "Back in five."

"Makes me a little sad," Shane says. "She deserves something better than divorce with nothin', don't you think?"

"Who?" Ed asks. He hasn't made up his mind about divorce.

"Dude, where's your head at?"

Seems Warren's elected himself. He knocks on Ariel's open office door. "You busy?"

"You're talking to me?" Ariel asks, truly surprised.

"I can come in?"

"What do you think about our talking only in questions to each other?" She earns a small smile from her former friend for it.

"I need to shut the door."

"Go ahead."

Warren's mass fills the frame before he closes them off from all the dozens and dozens of prying eyes. He sits down opposite her. "You probably don't know. I don't know how you would, seeing as how nobody talks to you anymore."

Ariel looks with ennui at the man's familiar girth, listens to his baritone. She is beyond crying by a good number of weeks. Pain is just pain. "Yes?"

"Javier has—hum. I think Henny has a grip on his—" He clears his throat. "Look. He's decided to go to the owners with sexual harassment. He's telling anyone who'll listen. Fuck, Ariel. You're in deep."

Ariel runs her hand over her face. "Mmm."

"He's saying you forced him to have sex or he'd lose his job."

Ariel looks at her watch. "Well, I have to go get the kids from camp. Hubby doesn't do anything anymore. Thanks for the heads-up."

"Ariel."

"No, really. Thanks." She stands.

Muzzle come walkin in when the rest the family gone to bed. They dint change no locks. Pops out the house tonight long enough he not back till morning. Fearius feel like he starin down a ghost lookin at Muzzle, an right the same time, Fearius starin at his own salvation. His hit walking straight into the alley with no way out, cant even jump the fence.

Fearius stand. Cribs keep playin, showin some platinum record col-

lection hung up in a room the people never barely visit but for dusting.
Peace the only thing worth payin for, Fearius think.

Muzzle say, "Danny, I need me some cash money."

What he call Fearius? "Say?" He squint his eyes.

"You heard me. Go get it."

"For serious? You come here to do this?"

"Word out, Danny. You the big hit man, hey. Go on an get yo gun
o get me all the green you got." Muzzle raise his shirt show a pea-
shooter .22.

Fearius put down the remote control on the table. In they own
house? It why Muzzle do exactly what he doin. He gotta know Fearius
think about the Moms and sisters. Muzzle already know Fearius not
gone do nothing under the roof on Orchid Street proper. He look at his
fucked up bro in the TV light. He wastin away, just wastin hisself into
nothing. He stink. Muzzle stink and shake both. Fearius feel like he be
inside a movie, someplace where stuff pretend. Fuck, Muzzle gotta be a
pretend thing the way he strung out.

How it ever come this far?

"Moms bank most my green," Fearius tell his brother.

"Gimme all you got, o the sisters gone hear somethin ugly. Sounds
the babies not forget anytime soon." Muzzle kinda pacing but not liftin
one his feet like it glued down to the carpet or he cant feel it.

Just then a baby chirp from the back. Both him and Muzzle go still.
How this not some kinda sick joke? Muzzle gone follow Fearius when
he go to his room? Fearius heart start thumpin. He might could pretend
he dint know who come into the house. Maybe he just try an save the
whole family from bein broke into and not see who he shoot.

Muzzle know Fearius cant never deny him nothing. It go way back to
when Muzzle beat the innards out Fearius every month. Still, Fearius
hide stuff from Muzzle, things in Fearius own heart and in his own
head that Muzzle cant never get at. Michael Bruce Harris never get
everything that Fearius have, never.

"I goin, bro," Fearius say and walk away casual to find him some
somethin. Muzzle stay in the front room. Maybe Muzzle need to keep

lookin out the windows. More n likely he cant care less, just bein lazy. He need to get high again soon.

Fearius dont got but three or four C and the usual work stack a fins and shit. Enough money still to get Muzzle ODed easy. Fearius reach into his hiding place an pull out his short president stack and the Jericho both.

One fluffy, one heavy.

He think on Moms and the babies in the house. He think on Blockhead. Theys just no way. Not here, probably not never.

Mexico smell like tacos and rose petals, yo. He know it. It just have to.

24

This July morning, dawn arrives dressed in the colors of smoke. It is no wonder. It pulls behind it a day on fire. One must confront New Orleans heat directly. "Hello, hot day soon to come," Prancie says aloud.

She did not sleep at all last night. She has not slept well since supporting Joe through his ordeal, but now she finds sleep to be only wasted time. She has so much to write, so much to record. Meals and their times. Observations of foes and their actions. Night provides much better cover for her work. Her husband snores audibly from the guest room for a solid ten hours.

Joe has begun legal proceedings, he claims, and he continues to insist she pursue a relationship with another man. This, above all else, displeases her. What a ridiculous notion with eventual court proceedings on the horizon. Does he think her so dim as to not see his plan to leave her with less than nothing? No, she will not alter her moral convictions at his bidding.

He additionally persists in baiting her with terrible language and foul names, but she will not succumb to his taunts. She will not give him the satisfaction of the hatred he so desires from her. If she hates him, he will feel justified in his actions, but Prancie will not allow his victory.

Something, she notices again as she looks at the seven journals spread before her, has gone awry, possibly, but she has no time to allow worry into her life at this juncture. Her journals had been so orderly, so lovely in their uniform penmanship. In the last months, the mouse and the moths have come more frequently. They must be to blame for the now significantly pronounced change in her handwriting. Still, the journals are a source of inspiration, and rereading supplies much of her current sustenance.

Prancie goes to wash. She has a day of making groceries planned so that she might continue the increased feeding. First to the farmers' market. She would like to choose from the fresh cheeses for a keynote ingredient. From behind the guest bedroom door come Joe's uninterrupted exhalations.

After undressing, Prancie weighs herself. She has not had to worry about her size for the entirety of her life, however she has noticed a continued dropping of digital numbers in the last while. Since Joe's cancer. How he could have overcome such an invasive intruder remains beyond Prancie's ability to understand.

The nude figure in the mirror looks much like a slight, pubescent girl's. See? The girl is very pale. She has taken care to stay out of the sun's damaging rays. Her breasts do not yet need a brassiere, but wearing one that included some padding might flatter her slim figure. There. See? There! A faded scar. The shape resembles a scythe.

Philomenia, eight years old, rode her bicycle down the boulevard away from the Sacred Heart Academy. That day she had learned the place of New Orleans in relation to the rest of the world. It sits at the end of a river, beneath an oval of lake, near the Gulf of Mexico, in the south of North America, a great distance away from the founding Sacré Coeur in France located in the continent of Europe.

Philomenia pedaled not so much looking at the pavement as she did the imaginary map of the world spread out in front of her. What a grand and colorful place, this globe of theirs. She decided then that she would see all of it. Inside the irregularly shaped landmasses lay the freedom of her future. She would travel for years in glamorous dresses and meet her husband in an exotic destination. He would be a spy, or possibly an ambassador. Philomenia liked the idea of both the words, although she was uncertain as to the responsibilities of an ambassador other than to be a spy without having to remain a secret.

In the imagining of her future husband, Philomenia did not see the workmen's truck filled with tools ahead of her. At significant speed, Philomenia weaved her way around the coast of Australia and directly into a pointed shovel protruding from the rear of the truck bed at an angle.

Prancie cups the breasts of the slight girl with her chilly hands. Neither of them has been off the continent.

The farmers' market at Riverbend spreads itself across a portion of a warming black asphalt parking lot. Three large white rectangular tents shelter local fare, including honey, and today, Creole tomatoes. Prancie searches for the cheese maker's lovely rounds. She stands holding a small bunch of parsley when the mouse begins to chew. No, no. Not now. The moths come in and blanket the spread of produce. Prancie can barely see the celery for all the dusty fluttering.

"I can help you?" a buxom African American woman asks Prancie, laying her dark hand on Prancie's arm across a pile of Vidalia onions.

Prancie tries to blink the moths away. It has not worked for some time. She says into the beating fog, "I may need to rest a spell. Is there a seat?"

"Oh, here. Oh, now. I have a crate." The woman comes around from the other side of her booth and steers Prancie to the back side.

Prancie can barely see for all the wings.

"Sit down. Sit." The woman places her hands on Prancie's shoulders and guides her down to sit on a milk crate.

"Thank you," Prancie says. "I'm sorry."

"Out on this blacktop, the heat can get bad even at this time a mornin'. Don't know why they stick us out under the sun the way it cook the vegetables and grit up the honey."

Prancie stares at the moths, listening to the woman's comforting voice. She does not care what is being spoken.

"Here," the woman says, "I know what you need." She walks away towards what Prancie thinks is an automobile and returns with a dampened towel or washcloth. "Put this on your forehead. You just havin' a flash."

A flash? Oh. A hot flash. Philomenia finished with that three years ago.

"I know how it go," the woman says and chuckles. "I know exactly."

"Thank you," Prancie says again.

"Sugar helps too, like with diabetes. The nectarines are something wonderful, ya heard?"

Prancie stares into the moths. She can hardly see the woman's face with the interference. "Yes. I heard."

Prancie must find a way to address the insurgent pests. Regular driving will become difficult, as will other things.

She returns home. Twice in her one-mile outing people chose to honk at her. Prancie does not care about the impatience of others. She must get back safely.

So it will be gumbo again this evening, duck and andouille. Prancie did not secure the cheese she needed, but she can count on gumbo any day of the week as the vehicle for her special ingredient.

When she looks at the clock, she sees time has escaped. Two o'clock. Prancie arranges her purchases on the counter and pulls her cutting board from the cupboard. She could likely cook the gumbo blindfolded.

She sprinkles flour over the melting butter for the roux in the cast iron. Joe enters the kitchen.

"You've been away for oh-so-many hours, Philly Steak."

"I was shopping."

"I see," he says. "What's the grub tonight?"

"Duck and andouille gumbo," she says honestly. Why should she hide her menu?

"Awesome. High five."

"Sorry?"

"The clock's tickin, wife. Aren't you even curious about being with a man besides me?"

She so wishes he would give up on the pursuit. "I'm a married woman," is all she can think to say.

"But you won't be forever," he answers. "Come on."

He should have died. He did not.

"Oh," he says. "Ed found this and printed it up for me. He ordered high-speed internet." Joe dramatically pulls a folded piece of paper from his back pocket and places it on the counter beside her cutting board. "Read up. Think about getting that other lay, Cheese Steak." Joe leaves the kitchen.

The page is only half full:

Presentation

The age of onset is variable, ranging from 30 to 60, with an average of 50. Death usually occurs between 7 to 36 months from onset. The presentation of the disease varies considerably from person to person, even among patients from within the same family.

The disease has four stages, taking 7 to 18 months to run its course:

1. The patient suffers increasing insomnia, resulting in panic attacks and phobias. This stage lasts about four months.
2. Hallucinations and panic attacks become noticeable, continuing about five months.
3. Complete inability to sleep is followed by rapid loss of weight. This lasts about three months.
4. Dementia, turning unresponsive or mute over the course of six months. This is the final progression of the disease, and the patient will subsequently die.

Treatment

There is no cure or treatment for FFI; hope rests on the so far unsuccessful gene therapy. Sleeping pills have no effect.

While it is not currently possible to reverse the underlying illness, there is some evidence that treatment modalities that focus upon the symptoms can improve quality of life.

Prancie tries to remember what a modality is. It rests on the tip of her brain, at the very top. Her gray matter feels conical today. She stirs at the bits of browning roux paste, making certain it does not burn.

"Phil Phil," Joe says, returning to the kitchen.

Prancie takes the thick wire handle of the cast-iron pot in both her hands. She lifts and swings with all her might. It finds his head. The vibration of the blow travels through her bones.

Cast iron, she thinks, makes a wonderful sound against a skull. Joe falters and falls to the tile. She swings twice more at his prone form.

Cerise convinced Roy to come up to the park with her, and she's happy she did. She can tell by his step he's enjoyin' the place too. He's carrying her easel. She's got a wooden box of paints with a handle on it that she holds with her claw. She can just get the fingers through, she discovered, so the right hand's startin' to be good for something. It works for grocery sacks also.

"Ha! There you go. That what you thinkin' of painting?" Roy points at a No Fishing sign by the pond.

"Just for that, I'm gonna paint you, Roy Brown. What you think of that?"

Roy looks at her with the smile behind his eyes, something better than butter on warm bread. She loves nobody else more in this world. They keep walking around the path, and Cerise takes Roy's free arm. It's a beautiful day.

Prancie skirts the red puddle coming from Joe and leaves the kitchen.

Prancie will have a cognac. On the way to the parlor, she finds the creaking floorboards, each complaining one of them. She stops and bounces her small weight on every dark brown plank. Here you are and here you are and here you are too.

Prancie inserts the key in the lock and turns.

She returns to the bottle of Hennessy. Its color and shape both call to her once more.

She pulls the corked cap. Straight from the bottle, Prancie swallows a goodly amount, what she imagines to be approximately a half cup.

Prancie does not expect Joe to notice. Prancie does, however, need to sit awhile and consider the results.

25

The supply run out the second time in one week. Brick scramblin to find enough on his own with everybody runnin scared away from all Alphonses people. It not what Fearius worryin about so much though. It comin on three weeks since Muzzle first snitch an Alphonse go in. Fearius aint got but one week left before they see to him goin out this world. He have a sense about it. Nobody say nothing, but he know it. He have numbered days.

Mexico be under Texas. Fearius remember from social studies. He know words like chalupa and burrito and puta, but the rest gone be harder. He happy the American dollar still worth somethin. Money always make steppin through foreign territory easier.

Fearius get the call from Brick sayin to quit for the day. Before the giant hang up, it his favorite thing to tell Fearius the day count on Alphonse. "Nineteen days, nigga," he say.

Fearius can fuckin bring it in Mexico. He work an be the next Tony Montana, buy a house on the beach an put up Moms and maybe Klameisha in luxury. He gone have his own lieutenants lookin out. He gone have a bulletproof Hummer an a supply a chocolate color maids dont wear no underwear under those little ruffle skirts.

He take the I-10 to Houston first, right? It the road there, he pretty sure. He need to start puttin clothes in a suitcase.

Fearius enjoy the nature by the river, even if walkin it make his way home longer. Not many people ever up here which he like. Most days it almost dark when he get back, sometimes the sky already showin stars.

Lately he notice the moon come out a lot in the afternoon. He can even see it from Pigeontown. He wanna know what it mean when the moon out in the afternoon. Maybe it always there. Might could be he develop better eyes. Carrots be good for the eyes, an he like the cooked ones Moms make with brown sugar.

He look for wildlife every walk on the levee. So far he seen him rats an the big things, nutrias, a wild dog pack with two coyotes in it, the long neck white birds that come in two sizes an the long neck gray bird cousins. He seen three straight up alligators at different times and on a foggy morning something he think a pig with tusks. Theys those squawkin green birds like little parrots. Lots of funny bugs with armor and pinchers and what. Butterflies.

Today dont offer up much. Fearius like to see him a deer sometime, or a big yellow cougar come walkin with fat paws out the scraggly woods right by the river. That be something. Maybe they grow em in Mexico.

Despite himself, Ed's beginning to feel bad about Ariel. She's not eating and mopes around, crying routinely late at night. She's told him at his insistence about the other man, and it now sounds like this Javier guy is a real asshole. Ed doesn't want to have to explain to the kids why their mom lost her job, especially under the circumstances. A potential lawsuit is nothing he ever believed he would have to contend with.

Well, he'll talk it out with Joe at the Rose. Ed goes out the front door and is hit by a blast of heat. July officially initiates the torture, he's come to learn.

For the last two weeks or so, Ed's wanted nothing more than to fuck his wife. Just ball. He wants what Javier wanted. He wants what the guys in the Rose staring out the window want. His desire fascinates and appalls him. He will not roll to her though, on her far side of the bed. She has to come to him.

Ed cuts across the grass. Joe doesn't care, although poor Philomenia probably does. Joe's spent a little time outside on his lawn lately, at Ed's encouragement. Getting outdoors and being close to the ground helps everyone. Green and sky blue are the most calming colors around. And a good golden amber, about the color of a Pilsner Urquell. Naw. He doesn't know about amber.

He takes Joe's steps two at a time. It's beer hour.

The doorbell rings. Prancie places the bottle of cognac on the end table. She will have even more in some time. She thinks Hennessy is a delicious vehicle to another place. Prancie will be there promptly.

She expects Ed. He stands beyond the sheers on the other side of the glassed front door. The oval beveled insert glints in the afternoon sun.

"Hello," she says as she opens the door.

"Wow. Ah, sorry. I thought you'd be Joe."

"I have never been Joe."

"I didn't mean that—"

Prancie holds up her hand to stop him. She surveys the drunk. He has destroyed her. At every turn. To befriend Joe in this last month proves her early thesis. A moth flies between them.

Ed swats. "What do they call these?"

"Pardon?" He saw it?

"This kind of moth."

No. She will not engage in polite conversation. "I don't know."

Ed Flank stands and waits for something more that will not come. Finally, he asks, "Joe's ready?"

She gets to say the words she has been planning for nearly half a bottle of cognac now. "No. Joe is indisposed." Prancie looks down to her hand. Freckles of blood have dried to a light brown on the back of her right wrist. "He sends his apologies."

"His stomach's bothering him again, I guess."

"We can suppose," Prancie says and closes the door.

It is not enough. It is not even close. She returns to the parlor.

Ed stands on Joe's porch and plops his hands on his hips. Yesterday, Joe had confirmed their regular visit to the Rose today, hell or high water. They even toasted to it. What's up?

Ed knocks again. Something feels not right. He looks behind him. He goes down the porch steps and looks both directions on the street. Uh oh. There's why. Daniel Harris lopes up the blacktop in Ed's direction. He can tell from the way the kid walks that he's carrying a gun. Ed knows how to tell now. Power is power.

Ed's not done anything to instigate another confrontation since that night, he doesn't think. He hasn't 'fucked with' Daniel 'n his. He hopes he hasn't.

Prancie has never forgotten a word Joe has said to her. She does not think so at the moment. Regardless. She knows the location of what she needs as well as what to do.

Trying to watch out for Daniel, Ed goes up the steps and knocks again. Philomenia doesn't answer the door a second time. Through the sheer curtain, beyond the foyer, someone moves around in the formal living room. Ed watches and then slaps at the glass oval repeatedly, his wedding ring clinking loudly. The person inside ignores Ed's racket.

Behind him, he feels Daniel approach on the street and stop. The hairs on the back of Ed's neck stand up. "Don't go breakin' down no doors, Rescue Man," the kid says.

The silhouetted figure finally moves into the foyer. Ed knows, from the size, that it's Philomenia. He hopes she'll let him come in until Daniel leaves.

She swings the door wide open with a flourish and steps back. It smashes against the wall behind. "Ed Flank," she says flatly and lifts both her arms. She holds something. It takes him a second to recognize the object. She levels an enormous revolver at his head.

Fearius see somethin he not sure all real.

Rescue Man be backin down the steps away from witchy Miss Philomenia an then all a sudden he dive into her big ass bushes. She be packing. She really fuckin packing. Philomenia gots herself a gun, and she pointin it at Rescue Man.

What happen with Fearius life that everything seem outta a game or some such he dont know. But there it be, presentin itself on this earth in the daylight. He like twenty feet back, standin in the street, and it goin down plain as a face, or a hand in front a face. Whatever they say. Fearius reach in his pants for the Jericho.

The gun blast hurts Prancie's wrist. She did not expect it. Behind the moths, the man has become lost in the ginger. She can hear him in there. Leaves rustle. They wave green shadows behind the moths. She pulls on the trigger with her finger again, but it does not go as easily. There! It fires! Joe warned her that subsequent shots would be more difficult to move into the chamber without cocking. There! Again!

The tiny lady be tryin to kill Rescue Man with a .45. She come down off her porch and wave around the big gun at her ginger plants. Fearius hold his place, watchin the scene, when Rescue Man come racin like a dog out the bushes on all fours. He struggle up onto his feet.

Fearius gots the Jericho ready. Ol Philomenia put another shot into her ginger. She blind now? Maybe she losin her sight. All the days Fearius ever know her, they always something off about the lady.

Rescue Man run then. He motherfuckin run at Fearius standin in the middle the street an hide behind him. What the fuck? Fearius gone be a wall? Maybe. Rescue Man hold on to Fearius shoulders, press his head into Fearius back. The man crouchin.

OK. Sure. Fearius a big wall. A big mofo wall. Hell yeah. He can rescue Rescue Man. Fearius point the Jericho at crazy ol Philomenia and wait for her to see him. Showin her she best stop her shit now. But she turn around blinkin with her head tiltin up like she only followin a smell. She step out into the street. Her eyes way wrong, wagglin around, showin the whites. Nuh uh.

Fearius back up, bump on Rescue Man.

They be a noise and then Fearius chest feel hot. Something go funny with his knees. He step around a little doin a dance he dont know the moves for, and then he on the ground. He try raise the Jericho but some reason his hand not workin right. Rescue Man sit down right behind him. Fearius sorta on top Rescue Man. Maybe he help Fearius out with liftin the gun. It always be heavy.

She believes she has gotten him directly. The shadowy mass drops onto the street. There. She is done. What the future might hold is not hers to know.

Prancie raises the revolver toward the mouse. It chews beneath her jaw. She knows. She knows it is not real. Fresh herbs rest on her counter. She could still feed more mouths real food. She was a girl once, with a scythe scar, who wanted to see the world. Prancie pulls the trigger hard.

Ed watches the top of Philomenia's head shower down around her onto the street. She is suddenly a marionette with cut strings, collapsing into a heap of thin limbs and a ruined face. Nothing makes sense. He can hear nothing but the echo of the gunshot in his ears.

Sitting on his ass, Ed moves his shaking hands over Daniel, lifting the boy's shirt. He has been shot in the chest. The hole in the top of his rib cage makes a sucking noise as Daniel tries to breathe. Ed considers CPR, but he doesn't know what to do about pumping on a sternum so near a bullet wound. He thinks he remembers a moment from first-aid class that told him not to do it. Ed presses his palm over the hole.

The sky has caught the kid's fascination. He trembles in some kind of seizure. Ed becomes aware of the expansive pool of bright red blood for the first time in the brilliant daylight. It seeps around Ed's legs. Where is everybody?

God. This cannot be happening. He is just a boy. His skin is as smooth as Miles'. He is just a boy.

Ed looks up and sees the moon through tears.

He picks up the boy's head and places it in his lap.

Fearius feel warm. The left side his shirt wet, but he feel fine. He spot the moon again up in the blue sky. A great big bird come over and block out the light. A hand go on his face, nice and soft.

"It's Ed," a man say. "It's Ed. I'm here."

Ed? Oh, yeah. It time. "I gone get rescued, right?"

26

Cerise and Roy turn the corner onto Orchid. The sirens they kept hearin' have to do with their own street. No, no, no, no. Something terrible has happened. Two ambulances and way too many police cars are parked every which way. A big part is marked off with yellow police tape. From across the street, another police car come pullin' up with its siren on, turn hard, and stop.

Cerise starts jogging. "Don't you dare, Cherry!" Roy yells. "You ruin one hand already!" Roy catches up to Cerise and takes her arm.

"Shh," he says. "Shh. We find out. You not gone do nothing right now." They have most of another block to go.

"Oh, what happen?" Cerise walks fast as Roy lets her. "What happen?" she asks. "You don't see Marie's car, right?"

"Aw, hell." Now Roy's understanding. Much as they enjoy some of their neighbors, the thought of their daughter being hurt sinks down to the bone like a fishing knife, fast. They both twist their heads around, lookin' and lookin'. "I don't see her car," Roy says. "I don't see it. Thank you, heavens, I don't see it."

They keep walkin fast till they get up to the yellow tape. There's blood all over, wet in the street, with little stand-up triangle markers around. It's horrible. Miss Philomenia and Joe's front door's open. Walkie-talkie noise comes from every direction, and there's lots of people going in and out the open door. They wheel somebody out the house right then, the head of the person on the gurney covered in bandages with blood showing through. Cerise puts down her wooden suitcase and lays her good hand on Roy's arm.

The paramedics yell for all the police to move and go down the porch fast.

"It Joe," Roy says.

"You can tell? Maybe. It gotta be, right?"

"It him. It Joe. I know his drivin shoes he wear."

"He's beatin' the cancer though, I heard. You see Miss Philomenia?"

"No." He looks around, lifting his head high and standing on his toes. "No, I don't."

"Our house is in there," Cerise says right as she figures it out. "We can get in. I'm goin'." Cerise slips under the yellow tape quick before Roy can catch her.

"Cherry!" Cerise knows her husband's trying to protect her from seeing things that hurt, but she's strong again. She's a good helper, and she knows everybody on the block. Probably the only person besides Miss Philomenia.

A policeman stops her. "Sorry, ma'am, you can't be in here." He's Chinese or maybe Thai or something. When did New Orleans get Asian folks to lose their minds and start working for the city in a uniform?

"It's my street," she says. "I live here."

"Where?" the man asks and raises his hand, snapping at other policemen and indicating something. There's a couple of lady officers too.

"Is that Joe?" Cerise can't help but sort of strain against the policeman's arm. She has to know who all is hurt.

"Ma'am, the paramedics need to get to the hospital."

Roy steps up. He's still carrying her easel and now Cerise's box of paints too. "That's Joe," he says. "Joe Beauregard—what's the rest?" he asks Cerise.

"Beauregard de Bruges," Cerise says.

The cop snaps his fingers again, this time louder. "Hey, Martin. Now."

"What happen?" Roy asks.

The policeman just keeps snapping.

"What happen?" Roy asks again.

The cop can't seem to get the person he wants. "Which one is your house, ma'am?"

"*Our* house," Roy tells the man. "That one." He points.

Cerise keeps lookin' around for clues. She never imagined so much blood but at a butcher's. It's horrible. The street smells like iron. There's an ambulance with its backside facing away from them, and suddenly she thinks she sees Ed pacing by the edge of it. He's covered head to toe in blood.

"That's your house?" The policeman points the exact same direction as Roy at their house.

"That's where I'm pointin'," Roy says. "What happen?" he asks for the third time.

"That house. That's your house."

What is wrong with the man? "What the hell?" Cerise asks the fool.

"Excuse me," the cop says. "I need to bring over a detective to question you. Please stay here."

Cerise keeps looking and knows it's Ed over there. Soon as the cop turns his back and starts walking to fetch a detective, she escapes, detouring around the mess in the middle of Orchid Street. It's a mess for real, something she knows ain't a happy ending.

It's him. It's him. She starts jogging over best her legs carry her.

The man's face is completely streaked with tears and blood. He looks like he decided to swim in blood. How's he still standing? He's pacing, pacing, when he sees Cerise.

The man howls, and then he bends over and starts bawling. He stands up again. He holds out his arms. Cerise goes into them straight away. It has to be bad.

Ariel sees the lights of all the cop cars, an ambulance, and the yellow tape spanning the width of Orchid and makes a T-turn in the street.

"The police are at our house!" Miles yells.

"No, we don't know that," Ariel says. "They're just near our house." Her stomach pulls up into her ribs. It takes all she has not to drive down and fling open her car door, screaming after Ed. Has he committed sui-

cide? "We can't park there right now. Let's go get some milkshakes."
She can call Sharon or Indira from Baskin-Robbins on Carrollton.

Ella starts crying in her car seat. "Where's Daddy? I want Daddy."

"Daddy's okay, sweetie." Ariel glances in the rearview. Ella's twisted
around, staring. Something horrible has happened.

Ariel pulls into the parking lot across the street from the bar—what's
it called, Flanagan's?—that was in the news during Mardi Gras. In her
head, Ariel can still see the guy's arrest photo. A big lunk of a bearded
bartender overserved an underage girl, and she died in their bathroom.
Ariel used to feel comforted by the fact that the Belle was outside the
college circuit. Now she could care less. Now she needs to know what's
happened on her street. She has to distract the kids somehow first.

Ariel turns off the engine, and Miles opens his door. He's out and
inside the ice cream parlor before Ariel can help extract Ella.

Inside, Ariel hears Miles already talking to a blinged-out young guy.
Her son says his father's getting arrested. "Cops are all over," he says.
"I'm tellin' ya." Miles nods exaggeratedly and pushes his pants down
on his hips.

Ariel strides over to her son and picks him up by his armpits, pivots
around, and carries his heavy boy self outside. She sets him down but
holds on to his arms. "I don't know who you feel you want to impress,
but it's not me. Do *not* scare your sister, Miles, and quit with the shit.
Now." Ariel is as serious as she's ever been.

Ella follows them out.

"It's true," Miles says. "Dad's going downtown."

Where the fuck has her firstborn child learned these expressions?

"Why?" Ella whimpers, holding small fists at her stomach.

For all Ariel knows, it's true. The massive police presence has her
scared to near meltdown. But Parenting 101 says the kids need to see
her calm. "Your father would have called me," she tells them. "I'm sure
the police are there about a neighbor or that bar. An old man probably
drank too much beer and fell down. Pull up your pants, Miles. Let's get
some ice cream."

Ella chooses bubblegum ice cream, a bad idea Ariel doesn't have the
wherewithal to stop. Miles pushes and wins a banana split with three

scoops. He knows something's up, no question. Ariel's not helping by acquiescing so easily. They sit in an orange formica booth while Miles eats cautiously, head down, staring out past his eyebrows through the plate-glass window.

"I'm going outside, guys, okay?" Ariel tells the kids.

Ella digs out a bright, drippy pink gumball from her ice cream with her fingers. She nods.

"I can see you through the window," Ariel says.

"Are you going to call Dad?"

"No, but I am going to use my phone. It's rude to talk on them in public."

"Whatever." Miles jams his plastic spoon into a banana slice, but Ariel can see he's upset. He wants to know too. She's impressed by the front he's learned to put up so well.

A bell rings on the door as she leaves. Outside, Ariel finds Sharon Harris' name in her contact list and punches it. The phone rings and rings. Ariel's directed to Sharon's voice mail. "Sharon, it's Ariel. I have the kids and saw the police on the block. I didn't know if I should bring them home. Can you call me? Do you know what's going on?" Ariel hangs up.

She can try Indira.

On the fourth ring, Indira answers. "Hello," she says.

"It's Ariel."

"Hello," Indira says with little change in her voice.

"Ah, hi. Are you home? Do you have any idea what's going on?"

"I'm in my office."

Of course she is. "Have you heard anything?"

"Sorry. What?"

Indira obviously knows nothing. "Something's happened on our block. I don't mean to alarm you." Ariel looks through the glass at her beautiful children. Her insides come apart. "There're cops everywhere, and an ambulance. We should probably get home. I tried Sharon, but she's not answering. It looks horrible, Indira."

"What has happened?"

"I'm up at the Baskin-Robbins. I had the kids with me."

"But what has happened?"

"I—" Ariel looks again at Ella and Miles. "I have no idea, but our street's crawling with cop cars. There's an ambulance. There's yellow tape. I just don't know." Ariel realizes she wants sympathy from Indira. Ariel also understands she's not going to get it. "Listen. I think I'm going to go over there. Do you want me to call you back?"

"I'm nearly done. I'll do the same."

"Who knows. Probably something with Tokyo Rose, let's hope." Miles is taking Ella's gumballs. Ella's hitting Miles with her spoon. "I have to go. I'll see you."

"Good bye."

Ariel hangs up. She needs to get home. Right now. Kids can deal with trauma pretty well, she's read. Sometimes better than adults. Ariel has to know. She sticks her head in the door. "Let's go. Come on. You can take your ice cream with you."

"Cool," Miles says.

Cerise sees Ariel trying to drive up to her house with their kids in the back of the car. Uh oh. Cerise knew some other people from Orchid were gonna need a lot of help. Ariel's likely one of 'em.

The lady can't get at her driveway and house. Cerise walks to the edge of the yellow tape. They're allowing her old careful person to stay on the inside now, but she has to step around the evidence markers and all the blood. Cerise's wiped herself up some. She hopes they can wash off the street sooner than later. They all can't be made to look at it for days more. Maybe Philomenia's estate will pay for Daniel's funeral. Who knows. Cerise wishes she could find where Sharon and Nate are. Likely the morgue, but she's not sure. They're most definitely gonna need some support.

Cerise has her own police person now, a young lady, who's in charge of making sure Cerise fills in neighbors coming home from work or school or wherever. More it's that Cerise can tell the police what people can come past the yellow tape and go home and which ones just want a beer at Tokyo Rose or to take a look around.

It's all so sad Cerise can hardly think on it. Now, though, Miss Ariel needs to know where her husband is and that he's not hurt. Not hurt physically. The poor lady comes up shaking, holding her two children's hands. They have ice cream, but both are spilling it out their cups looking at the street and all the police people.

"We need to talk, Miss Ariel," Cerise says, nodding, trying to show it'll be okay. "We can all go into your house. Come on. Duck up under here."

Cerise watches the smart boy she forgets the name of—it's a musician, an old one—look up at his mother's face. This mess gonna affect a lot of people. The little girl starts crying.

"Shh," Cerise says. "It's gone be alright. I promise." She tells the lady cop, "These are Ed's people."

The woman nods, frowning, being official and putting her hands on her big belt with all its different weapons strapped on it. They got so much these days, pepper spray and those tasers along with clubs and guns. Too bad it seem like the NOPD not doin much at all with all their stuff to stop the ones who need stoppin'.

Cerise holds up the yellow tape. Ariel and her kids walk under. "Let's get them set up with a video," Cerise tells Ariel.

"I want Daddy," the little girl cries.

"Yo, what happen?" the boy asks. He stares at the red street, his head following the runoff of blood into the gutter. "Whoa . . ." The boy suddenly goes white and drops his ice cream. He races up his porch steps. He tries to open the front door then starts banging on it. He pushes the doorbell over and over. "Dad! *Dad!!*" He bangs the front door again.

Ariel stops in her tracks. "Jesus, Cerise, I don't, I'm not sure I can do . . ."

What in hell has Cerise made these poor people think? "Oh, no, no," she says. "Ed's alive. He alive. Hang on. He's not here, but he alive and he gonna stay that way. I just don't think he gonna be okay for a real long while." Cerise reaches down with her good hand and touches the little girl's pretty hair.

They get up on the porch, and Ariel goes in her handbag for something. "Miles, he's not here," Ariel says.

"I promise I'll be good. I promise!" The boy breaks down sobbing, crouching against the door.

·"Miles, get up. Miles," Ariel says. "Dad will come back."

"I don't want a recarcerated dad!" the child hollers into his knees.

"What?" Ariel asks, giving her daughter's hand to Cerise to hold while she bends to the boy. Ariel rubs his back. "What, Miles?"

"I want Dad!"

"Hey, hey. Miles. Look at me. Shh." She keeps on rubbing.

"I promise I'll be good. I don't want a, I don't want a dog dad or a ant—" The child's just hitchin' with his crying.

"What?"

"What if he comes back . . . what, what if I don't know it's Dad?" The boy starts wailing like Cerise saw his father do just a short time ago.

"Are you talking about reincarnation?" Ariel asks. She takes the boy's chin in her hand. "Miles, listen to me. Just listen."

When the relatives arrive, Ed is mowing Joe's lawn. They pile out of a large pickup truck with a rear seat. Four kids and a mother and father. It's not what Ed would have predicted for a cousin of Joe's.

Joe still lies in a coma. The police took two weeks to find his closest living relative. Evidently this is the man from Alabama. Ed stops pushing his manual mower and holds out his hand in greeting. "Hi," Ed says. "I'm Ed, a neighbor."

"Damn, I haven't seen one of those since I was a kid." The man points at the mower. He has a pronounced Southern drawl.

Ed shrugs and wipes sweat off his brow. "Good for the environment."

"Yeah, well. I'm Lou, short for Louis, and this my wife, Terri." The man points at his rumpled-looking kids. "Jenna, Jacob, Jessica, and Jerry."

"Hello, everyone," Ed says. "Welcome."

"You're the man been visitin' Joe," Lou says. He is very tan.

"I guess I am," Ed answers. "Huntsville's near Tennessee, right?" Ed directs the question to the woman, but she only looks to her husband.

"Yeah, not too far from the border," Lou says. "Makes for a long trip."

The woman plucks at her T shirt, fanning herself off.

"New Orleans in July," Ed says, smiling. He wants to tell them that it's his fault that Lou's cousin is in a coma and his cousin's wife killed herself. He wants to tell them that they are allowed to force him into labor. He will haul rocks up hills. He will hoe a field. He will do penance the rest of his life. "Good and hot till mid-October."

"There's air-conditioning in there?" Lou asks, tilting his head at Philomenia and Joe's house.

"Sure. Better you guys than nobody, right?" That came out wrong. "Let me get the key. I mean, you know, it's better to have people in a house than not, right? Houses shouldn't sit empty." Shut up, Ed. Get a grip. "I'll be right back."

One of the children has some kind of disability. She wears a wooden slab of a shoe and stands crookedly. Ed goes in his front door.

"Ed?" Ariel calls out.

"The Alabama people are here. Just getting the key."

Ariel comes out of the family room. "You doing okay?"

"Hot," he says, taking the key from the foyer table.

"Don't get overheated. You want some water?"

He shakes his head and goes back out.

Lou, his wife, and his four Js are swarming the exterior of the house. Ed's reminded of ants surrounding a large crouton, figuring out how to carry it away. Lou's gone down the north side. Ed sees him reaching into ferns. "Here it is," Ed says, holding up the key.

"Ain't no pool," one of the boys calls from the backyard.

"Foundation nice an' dry," Lou says to Ed, brushing off his hands.

"They took very good care of the property," Ed says. He wants to tell the man that Joe's head resembled a watermelon as much as it did a head the first time he visited. He wants to tell him how the doctors had to take off a piece of skull so his brain could swell out the hole and how poor Philomenia was cremated with no funeral.

Ed wants to tell every person he meets. "Really good care," Ed says. "Here you go." Ed hands Lou short for Louis the key. "I cleaned it up in there, but the fridge is emptied out. Let me know if I can help you find a grocery store or anything."

"We got a cooler in the truck. Stopped at the Wal-Mart off 65."

"Or directions to the hospital or anything."

"Yeah, alright. Thanks."

"Okay, then." Ed wants to explain when there's no explaining possible to a man who could care less. "Well, I'm going to finish the lawn."

Lou nods and calls his brood. "Git over here now!"

Ed sets to his task, to mowing Joe's lawn, to rolling his boulder up the mountain.

Night-blooming jasmine drifts from Philomenia's side garden. Ed sits on his porch with his ice tea and stares into the dim light of the streetlamp behind the live oak.

Ariel comes out the screen door. "The kids are down," she says, sitting. "Mmm. That smells good." She takes his hand.

They just sit. Half an hour must pass.

Ariel shifts in her seat. "When you're ready to talk about it, I'm here."

She's said the same thing most every night since the shooting. He tells her parts sometimes, but he can't get out the whole truth of it. He cannot fully confess. He's only revisited what he told both the police and sweet old Cerise.

Nobody in the living world knows what he did.

Ariel helped him mop up Philomenia's kitchen. With hoses and brooms and bleach, Ariel and Cerise and Roy and Ed cleaned up the street when the yellow tape came down.

Sharon and Ariel have become friends. Ariel cooks a second dinner some nights and carries it across to the Harrises.

Ed's imperfect and beautiful wife has taken a leave of absence from work. She may or may not have a job after the corporate investigation is done. It's okay. They both believe there are more important things to worry about.

He watches her now, since that day. Ariel hugs Sharon every time they see each other. She's learned all of the woman's grandchildren's names. Ariel reads stories to their own kids. Standing in the doorway one night after wandering the house aimlessly, as Miles and Ella giggled on either side of Ariel, half hidden behind a giant adventure book, Ed realized suddenly that she has always read to them.

Now. Here on the porch. If he doesn't now he may never.

"I hid behind Daniel," he says.

Ariel is silent.

"Philomenia shot at me four times. I hid. First, I hid in their ginger bushes."

"Of course," Ariel says gently. "Anyone would. What else could you have done?"

"You don't understand," he says, and his voice breaks.

"Sure I do. I'll understand anything you want to tell me. I swear."

"When I ran out of the bushes, I *hid behind* Daniel," he says. "Philomenia shot him because she thought she'd get me." There. He's told somebody.

"Okay," is all Ariel says. "Okay."

"He had his gun out aimed right at her. I hid behind Daniel because I thought he was going to shoot. Or she'd stop because she'd see his gun. But he didn't shoot. I got somebody killed, Ariel. I killed a boy."

Ariel nods, and Ed can see something change in her. She raises her hand to her mouth. He watches a tear roll down her perfect cheek. She nods. "Okay," she says. "Okay, I understand."

"I'm going to tell Sharon," Ed says.

Ariel sits and says nothing. Finally she says, "No, you're not."

Inside, as they ready themselves for bed, Ariel knows that she can keep Ed's secret for the rest of her life. She will tell him that. Sharon has already talked about her sons and their guns and what part of New Orleans they got themselves into and how Daniel's days were numbered, how he gave her money she knows came from the wrong place and how she's had a sense since she gave birth to Daniel that he wouldn't live to see his sixteenth birthday.

The boy wore a dress shirt in his coffin. Blue. The pants, Sharon said, weren't quite long enough, but you couldn't see the bottoms or his feet.

Now. Now or never. She loves him terribly. Ariel goes to Ed and wraps her arms around his pale, warm torso.

Cerise finds herself so proud of her daughter she doesn't know what to say. Marie brings what has to be twenty cars full of her old high school friends and all their families to the block party benefit to help with what the Harrises owe for Daniel's burying costs. There's so many kids that the street feels busting full of life.

Cerise requested her lady cop friend and one other from that day to be assigned to guard the street ends. Cerise already brought the woman ribs and potato salad and what musta been a dozen deviled eggs. The lady cop's pretty happy. And fat. She keeps thanking Cerise for the feeding.

Two bands are getting ready to play, courtesy of the young manager fellow at Tokyo Rose. He donated four kegs on top of the bands, and the blond man who's always around is workin' the taps. Cerise hears he was a friend of Joe's. He's talking to anybody who'll listen about a new hurricane way out over warm waters.

Ed's not drinking, she sees. She understands why.

Cerise should try to get done with what she wants to before she's too emotional. She can do it. She's a surfer, after all, just born in the wrong place, before her time. She's been chewed by sharks and lived to surf another day. Hang ten.

Cerise looks at all the people, probably over two hundred, easy. She has to find Klameisha. There. She's off on her own lawn overseeing a gob of toddlers. Good for her. Klameisha's a watcher too. "Klameisha," Cerise says normal, not trying to get any other attention. Cerise waves her claw hand on purpose and walks over. "Hey there. We can both watch the kids a spell."

Klameisha smiles, looking sad and pretty at the same time.

"I have something for you," Cerise says.

"Naw, Miss Cerise, we're going to make it from everybody else here, but thank you."

"No, listen. Your brother told me something before he died."

Klameisha looks scared.

"He wanted you to go to college," Cerise says.

"Naw . . ."

"I got five thousand dollars to start you off. He wanted it. I swear on my left hand."

The girl stands staring. Cerise can see why Daniel chose her. Even now, she keeps her eye on all the kids. "Daniel wished it?"

"Yes, he did."

Daniel's sister squares her shoulders and lifts her head.

Good enough, Cerise thinks. Good enough.

EPILOGUE

Some of us choose to stay for Katrina.

It's okay to ask. Everyone does.

The plainest answer is that we decide to stay because it is the only thing we know to do. And we decide to stay because we want to stay, because our bargeboard houses and shotgun apartments are all many of us have. They hold meals, and photographs, maybe a mother who requires dialysis or a dog frail with age. Finally, we stay because there is no other option. Our payday hasn't arrived and we do not own cars and we cannot afford to take a bus to some town or city where we have no family.

Divided, those of us living Uptown on Orchid Street stay and go both. We fill our bathtubs with water and our cupboards with sardine tins and canned ravioli. Or we pack our cars with unnecessary things, bad paintings of leaves and a doll's lavender glitter dress and a dozen identical T shirts printed with a picture of a boy named Daniel. We will worry for snowy egrets and palm trees and old roofs.

In the dark days afterwards, one of us will find, while searching for candles, years of an odd, sad life written in journals. A husband and wife will find forgiveness. And those of us living Uptown on Orchid Street inside the big lasso of river, on the beautifully high ground that does not flood, all of us down to the last baby, will eventually find each other again.

ACKNOWLEDGMENTS

The first words of this novel appeared on a laptop in Toronto. My husband, Joseph, and I had picked up the computer, on sale, in Memphis. At the time, I'd counted the laptop among what I thought to be the minuscule sum total of all my worldly possessions. Hurricane Katrina had reduced our city, and me, to something whipped and dispossessed. I thought I might try to write a swan song for New Orleans.

Most everyone knows what happened in the days after Katrina, which governing bodies failed us miserably. But so many people, thousands and thousands of them, gave and fed and cared. Before Memphis, before our trek to Canada, I'd evacuated to Lake Jackson, Texas. I am perpetually ashamed that I didn't have the sense then, or in the following months, to properly thank the family who made room for me, who bought me birthday presents, who cried alongside me as we watched New Orleans drown on their television screen. For generosity beyond reason, I wish to thank the Suazo family: Matthew, Stacey, Jason, Claudia, and Isabella. I honestly had nowhere else nearby to go, no other offers for shelter. You gave me far more than that, and I am forever in your debt.

Joseph and I made it from Texas to Memphis, where we walked into the Office Depot and afterwards a barbeque joint, and where, after a long teary night of debate, we decided to immediately return to ruined New Orleans. I'd been gone less than two weeks. So many friends had left pets. *Maclean's* magazine had asked Joseph for his story. So back we went. Jarret Lofstead and Raymond Boyden, thank you for your humor and protection and company. Lance, thank you for the shelter in the dark. Jennifer Kuchta, thank you for choosing a house on high ground and for keeping the light on all the months we were later away. Rick Barton, thank you for finding us a room in Baton Rouge and for finding a way to keep UNO alive. You saved far more of us than anyone I know. You were our island in the flood.

Peter Schock, I have no idea how you did it, but you managed to hold together a madly far-flung English department. Thank you for those semesters under the bridge. Jeni, you gathered many of us through e-mails, a little tether to life for us. Thank you. Samantha, your Toronto apartment rocked.

Some of us made it back eventually. Near and far, indefatigable friends and graduate students and neighbors prompted me to continue writing with gifts of music and wine and stories and food and company. Thank you, one and all: Gord, AC and Bill, AK and Jackson, Rakia, Marcus, Steve, Brandon, Joey and Sarah K, David Parker Jr., Barb, Casey, Jen V, Rachel, Arin, Chrys, Lish, Trisha, Bill and Nance, Sarah and Simon, Corey at the bank, Kris, Kim, Joanna, Allison and Gavin, Pete, Ashley, Sophie, Sean, Will, Dawn, Erica, Jim, Kelly, Emily, Philippe and MS, Julian, Gwen, Alexis, Sonja, Mitch, Gabe and Julie, Sterling and Dale for your smiles in the park, Karen and Steve for a respite on Dauphin Island, Grim Jim, Dinty, Lee, Susan, Bill Gullo and Rachel, Darren and Leslie, Joel, Matthew, Nicole, Francis Geffard, Eddie and Bob. I have forgotten to name others of you, without question. I will tell you thank you in person.

I used a number of books for reference along the way. Thank you, Abram Himmelstein; your Neighborhood Story Project series is a font of authenticity. C-Murder, thank you for *Death Around the Corner*.

Dear family, you are my backbone. Without all of you, I would not have found the strength to finish this. Beautiful sisters Meg and Emily, I love you beyond measure. Your families, Lance, Steve, Amelia, Alex, Otto, and Eli bring me so much sheer, unadulterated joy. Cheri, Franz and Edna, Travis and Ally, Spanky and Mel, Josh and Bethaney, Katie, Jim, thank you for making me laugh, for helping me to remember that life should be lived with gusto and beer drunk from a cold glass. Blanche, Veronica, Sue, Mary, Suzanne, Frank, and families, thank you for keeping my husband whole. Julia and Jacob, David, Megan and Michael, Barbie and Rudy, you are often in my thoughts. Karen, we will visit soon. Promise. David S, you changed shunts and bandages, and for that I am grateful. Mary Anne, who knew a mean stepdaughter could grow to so love the woman her father married? Sweet Mom and kindest Dad, you created my world. I wish I could give back the tiniest piece of what you gave up for me. This novel comes directly from the heart you filled.

Some strangers took a chance on me when nobody else would. I have held you very close ever since. Michiko, I know this is the start of a long friendship. Rob McQuilkin, Super Agent, you have no equal. Your support and encouragement are unwavering, your belief almost surreal. You got my back, and I adore you for it. Jennifer Jackson, editor extraordinaire, I couldn't have done any of this without you. You wear a big ol' Viking helmet and carry a sword for me. Thank you doesn't come close to saying enough, but thank you from the bottom of my heart.

And finally, at the end of it all, Joseph, my husband, here you are. I see the porch swing, love, and we're in it together.

ALSO BY AMANDA BOYDEN

"*Glorious, modern, satirical and funny. . . . Utterly realistic, compelling, artfully done, and also relevant. . . . A first novel of complex truth and beauty.*" —San Francisco Chronicle

PRETTY LITTLE DIRTY

Lisa sees the life of her gorgeous best friend Celeste Diamond as just about perfect: she has a gigantic house, two older sisters to coach her through the hazards of high school, and loving, lively parents. As Lisa's own home has long been a place devoid of joyful noise, she joins the Diamond household, slipping into their routine of sit-down suppers and soaking in the delicious normalcy of family life. But what begins as the story of two young women living a charmed existence soon swirls into an intoxicating novel of art, music, and self-destructive impulses.

Fiction/978-1-4000-9682-4

VINTAGE BOOKS
Available at your local bookstore, or visit
www.randomhouse.com